VICTORY AND DEATH

VICTORY AND DEATH

The Planewars Saga: Book One

RUSSEL FRANS

Worlds Collide Publishing

CONTENTS

Prologue – The Council of Kings (pt. I)	8
Chapter I – The Battle of Harmony Valley	16
Chapter II – Magnid Hathey	34
Chapter III – Family and Friends	44
Chapter IV – The Blade	64
Chapter V – Past, Present, Future	71
Chapter VI – That Which Cannot Be Killed	89
Chapter VII – Kratan Vythor	104
Chapter VIII – A Trail of Tears, a Trail of Blood	111
Chapter IX – The Winter Cold	125
Chapter X – Paxon Gorthös	143
Chapter XI – Fates	157
Chapter XII – Thy Home, But Not Thy Castle	180
Chapter XIII – The Hunted	202
Chapter XIV – Hazeus Nightstar	226
Chapter XV – Rebellion	241
Chapter XVI – Reunion	263
Chapter XVII – The Spring's Breeze	276

Chapter XVIII – Storms on the Horizon	297
Chapter XIX – The Battle of the Lakewoods (pt. I)	318
Chapter XX – The Battle of the Lakewoods (pt. II)	347
Chapter XXI – Braennor Hakan	372
Chapter XXII – The Long March to Certain Doom	379
Chapter XXIII – Magic	394
Chapter XXIV – The Final Obstacle	413
Chapter XXV – Agan Winnefore	440
Chapter XXVI – The Immortal Wizard-King	454
Chapter XXVII – A Change in Weather	485
Epilogue – The Council of Kings (pt. II)	491
Appendix I: Ranking of the Armies of The Vastness	497
Appendix II: Glossary of Characters	498

Victory and Death

The Planewars Saga: Book One

by Russel Frans

WORLDS COLLIDE
PUBLISHING
(Trademark pending)

This is a work of fiction. All names, characters, places, and events in this book are either the product of the author's imagination or used in a fictitious manner. Any resemblance to actual persons, actual places, or actual events is purely coincidental.

Note: If you purchased this book without a cover, you should be aware that this book is stolen property. It has been reported "unsold and destroyed" to the publisher, and neither the author nor the publisher has received payment for this book.

No generative artificial intelligence tools were used in the creation of this work or cover art, nor is permission granted for these to be used in the learning of such tools.

VICTORY AND DEATH

THE PLANEWARS SAGA: BOOK ONE

Copyright © 2024 Russel Frans

All rights reserved.

ISBN paperback: 979-8-9903437-2-6

ISBN e-book: 979-8-9903437-1-9

Cover art by Mark Smylie. Maps and interior art by Russel Frans.

Edited by Robin J. Samuels, Shadowcat Editing.

Worlds Collide Publishing

Spokane Valley, WA

Trademark pending.

worldscollidepublishing@gmail.com

First Edition: March 2024

Acknowledgements

First and foremost, I want to thank National Novel Writing Month (known to insiders as "NaNoWriMo") and the people that run this event every November for inspiring me to finally put words down onto the page. What an amazing challenge, what a bright community, and what a worthwhile endeavor for anyone who has ever thought "it would be fun to write a novel, but who has the time?" It taught me that my time is what I make of it.

I also want to thank all of my earliest readers, including Casey Scott, Joe Ledahl, Joey Hewitt, and my longest-running fan of all, Jocelyn Frans. You were there for the roughest rough draft and gave me some of my best feedback. This book wouldn't be what it is today without you.

A most sincere thank you to the inimitable Mark Smylie for his amazing talents, of which I now have a new favorite (see cover). Thank you to Robin J. Samuels at Shadowcat Editing for your keen eye and expertise. And thanks to both of these parties for their invaluable insights into the world of self-publishing.

My thanks also to the talented writer, Megan E. O'Keefe, for the insights into the world of authoring. Cheers to your successes!

And if you are holding this book, reading this now, then my most sincere thanks to you. A story is nothing without anyone to read it.

For Owen.

Thanks for reading with me and telling me to publish.

THE TWENTY-SEVEN KNOWN WORLDS, AS

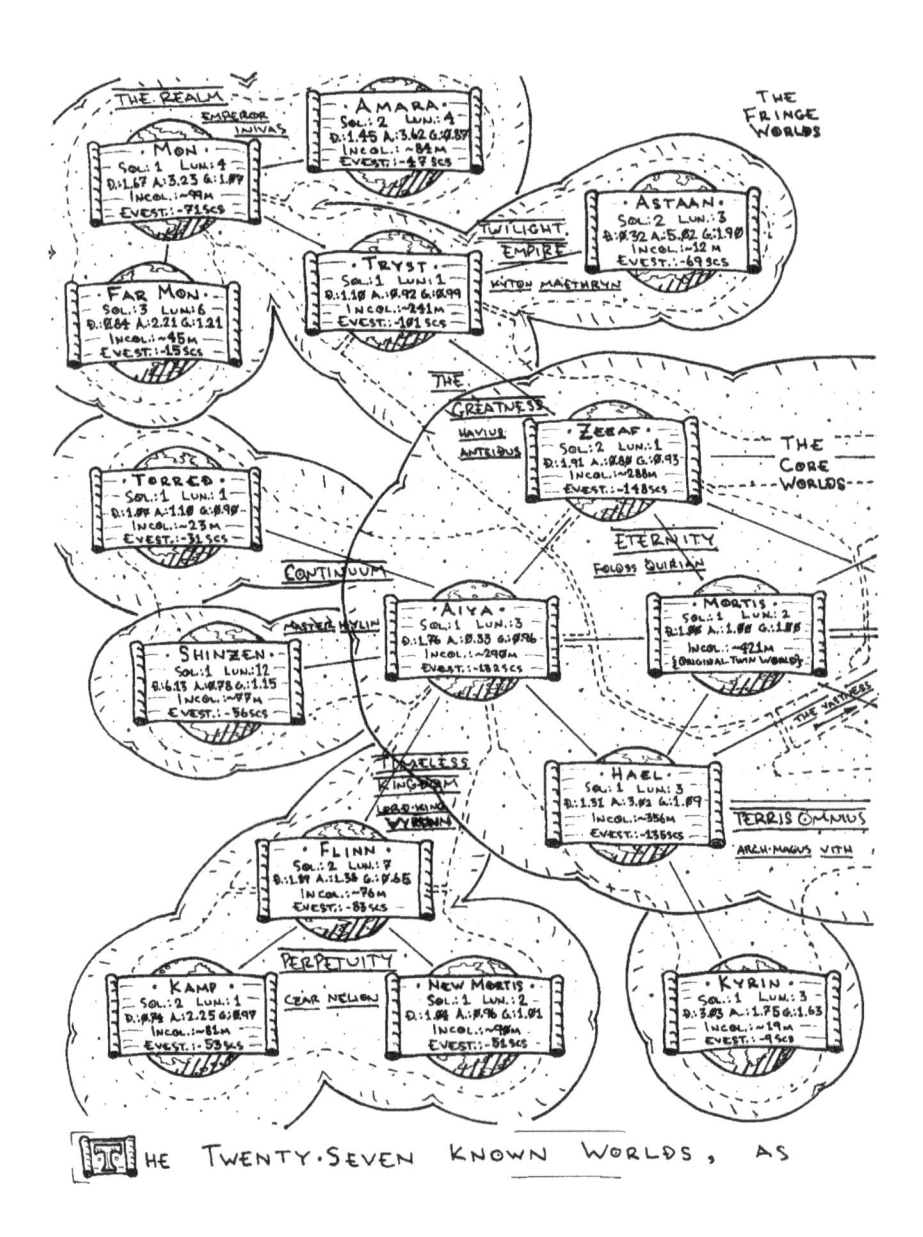

ASCRIBED BY THE CONSENSUS OF SAGES. {SCS 343}

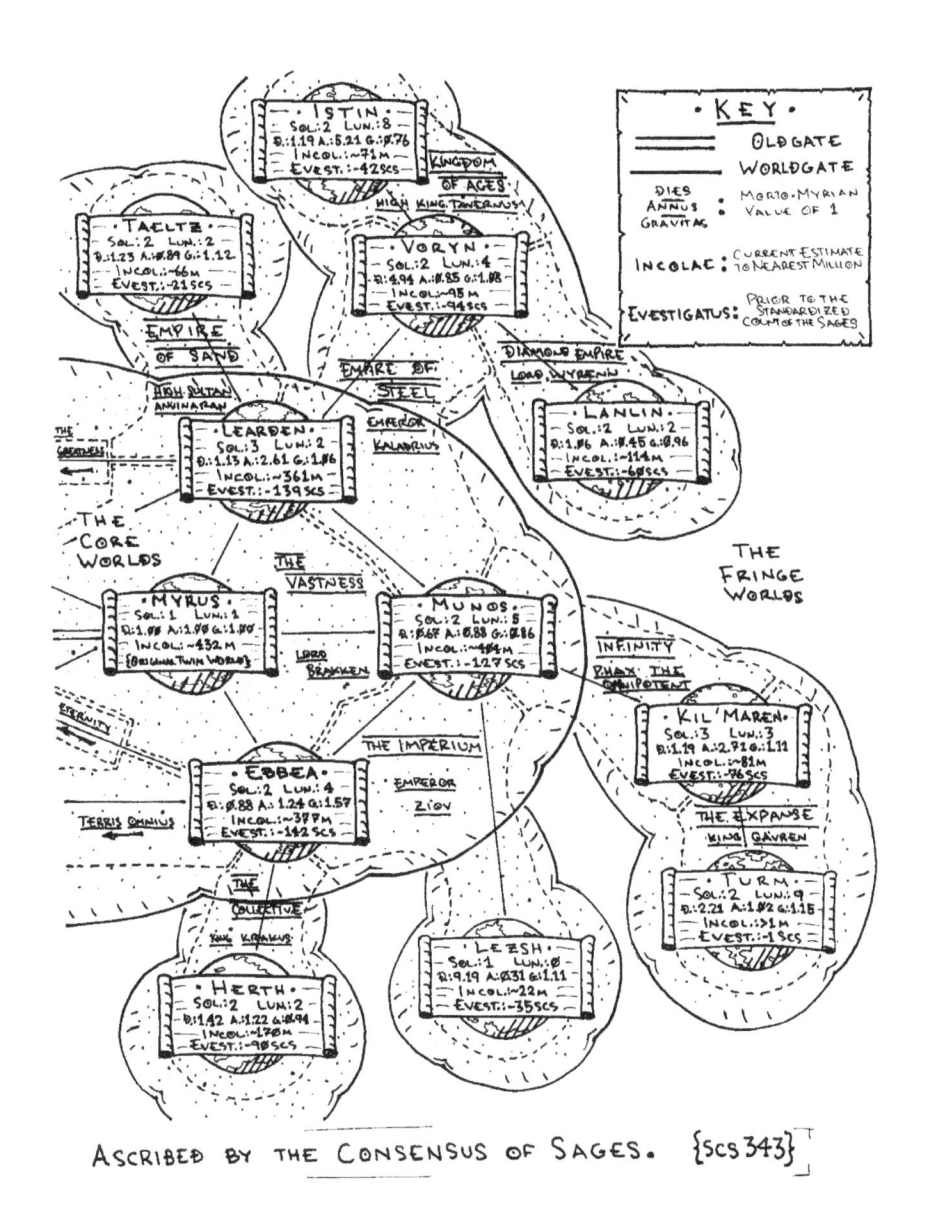

Prologue – The Council of Kings (pt. I)

"It cannot be done," declared King Horrin, somehow piercing the low roar of all the men speaking before him. "It is simply not possible."

Duke Garreth Jacob turned his attention to the older man. As did most in the council.

Assembled in this darkened room, in the frosty mountains of this remote and punishing world, were several of the most powerful mortals in the entirety of the domain.

Smoke from a tobacco pipe wandered lazily upward, playfully defying this world's pull, lit only in the scintillating pattern of the candelabras. They sat about a large oaken table with a fine finish. This was the mountain retreat of one of the noblemen here this night. The trappings were fit for a king.

But the cold night and the fine furniture both were ignored at this moment. Because kings of men assembled in secret for one purpose.

Upon the large table sat a letter. It was the letter Duke Jacob had received, though each of these noblemen had received a copy of the same. It was from a general in another Dominance entirely. He was an enemy to the men in this room, by the laws, however he appealed to them as allies.

The letter spoke of wild and blasphemous things. It spoke of a word so illegal that some might be executed even just for reading it. In fact, these kings of men in this room now would surely be executed if they were found.

This letter spoke of rebellion.

"You see, the Arch-Magus is no mere man," Horrin continued. "Even we kings of men fall before a sharpened blade. Splay us and we will quiver and die. Behead our meager frames and we will cease our chattering."

His eyes, already steely, grew frigid.

"The Arch-Magus has survived attempts at each such thing – and worse – with no more than a scratch. I have ruled my remote province for longer than some of you have been alive, and I daresay many of my subjects are more loyal to me than they are fearful of that Wizard, but I am only a man. The Arch-Magus is an immortal Wizard-King; he is a *god*. One does not overthrow a god, gentlemen."

King Horrin let his stern face punctuate his statement.

Garreth had always admired King Horrin, as most in this room surely had. His was a relatively small and wealthy province in the highlands of the world known as Hael. The world was the home of all the nobles here at this meeting, true, but King Horrin held something of a privileged place. His province had many mines of iron, gold, and even gemstones. Though these were all, of course, property of the Wizard-King, just as the towns and people were, his wealth was tremendous, nonetheless. Perhaps a greater value than any of that, his province was remote enough from the worldgates, through which the Planewars spilled regularly, that his people knew relative peace.

Horrin was a rather tall man. His age had made him frailer, but his frame was surely once fit as a soldier. A dark, short-trimmed beard complemented his black-and-white hair. His garb was of a fine cut, and a simple crown of gold adorned his head. Though each man present was indeed some high-ranking nobility, Horrin had a certain air about him. He commanded attention, even among kings.

And he seemed to think it was folly for any of them to be here.

Suddenly, voices from most of the men at this table erupted at once.

"I could rally my lord generals! I say we try it!"

"And those lord generals would watch your head roll at their feet, fool!"

"Let us but take a moment to discuss."

"Every moment we discuss is another moment the Arch-Magus's assassins likely close in on us!"

"It is foolish not to consider."

"You are a fool. You are all fools!"

Garreth could only sit and listen to the chaotic orchestra of dissenting voices. Every man here was a high noble, except for him. There were kings of men and two high counts. Garreth was but a duke. His own king was not even present here, and only provinces larger than his had high counts.

If he'd give it but a moment's time, the voice in the back of his mind would ask him what he was even doing here – why he had been one to receive a copy of this letter.

But, no matter the reason, he had received it and he was here. So, he would make himself heard.

Duke Jacob stood. He was at the opposite end of the table from King Horrin, whom most of the nobles had been addressing when they weren't arguing with one another.

King Horrin simply looked to Garreth, an expectant expression on his wizened face. Slowly, one by one, the other noblemen quieted and turned their attention to Duke Jacob.

Garreth had spoken in front of hundreds before. Never, though, had he had an audience of kings.

He cleared his throat.

"Gentlemen," he began, "there has to be a way... There *must* be a way to destroy him."

He saw the looks of disdain from some of the men present.

"What would a boy know?" scoffed King De L'Ardent from his seat on Garreth's left.

King De L'Ardent was a middle-aged human, though his years had not treated him well. His province, on the shores of the very same continent where the Arch-Magus made his home, was wracked by storms and war and unrest. His punishments from Vith were harsh indeed. He had one hand, as the other had been burned to a mangled stump.

Rumors said he had been touched by Wizard's fire itself. A beard that was more gray than brown covered his chin, while his mustache was closer to white. His eyes were serious and his tone even more so.

"You've not served in battle," he went on, "nor lost your cities to the Planewars. You've not suffered a famine, nor have your people borne a great plague. I'd bet gold against garbage that you've never been under the Wizard-King's gaze."

He straightened up, squaring himself with Garreth.

"You're not even a king."

Perhaps he was right. Upon what basis could Duke Jacob speak here at this council? He was outranked by every other noble here, and he was likely fifteen years the junior to the next youngest. He was no boy, but he was a mere twenty-three years of age, by the Count of the Sages. His political power was miniscule compared to any other nobleman here. Why had he received this letter?

And yet, he was eternally grateful that he had received it.

The twenty-seven known worlds and all the mortals on them were locked in the Planewars. They had been for centuries. The boys of the Dominances went to war for Immortals who would never know their name nor care whether they lived. The people of the multiverse were starved and deprived and marched to war. Wizards fought each other for control of the many worlds; as they had from before Garreth was born, as they would long after he died.

Unless they could change it.

The small audience still awaited Garreth's reply to the embittered king. But he chose to ignore the man's questions and direct his response to all of the men.

"Are not the gods dead?" Jacob pondered. "If Vith were truly a god, do you think we would be here now? Do you think that kings of men could spirit away to a secret meeting in the darkness of night without their *god* knowing? No, a *god* would not allow for such a thing. The Arch-Magus is no god; he cannot be *immortal*…"

Jacob's thoughts raced.

"Even..." he continued, "even mighty evergreens eventually fall and are consumed by the forest. Lo, even vast mountains, the Sages tell, bow and crumble to the constancy of the sea." His thoughts came more clearly now. "Yes, and if a mountain can fall, then who is to say that *we mortals* are not that ocean that would claim the honor of toppling the Wizard?"

King Horrin eyed the duke, but his expression was measured and unreadable.

A low murmur again began to fill the small building. With tensions high, the murmur wavered and turned once more into the low roar that had filled the chamber moments before.

Garreth decided to sit back down. Standing was no small task on this world, called Kyrin. The weight of everything on this plane was amplified, and it had a truly punishing effect. The letter that sat upon the table lay almost completely flat, pressed by the unseen powers of this place. Even the air here somehow felt as though it was slowly crushing him to death.

There were stories from the histories that battles had been drawn here, though Duke Jacob could hardly imagine how. Perhaps, if they truly wished to rebel, they could draw their people here, and protect the gate from Hael with all their forces. But what life could the people of their Dominance make for themselves here on this harsh world, this place of ogres and giants?

I must stop, thought Garreth. *I mustn't keep doubting it. General Vallon says he will overthrow his own Wizard-King. We must be there at this precipice as well. We must take this chance.*

Duke Jacob was about to enter the fray of the men all speaking at once when King Horrin stood. It clearly required much of him, on this harsh plane, but he showed not even the slightest strain.

Almost immediately, the group quieted again.

"If we kings of men, hiding here on Kyrin, could somehow fuel armies and slay gods with our secretive words, then perhaps this discussion would be worth continuing."

Horrin's words were harsh, but his tone was measured and even. He looked directly to Garreth now.

"And if whispered strategies and fool's hope could raise the ocean and topple mountains, young duke, then perhaps we *would* strategize and perhaps we *could* hope. If you were able to show me even one Wizard that could be wounded by any mortal weaponry, then *perhaps* we could spend our time on the philosophy of who should rule and who should not. But none of us here has seen a Wizard bleed. None of us here need bother to debate the right of our Wizard to rule."

He sighed lightly before going on.

"Each of us knows what punishment awaits us for even uttering such fantasies. I recommend you each burn your copy of that letter and never speak of it again. I suggest you deny at all costs your presence at this council. We will hope our absence from our duties has gone unnoticed. May the Arch-Magus forgive us."

And with that he turned from the large table. He walked from the barely lit room of the squat building in the snow-swept valley and left.

Garreth and the council of kings watched him go in a desperate sort of silence.

Part One:

The Rule of the Immortal Wizard-Kings

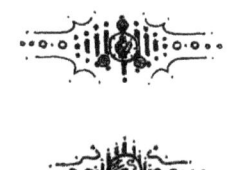

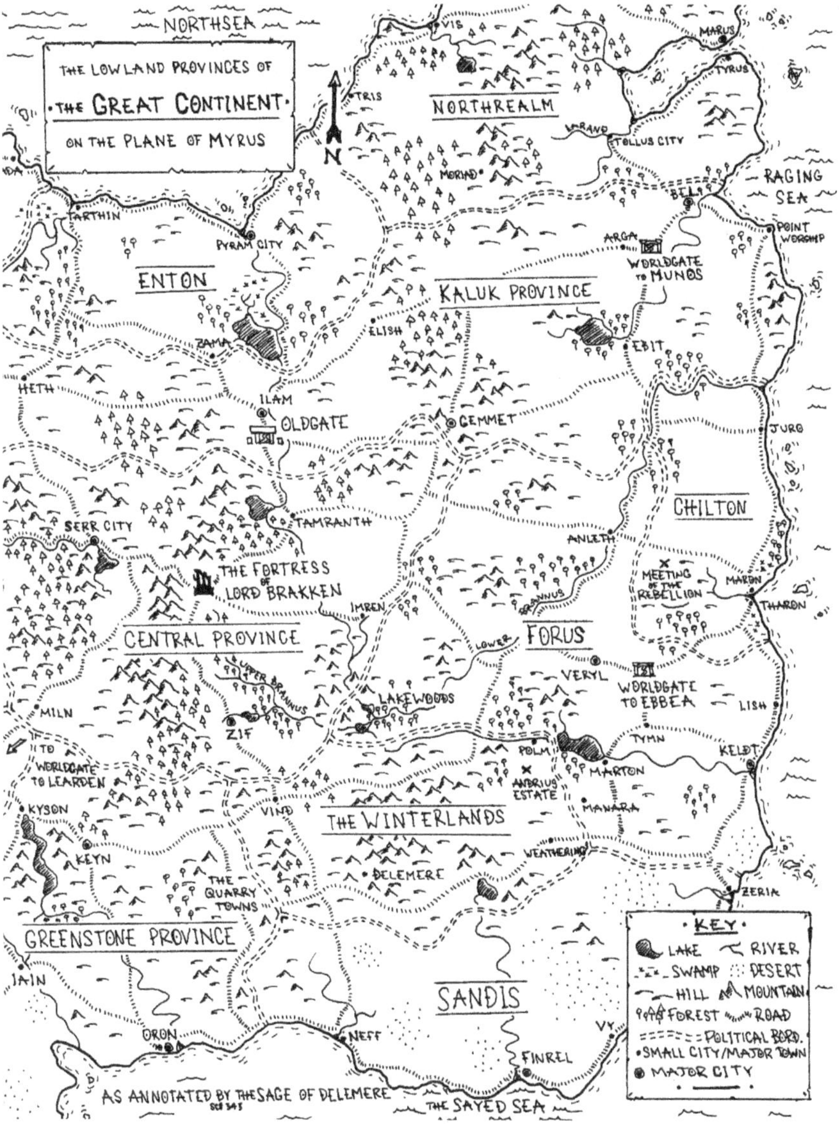
NORTHSEA
THE LOWLAND PROVINCES OF
THE GREAT CONTINENT
ON THE PLANE OF MYRUS
N
VIS
MARUS
TYRUS
TRIS
NORTHREALM
TOLLUS CITY
MORIAD
RAGING SEA
TARTHIN
PYRAM CITY
BEL
POINT WORSHIP
ARGA
WORLDGATE TO MUNOS
ENTON
KALUK PROVINCE
ELISH
ZAMA
EBIT
HETH
ILAM
OLDGATE
GEMMET
JURO
CHILTON
TAMRANTH
SERR CITY
ANLETH
THE FORTRESS OF LORD BRAKKEN
MEETING OF THE REBELLION
MARON
THARON
IMREN
CENTRAL PROVINCE
LOWER
FORUS
VERYL
WORLDGATE TO EBBEA
UPPER BRANNUS
LAKEWOODS
MILN
ZIF
LISH
TYMN
POLM
KELDT
TO WORLDGATE TO LEARDEN
ANDRIUS ESTATE
MARTON
KYSON
VIND
MANARA
THE WINTERLANDS
KEYN
WEATHERING
DELEMERE
THE QUARRY TOWNS
ZERIA
GREENSTONE PROVINCE
KEY
LAKE
RIVER
SWAMP
DESERT
HILL
MOUNTAIN
FOREST
ROAD
POLITICAL BORD.
SMALL CITY/MAJOR TOWN
MAJOR CITY
JAIN
SANDIS
ORON
NEFF
VY
FINREL
AS ANNOTATED BY THE SAGE OF DELEMERE
THE SAYED SEA

Chapter I – The Battle of Harmony Valley

The sun beat down on Artorus like a waterfall of heat and light. This plane had three suns, one at zenith as another was slightly closer to setting, and still another was following them upward into the sky on its slow journey. Many months from now, the three fiery balls would be bunched closer together, and their heat would not be so harsh.

This world was called Learden.

Artorus did not like the heat in this place, but it wasn't what bothered him at the moment. He knelt down beside the body of a man – no, a boy – lying in the ashen dust, staring back at him with the eyes of the dead. The expression was a common one for those felled on the field of battle: pain, agony, and regret in those last fleeting, gasping moments of life. Artorus felt an all-too-familiar pain.

It was not as though Artorus was unused to death; he'd seen more of it than he could ever recount. In fact, most people he'd ever known rested with the fallen gods. Most of these went well before their time, but such is the way of the soldier. He forced himself to see the spectacle before him and to feel every detail, nonetheless. And staring into this boy's eyes told him the story of his own life. The boy was a soldier, born to fight and die for the Wizards.

Artorus was not a spiritual man, but he quietly said a quick prayer to Koth over the boy's body and closed the corpse's eyes. It was a prayer he'd heard his sister use for the living; he wasn't entirely sure if it was appropriate for the dead. But this maladroit prayer from this impious general would have to suffice.

In truth, Artorus had rarely said any prayers for his fallen. He wanted to do something more than simply feel their loss; he wished there was a greater force at work in the multiverse which could grant some solace – to the fallen, to their families, to himself, to anyone at all... But the prayer was like a glove that didn't fit his hand.

Far too many to pray for this day, anyway, Artorus thought as he stood up and scanned the field before him.

The general Artorus Vallon of the Fifth Planar Army was a commanding figure, despite the fatigue and filth of a sleepless night and a bloody battle. From walking about and crouching on the ashy slope, his heavy cape collected more grime and gore at its frayed ends than even the prior days of battle had already accumulated. The gold-trimmed, deep red cloak hung loosely about his worn armor. His was half-plate – armor that provided considerable protection, but was neither so invulnerable nor so cumbersome as the heavy field plate that some of his shock troops wore. His armor was once the color of polished silver, with many insignias of rank and standing, now dull gray with the stains of blood and the scars of a thousand sword strikes. His short dark beard and trim hair were much cleaner before days spent on the battlefield, and his almond skin shone from behind them with a thin layer of perspiration. Dark brown eyes were deep-set in his face, and they told a story of sorrow to those who peered long enough. His muscular frame moved with all the training a lifetime in the armies of the Planewars could provide, and the tassels of his rank swayed sleekly with his fluid motions. A very fine broadsword hung at Artorus's hip, both scabbard and hilt showing countless battles of wear, though not concealing the craftsmanship with which even the Wizard-King might be impressed.

A hot wind picked up dust and ash as it blew through the battlefield. For as far as he could see in the sunlit haze, bodies littered the slope of the mountain and stretched into the shallow valley ahead. The sparse foliage that had previously dotted the landscape had mostly burned off with the patches of grass and left a smoldering scene of blood, spears, and skeletons. The smoggy valley blocked his view of the forest of peculiar trees and the bay beyond that which his men had scouted days before.

This world was his home during these months of deployment, but Artorus was born on another world entirely. Artorus called the plane of Myrus home. Where Learden had shrublands and forests of tall and lanky trees, Myrus had broad-leafed and full-bodied trees and flowering bushes of all colors. While Learden was covered in huge swaths of desert and arid landscapes, Myrus had innumerable lakes and endless rolling green hills. When Learden summers dominated the world for months and months, Myrus would move easily through all four seasons.

This war eternal had raged on across each of the many planes for the whole of Artorus's life, for the lives of his father and his father's father – and long before that. The Planewars were all Artorus knew – all anybody knew. Life and war were all but inseparable, and not a single village on a single world amongst the endless æther was free from the bonds of the raging warfare.

Artorus served a Wizard called Lord Brakken: Lord Brakken the War Maker; Lord Brakken the Eternal; Lord Brakken the Cruel. The dominion of any Wizard-King was called a Dominance, and this particular Dominance was called The Vastness. Artorus's homeworld of Myrus was Brakken's very seat of power, but The Vastness stretched across portions of three other worlds and was frequently embattled through the worldgates to others.

The *entirety* of one world, and *millions of souls* on three other worlds bowed to the Wizard. The Vastness was, in fact, one of the largest Dominances among the planes, commanding likely more of the multiverse's peoples than most any other Wizard's. The Sages told of a number that is *beyond millions*, just as millions are beyond thousands. Artorus never committed the word to his memory, since thinking of so many mortal people at once boggled his mind.

But, still, this was not enough for the Wizard. Brakken would not stop until *all* the worlds were his.

The immortal Wizard-King was nothing if not ruthless. He had leveled entire cities and slain millions in his conquests. Living his entire life under the Wizard's rule, Artorus could not compare his Wizard-King to any of the sixteen others in the multiverse, but he doubted very much that his was different from any of them, despite what the propaganda machines would have the people believe. Some called the Wizards the ultimate beings, some called them living gods, and some only called them a fact of life.

With a Dominance larger than any other Wizard, Brakken also had more enemies than any other. One of Brakken's rivals in the perpetual war was the Wizard-King called Kaladrius. Each Wizard fought the others for Dominance over the twenty-seven worlds and the souls therein. Sages and mortal philosophers have all debated the true intent behind the warring of the Wizards, but as far as Artorus could tell, it was a pointless topic. Kaladrius and Brakken had fought for hundreds of years, and they would continue to do so no matter what motives mortals might dream up for them.

Not unlike his own Wizard-King, Kaladrius was a bloodthirsty and brutal emperor, who marshaled his forces ever onward against the endless assaults of his neighbors, trying desperately to gain ground on one world or another. At present, the Fifth Planar made battle against one of Kaladrius's armies known as the Fourteenth Colonial Army, under the command of a General Hemmet – a rather resourceful dwarf.

And so, all the while, as Wizards made bids for the control of greater Dominances, the mortals spilled their blood and died for them – mortals like the nameless boy amid the ashes at Artorus's feet.

"Sir!"

A soldier approached from behind, the clanking of armor indicating he saluted as he came to an abrupt halt behind Artorus. Artorus recognized the voice. The general turned to his subordinate and found a familiar sight.

The soldier was his lieutenant, Rreth, a large human with plenty of scars to support his battle-hardened demeanor. Artorus had long surmised that Rreth had some dwarven blood in his line; his beard was thick, his form sturdy, and the general had seen Rreth take blows that would surely have felled most. He was a dependable soldier, a good leader, and a friend. Artorus returned the salute.

Though many armies of the other Wizard-Kings differed in ranking systems, in most of the armies of Lord Brakken, a general's highest-ranking subordinates were his lieutenants. Lieutenants each led a small number of high commanders, and the hierarchy continued on from there. It was good to have a man like Rreth for a lieutenant. He could just as easily wade into the combat and inspire the troops as he could give orders and direct the activities of the army. Each skill was put to the test often.

Rreth was one of the Fifth Planar Army's two lieutenants. And, more important than any other of an officer's qualities, Artorus had to be able to trust his lieutenants. Rreth was a man he could trust.

"The preliminary reports are in, sir," Rreth informed his general, "and the numbers don't look as good as we'd hoped."

Artorus frowned.

The lieutenant continued, "However, as you planned, it looks as though Kaladrius's forces have withdrawn down the valley and toward the bay, making for the fortress on the island and abandoning their siege weaponry in order to cut through the woods. Sparse as these odd trees are, the siege weaponry can't manage the woods very well. They tried to burn it all, but our scouts salvaged some of it." Rreth concluded with a grin, "Looks to be a couple trebuchets included in the salvaged pieces."

"I take it then, that our engineers were correct that a trebuchet shot could span the breadth of the woods?" Artorus asked.

"Yes sir," the lieutenant replied as his grin widened, "looks that way."

"Good news, my friend," the general said as he began to walk down the slope toward the encampment.

His lieutenant followed.

"Have the engineers make all necessary repairs and position a crew with heavy guard to begin firing on the far side of those woods immediately. Cancel the construction and bring all the completed weapons to bear as soon as possible. I don't want to waste any time, Rreth."

"Yes sir," the larger man repeated. He saluted once more, and then hastened down toward the construction site where their own siege weaponry could be seen.

There, long spans of wood were being carved and bent into shape with a dozen workers toiling in the heat on metal joints and bracings. Hasty canopies were the full extent of the respite most troops received from the relentless heat this day. They made light encampments in an effort to remain as mobile as possible on their assault. They always left the heavy tents and blankets in the center of the carts, allowing for the lighter gear to be unpacked and repacked with ease. It was a trick for warmer climates that Artorus had picked up from his last general.

Artorus passed a few patrolling groups of men on his hike down the hillside who stopped to salute the general, but many were either collecting or burying the dead from the morning's battle.

Just as Artorus was reaching his command tent, the guards stopped in the middle of their salute and looked past him with shock on their faces.

"Not again..." the general muttered as he spun about, sword coming halfway out of his scabbard by reflex as his eyes scanned the slope behind him.

Over the hill, emerging from the bright horizon, he saw a terrible sight. Goblin wolf riders– dozens of them – raced at the defenses, and then the hulking form of an ogre crested the hill, teams of orcs pulling at thick chains that ran to iron collars and shackles around the huge limbs of the creature.

"Dammit!" cursed General Vallon as he clicked the sword back into its sheath and called orders to the men that were not already grabbing weapons and forming battle lines. He ran as fast as his heavy armor and fatigued legs could take him over the loose piles of ash. He could clearly make out the goal of the strike force: the siege weaponry.

Rushing past a group of soldiers scrambling out of their canopies, armor donned hastily or not at all, he looked to the lead individual.

"Spear!" the general called, his tone commanding.

The lead soldier grabbed a spear from one of the men behind and tossed it to Artorus. Not breaking stride, he caught the spear in one hand as he used the other to press down on the handle of his sheathed sword to raise the scabbard out of the way of his hurried gait.

Thin, scattered lines were quickly forming in front of the siege assembly area. *These men will be trampled,* thought Vallon, and he picked up his pace.

Goblins were vile creatures, lesser cousins of the orcs, and their leathery skin ranged from sickly gray to putrid green. The Fifth Planar fielded no such creatures among their ranks. Most of the men referred to them in a slur, *gobs,* and they were not well liked even by those on their own side. Though they were not large, rarely topping three and a half feet in height, goblins' frames were packed with wiry muscle, and the creatures were notoriously hard to land a blade on. Their most outstanding feature, however, was undoubtedly their hideous faces: gnarled, pocked, sparsely haired things with twisted, pointed noses, set with spiteful red eyes.

The goblins themselves were, however, not truly the problem; even several dozen of them could be repelled easily, unmounted. The true problem was that, supposedly since the Wizard-Kings discovered the vile creatures on the plane of Ebbea, the goblin race was very adept at rearing and training for battle the monstrous beast known as the mountain wolf. Mountain wolves were much like their more common ilk, if quite a bit more massive, but with many centuries of breeding so that only the largest, most fearless of their race ever lived past pup; perhaps thousands of years of breeding for battle fueled the rage of these monsters. Inbreeding had long left the mountain wolves with ugly features like patchy fur, snaggleteeth, or occasionally no tails. But, most goblin riders rode wolves as large as a mule. This meant that several dozen goblins mounted on several dozen of their wolves was indeed a sight to be feared. This was likely the largest unit in the opposing cavalry regiment.

The riders raced forward, the huge gray wolves throwing ash and dirt up as they sprinted rapidly down toward the scrambling troops hastily bringing weapons to bear. Artorus could only keep running toward the thin battle lines between the attackers and their target.

Then the first riders crashed into the defensive lines. Teeth, claws, and blades rent flesh and snapped swords as men were trampled underfoot. Artorus could hear the screams of his men as he was dashing toward the melee despite the complaints of his aching body.

Lieutenant Rreth had acquired a halberd when he'd seen the attackers and organized the men into defensive lines. He stood now in the last line of men before the scrambling engineers and craftsmen. A surprise attack was not jarring to him anymore; a call to arms was like an old friend that didn't always bring good news. He had come to expect battle at any moment when he was deployed. But these beleaguered troops were already exhausted from the morning's fighting, and this assemblage was a ragtag mismatch of support personnel and a handful of fighters fresh out of the infirmary.

Rreth was what some had described as an exceptional soldier. Like most men among the planes, he'd been born to a life in the armies, but unlike most men, he was a skilled warrior and superb leader. He actually enjoyed the thrill of battle for most of his career, but that all changed when he joined the Fifth Planar and met Artorus Vallon. Enjoyment and thrill were replaced by honor and duty, more powerful forces by far.

General Vallon was different from every other general that Rreth had met. While most generals drooled at the chance to please the Wizard-King, Vallon was eager to please his men; while most generals sent their troops to the slaughter if it might gain them some strategic advantage, Vallon saw the value in an army that was fit, trained, and healthy; while most generals despised their task and wanted only to climb closer to a bland bureaucratic role somewhere near the feet of Brakken, Vallon wore his charge like a shining crown of gold, proud to serve the men of his army.

Vallon had many scars from the Planewars to be sure, and the armies of likely five or six other Wizards had surely vied for his general's life, but it was not pain or fear that fueled his passion. Rreth couldn't quite place what it was, but something drove Vallon on – not like a whip at his back, but like a treasure just beyond the next hill. His spirit and his ability to lead were drawn from a well of some unknown vigor that had always made Rreth curious.

But a soldier does not ask such questions of his general. Whatever force drove General Vallon to strive for victory, the lieutenant gladly devoted his life to this man, who would risk life and limb for his own soldiers.

And so Rreth and a couple dozen others now stood between charging cavalry and their goal. He had spotted Vallon rushing to their aid, and Rreth would hold the lines until his general could arrive and pull off another miraculous maneuver.

A huge wolf barreled toward Rreth, its rider having been felled by a thrown spear from the side. He dug his left foot into the soft earth and rammed the butt of the halberd beside it as he tipped the pole arm forward and leaned hard on it.

The wolf arrived, a flurry of raking claws and snarling fangs. The immense weight of the beast crashed into Rreth, but his stance held. Easily twice the large man's mass, the charging beast was impaled by the weapon, and the blade of the halberd emerged from the back of the wolf, skin tearing, spine cracking. This, however, did not stop the giant wolf from its gnashing as its body slid past the head of the weapon, an explosion of furry gore behind it. Rreth scowled at the gruesome sight as the dead – yet still fighting – creature slowly approached his face. The gnashing slowed and finally stopped as the beast's mouth, teeth of all different sizes protruding from it, came to a halt just inches before Rreth's scarred face.

Rreth gave the beast a snort of satisfaction as he dropped his halberd, now slick with the dark blood of the wolf, and the massive creature fell the rest of the way to the ground. The lieutenant slung the battle axe into his hands from its place at his back. He looked up to those front lines, now barely visible through the half dozen riders that had already broken through. His eyes met the gaze of one particular gob.

This goblin was the leader of this unit, the insignia of a captain of cavalry in the armies of the Wizard-King Kaladrius emblazoned on his chest. Most of the goblins wore little or no armor, though many of the wolves had spiked bits of metal and plating affixed to one part or another. This rider was wearing full plate of a ruddy brown, rusted hue, with a small tattered black cape fluttering behind him, and the creature's wiry muscles bulged from under the dark armor. Only the head of the gob was fully exposed; a long-since grotesquely broken nose nearly hid dark, hateful eyes of crimson set in a twisted and heavily scarred face of greenish-gray. His wolf mount was barded with a wicked helm and spiked plating, all caked in blood. In place of leather reins were spiked chains, and the goblin tightly held them in one of his gnarled hands, while the other gripped a large scimitar – big enough for a normal man.

His opponent locked eyes with Rreth, snarled, and spat an unknown insult in the gob tongue through his fang-like teeth. His wolf was still finishing chewing on an unfortunate swordsman of the Fifth Planar.

Rreth glanced around and found no allies nearby. All the men in the last line had broken off to engage the attackers or they were lain low in the ash near his feet.

His halberd, too, would be of no use. He could not spare a minute or two to wrestle it from the wolf corpse.

Then, two more wolf riders trotted up to either side of the gob captain. It was not common that Rreth felt fear on the battlefield, as adrenaline typically drowned it out. He felt it now, he was surprised to notice.

Vallon'd better get here quick, thought Rreth, as he tightened his grip on the large axe in his hands.

With a long spur into the side of his monstrous mountain wolf, the gob captain charged directly at Rreth, his two riders in tow.

A young half-dwarven man stood at the front of the battle lines as the bulk of the goblin wolf riders were still charging at them. The other soldiers affectionately called the stout man, sporting a bushy braided beard that jutted outward, "Stub." Stub was unshaken at the fearsome sight as he gripped his war hammer and small wooden shield. Sages tell of the old hatreds between the dwarves and the goblins, but this half-dwarf never cared about that. He had been raised by his human mother, his father long since dead on a forgotten battlefield on a foreign world. About now, though, the soldier could begin to see a reason for the hatred; gobs were vile beings. There is glory in battle, perhaps even a kind of enjoyment in a sound victory, but what these creatures' faces showed was pure bloodlust. All the races were at war, it was true, but gobs were bred for battle – they knew no joy outside of the slaughter.

Already, the men that had begun this skirmish on either side of Stub had fallen under the curved blades and thunderous paws of the riders and their beasts. Two more riders now were heading straight for him. His grip on his weapon tightened though sweat stung his eyes. He raised his shield high, preparing for his glorious end as the wolves drew ever closer.

Then, something that Stub did not expect occurred. Coming from somewhere outside his vision appeared a figure in shining armor. He whipped an elaborate sword from its sheath and, in the other hand, maneuvered a spear to point at the incoming cavalry.

The honorable General Artorus Vallon skidded to a halt in front of the two charging wolves, dust and ash flying up as he thrust his brilliant sword, shining in the three suns, into the earth beside him. The general quickly set his spear for the charge, and before the rider could react a terrible howl indicated that the spearhead found its mark. Stub found it hard to move as mere feet in front of him his exalted general fought with almost blinding speed before an onslaught of horrible beasts.

Stub had come to the Fifth Planar only recently, but he saw now what he'd heard from his fellow soldiers: in Artorus Vallon, the Fifth Planar had more than a general; a true hero of the Planewars stood at the head of this army. Many in The Vastness told stories of this man's skills in combat. Now Stub watched it for himself.

Artorus held the spear tight, but it snapped under the immense weight of the charging wolf. Half expecting the creature to tear him to shreds, spear or not, he had little choice but to duck as the goblin yelped and flew directly over him. Artorus dislodged his hefty sword from the ground in the same motion as he stood from his crouch. Spinning to gain the momentum he would need, he came around just in time to catch the other rider who was passing him on his right. A goblin scream sounded, and he watched a writhing arm fall in front of him with the wickedly curved, rusty sword still clutched in its grasp. The great wolf that the rider sat upon slid to a halt at the rider's command, but between the loss of his arm and the abruptness of the stop, this goblin did not also stop with his mount, and was instead thrown to the ground. He rolled to a stop, either unconscious or dead. The wolf, however, seemed no less interested in Artorus without its rider.

Artorus glanced back to see the spear-impaled wolf still writhing and sputtering blood from its mouth; it would not be tearing him to shreds after all. But another sight caught his eye: the goblin that had been thrown from that dying wolf was getting up, wincing at a broken arm, and stumbling on a leg that was in no better shape.

So Artorus was faced with a still-very-capable mountain wolf and a wounded goblin. Though it was likely that more cavalry bore down from behind him, he was forced to continue facing away from the assault as the huge wolf charged him. The general dashed to his left and, with a vice-strong grip, clasped the stumbling goblin by his broken arm. The scream was piercing, and the goblin's half-attempted swing at the general was quickly abandoned, another sword falling to the ashen earth. As the pattering of the wolf's paws in the soft earth rapidly approached, Artorus wrenched the goblin's arm, eliciting more screaming, and shoved the goblin directly between himself and the charging wolf.

The general's ploy seemed to work brilliantly as the raging wolf connected with flesh and proceeded to rend, not seeming to notice or care that the flesh was not of a man, but a goblin. Taking careful aim as the goblin's last screams fell silent, Vallon quickly closed the short distance with the wolf; its head was still lowered, teeth in the goblin's neck. Artorus swung a precise strike at the base of the wolf's skull, and a snapping sound was heard as the wolf's spine was cleanly severed. The massive body fell to the ground with a great thump and another cloud of ashen dirt.

Artorus glanced up at his lines of battle-wearied men, his face drenched in sweat and quickly collecting a layer of ash. His breath came in huffs, but the sight before him made him forget all his fatigue for just a moment. The lines of various races of humanoids – men, dwarves, and others – all looked to him with astonishment and let out a great cheer in the sun-drenched battlefield.

He couldn't help but smirk. Though, there was one man in front, who had not joined in the cheer but remained quite serious – a half-dwarf as best as the general could tell. At first, Artorus was curious.

Then, the man hurled his hammer directly at Artorus's head.

Rather surprised, the general began to duck, but he could already tell the throw was too high. That was the moment Artorus heard the thudding of more wolf paws from behind him. Spinning about, he saw just as the war hammer had smashed into the chest of a goblin rider, dismounting him. Already, though, the mountain wolf was on top of him. Artorus was caught with a claw or two digging into his leg, and what seemed to be the weight of an elephant slammed him to the ground.

The general heard another roar from the men behind him, and they charged up to his side. Much to Artorus's relief, as he writhed under the massive form of the wolf over him, the beast was quickly enveloped in a shroud of soldiers, spears, and blades. Before the wolf could get much more than scratches on the general, it turned its attention to the men around it and was shortly felled.

With more and more troops coming to defend the siege machinery, called by the sounds of the skirmish, the wolf riders had nearly all retreated or fallen, but the damage was done. Several of the riders, having broken through the lines early, had begun the slaughter of the engineers and craftsmen, at least one of them starting a serious blaze amid the mass of wood.

Kaladrius and his alchemists had somehow crafted a sticky, extremely flammable substance that the goblins termed "magic mud." Artorus had seen it burn many of his troops alive. And the result on this day was a flaming mass of screaming men and ruined weaponry.

Not having the time to fully assess the damage, Artorus could already tell they had lost at least half of the weapons, but it was not quite yet time to mourn for weapons or engineers; a huge form still thundered toward the men, much slower than the wolves, but with a terrible speed all its own.

Artorus strained hard to stand. One leg bled rather heavily from the claw wounds, and the other simply cramped from exertion. Still, he held to his blade, and he managed to steady his legs beneath him.

An ogre is something no soldier ever wishes to meet. While smaller than their greater cousins, the giants, ogres were a special creature of rage unparalleled. Ogres were nearly incontrollable, and it was uncommon for armies to field them. But tacticians generally agreed that, if one were to position an ogre wisely enough, few forces short of a Wizard's unholy touch could cause such carnage amongst one's enemy.

The huge brutish creature appeared mostly like a human, but with an overemphasized musculature, some bulging bony protrusions, and scraggly knotted hair about most of his head. Its skin was probably as thick as the heaviest armor, and one swing of the terrible monster's arms could clear entire defensive lines. It was easily six feet wide and almost twice as tall.

The ogre charged, the orcs having long since loosed their hold of his shackles, spurring him in the direction of the fray with the rattling of their chains.

Though most probably considered it, none of the men of the Fifth Planar Army would dare run while the great General Artorus Vallon held his ground at their lead, and they stared into the face of the charging ogre.

Artorus swore under his breath as he thought *This can't be the place I die.*

But he steadied his sword and pulled for his aching muscles to stand ready. Though ogres never hold one sight for very long – something about bad eyesight – the general could swear the beast was staring straight into his eyes with cold, calculated bloodlust. With humongous thundering feet rapidly closing on him, Artorus took what might have been the last breath he would ever need.

A tremendous snap and a great whir sounded over the assembled line of men. A huge spear, as long as a tall man and thicker than a forearm, with the first half consisting of metal and the rest sturdy wood, streaked over the heads of the troops. The ballista bolt struck soundly between the collar bones of the ogre, whose run quickly fell into a jog and then a stumble. The look on the beast's face was one of confusion as blood began to pour from its mouth.

Finally stopping not two dozen feet before Artorus, the creature wobbled, wavered, and fell forward.

A large dust cloud and a sickening crunch blinded all of Artorus's senses for a moment. As the haze slowly cleared, three things were revealed to the general. The first was a mountain of bleeding, twitching flesh, peaked with a gory spear-like tip protruding upward, where the ogre lay dying. The next was the dozen or so orcs that had marshaled the beast who were quickly making their retreat back around the hill from whence they came, with a half dozen of the goblin riders at their flanks. And also revealed was the fact that there was, at least, still one working ballista among the siege weaponry and men smart enough to man it.

The general huffed as his armor suffocated him, the ceasing battle finally allowing him to realize how much his lungs burned for oxygen. He unclasped his chest piece and the heavy plate fell to the ground with a thud. Around him his men mostly stood in disbelief, some searching for the bodies of their friends and just a few celebrating their victory with clasped hands and praise for their general.

Assistants rushed to help Artorus with his armor and wounded leg as he congratulated the men on a job well done. But he still had work to do. He limped his way around the site of the melee thanking his men for their bravery and skill and observing the honorable fallen.

The honorable fallen...

The death was nearly too much as he passed body after body. These were supposed to be the men who had survived the trials of this combat. They had not even cleaned the field of the night's bloodshed before more carnage was created, ending yet more young lives.

Artorus stopped as he came to a sullen sight. He stared at the remains of the half-dwarf that very well may have saved his life with his thrown hammer. It seemed he fell to the wolf's maw before the men subdued it.

"What was his name?" he asked one of the men who was preparing to move the body for burial.

"I'm sorry my lord, I do not know," replied the squire who was wrapping the corpse in cloth.

"We called him 'Stub,' sir," replied another voice from beside the general.

A dirtied half-elf stood with wounds still bleeding as he stared at the fallen half-dwarf.

"I never actually knew his name. But he was a good man, a good soldier, sir," the half-elf finished as he saluted to the general and hobbled off to have his own wounds tended to.

"Stub," Artorus repeated to himself, and the squires carried the body away.

Not even a true name by which to be remembered... he thought.

Another mishandled prayer to Koth for a name that was not his would have to suffice.

In all the many years Artorus had spent on the battlefield, the deaths were still so powerful to him. Most men of war had become numb to it, but Artorus could not. He had promised a fallen friend long ago. Artorus Vallon would never stop feeling the sharp pain of death until the Wizard-King was dethroned and the Planewars were ended.

Artorus had secretly been planning a rebellion for more than four years now. It was still barely more than clandestine letters to the right people, or what he'd hoped were the right people, and a few select agents in safe houses around the whole of Myrus – whispers on the wind – but in those four years a momentum had built, nonetheless. The men of his army didn't know of his plan – not yet. They probably wouldn't even follow him on his fool's quest. But soon, the death would stop; it had to. All his life he'd borne witness to death and carnage – he'd *created* death and carnage – at the whim of a madman. Lord Brakken the War Maker had owned Artorus since he was born. Artorus did not choose a life of military service; he was one of hundreds of thousands of beings that were born to it – millions upon millions of lives across the myriad planes to fuel the never-ending wars of the Wizard-Kings.

Of those twenty-seven known worlds, Artorus had visited five of them. Being in a Planar Army of The Vastness made Artorus more well-traveled than most mortals. But on every world Artorus had visited was the same sad story: despair, carnage, destruction.

It would all end soon, or Artorus would die trying to end it. The mass of bloodied corpses that littered the ground around him stood testament to that simple fact. It had to end.

"General," called a melancholy voice from behind.

Artorus turned to see three men bearing a stretcher, and on it, a corpse. Even missing his right arm, and the rest burned badly, Artorus could tell who it was. The general stared at the corpse for a silent moment then nodded solemnly to the men.

Not him... thought Artorus with a sick feeling twisting his gut. *A non-believer's prayer won't suffice for this brave soul... Nothing will soothe this loss... It all has to end...*

The dull-eyed troops carried away the remains of the once-mighty Lieutenant Rreth.

Chapter II – Magnid Hathey

Twelve years ago, Artorus was a captain in the Fifth Planar Army, promoted after a nine-month tour of duty on a strange world known as Ebbea.

It was a harsh place, to be sure. The Sages told of the pull that each world exerts on the beings there, forcing them toward the ground; they called it *gravity*. The gravity of Ebbea was somewhat stronger than most of the worlds, or so they said, and it made for interesting effects on the body, not to mention the fauna of the world. Supposedly, this was where orcs and goblins were first found, accounting for their greater muscle mass.

Artorus always took care to hear the tales told by the people and the places he encountered, though at his core he was a man of duty, not a scholar. No thoughts of rebellion had yet pervaded his mind, and he was still married to a woman he loved dearly.

Being promoted to a captain was a great honor for the young Artorus. He'd entered the army as a simple foot soldier and made his way to the rank of sergeant shortly after that, but sergeants were numerous and they were still enlisted men. Captain was the entering rank for officers in the armies of The Vastness. Now that he was an officer, what new challenges would he face? Would he prove a good leader for these men?

Returning to his home world, called Myrus, from the long months of battle, Artorus was happy at the prospect of seeing his wife again.

Just thoughts of her would lighten his pack and brighten gloom from days of battle, but he still had some time yet before he could see her. The Fifth Planar Army was no longer on tour, but there was the debriefing for the officers, the recruitment, and intensive training that would take up the next nine months or so. But he was home, nonetheless, and being on the same world as Elsa brought him joy.

And Myrus herself offered beauty too. This was one of the original twin worlds upon which history as it is known began. The three original mortal races – man, elf, and dwarf – each called the Twin Worlds home originally. An old place, replete with stories of the great long-lost cities and ancient forests. It was true that nearly every larger city had been razed more than once in the Planewars, but some of the oldest villages in the known worlds dotted these lands – older, they say, than the Wizards' rule.

But no story and no sight Myrus could offer would compare to the chance to see Elsa again...

"... And don't forget to look into the grain problem," ordered General Hathey to one of the lieutenants, as he slowly walked through the fort. "An army with sick horses is no army at all. I don't care if we're not deployed."

The general smiled at the lieutenant – a human named Thatch – and then the subordinate saluted and headed off toward the stable area.

General Magnid Hathey was a doumir – a child of both dwarfdom and elfdom. The doumir were interesting characters, with most being awkward sorts of creatures, but the rare exception was an impressive being: all the sturdiness and mirth of a dwarf with the unequaled grace and wisdom of an elf. Hathey was certainly one of those exceptions. The general had a short, kempt beard of dirty blonde that complemented his long, light, tied-back hair, barely revealing his slightly pointed ears. A pale skin tone helped all the more for his vibrant green eyes to shimmer in the bright spring morning like shining emeralds. Not quite lean, but certainly not heavily muscled, the general stood at about five feet and wore loose-fitting and rather fine clothing when not in battle. More noticeable than any other trait of his, though, the general often wore a smile on his face – something rarely seen on a general of the Planewars. He spoke with wisdom and he treated his men with fairness, and so was well liked among the soldiers and officers at his command.

Artorus was no exception; he'd decided that he very much liked being in Hathey's army. He'd been transferred along with his regiment over to the Fifth Planar Army barely more than a year prior, and his former general was not nearly so enjoyable. General Jokon was a cruel half-orc who, though undeniably talented on the field of battle, would not blink at the sacrifice of thousands of men if it would gain him a strategic advantage. Jokon's Third Planar Army was often selected for the most brutal deployments and usually had both a high rate of casualty and a constant influx of new recruits and transfers. Such as it was, Artorus was happy when the call came to join the Fifth; more men were needed for an extended peacekeeping campaign currently based on Myrus. Of course, war rarely went as planned, and the Fifth Planar was called to other worlds to reinforce other Planar divisions, such as their time on Ebbea.

"So you see, home for an army is simply where the general makes it, gentlemen," Hathey continued with his usual smile, as he strolled with Artorus and the six other newly promoted officers. "The best part of a lifelong soldier is the unparalleled adaptability, learned in youth and kindled through constant reinforcement."

Hathey saluted at a small group of soldiers who had stopped their meal to salute their general as he passed.

"As you were, men," he said, nodding to them.

There were several more stops on their trek through the camps. Basic instructions came with each stop; the stables had taught the officers the importance of good feed, the mess tent held a lesson on letting soldiers rest and rejuvenate, the smiths taught of the integrity of an army's equipment, but the small group finally reached their ultimate destination on this trip.

"This is the primary lesson which I share with each of my officers," the general said as he stopped and motioned to the mortuary. "And it is how my army operates."

He turned about, facing the group of officers, the smile dropping quickly from his expression.

"War is death," he said plainly.

Those bright green eyes suddenly took on a certain intensity without the general's usual smile, and he directed that intensity at each of the seven men in turn.

"War is pain; war is starvation and disease; war is desperation and solitude," the general continued. "War – is – death."

Each of the seven men had the experience with death that a life in the military would bring, and none of them were new to it by any stretch, yet somehow, hearing it from the normally cheerful man lent a certain gravitas. It was as though the general represented the one stronghold of mirth and vitality in a world of gloom and death – *many worlds* of gloom and death – and now he stood in front of his men and told them precisely otherwise.

The dwarf next to Artorus, named Hoggin, who joined the Fifth Planar as a commander, could only glance away as Hathey's gaze passed over him. Most of the officers squirmed under the general's gaze, but Artorus was last in the lineup and he knew this was a test of sorts.

It stung to think of all the deaths Artorus had witnessed as the general looked into his eyes last, holding his gaze for a long moment. At once, so too did cold, dead eyes stare at him from a thousand memories of a hundred battles: men, women, and children, each with that same exact look on their face. He'd not felt such pain from the thought of death since his first days on the battlefield, yet now he felt every death from then until now as the general's eyes were locked with his. The feeling nearly crushed Artorus.

"Only a sadist and a sociopath would take enjoyment from war," Hathey finally continued after the painfully long silence. "You'll find no such man in my army."

General Hathey waited for something – a question, perhaps.

"Sir, pardon me for saying so – I mean no offense, but—" Artorus began.

"Now that you are an officer in my army," Hathey interrupted plainly, "you needn't apologize for anything you say to me in good taste, Captain Vallon. You cannot offend me with your input; it is the very reason I've promoted you." That smile of his returned as he nodded to Artorus. "Please, continue."

"Sorr— uh, right, I won't, sir," stuttered Artorus. "Well, my question is this: you speak of how no man should find enjoyment in war, but you yourself are a cheerful man. I do not think you could find a soldier in your army that has not noticed that, sir."

"Rightly so," responded the general as he began to pace in front of the small group. "For you see, an officer, and a general more so, can and *must* separate himself from war on a philosophical level. Our job is war, gentlemen, do not mistake me, but we, as people, are more than a job. War is the purpose for a general to be a part of an army, war is his task, but war does not *make* the general. Only he can do that for himself." The finely dressed doumir sighed deeply before continuing, "The death and dismay I have seen could fill the volumes of a Sage, but all of the pain cannot stop me from being who I am. And an officer in my army shall do the same, or he shall return to the ranks.

"Each of you will look upon and ponder the deaths of any soldier in your charge. Most men in the armies of The Vastness have become desensitized to the death, but here in the Fifth Planar, we must feel it sharply. While the others lose themselves in war, we remain clear-headed. While the others will not be the same when they return to their families on leave, we shall retain that which makes us who we are.

"Is it painful? Is it difficult? Will it wrench the very soul of my officers?" He had stopped pacing again, turning back to his listeners. "Most assuredly. But will it be a worthwhile cost to pay?"

He sighed once more and spoke earnestly.

"It will."

The group was dismissed shortly thereafter, but this first lesson from his new general would return to Artorus's thoughts for years to come. And those years passed quickly while Artorus was in Hathey's army. Being based on his home plane meant that he could see his wife a precious few more times a year.

Artorus studied his general intently in this time. He was neither a brilliant strategist nor an impressive warrior on his own, but he could lead men and inspire greatness in those around him, and so his army was unstoppable. Performing exemplarily under the leadership of the general, Artorus was promoted to a commander, and then a high commander, and eventually to Hathey's top lieutenant. Advancement through the ranks like Vallon's was rarely seen in Wizard-King Brakken's armies, and he was as surprised as any of the other officers about it. But Hathey must have seen something in Artorus that Artorus did not even see in himself, and he found the general to be more than just a superior officer – he was a friend.

Now, five years after Artorus had joined Hathey's army, they had deployed to a world known as Munos to be committed for a massive war effort to reinforce a crumpling defense against a Wizard-King calling himself Emperor Ziov. This was a new opponent to the Fifth Planar – or, at least sporadic enough in the span of the Planewars that the two Wizards had not drawn battle in Artorus's lifetime as far as he was aware. The Fifth Planar had just come through the worldgate in an assignment to reinforce the Nineteenth Planar Army as the last few remaining forces Brakken held on this continent of Munos.

The plane of Munos was practically the opposite of Ebbea. The world's pull was light, making marches easier and allowing for some truly spectacular maneuvers from the more acrobatic fighters in a pinch. But the days were short here, which could disorient a soldier almost as much as Ebbea's gravity. A sleep-deprived fighter is not much of a fighter.

"Lieutenant Vallon," called General Hathey as he pored over maps on a hastily erected table amid still-rising tents.

Artorus, gleaming in his new set of armor, cape fluttering in the cool wind blowing in from the sea several miles west, approached from where he was helping men unload spears from the carts. Humorously enough, the spears would almost seem to spring up in the low gravity of

Munos, making for some comedic scenes among the soldiers as equipment would fly from their hands and they would trip over their own feet, overcorrecting their balance.

"Damn." Hathey grinned. "I was just getting used to calling you 'high commander.'"

"I won't apologize for your mistakes, sir," retorted Vallon, straight faced.

Hathey let out a hearty laugh.

"You know," the general admitted, "sometimes I think I only promoted you so that I could have someone with a sense of humor following me around more often. You're lousy with a sword, you know!"

Artorus smirked.

"Now stop distracting me," the general went on. "I'm fearful that our hold of this worldgate is tentative, at best. I want you to lead the reorganization to ensure our supplies don't get disrupted here."

Hathey glanced around at the terrain that surrounded them and cursed softly, "Wizard's fire! The way this valley climbs in all directions, it could be a death trap and we'd never see it coming. And if I were one of Ziov's generals, I'd pinch our crumbling defenses off right here and now."

Soldiers and officers were all milling about, busy with their own tasks as the two stood over the small table.

Artorus nodded in agreement. "And, sir, what do you know about this Ziov?"

"Nothing but the fact that he's a bloodthirsty tyrant, bent on multiversal domination, who will slit throats and bury kingdoms to get what he wants," replied Hathey in a matter-of-fact tone.

Artorus cleared his throat.

"I realize he's a Wizard, sir. I was wondering what else you know about him."

The doumir smiled and opened his mouth to retort, but his smile quickly faded as he glanced behind Artorus.

Shouting sounded from the south side of the camp. Then noise erupted from the northeast as well, and soldiers dropped barrels and tentpoles for weapons and shields.

"There's that ambush..." muttered Artorus as he gritted his teeth.

Artorus began to charge toward the southern disturbance, drawing his long sword. A strange noise stopped him, though. Some sort of scraping metal, with a soft grunt.

Artorus's stomach wrenched as he halted and turned around, somehow already knowing what the sound was.

Lieutenant Vallon saw General Hathey, leader of the Fifth Planar Army, mentor, and friend for six years, trembling as two feet of blade protruded slightly upward from his chest, dripping blood in the wind. The general fell to his knees, a look of shock on his face, and Artorus saw a cloaked dwarf behind him.

High Commander Hoggin, who had stood beside Artorus all those years ago and met the general with him, now stood over the dying doumir with a sick smile stretching across his dark face, and he spat on the ground beside him. He hissed something at the fallen general. Artorus only caught "... paid well."

With a scream, Artorus charged now for his general's assailant. As men were running in all directions, only a few others had noticed their leader fall.

Hoggin rapidly withdrew his blade and retreated with four other figures that Artorus thought he recognized, similarly cloaked, blending into the chaos about the camp. Artorus was determined, however, not to let him get away, and he called orders to the nearest troops around the command area as he ran. But a new noise stopped him one last time as he was passing the fallen doumir.

"Vallon," called a sickly voice. It was painful to hear.

After a desperate glance into the swirling mass of bodies where the dwarf and his conspirators fled, Artorus quickly approached his fallen friend.

"General! Hold on, we will summon the surgeons," cried Vallon, but Hathey held up a bloodied hand.

"It is of no" – a cough spurted blood onto the general's beard – "no use..."

The doumir's eyes were slowly becoming distant and he slouched as Artorus tried to hold up his head and shoulders.

"Please, sir, just hold on."

Artorus felt tears welling in his eyes as frantic soldiers could now only stand around him, seeing their general with a mortal wound. The crowd grew as the sound of the battles moved farther away from the camp in either direction.

"I lied to you," Hathey managed to say between coughing, blood still dribbling from his mouth, "I lied..."

"No, sir," Artorus said.

He was unsure how to find the words for the dying man; all of the soldiers were quiet.

The general continued, "I did... You are good leader... and a much finer s-swordsman than I ever was."

He was using the last of his breath for a quip? A pained smile reached the doumir's lips as his shining eyes were locked with Artorus's.

A strained laugh finally released the tears as Artorus shook his head.

With a shaking hand, Magnid Hathey pointed to the table at which he'd been standing.

"R-read the letter," he sputtered.

Artorus glanced at the table, but remained at the doumir's side.

The general managed his final words: "War... is death... Artorus..."

His grip tightened on Artorus's forearm, then the general spasmed once and fell limp.

As the sounds of fighting grew more distant still, a solemn silence held all the various soldiers and officers for some time.

Artorus embraced his friend and mentor.

Many moments later, Artorus was sitting stunned at the table next to where his general had fallen. He held a cloth in his hands, but the blood would not wipe from his fingers.

The attacks were simply a distraction for this assassination. It appeared Ziov thought Hathey to be a threat and must have paid in bags of gold to have him betrayed by his own officers.

Numbly, Artorus set down the bloodied cloth and opened the letter that was lying partially under the strewn maps, wax still soft on the seal.

SCS 337, 9th Day of 5th Month

To: Lord General Kremaine and staff,

This letter of recommendation for succession, should the worst happen, shall effect in full my judgment for the assumption of leadership of the Fifth Planar Army. This letter replaces all previous recommendations. Let it be recorded that I recommend for my replacement with the highest regard, the honorable Lieutenant Vallon.

Signed,
General Magnid Hathey,
Fifth Planar Army

Chapter III – Family and Friends

As it turned out, the goblin riders and their ogre were just one of three surprise assaults that struck shortly after third sunrise on the fourth day of the Battle of Harmony Valley. General Hemmet had engineered what he'd hoped would have been a safe withdrawal for his forces against the proven superior tactics of Vallon. But Vallon's army managed to repel each assault and disrupt their retreat enough to take the island fortress a few weeks later.

Mala always did have an ear for tactics, and her brother would often submit to her wishes by humoring her with battle plans, tales of maneuvering vast forces, and poring over maps at all hours of night. And, truth be told, Mala wouldn't ever refuse a story of a good swordfight.

It was comforting to have Artorus home again. Of course, simply seeing him was rewarding in itself, but also, they had work to do.

Mala Andrius was a noblewoman and made the effort to carry herself as such. All the years of lessons at her father's behest had obviously had their intended effect, but even more so, Mala found it allowed her to get what she wanted from the people in power – it was a useful tool.

Mala's auburn hair fell just to her shoulders, and she often pinned it back with simple barrettes. Though her status gave her wealth, she saw no need to display it in her clothing; it was clean, it was of good quality, but not made of expensive silks or embroidered linens. She was a somewhat tall woman whose soft blue eyes, her brother always reminded her, tended to show exactly what she was thinking.

Mala smiled at the thought of having her brother back home. It was time to get to work.

"Honestly," Mala said to her half brother in her calm, commanding voice, "I think we're not moving quite quickly enough. There is more I can do from here."

"Mala—" he began to retort, but she interrupted.

"I know, I know. 'Patience is a trait of a great strategist.' You've said it before. But is not *initiative* important in war?"

She raised an eyebrow; the answer to her question was obvious.

"Of course, Mala, but initiative is nothing without the means to act on it," he stated. "And more than three centuries in absolute control of everything in all the worlds *pretty well* proves that the Wizards have had the initiative for some time, I think." Artorus shook his head slightly before continuing. "I've been over it in my head a thousand times. The only way I can see to truly shake this empire is from the outside. Of course, I've just set Kaladrius back a few months in that regard and Phax has been on the defensive for some time now. Really that leaves only that vile creature, Krakus, or the maybe the crazed Ziov, or perhaps some combination of the lot... unless Quirian is going to break the Hundred Years Truce..."

Artorus shook his head again.

"But," he admitted, "even if the thought of somehow working with those Wizards didn't turn my stomach, Lord Brakken is not stupid. Even in the heat of battle, you hear the calls of the horns and you see the maneuvers of the unit before they charge you. Brakken will see anything I could possibly do to aid his rivals militarily and squelch it; and then you would have a rolling head for a brother."

"Don't say that," Mala pleaded quietly.

"Mala, war *is* death," he told her, his tone darkening some, "and we presume to bring the fight to the very doorstep of the beings whose existence is defined by warfare. It is like seeing the ogre tear your troops apart like paper while weapons bounce off its hide and then grabbing a spear to charge it." A sigh escaped him. "I do this because..." Artorus continued, looking away, "well, because I must, but I do not have illusions that I will survive it."

"Artorus, our letters across the multiverse are brilliant," Mala pleaded softly. "With my knowledge of the nobility and your knowledge of the military leaders, we know so many who might have the power to help us make a change. And already we've rallied hundreds of able and willing souls to our cause right here, in The Vastness. We are hidden well throughout the plane. You have to see that we're making a difference. You have to see that we can disrupt this Dominance from within. Let the future of this empire one day rest in the hands of *its own people*." She sighed. "I simply fear the longer we delay, the more chance there is we are discovered. No matter how carefully we addressed and delivered those letters, we are advertising our blasphemous and illegal intentions."

"Strange to hear you call action against the Wizard 'blasphemy,' Mal."

"Don't change the subject," she said, returning the smirk.

"But I'm so good at it," her brother retorted. "And you've got to do what you're good at, right?"

"You're good at strategy... You're good at inspiring those you lead, you're good at swinging your sword around, but you have *never* been good at debate. So don't change the subject."

Artorus laughed at this.

"You remember that time your father wrung my hide for telling him how to administer his staff?" Artorus's eyes sparkled the way only a youthful tale of rebellion could make them. "Right as he was in the middle of chiding me for ruining another set of clothing? He chased me around the house, his face red with the alcohol and the anger, and there I was: mostly naked, still covered in mud. How's that for a debate?"

His laugh was earnest.

Mala laughed heartily in return. In truth, she didn't remember much about her time at home with Artorus – he'd left for the armies when she was just four years old, but he always had stories for her from that brief time – stories about her as a babe, stories about life with their mother, stories that felt like home.

Somehow Mala felt that the young man, only five years older than she was, had grown so much faster than he should have. Perhaps it was the loss of his father at such a young age, or perhaps his struggles with her own father, trying to play a paternal role for a rebellious son. Even from a very young age, she did remember the fights they would have – the two men of the family.

At that time, she only wished it would stop. Like so many things, though, Mala never truly knew how much she needed the company of her brother until he was taken from her. Even at four years old, the clarity of the situation was her most powerful memory from childhood.

She still had a clear image in her mind of an older brother, holding a practice sword and standing in the bright doorway out of the manor house of her father's estate. It was a complex memory, as it filled her at once with peace and love and sorrow and shock.

A brief pause followed. The crackle of the fire and the warm light it cast in Mala's study were a comfort as the two siblings thought back to simpler times.

"You're right," he finally said. "The pace of our recruitment is not adequate, and the task is perhaps somewhat more accomplishable with even our current resources than I imply. Sometimes I think I stall at the thought of bringing more people into our plot simply because of the danger we will face. But that was always the plan. We always knew this was a deadly task. The liberty will not come without facing the dangers."

Mala couldn't help but smirk. He often agreed with her after time enough to think. *You're right* was practically a tag line when Artorus spoke with her. She wasn't actually sure if it was her ability to debate or if it was something Artorus did of his own accord. But she'd hardly argue it.

"I just can't recklessly risk the lives of those we've already swept up in our plot," he continued, "and I *can't* lose you too, Mala... I just can't..."

A sharp pain shot through her chest. She thought of Elsa: her golden hair, her endearing smile, her endless love for the only brother Mala ever had. Mala missed her sister-by-law so much. It was painful every time she thought of it. Elsa took with her to the grave so many things: the greatest happiness Artorus had ever know in his war-torn life, a shining example that life within the Planewars was not truly void of serenity or love, some of the best cooking Mala had ever tasted… the unborn child in her belly…

"I miss her too," she said as a tear fell from her eye.

Strange, she thought in introspection, *I seldom cry for her anymore.*

Another pause in the low-lit meeting room. Then Artorus spoke, this time with renewed resolve.

"For her, we must push on. To prove to the Wizards – to all people – that hope did not die with that amazing woman." He began to nod as he spoke on, "She is with Koth, isn't she, Mala? Watching over us?" Mala nodded. "Then for her, we will end this soon. We will stop the wars that have claimed so many – *so many*."

"We will," Mala affirmed, "for her."

Taking a deep breath, Artorus shook his head.

"There is still the matter of the Wizard-King himself," he said in a more thoughtful tone as his tactical mind returned to him. "We've been putting this off, but it has to be discussed. These creatures are not like you or me, Mala. They do not bleed when they are cut. They do not die when they are run through. They can kill us with a thought and a wave of the hand. I've seen Wizards lay hundreds of soldiers low. Some contend that they are gods."

"They are no gods, my brother," Mala calmly replied. "Koth will guide us. You say you don't see how, but Koth will guide us; *he* is god, not these Wizards."

Mala's religion, known as Kythianism, was the worship of Koth, the Lord of Truth and Justice.

All existence is an extension of Koth, known as Kythia. All faithful Kythians believe that both Truth and Justice exist everywhere in the multiverse as Koth's will, but certain things can cloud them. A Kythian must become closer with Koth to pierce the Fog of deception and evil and see the multiverse with the True Sight.

Though evil was certainly present in Kythianism, it was not such a fairy tale as some of the other religions that created some devilish figure to be the embodiment of evil in mortal-kind. No, Koth was Truth and Justice, but mortals were imperfect. The Fog could make good men act poorly. Beings like the Wizards perpetuated the Fog as they were *very* far from Koth, but the Lord of Truth was always there to guide his faithful.

Mala was far from achieving True Sight, but like all Kythians she practiced it through prayer, words, and actions. It was said that Koth watched over all those who followed his ideals, both in life and in death. True, it was one of a large number of religions that existed in the numerous worlds, and each religion had its zealots. But Mala was a true Kythian and she had no doubts.

It had always disconcerted her that Artorus was not a believer. But then, the Fog can envelop even the most heroic, for not bravery, nor might, nor intellect is a substitute for the True Sight. Mala had much work to do, but she strived always to honor the Truth of Koth.

She and her brother discussed these matters from time to time, but he would always retract when the topic was broached. He had suffered wounds deep enough that the Fog obstructed his every thought. One day, perhaps, he could see Truth, but Mala knew it would take time.

Typhondrius tried his best to be patient, which was not normally difficult for the precise elf. He knew the Master Artorus had only just returned, and he knew the Lady Mala was never comfortable being away from her brother for long. His last deployment had lasted nearly eight months – so he allowed his ladyship her time with family.

And, if he was honest with himself, Typhondrius had spent most of his life waiting. Waiting to serve, waiting to be of use... Perhaps even waiting to die...

Typhondrius was an elf of tall stature – as elves go – and determined poise. He dressed well and had a noble air that distinguished him from most. His right ear, though, told a tale of violence in his past, as it was nearly missing and only mutilated flesh remained as a centerpiece of a large burn mark that covered much of the right side of his head.

He was leanly muscled beneath his loose clothing; in fact, he'd been practicing with a blade lately, taking up lessons with one of the recruiters that recently moved into the compound. But Typhondrius's true task was administrative in nature, and in most capacities, he functioned as a servant for the Lady Andrius though she called him friend.

The compound was beginning to get a bit crowded, actually. With the inclusion of his sword master and the other teachers and tutors, Typhondrius now counted a grand total of fifty-four guests in the compound; from dwarven officers of war to human politicians and elven bureaucrats, each had given up their life somewhere in The Vastness to go into hiding and join the secret rebellion. It was a large compound, true, so fifty-four was not nearly an impossible number, but already new constructions were being prepared for further guests.

These rebels aimed to release the imprisoned lands from the immortal Wizard-King. Being an outlaw himself, Typhondrius could hardly begrudge them their illegal plot, but the lengths to which the lone elf could help were minor. And so he assisted the Lady Andrius and the General Vallon in any way he could.

The servant looked down at the letter in his hand. It had only just arrived late in the night yesterday, but he'd wanted the general to get his rest. And now, in the late morning of the summer, it seemed the urgency of the document – if he guessed right – would outweigh politeness.

Lightly, he knocked on the door of the study.

"My lady?"

Mala called for her servant and friend to enter the room. She had heard him shuffling outside the door for a short time now. She smiled as he entered, both as a kindness and because it warmed her heart to think of the good elf's immutable patience. How long had he waited before she even detected him?

He held in his hand a letter, and immediately she knew.

"This arrived—" he began.

"Last night, from a runner," she finished for him, unable to hide her excitement. "I know, Typhondrius. But is it what we'd hoped for?"

"It is indeed," Typhondrius replied. "It is addressed to you, Master Artorus." He approached the general, who stood as Typhondrius bowed to him. "It is good to see you, my lord."

"Noble Typhondrius, the pleasure is all mine," Artorus responded in mock flourish, which dissolved quickly as a large smile stretched across his face.

He grabbed the elf by the shoulder and squeezed endearingly. "I missed you, Ty."

Unable to resist the man's smile, as could few, Typhondrius returned it and admitted, "Likewise, Master Artorus."

"So it's true?" asked Artorus.

Mala was now standing as well as she laid her hand on Typhondrius's shoulder and peered over it at the letter.

"It really is from the Sage of Delemere?" Artorus asked, awestruck.

"Yes, the personal seal confirms it." Typhondrius nodded as he handed it over to Artorus. "Let us hope there is some good news in it."

Artorus opened the letter. It was written on fine paper, in fine ink. Mala had been raised as a noblewoman, and she recognized goods of high quality. She had sent perhaps thousands of missives in her duties as the magistrate of timber management for the southern lowland provinces, but none were of a quality such as this.

She'd never had interactions with Sages; mostly no one had, but by the look of this piece, their penmanship alone seemed deserving of a reputation. It was getting harder still to conceal her girlish excitement.

Sages were intriguing beings. They were said to be immortal, and Mala had no reason to disbelieve it. Supposedly this Sage of Delemere had been there, in his reclusive mountain keep, since before the Planewars. Delemere was a tiny monastery, very high in the mountains of Mala's home country, known as the Winterlands, and by all accounts the Sage made a journey from the mountains exactly four times each year to various destinations on-world and off, but always to collect knowledge. It was said that there is no knowledge in the twenty-seven worlds that one Sage or another does not know. Since childhood, the Sages had fascinated Mala immensely.

Artorus scanned the document and his brow furled in thought. And when he caught the expectant gaze that Mala was displaying, he set the letter on the table beside them so they could all read at once.

SCS 343, 12th Day of 9th Month
To the distinguished General Vallon,

Dear human, please let me begin by saying I cannot endorse any actions which I surmise to be planned behind these questions. As a Sage, it is not my place nor my desire to interfere with the activity of mortals. We are scholars, we are scientists, we are observers, we are recorders; we are not participants. As teachers, too, I am however obliged to respond to your questions to the best of my ability. And, per your request, I shall respect their secrecy.

You ask how Wizards came to power and how the Planewars came to be.

In history, it is usually quite difficult to pinpoint a single cause for latter effects. And the Planewars have been going long enough that only a Sage could hope to answer the question in confidence, I believe.

It is not entirely common knowledge that, long ago, before the outer worlds were known to even Sages, before orcs or giants or griffons or the merfolk were known, the Wizards were a subservient class – an instrument for those in power. They lived among dwarves, elves, and humans and ruled over none. Much as today, however, they were widely thought to be the only creatures capable of wielding magic.

Like most beings, men feared that which was more powerful than they. To the historian's eye, it would seem ironic that the Wizards of old held but a glimmer of the power the Wizards now know. Though men wished very much to keep these instruments of their bidding, the Wizards did eventually come to realize that the mortals could not contain their powers.

It started with just one of their kind. And thus shall the name of Gorrithas forever live in infamy. It is agreed, in tales now long lost to mortal historians, that other Wizards had slain their masters before Gorrithas. He was, however, the first Wizard to take land and title from his king for himself and become the ruler of a land – the first Wizard-King, one might argue. Every powerful man who held ownership of a Wizard had good reason to fear for his life after this. And thus, with the Wizard's flame, did the rule of mortals end.

The twin worlds of Mortis and Myrus were all that was known to history at this time. If one is to consider the history of the Planewars, though, we must consider how the new worlds became known.

Nearly seventy-two years to the day after Gorrithas had seized power, he was slain by his protégé, who would later come to be called Master Fadrus, Lord of the Darkness and Bringer of Worlds. And it was this being that found the most important of secrets: that our two worlds were not all of existence. Just as the great forces tied Mortis and Myrus together in the vast æther, so too were there other worlds tethered as they spun through the great emptiness. Fadrus somehow discovered this fact, and he learned how to pierce The Vastness and go to these other worlds.

The Wizards of this time worked together to create the worldgates, strange as that may seem to a modern observer. This is yet one more topic about which the order of Sages greatly desires more information, as exceedingly little is known of how this process worked, how Fadrus came to know of it, or why the knowledge was eventually lost with him.

Things went on this way for some time – nearly one hundred fifty years, known as the age of expansion. And when it was discovered that the seemingly infinite worlds were, in fact, a mere twenty-seven, the cooperation and the construction of the worldgates stopped abruptly. Records of Fadrus disappear entirely, and many other Wizards came to prominence as they battled for Dominance over one another.

Let it be said: many Sages have commented on the strife caused by the most greedy and bloodthirsty tyrants of mortals – strange as that may sound now – but man hath no wrath like that of Wizard-kind. A new epoch was born as empires sprung in a hundred directions to dozens of new worlds. Each Wizard-King hastened to claim the worlds as their own. The conflict escalated through a long and intricate series of events, and we now call it the Planewars.

It has now been more than three centuries of war by the Standardized Count of the Sages.

So, you ask how things came to be this way. Having the sight of a Sage, I now see no other way things could be. The mighty Wizard-Kings are a force beyond all others known to history. True though it may be that the God-Kings of old were said to be mighty – perhaps mightier than the Wizards, it would seem that they could not have dreamed up the conflict in which the once-called "civil races" now live.

This is my briefest answer to your question and further correspondence would be requisite to further detail.

Your second question asks of how a Wizard might be killed.

In this discourse, I must apologize, as I have very little information for you. I've had few interactions with Wizards. I've not seen a Wizard killed, and it is certain that they do not die of age, as a mortal would. And yet, the histories all agree with certainty that there are fewer of them now than there were; I can attest to this with my own observations. In times past, when they were subservient and weaker, the Wizards numbered in the hundreds. One relatively reliable figure by the Sage of Timmanthy recorded two hundred seventy. As you know, there are now seventeen Wizards known to the multiverse, and it seems highly doubtful that there would be any more about which the Sages do not know.

Be warned: conjecture will breed misunderstanding and misdirection as easily as it breeds knowledge and understanding; a careful hand is required.

In this dangerous realm of conjecture, one could expound. Sources do agree that Wizards who committed an egregious offense to their masters in the age that they served mortals were destroyed. Very little was said of how exactly this was done, other than a few mentions of certain "Councils of Judgment." It is rather clear, both from the histories and from modern observations that wounds which would kill a mortal are little more than an inconvenience to a Wizard.

> Though I have further hypotheses concerning this matter, I'm afraid that, until such time as I can formulate a proper theory, I would not share them in written correspondence with one such as yourself. I'll likely make it a topic of minor research in the coming decades.
>
> May you always be observant.
> With both sight and knowledge for the worlds,
> Kellos, Sage of Delemere

The three stood over the letter in a long silence as they read and reread, until finally Typhondrius spoke.

"My lord," he said, "I am sorry."

Artorus looked up from the letter to meet Typhondrius's eyes with a quizzical look.

The elf shook his head. "It does not seem that this news is quite so good."

Artorus waited a moment before he responded, formulating his words. "Ty, I've led hundreds of thousands of men in my days as a general, into battles that might very well have spelt their doom – every last one of those men. Even with a full complement of scouts, it's hard to know much about your enemy, but I've marched men through worldgates to hostile planes without any chance to garner intelligence." He held the elf's gaze, as one finger of his prodded the letter. "So, trust me when I say: I can work with this. This is *information*; perhaps the deadliest weapon in war."

Artorus shook his head and chuckled as he continued now to both of them. "To be truthful, I half expected this Sage to turn us in the minute he saw the letter – you both know of the contingencies I put in place for this."

Typhondrius raised an eyebrow. "I see your point, Master Artorus, but perhaps I missed something in the letter… I took it to state that the

Wizard-Kings are incredibly powerful, they live forever, and cannot be slain by mortals." He looked to Mala and her brother in earnest inquiry.

"And that may be exactly all we gain from this in the end," Artorus admitted with an open-handed gesture, "but tactics are my specialty, and I shall pore over this until I've deciphered all possible courses of action for our sorry band of hopefuls." He grinned mischievously at Typhondrius. "First, I'd like for you to get three copies of this drawn, Ty. One for each of us. We represent an important difference in perspective that I think will someday serve this rebellion well. We must study this."

Artorus's grin faded into a thoughtful expression as Typhondrius nodded to him and took the scroll back.

"It is funny, isn't it?" pondered Mala to the pair. "Clandestine letters have made up a majority of our rebellion so far, haven't they? But we never thought we'd get one from *him*. I think this marks a change in direction for our plans..."

Even as her mind raced with thoughts, Mala looked at her brother with a smile. It seemed as though she would get her wish after all; things were likely about to start moving more quickly.

For what had become years, Lord Landais Ormond had been exchanging illegal and entirely blasphemous letters with one Lady Mala Andrius.

Lord Ormond was a simple city administrator. Like most every noble, Landais was born into his task. His father's only son would follow him as a city administrator wherever the Wizard-King might have need of him. But Landais was not his father.

The late Lord Korin Ormond was known more than anything for his devotion to Lord Brakken. So far had his loyalty extended that, when the War Maker told him that Waterrun, his mining village nestled in the mountains of Central Province, had failed to meet their quota, he gathered the foremen in the town square and had them burned alive.

So far had Korin Ormond's loyalty extended that, when the people of Waterrun gathered to seek their own justice from their city administrator, he chose instead to offer up his wife and children to the mob, and then burned himself alive in his offices.

Landais Ormond was not his father.

Even at the tender age of twelve, he remembered with haunting clarity that very thought resonating in his mind as the flames reached high in the sky and the mob of citizens argued over what fate they thought appropriate for the still-burning nobleman's family.

As it turned out, they decided to spare the lives of the remaining Ormond family.

The young Landais would eventually go on to serve as a nobleman administrator himself. Over the years, Landais was assigned to several different assistant positions for other nobles, far from that mining town, until such time as he was ready to administer a city of his own. Then the new homes in new cities came and went, and each time he moved to a grander and grander city. It seemed he was good at the task after all.

In every city, though, Landais could not forget that lesson from that fiery night in the mining town. He remembered a gathered people who had been oppressed by the nobility their whole life – who had likely already forfeited their lives by choosing to rise up against their master. They still managed to elect compassion over vengeance for the family of nobles.

From that time and for all time, Lord Ormond had done everything to pay this debt back to the people of The Vastness. The populace was his greatest charge; it was his only charge.

And, until recent years, this had meant mostly a never-ending task to keep the city of Manara out of the eye of the Wizard-King's heavy-handed rule. Ormond was good at this. He had mastered the bureaucracy of The Vastness to such refinement that even the most miserly tax collectors of the imperial treasuries could find no cause to punish the good people of Manara. Not one boy was recruited to the armies early and not one bale of grain was sent from Manara late.

There were many who called Manara "the City of Grains." Its moniker came from the vast expanse of fields surrounding it and the numerous granaries and mills that lined many of the streets. Manara's harvest and export was one of the more impressive grain productions of any city her size.

The latest counts placed Manara's population in the several thousands. Though it was rather far off the heavily trodden roads of The Vastness, it had gradually become a sought-after destination for tradespeople and craftsmen as the population grew, since it was protected from the harsh weather by its surrounding mountains and protected from the Planewars by its relative strategic unimportance. This had allowed it to slowly accumulate an impressive harvest every year. So subtle had her growth been that even bandits and highwaymen seemed to ignore Manara with only minor patrols protecting the roads.

Manara was like a fragile secret. Her people were fed and they were generally happy. And this was not at all a common pair of traits in any peoples of The Vastness – in all the Planewars, likely: fed and happy.

So why had Lord Ormond now thrown in with outlaws, blasphemers, and rebels? Why had he involved his entire populace in a foolhardy plot to overthrow the immortal Wizard-King?

Because no matter how happy the people of the City of Grains were, they were still mere fodder to Lord Brakken. Landais's every action was bent toward keeping the all-powerful Wizard's eye away from his city, and it would only be a matter of time before his administration of Manara conflicted with the hell-bent goals of the militaristic dictator. Landais knew this in his heart, and he had known it ever since that night he watched his father burn.

So to protect the good people of Manara, Lord Ormond had endangered them. His staff; his friends; every man, woman, and child of Manara was put at risk.

He was placing an immense amount of trust in Artorus Vallon and his sister. But in all his interactions with other nobles and with soldiers – with anyone who served Lord Brakken – Lord Ormond had never met two people as honest as them. When General Vallon spoke of freedom, he spoke true. When Lady Andrius spoke of saving the people of The Vastness, she spoke in earnest.

And if there was any one thing that would fulfill a long and laborious life of leadership, it would be seeing his people to freedom. It was likely not even a concept they could recognize if it were in front of them, but Lord Ormond intended to show them to it nonetheless.

Landais sat at his desk in the administrative building of the prosperous and bustling city of Manara. A pleasant fire crackled in the hearth on the side of the room. His chair was padded and his desk polished. In fact, most of the things Landais now had in life were far beyond the imagination of most peoples of the multiverse. Compared to the soldiers dying in the muds of Munos, or a humble farmer fighting for his life from roving bands of orcs in the harsh lowlands of Astaan, Landais Ormond may as well have been a king.

We crave not the accoutrements of the flesh, but of the mind and of the soul, Landais quoted to himself from a notorious and banned author of Myrus's past. *One gains their wealth not by way of gold, but by way of justice. One gains their power, not by way of armies, but by way of knowledge.*

It was a manuscript titled *On the Premise of War* by an elven philosopher and writer – and, eventually, martyr for the cause of peace – named Phyrus Akrenemous.

In truth, were the agents of the Wizard-King to search his offices and residences, they'd likely find more banned books than production ledgers.

This very moment, he had a book on his desk in front of him: *The History of Morto-Myrian Politics* by a dwarven scholar called Koûrum Onton. It was heretical simply for acknowledging and describing forms of government that did not involve Wizards. It was historical, from a time before the Wizards came to power. He had to admit to himself that in the past he had thought the concept to be dead and buried, as well, but in these recent years, much had changed.

In recent years, there was a cause for hope.

Even if it was kept secret, like a dying flame hiding from the eyes of an enemy, hope now existed. If Landais had to devote every last waking hour yet remaining in his life, he would see this timid flame grow to a roaring inferno; a signal fire to call to all the peoples of the twenty-seven worlds. The people of the multiverse deserved a chance to govern themselves.

A knock at the door gave him a slight start.

He covered his reading material with a shipping ledger.

"Come in," Landais called.

The door creaked open, and an elven servant named Chara poked her head in.

"Pardon my lord," she said sheepishly, "but Master Grenn is insisting I ask you once more about your dinner. Are you ready?"

Landais couldn't help but chuckle. Grenn was a friendly dwarf and inspired chef who had been in his employ for nearly a decade now. He regularly played a little game with Lord Ormond, as he worked into the late evening hours, where he would refuse to leave the kitchen without forcing his master to eat a supper. He was truly a good man.

Grenn didn't know of the plans for rebellion. Chara didn't know either. So many of the people close to him had no idea of the terrible danger he'd put them in, and they could not. One day they'd all know, but it would not be any day soon. For now, secret shipments and secret grain stores that were small enough to be overlooked were his contributions to the cause.

"Of course, of course," he conceded to his elven servant. "Although, before you tell the good chef you have defeated me, would you do me a favor?"

"Sir?" Chara said with a nod, as she stepped fully into the room.

"Please, come and sit," Ormond beckoned.

She pulled the door closed and made her way toward Lord Ormond.

Carefully, as she had turned to latch the door, he adjusted the ledger to make sure it fully covered the book beneath it. Then, Chara took a seat in the chair across from him.

He clasped his hands and placed them lightly on the desk in front of him as the fire continued to crackle gently. Chara was a beautiful young lady. Many of the younger male staff around the administrative building talked longingly of her. But she was shy, and she writhed under the clumsy advances of the gardeners and carpenters and farmer's boys about town.

"Chara, how long have you worked for me?"

"Eight years, m'lord," she replied promptly. "Why do you ask?"

"Well, in that time, have you ever known me to give you unsound advice?"

"No, m'lord."

"Then may I have your permission to speak plainly?" Landais smiled politely at his servant.

"Um," she hesitated, "of course, m'lord. I don't rightly think I could refuse my lord."

"Please, Chara, I implore you to refuse the plain speech of anyone who would not treat you with respect."

Chara flushed at this. An elvish girl, slight of build and slight of demeanor, she clearly was made to feel inferior by the other staff. Landais guessed that, in quiet hallways and behind closed doors, there are many who did not show this girl respect.

"I mean that," he continued. "And you can tell them I said it, if you must."

She swallowed her discomfort and regained her composure. Her response was a simple nod.

"Well, I do hope you'll take this advice as it's intended… But did you know that our friend Grenn is not just a talent in the kitchen, but he also has a skill for poetry?"

She looked surprised at this fact.

"No, m'lord! Poetry?"

"Yes," Landais pressed, "and you must promise never to tell him I revealed this next part to you. He'd surely burn my soup every evening for a month." He squinted conspiratorially to his servant. He could see her curiosity was piqued. "But I've even seen a poem about you, Chara."

He paused to let the realization strike her. If she had appeared put off or discomforted, he would have dropped the matter. But instead, a smile creased one side of her mouth.

Landais went on. "I do believe there was a line about 'his orchid among the grains.'"

"M'lord," Chara asked, attempting to wipe the grin from her face, "why are you telling me this?"

"Because," Landais admitted earnestly, "I think those in this multiverse with gifts should share them. If a gift can improve the lives of others, it should be made to do so. I, myself, appreciate the gifts the Master Grenn offers in the kitchen. But his gifts of poetry are not for the likes of this old man."

And your gift, young lady he thought, *is that of kindness. Perhaps the most precious gift of all.*

He smiled to his servant once more and then gestured politely toward the door.

She looked thoughtful for a moment and then hurried out of the room.

Later, over a cup of truly delicious soup, Lord Ormond's illicit reading material had multiplied into several volumes of banned topics, written by martyred writers. He was glad to have the sustenance, as he would be working late this evening.

Chapter IV – The Blade

The position of High Justicar was not a title easily earned. It required undying loyalty; it required great skill; it required blood – so much blood. Gnarrl had spilled rivers of blood, and Gnarrl had undeniable skill. And why shouldn't Gnarrl be loyal to Lord Brakken? Brakken the Eternal represented both power and stability. Brakken the War Maker was a god... or so he would have most of his slaves believe. Gnarrl knew that Brakken the Cruel was no god. All the gods were long dead, as best Gnarrl could tell. But Gnarrl had most certainly seen his Wizard-King do amazing things with that magic of his.

Once, the justicar had reported to the field of a battle to give Lord Brakken requested intelligence on one of his kings. As it so happened, at that time, no less than three dozen orcs raged out of control on the battlefield, breaking through Brakken's lines of guards and barreling at him with great swords and full armor. Brakken let them see his eyes – that stare that so many would claim is pure divine wrath. The Wizard-King froze the greens in their places.

But Brakken called off his men that had immediately descended upon the now-helpless orcs. Instead, he raised his hand and bellowed a noise that Gnarrl could only describe as a roar. Every last green was enveloped in a torrent of flame that erupted from their feet and leapt into the sky. It soared hundreds of feet, billowing smoke and radiating heat.

That patch of ground did not stop smoldering for three days.

So Gnarrl was loyal to the man that could do this. But Brakken was no god. If the War Maker were a god, why would he need a High Justicar?

The reason was simple; of all the mighty powers these Wizards could command, none of them were subtle. Few would rightly call Gnarrl's technique subtle, but the High Justicar was head spy, head bounty hunter, head torturer, and head assassin in Brakken's empire; in comparison to his Wizard-King, he was the very picture of subtlety.

And he did not fail. There was only one punishment for failure in The Vastness and it was death.

"Please! Don't kill me!" A desperate plea broke Gnarrl's contemplative wanderings.

Gnarrl was an impressively large man. He was of half human parentage and half orcish. He had not known his mother in his early life, discarded as a babe. He had been raised as much by the disgusting greens that found him as he was by the harsh streets of the city he eventually found. Much too smart for either teacher, though, he had grown into his own place in The Vastness.

Gnarrl was muscular and sleek, an obvious killing machine to any trained to look for such traits. He always carried his two black-hilted, slightly curved daggers, and they complemented the black leather armor that clung tightly to his predatory form. He had a large, heavy cloak of the deepest gray that normally hung over his head and concealed his body, but it was now slung at the entrance to the torture chamber. His dark face was fully visible in the torchlight. Fangs jutted from his lower lip a half inch or so, which accentuated his wide, stubble-grown jaw. That jaw usually carried what most would take for a scowl. While half-orcs would often display much more of their green-ish features than human ones and were regularly mistaken for full-blooded by civilized folk, Gnarrl just might be mistaken for a large and ugly human from afar – given a dark enough alley.

Perhaps the most menacing feature of the killer, the dark green eyes of the justicar were speckled with the sickly yellow of orcish eyes, glinting in the dancing fire light, and they locked on the half-elf tied to the torture table beneath him. Gnarrl stared with quiet, depthless intensity.

"You know something of what the High Justicar does for your Wizard-King, yes?" Gnarrl said in his thick, low, and smooth voice.

The captured man nodded slowly.

"Then you know I will kill you, half-elf," he continued, allowing menace to claw just under the surface of his calm voice. "If you tell us what we want to know, you can at least make that death a quick one."

He glanced up at the row of torture implements hanging above the captive.

"If you do not tell us, we will resort to these." He smiled with what could almost be called pleasantness. "Now what did you say your name was?"

Shaking as tears rolled down his cheeks, the half-elf could not move any part of his body much for the bindings, but his eyes could still clearly see both his captor and the collection of tools upon the wall.

Gnarrl thought briefly of his mother, as he often did when people wept under his menace. He remembered the confusion on her face at the teenage boy standing over her. He remembered the bright color of her blood as it seeped from wounds in both kneecaps. He remembered the moment of horror when she realized who he was. He remembered satisfaction, pure and freeing.

For many years, he searched for his father, but there was truly no way to tell which of the beasts had raped his mother and spawned him. He'd sufficed for years to simply kill any of them, but he found the endeavor only as fulfilling as any bloodletting might be. It was good practice, at least.

"M-m my name is Forian." The man sniffled. "And I came to you to tell you that whispers of rebellion have been circulating. I-I do not know more than that." The captive whimpered, "I came to you!"

The justicar sighed. "Well, I can't say I won't enjoy breaking you, Forian, but I did actually have other things to do this evening. You're sure you don't want to tell us who is behind this 'rebellion?' Where they are hiding? How many of you there are?"

"I can't! I don't know!" the captive screamed. "*Please*! I came to *you*!"

Slowly, deliberately, Gnarrl reached for one of the longer curved blades hanging from the wall. Its specialty was carving the chest and abdomen, so he wouldn't be using it immediately, but he always found it to be very motivating for his guests.

Shortly afterward, he found himself having to retrieve an instrument that was more immediately useful. He began to crush fingers, always starting with the pinky. Screams filled the chamber as the justicar worked.

An hour later, the High Justicar entered the large room of Lord Brakken's study, cloak now draped in its usual place about his shoulders, but the hood off when he met with Brakken. He always thought that "study" was an interesting title for the place, since it held few books, and he'd never seen the Wizard-King study anything here. The War Maker never slept, not one minute of his incredibly long life. But this moment, he was doing the closest thing to it, as far as Gnarrl could figure – some kind of meditative state, sitting on an oversized pillow in the center of the room.

Brakken was stable. Gnarrl could depend on Brakken to do what was necessary.

"What?" Lord Brakken demanded in his deep, regal voice as soon as the justicar had entered the room.

"My lord," Gnarrl began as he knelt in the entrance to the room, on a special patch of tiles for this specific purpose laid at the entrance of all rooms that the Wizard-King frequented. "This rebellion which we've discussed; it seems to have gained some momentum in the lowland provinces here on Myrus. We captured a pitiful half-elf who has told us of the small hideout they used, but little more. I've dispatched assassins to the location, but I surmise they'll have scattered when they realized the half-elf has not returned."

Slowly, exuding power in every motion, every flexing muscle, magic nearly crackling in the air around him, the immortal Wizard-King, Lord Brakken of Myrus, stood from his seated position in the study and breathed deeply. The creature was at least seven feet tall – even taller than Gnarrl's impressive height – and his frame was heavily muscled from head to toe. His long dark hair fell about his head and shoulders evenly, but never concealed his intense, human-looking face.

Brakken was powerful. Gnarrl could appreciate the sheer might the Wizard held in his every action.

Both muscular arms protruded from sleeveless robes, his right arm having tattoos of the blackest ink coursing up and around, somewhat resembling flames creeping up his limb. His large chest fully filled the lordly robe that he was wearing: extremely fine, extremely rare silks, embroidered with gold and silver, probably a cost as expensive as a village could muster in a year. Brakken's colors of choice were usually a rich gray accented with metallic hues, but often he chose to cut the colors with a sash of vibrant orange or crimson red to imply the power that he commanded over the drab world around him – or some such dramatics. Even his boots were cut of the finest leathers, from worlds far enough away that they might cost exorbitant sums. Atop his head sat a simple crown of brilliant gold, brighter than any in the empire, with a single blood ruby set at its front – an unmistakable symbol of Wizardry. The kings of the land all had crowns of gold, with lesser nobility having lesser metals, but only the Wizard-King was allowed the blood ruby.

Brakken was regal. Gnarrl knew that the mortals of the multiverse would always bow to the power of the Wizards. Rightly, this was how Gnarrl was one of the most powerful mortals in the multiverse: by being one of the most useful mortals for the Wizards.

"Who is king of the land that this being was captured from?" The large Wizard filled every corner of the room with his deep voice as it reverberated from thick stone walls.

"It is King Perrinor of the Kaluk Province, my lord."

Like every other being in the multiverse, Gnarrl avoided the gaze of the mighty Wizard. It was said that their gaze held more power than most humanoids can bear, and many have died merely from looking into a Wizard's gaze. Of course, Gnarrl doubted this, but he did not want to display impertinence in the presence of his Wizard-King.

"Kill him," the Wizard said plainly. "He shall be the first message to our subservient kings that I do not suffer rebellion from these lowly mortals. All other kings can expect the same if rebels are caught by us in their lands."

The regal voice of the Wizard-King seemed to reflect off of each wall and swirl around Gnarrl.

Brakken was decisive. Gnarrl could always follow a command given by Brakken, to all required detail.

"Of course, my lord, I shall do so immediately. I will make it messy."

Gnarrl grinned down at the floor where he stared.

"No," the Wizard-King retracted, "on second thought, I want to do it. You continue this hunt and I will summon Perrinor and the other kings. Why send a message, when I can show them plainly?"

Brakken was intelligent. Gnarrl enjoyed the thought of the lowly kings watching in horror as one of their own was drawn and quartered at their feet. It would be beautifully effective.

"You will find these so-called 'rebels,' and you will slay them like the vermin they are. Whoever claims to lead them... I will have his head."

Unceremoniously, the Wizard ended the conversation by turning and walking back toward one of the large windows on the far side of the study.

"It will be done, my lord," Gnarrl said as the Wizard-King walked.

Gnarrl stood and exited the study, calling for two of his assassins. The two most skilled of his subordinates were never far from Gnarrl unless he commanded it so. They would arrive quickly. Gnarrl headed for the stables, an outbuilding close to the outer fortress wall, as he awaited them.

Once outside the main citadel, Gnarrl could catch glimpses of the world Lord Brakken called home. His fortress stood among the great mountains of the Central Province of Myrus, the focal point for all of the Wizard-King's power. Everything that happened on several worlds at some point, in some way, came through Central Province to the fortress for Lord Brakken to approve or deny.

It was a mighty fortress, built hundreds of years ago of more metal than stone. Spikes topped the huge walls and no being could possibly mistake this place for anything other than the home of a Wizard-King.

As the justicar's two assassins reported to him, he called for the horses. In all The Vastness, likely all the multiverse, there was no finer breed of horse than the Linium. They were bred for the greatest of tasks, and had been since time immemorial. The mightiest generals of The Vastness rode them into combat. And, though they came in many colorations, only one was bred to be the very largest and strongest among them: the Midnight Linium. Perfect black, mighty, and regal, this was the only type of horse the High Justicar ever used. Nobles would pay for them in costs that could likely buy armies or castles.

As the three assassins rode out of the huge gate and onto the mountain roads, they each had a Midnight Linium. The sight was fitting. The steeds were as dark as the tidings these killers would bring. The Liniums yearned to fill their massive lungs with the autumn air and sped to a full gallop as they rode out on their task.

The first of the autumn storms rolled up from the plains below. They were late this year. Gnarrl always appreciated a good storm. Dramatic weather for dramatic times.

Storms could not stop the justice of Lord Brakken. Nothing could.

Chapter V – Past, Present, Future

Mala had been feeling nostalgic lately, as she walked her estate. Week by week, more soldiers and other staff were arriving.

This very day, they expected a special guest: one Commander Orgron Braïun. She'd heard plenty of stories about the dwarven officer from Artorus, and she'd even exchanged a couple letters with the gentleman. He was a family man, with what sounded like an impeccable sense of propriety. He was exactly the caliber of person they would need if they ever hoped to bring about a new sort of world for mortals.

Still, it all contributed to the changes that somehow left a little soreness in her heart in the stiller moments. It was a strange side-effect of progress.

Mala sat in the estate library. Her family, on her father's side, had long been nobles and their historic family estate was located some distance from where she now studied. The estate of Lord Thorton Andrius and wife – where Mala grew up, and where Artorus spent the last free years of his life – was much closer to the Raging Sea, many miles to the east. The noble houses lay neatly arranged outside the larger city of Keldt, a bustling trading port and center of shipping and culture for the region. Much like every other large city on the Twin Worlds, it had been rebuilt perhaps three or four times after being leveled by this Wizard or that army, but it had a distinct culture nonetheless. Most textiles for the continent originated in Keldt, but her own father's task had been timber management, which she inherited from him.

It was more than twenty years ago now that they began construction on this satellite estate in which she now sat, originally to be a summer retreat in the cooler climate. But the war with Krakus had been escalating for some time and it had spilled into the world of Myrus, which had only recently forced Phax back through a different worldgate.

Fearing the impending strife, the family hastened the construction, intending to move there, but Koth saw a different Truth for Mala's parents.

As armies marched all around and battle engulfed Keldt, knowing the end was near, the nobles sent their only daughter with several of the servants, most of the guards, and as much of the considerable family treasury as they could manage to take shelter in the refuge on the high plains. They had promised they would be close behind. They wanted to save as many others from the surrounding area as they could.

Another vast army came from the sea and swarmed the land, killing all nobles – as they often did to assert their Dominance over a conquered territory. It was truly a brilliant strategy, as a kingdom without its magistrates and leaders would remain in disarray for quite a time.

Though Krakus was rebuffed short weeks later, the war had already collected the innocent souls, and Mala was left with the estate. Save for some extended cousins on other planes, the line of Andrius would end with Mala.

She had only been a girl then, but since that time, the Lady Andrius had resided in the high plains of the Winterlands Province and run the Andrius estate. She was able to manage her noble task well remotely, as timber management was as much about surveying forests and inspecting logging trails as it was about writing contracts for the harbormasters over in Keldt.

Up here, snow would frequent the terrain, blanketing the wide country in white winters, but the most beautiful broad-leaved trees blossomed in the other seasons. In good weather, it was a few days' walk from the small town called Polm that was the closest civilization. Polm itself was nestled in low hills as the terrain slowly climbed toward the mountains in the west, at the edge of a mighty lake called the Varean. In a time long passed, many noble families from Keldt would vacation to this beautiful area just north of her estate.

This library only had a few books that had been moved in before the war destroyed the original estate. The rest of the now-impressive collection had been built from purchases Mala had traveled far and wide to gather. Not all the tomes were even legal in Lord Brakken's Dominance.

Always Mala had had a fascination with knowledge, and though it was a foolish dream for a noble girl, she'd even written letters to the Sage of Delemere before. He hadn't responded to her silly inquests into things such as the origins of magic, the reasons behind the Planewars, even the nature of the vast æther between worlds. Though she had not expected a response after her first letters went unanswered, she'd never lost hope in the knowledge of the great Sages.

And now, staring at the fine calligraphy of the very Sage she'd always admired, she found herself to be that foolish noble girl again. Her copy of the letter lay to the side, as she preferred the original. A thirst for the information within was quenched only temporarily each time she read through it again. She was certain that her brother was right about this letter; there was the key to their victory somewhere in here.

She finished the letter for yet another time and then took a deep breath, pushing the original and the copy to the side to make room for the small stack of books she'd already collected from her library shelves. They were volumes of history – *A Brief History of Morto-Myrian Warfare*, *The Movements of the Wizard-Kings: an Analysis of Strategies in the Planewars*, *The Immortal Wizard-Kings and Their Dominances*, and more.

She cracked open the first of the ancient tomes and began her research.

General Vallon stood at the gate, dressed not in his official military garb, but with the unmistakable attire of a warrior and an officer, nonetheless. His fine broad sword still hung at his hip, and a cape moved lightly about in the cold breeze that spoke whispers of snow. Some time had passed at the Andrius estate, and though the waning warmth of autumn had held somewhat longer than usual this year, it was nearly time for the winter clothing. He had an assistant make a note of such in the inventories, and then looked back to his arriving guests.

From the entry gate to the Andrius estate, he waved to a small troop of soldiers as they climbed the last gentle slope up to the compound. Their leader, a hearty dwarf with an impeccable fashion sense and a long, neatly braided beard, was Commander Orgron Braïun, whom, despite his protestations, was called "Slick" by most of the troops.

The dwarf might not have even passed as a soldier to the untrained eye, were it not for his uniform. So well-kept was the middle-aged dwarf that his hobble was the only indicator he'd ever seen battle. He was an average height for a dwarf, perhaps four and a half feet. His hair was neatly parted and combed to the side, his beard was trimmed of stray hairs, and his collar was heavily starched and well pressed. While most dwarves had a penchant for ale and a belly to show for it, the commander was in good shape.

Braïun had a certain refinement to him that many soldiers had lost long ago. While some of the troops joked that "Slick" had no place on the battlefield, Artorus knew him well. The general saw the thick muscle, hearty constitution, and tactical eye under the prim exterior. And, of greater import than any of those, Orgron Braïun was a man who could be trusted – perhaps even more than most men in the Fifth Planar.

Commander Braïun brought the pre-arranged number of men who were personally selected to join the cause by Artorus and would each shortly take an oath to the resistance. Each had produced their own request for leave and represented a varied swath of troops from the Fifth, though the commander's heavy limp reminded everyone of his particular reason for leave.

His troops stated that during one of the surprise raids toward the end of the Battle of Harmony Valley, he'd stopped to fix his hair while the unit was attempting to maneuver around a unit of orcs – though Braïun's claims seemed to recount a much more tactical explanation. Either way, it was agreed that he had a clash with several of the large brutes and had bought his unit a precious few seconds while suffering a large gash on his left leg. It had healed well so far, but he'd be out of combat for a while longer. Artorus rubbed his own leg, only recently healed from that same battle, just one or two surprise raids earlier.

The commander had ridden a small horse for most of the journey, but had decided it would not be proper to remain mounted in front of his commanding officer, and so he hobbled the remaining distance, three dozen troops in tow. The general saluted his commander.

"Greetings, Commander Braïun." He met the eyes of the men behind him as well, "And to your... army."

The men laughed.

"And to you, sir," Braïun returned with a slight bow. "The journey was long, but quite worthwhile."

"Your meals are already prepared in the main building," Artorus informed the tired men before him, "though you're welcome to drop off supplies in the temporary lodgings on your way."

He paused, and then motioned rather sheepishly to the stables.

With so many more men here and the new barracks not quite yet completed, they'd been forced to make alternate accommodations. The additional six dozen planned to arrive in another two weeks should be able to enjoy the barrack's comforts immediately upon their arrival. And judging by the troops he'd selected for the first wave, they should be able to survive their temporary stabling without much complaint.

The men began to head into the compound. Though weary from travel, Artorus could see them energized by being here; at finally reaching their destination; at finally becoming a part of something better. Their salutes as they passed were sharp and their eyes clear.

All of the suffering these Wizards cause, thought Artorus, *will be over soon. We gain momentum now, we gain... initiative...*

He smiled. "Mala was right," he mumbled to himself.

"Sir?" the dwarven commander asked as he stepped up beside General Vallon, wiping his brow with a kerchief.

"Nothing," Artorus dismissed the question.

Braïun remained quietly by his side nonetheless.

"You need something, though, Commander?"

"May I speak freely?" the dwarf asked as he put away his kerchief and straightened his braided beard, tucking it neatly back into his belt.

"Of course, Orgron," replied the general. "You know you can – especially now."

A polite smile showed from beneath the dwarf's beard.

"I'm honored to be here, sir," Braïun started. "I believe it is the beginning of the end for the War Maker. The tension builds among the people, I can see it. And now I have the honor to be at the forefront."

The dwarf turned to meet Vallon's eyes. "Thank you... Thank you for that, General."

"I have you to thank, Braïun," the human said in return, placing a hand on the dwarf's shoulder. "One man with delusions of grandeur is just crazy. But a delusional man with fools to follow him is an army."

Artorus grinned. Humor was sometimes lost on the prim dwarf, but he blinked twice and smiled politely.

"Well, I'll simply take that as a 'you're welcome,' if you don't mind, sir."

"Fine by me, Commander," Artorus said, smiling, as his eyes turned to the men now in the compound. "And you truly are welcome, my friend."

The two treaded slowly into the compound after their three dozen troops.

"The Sage says there were two hundred seventy Wizards before," Typhondrius contemplated. "*Two hundred seventy*, but now there are only seventeen. One would think that we could find far more than we have about where they died and who killed them..."

Typhondrius shifted in his seat slightly before catching himself. A proper servant does not fidget. "In all my time at the fortress, I did not hear much discussion of the other immortals. Our task was mostly just to dote upon the master and receive our punishment if we were to misstep..."

But Typhondrius realized he was talking more to himself than to Lady Andrius.

"Mm," a distracted Mala replied, as she pored over a passage once more. "You're right, we should have heard more," she admitted thoughtfully, "but if I were a creature that everyone assumed was immortal and I owned the world, I suppose I'd be a little restrictive about this kind of information too."

Without looking up, she moved to the next book.

"Yep," she exclaimed, "here he is again! This is definitely one of our defeated Wizard-Kings. Apparently, he used to rule most of Learden – that's where Artorus just was. You'd think we'd have heard of him. He was one of the most recent ones to have been destroyed, it seems. His name was Jazaan."

"And what does it say about *how* he was destroyed, my lady?"

"Nothing." Mala shook her head. "It just keeps talking about his height of power long ago and then the decline of his empire... Wait—" Her eyes widened. "This might be something..." She excitedly read through the next couple of pages.

Typhondrius waited quietly. He fidgeted no more.

"Wow!" she proclaimed excitedly. "Yes, it has a description of the battle Jazaan had with Kaladrius."

Typhondrius did not have to try hard to be patient, as he awaited Mala to reveal the passage to him. All the years of service to an immortal Wizard-King had left him with an abundance of patience. The alternative to patience was a much worse fate.

Sometimes he hated his patience, but it could be a useful tool.

Finally, Mala set the book on the table so that they could both read the passage.

As Jazaan's provinces dwindled and dissolved, the old Wizard finally met his rival on the field of battle in the high mountains of the continent of Tinnea, on Learden. Histories hold no tales as great and terrible as those of the Immortals clashing. The armies fought and each Immortal commanded fury. But Kaladrius was mighty indeed.

Jazaan's world was lost to him. Descending from the peaks, beginning the retreat, Jazaan fled from his better. But he did become cornered by Kaladrius. Their transportation magics took them to the peaks and then back down, but Kaladrius would not give up.

Ice shattered and flames licked the skies as two Wizard-Kings fought one another. Immortal magics cleft the mountain. And it was during this fight that Kaladrius was able to cast his spell over Jazaan's mightiest troops. He took their souls from their bodies. Kaladrius had squelched any hope of escape for the doomed Wizard.

And the mighty Kaladrius was more powerful, and he called for lightning from the heavens above to strike down his opponent, and Kaladrius the Brazen claimed victory.

'Tis a strange occasion when an Immortal is slain; like lights from the very Æther, the Immortal death became a shimmer that captured all who viewed it. As Immortals do not have material forms, no account was ever given of his body and no burial performed. Kaladrius the Mighty became the king of Jazaan the Fallen's dominion evermore.

"Amazing," gasped Typhondrius. "I've—" he began, but then he hesitated.

He took a breath. If he could not be brave for his lady, who would go so far as to rebel against their immortal Wizard-King, then for whom could he be brave?

"I've seen some of these things this very passage references," he admitted in a more measured tone. "Lord Brakken has 'stolen souls' and 'called lightning' as this text states Kaladrius did. As best we tried, we could not avert our eyes to all of them... I believe there is some accuracy to this account."

Mala frowned.

"You know, Typhondrius, I've never seen a Wizard in action. I really hoped all the tales of their power were at least a little exaggerated." She motioned to the text. "Fire and ice and lightning... transportation magic and mind control? These things aren't embellished some?"

"I am afraid not, my lady," Typhondrius admitted darkly, then shifted in his seat.

There was the fidgeting again.

At once, memories Typhondrius had worked years to bury away deep within his mind began clawing their way back to the surface. He calmed himself with a deep breath.

"But you know I hesitate to speak of my years serving the Wizard-King." Typhondrius turned his eyes downward.

"You don't have to tell me if you don't want to," she said softly.

Typhondrius shook his head in reply.

"You are kind." He could no longer resist rubbing his scarred ear. "We presume to endanger hundreds or thousands – even hundreds of thousands – of lives and I fret over recounting my past."

He laughed softly, if only to cover a shudder.

If he could not face his past now, then when would he ever? Typhondrius took another deep breath, this one for courage once more.

"In my time as Lord Brakken's servant, I saw many things which I'd much rather not have, but most were merely the sick perversions of the human nobles who clambered to the highest positions of The Vastness."

He looked back to Mala. "No offense to either your noble blood nor your human blood, my lady, but I've seen noble humans do things that I do not think even a Wizard would do."

Mala smiled comfortingly to her elven servant.

"I am offended enough by them and their actions that your words only comfort me, Typhondrius. Go on."

The elf swallowed hard.

"Well, there were certainly times that the Wizard-King displayed qualities more dark than I can comprehend any mortal being possessing. I can't quite describe it, but the feeling you get at the base of your stomach when a wild wolf happens across your path and snarls at you, or the feeling of falling, not seeing, to what you think in that instant just might be your death; there were times that I got some such feeling merely from being in the same room as that Wizard. It was a twisting, tearing feeling in my chest, almost sickening.

"I carried cups and I gathered linens about the fortress. Mostly, I merely picked up dust, actually. But even these tasks were deadly around a being such as Lord Brakken. The master did not suffer inadequacies..."

Typhondrius sipped from a glass of water before he went on.

"Magic, as I've witnessed, is some limitless form of power. He shot flames from his hand and moved the earth beneath him; he commanded the actions and read the thoughts of men by staring into their eyes; he could even transport himself as the text states – it is called 'teleportation.' It made a strange popping noise as he would completely disappear, only to appear elsewhere in the fortress."

Mala listened intently and began to scratch some notes.

Then Typhondrius's shoulders slumped further as he sighed. He knew how visible his burned ear was. It was clearly no secret. But somehow he felt that if he but avoided discussing it, it might fade. He felt in some hopeless, delusional way, that time and ignorance could heal his scar. It could not.

"He did this to me, Mala," the elf said, motioning toward his ear with a trembling hand, his voice beginning to waver slightly.

Mala stopped writing and looked up at her elven friend.

"He did this to me the same day I fled from his fortress. I felt the mighty power of the immortal Wizard-King from only his bare hand on the side of my head." Typhondrius lowered his head. "I only dropped his drink... I had been on shift for three days, and the Wizard-King does not sleep. I was simply exhausted. I'm certain he would have killed me, but he became distracted when his assassin entered the room, and I was left to whimper on the floor."

Mala laid a hand gently on his shoulder. "It is okay, Typhondrius. You do not need to continue."

If Typhondrius could be honest with himself, this was perhaps the bravest moment of his ninety-nine years. In his years at the fortress, he had hardly even mentioned the master conversationally for fear any of his more sinister servants might be within earshot. And here he sat, plainly discussing him as the monster he truly was.

So brave... and yet, he felt terrified.

He had thrown in with this rebellious lot, but only after he faced destruction at the hand of the Wizard-King. Was there bravery in running away from the fortress that night? Was it bravery when the only alternative was certain death?

And could he ever make amends for living a life subservient to Lord Brakken for the better part of a century?

"I can't describe that feeling, when he used his immortal flame to burn me; it was not the flame of a candle or even that of a great hearth, it was something wholly different." He raised his head, once more meeting Mala's eyes. "But it is not the pain that prevents me from recounting those days... not the fear. It is knowing that I spent seventy-three years watching that monster murder, control, and enslave people with no more guilt for it than if he'd crushed an ant under his thumb. He'd killed probably *hundreds* of servants before that night, before it was my turn."

A grim look overcame his features, and he looked away once more.

"And I did nothing, my lady... I *watched*."

After a short pause, Mala pulled Typhondrius into her embrace.

"No, Typhondrius, you did not do 'nothing'; you are here now; you will fight him." She held the embrace tight. "And if you say there is truth to the words of these pages, then there is truth that even the immortal Wizard-Kings can be killed. And we *shall* kill Lord Brakken for his crimes against you – against us all."

Typhondrius did not return the embrace, as much as he longed to.

He was all but certain: if not for the Lady Andrius, he'd have succumbed to his pain and his fear, to his shame, long before now.

For a time, the only sound in the room was the soft crackle of the hearth fire.

Artorus breathed deeply in the thin air, gripping the hilt of his wooden sword tightly. The soldier struck at him, a high arcing strike, but Artorus was too fast for the young half-elf he faced. He darted aside the falling strike and thwacked his sword up against his opponent's shoulder, eliciting a yelp.

"Now two," called Commander Braïun from the side of the training yard. "Two men against the general!"

Artorus glanced at him with a smirk.

The half-elf rubbed his shoulder as he nodded to the human that joined the fight with his own wooden sword. The two of them spread to gain a flanking advantage on the general. Artorus just smiled at them cheerfully.

The two men both dashed forward at once, the human reaching him barely before the half-elf, who was probably slowed by his throbbing arm. Artorus leapt directly at the human, well inside his swing, but also sacrificing a good shot at the soldier. He heard the sword of the half-elf clap against the packed earth of the training yard as he grabbed for the human's sword arm, clasping his wrist tightly with his left hand. Artorus then stepped around to the back of the soldier, bringing his own wooden blade up to the soldier's neck from his right side. The half-elf weaved about the training yard attempting to find an opening to strike, while the human writhed about in the general's grasp, pain from the pressure points in his wrist causing him to grunt.

Finally, when the half-elf was close enough, the general pushed his captive toward the other combatant, whipping his sword around to rap him on the back of the head as the soldier stumbled. The half-elf aptly dodged the incoming human, only to find another square blow on his right arm.

Clapping came from the side. "Three!" called a smiling Braïun.

The two beaten soldiers looked nervously at each other as the half-elf again rubbed his shoulder and the human rubbed his wrist first and then his head.

This time, a much larger human thudded onto the training ground, most likely some orcish blood in his veins as he was of darker skin and an impressive build; his name was Jarl. Jarl held a very large wooden sword, resembling a fence post more than a practice sword, and grinned at all three of the others. His hairless head was marked with scars, and his muscles were barely contained in his training uniform. The human and the half-elf both nodded and came to the side of the large man.

Artorus swung a few practice strikes with his sword and smiled pleasantly at his three opponents this time.

Jarl charged first, swinging his large sword with great speed, forcing Artorus to block three times as he backed away in the face of the larger combatant. The other two soldiers, though timidly, did join seconds later, each taking a flank once more. Artorus did not let them keep their position surrounding him as he took the half-second opportunity between Jarl's swings to lash out at the human, forcing him onto the defensive and allowing Artorus to sidestep the next swing from the larger man and place a firm kick into the giant's side. Jarl grunted but slowed little as the three again took up their positions around him.

This time, the half-elf struck first – a high swing. Artorus ducked under it and tripped the unfortunate half-elf with a leg sweep, sending him sprawling to the ground, hitting hard. Artorus had only a moment as wooden swords from both his other soldiers came down at his head.

Rather than dodging away from them, the general dashed right between them, landing a glancing blow across the smaller human's back, as Jarl's defenses were better and his sword was already waiting to deflect a counterattack.

He had removed the smaller human from the fight and was intending to get out of reach of the larger man, but he felt a meaty arm reach around his neck from behind.

Hm, getting slow in my old age, Artorus thought, *but not too slow.*

Before the large man could even get his sword in a position to strike the general, Artorus twisted his wooden blade about and jabbed it back into the stomach of the large man. Surprised enough to loosen his grip, the large man's arm lost Artorus before his other hand could finish the swing of his sword. The huge wooden sword ended up colliding into the brute's own knee and he stumbled enough for Artorus to land another blow with his sword for good measure, onto Jarl's shoulder.

The half-elf had just gotten up, holding the back of his head where he'd landed on the hard dirt, and Artorus strolled up, smiled at him, and hit him once more in the bruised arm, eliciting one more yelp.

"Amazing," Commander Braïun called as he clapped.

The three soldiers collected their weapons and left as the general clapped them each on the shoulder in thanks for the sport. Artorus tossed his wooden sword to another soldier who then handed him back his regular blade.

"Excellent practice," the general called to the soldiers in the yard, "Three more hours, then assist with the thatching on the new barracks." He nodded to a few of the men around and smiled. "Jarl's not nearly as mean as he looks, He needs a little more sparring."

The large human reddened slightly.

"Thanks, Commander Slick," Jarl said somewhat scornfully to the dwarf on the sidelines as he frowned and rubbed his stomach.

Braïun smiled pleasantly through his braided beard at the large man.

Artorus stepped up beside his dwarven commander, the dwarf straightened his beard and tucked it back into his belt, and the two began to walk away from the training yard toward the library. They were silent a short while, taking in the nice weather that still clung to the Winterlands like a fond farewell. Artorus could stand to catch his breath anyway.

After a time, though, Braïun looked to his general.

"Sir?" the dwarf said inquisitively to his general as he hobbled beside him. "You could have – nay, you *have* – built yourself an impressive career in the armies of the Wizard-King. Your skill with a blade alone has started to become legend."

The dwarf paused but he wasn't done.

"We all feel the same about the Planewars," Braïun finished, "but I'm am curious what would cause a man who has come into such an esteemed career to wish to throw it all away."

He stopped, ostensibly to rest his leg a bit, but he clearly wished an answer to his question, if Artorus was willing.

Artorus met the curious gaze of his commander and his bright disposition faded slightly in the cool morning light.

"It is a tale I do not often tell, Braïun," he started.

"Then do not break tradition," the dwarf quickly replied. "I am sorry I asked, sir. It was rudely personal of me."

"No, friend," Artorus said, looking the commander squarely in the eyes. "I ask you to give up everything you ever were or ever could have been in the armies of Lord Brakken to aid me on this fool's crusade. I owe you an answer to that question, at least."

Braïun did not protest further.

Artorus continued, "Well, these days most of the men don't know it, but I was once married."

The commander nodded solemnly in recognition of where he already knew this tale must end.

"She was beautiful, Braïun. Every man says his wife is beautiful, but she was incredible; she was a goddess. Hair that curled merrily in swirls of golden light, the brightest blue eyes – like a crisp winter morning. And her love was endless. She could give her last loaf of bread to a starving boy on the street, even if it meant we would not eat that day. Everybody loved Elsa – dear Mala probably more than most."

Braïun smiled in thought as the general went on; possibly he was imagining the picture Artorus painted or possibly he thought of his own wife back home. Artorus always could tell that Braïun was the romantic type.

"Whatever happens with this rebellion, Braïun, I truly hope your family is safe." Artorus looked at his dwarven friend solemnly.

Braïun nodded thankfully.

The general looked away, out toward the stretching landscape that was now visible from their spot within the compound.

"I'll never forget the day she told me she was with child..." Artorus reminisced.

Artorus shook his head. After all these years, though he could remember it clearly, he had trouble believing it had once been true.

"I'd just come back from a short tour, probably a year before you joined the Fifth. I came home, and she looked at me, those sparkling blue eyes piercing my heart every time. Then she said it: 'We're going to have a baby.' I couldn't tell you if I cried, I honestly don't remember, but for the next three months all I could imagine was that beautiful babe. It was an extension of us; even after we grayed, then passed into dust, our child would live on." Artorus paused another moment. It was still difficult to talk about Elsa and their baby. "You remember Phax's insurgence a few years back? When his agents crafted a series of assassinations, and then a small army struck into Myrus as far as the Larand River? Our house was just on the other side of the Larand – a cottage tucked into the hills outside of Tollus City; it was so quiet. We didn't expect the action to make it so far upriver. Most of Phax's targets had been coastal. I had promised her we were safe."

Artorus sighed.

"I came back from gathering wood, and I immediately recognized the signs of a skirmish across the river." Artorus paused again as he looked downward. "If only I'd gathered it earlier... If only I'd not gone... If only we had just... left... The house was already burning, and before long, all that remained of my home, my wife – my entire life – was ash. I don't know if some fighting had actually happened on our side of the river or if Phax's goblins simply torched it for fun; I'll likely never know, but none of it mattered anymore...

"I contemplated death; contemplated drowning myself beside the charred remains of my family... I've been in battles and faced dangerous enemies, but I do not think I've ever been closer to death than that day... But something tugged at me; something wouldn't let me do it. My thoughts kept returning to my sister, to my men, to the life that still resided in the world. I buried what I could find of my wife and our unborn child on the fertile ground outside the yard of that cottage and eventually came to live with Mala."

The two officers had begun walking again and were now outside the library, where sconces still lit the interior and shone dimly through the stained glass that adorned the front doors as the sun climbed upward in the eastern sky. Braïun was quiet.

"At first," Artorus continued, "I hated Phax and his armies for what had happened. I began to hate all goblin-kind. But I came to realize... It wasn't the soldiers of Phax that I hated. I've been a soldier most of my life. We play our part in wars, but not because we're evil – it is simply our way. Neither you nor I have ever burned down houses with women or children in them, but even the vilest acts came from some orders through some officer of war. Hells, even those twisted goblins are just soldiers at the disposal of the Wizards. I had thought a long time that I should have picked a safer place to raise my family, but truly no place is safe in the Planewars. It's the Wizards that started this war and it's the Wizards that continue it. Mala and I talked about it for many, many hours, into many, many nights."

Artorus sighed once more, deeply this time.

"I'll tell you, Braïun," Artorus said contemplatively as he looked in at the dim flickering from the library building, where he imagined his sister studying, "I know that if it weren't for that woman in there, I'd likely be dead in that river. It was she that first mentioned the rebellion four years ago on one dark night. It was her mind that raced with the idea.

"And I believe in her – probably more than I believe in myself. She will stop this war; this *endless* war that claims lives every moment of every day. I can plan and I can act out orders, I can strategize and I can lead soldiers, but Mala is the true heart of this resistance. She is its soul." Artorus looked back to the commander. "And when we stand over the head of that creature, Lord Brakken, and the multiverse knows that the Wizard-Kings are not gods, it will be the end for the 'immortal' Wizards, and the many worlds may just know peace. And that is when I can rest beside Elsa and my child… only then."

Commander Braïun took a deep breath as he straightened his beard and nodded once more to the general.

"It is sorrowful," Braïun said seriously, "what happened to you and your family, sir. I have a family of my own, and your words of your wife touched my heart. My children mean the world to me. I cannot think of what I would do if harm was to come to them."

He looked now to the doors of the library.

"I believe you're right, General," the dwarf stated in solemnity as they approached. "That is why we follow you and your sister. I trust that this war will end by your hand."

Thoughts of Elsa were still ablaze in Artorus's head as the two opened the doors and entered the library.

Chapter VI – That Which Cannot Be Killed

Typhondrius awoke from a manic dream in a cold sweat. He had chills, but his right ear – or what was left of it – throbbed and burned, as hot as the hearth. This was not particularly new for him, and yet repetition never dulled the pain. And he was fairly certain those dreams were getting more frequent of late.

He tried hard to bury once more into the depths of his psyche the swirling terrors that revisited his mind. He knew he'd never be free of them – not truly. But at least he could seal them away for another day of productivity before nighttime brought them forth to menace him again.

It was nearly morning anyway; he could see the light of the sunrise creeping into his window. It would not likely be more than a couple more hours until the others arose.

He rose, prepared for the day, and walked the grounds in the new light of morning. Each of the guards Artorus had selected from among his soldiers was a man worthy of praise. Typhondrius enjoyed the company of the night watchmen on mornings such as this.

But, still, his thoughts lingered on his dreams. Brakken the Eternal was a fearsome being; he bent the elements to his will and he controlled the fate of worlds, but his most dreaded power was that of the mind. Brakken's gaze, it was told, held the power of the gods. All his adult life – for the seventy-three years until that fateful night he felt Brakken's flame – he served the Wizard-King, but in all that time, he never once looked into his eyes.

And now he was here with the Lady Andrius and the Lord Vallon to attempt to overthrow and kill that very creature he'd served for so long.

Typhondrius decided that he could not spend these valuable morning hours in peaceful walking and meditative thought; he had work to do. If this rebellion was going to have a glimmer of hope, no matter what territory they might win or how many mortals they might call to their cause, they would have to be able to defeat the mighty Wizard-King ... *somehow*.

Typhondrius had witnessed only a few of the many dozens of assassination attempts in his decades serving the Wizard. Most ended well before they ever reached their target, but a select few were able bring their blades to bear on the Wizard-King.

A dagger, Typhondrius recalled, had no more effect on Lord Brakken than it would a stone wall; they seemed to bend and break against his very skin. Sword, arrows, axes, or spears, Typhondrius could not imagine having any more of an effect.

But the Wizards *could* be destroyed; the Sage himself said so.

So, the power of a Wizard wagered against the knowledge of a Sage. Which would win out?

Typhondrius sat down in the library and began his research for the morning.

Sweat had beaded on Mala's brow. She was thankful to be practicing her sword skills again. Hands that spent a lifetime writing missives and tallying stocks still felt somewhat foreign with a hilt in them.

But there were new opponents to test these skills against at the compound these days. Orgron Braïun was likely one of the more skilled among them.

"My lady," the proper dwarf said through labored breaths, "the general has mentioned how you have much skill with a sword, but I must say I am impressed anyway."

They were handing off their swords to the next pair as they each reached for kerchiefs to wipe their sweat.

"You are too kind, Orgron,"

Braïun shook his head. "Kindness to a lady is never misplaced, it's true, but I speak in earnest, my lady. Your parry is swift, and your footwork is above par. I'd guess an unintelligent man crossing weapons with you would think that you lack strength as well, which might be his downfall, as you have a powerful swing."

Mala couldn't help but chuckle. "Good soldier, I'm not used to praise on the practice grounds. My brother only ever leaves me with bruises and lessons – and more lessons and more bruises." She laughed again.

"Well," Braïun admitted, "Artorus Vallon is practically legend for his skill with a blade. He is second likely to his Lieutenant Highblade, true. But the two of them represent perhaps two of the greatest swordsmen in The Vastness. I'd not want to spar with your brother regularly. I doubt my pride could handle it."

Mala wondered if he might have been cracking a joke, but he delivered the statement in a humorless sort of way.

The two reached a bench and both sat down to rest in the shade as the clacking of wooden swords was a comforting sound in their makeshift training yard. This space was once intended to be a huge garden, but Mala never did approve of wastefulness. She could not bring herself to devote monies and man-hours to the care of delicate plants from faraway worlds. And so this patch of ground that remained empty for so long had finally found its use.

"So, Commander Braïun," she chanced, "may I ask how you came to the Fifth Planar?"

The dwarf nodded. "I fought for many years with the Sixth Homeworld Army. They are noble enough, I suppose. But your brother has acquired something of a reputation among the armies of The Vastness – at least for those who pay attention to such things."

"Oh?" prodded Mala.

"Indeed," Orgron went on. "You see, it's no secret that most generals will charge their armies into the deadliest breach in hopes of impressing their lord general. Most officers of a high rank are only interested in climbing closer and closer to Lord Brakken.

"Rumor had it that General Vallon had been offered command of the Twelfth Planar after the death of General Kaeff at The Battle of Nine Mountains on Ebbea. The Twelfth Planar has long been said to be the last step in a general's career before making lord general. It had been Kremaine's before his own promotion and assignment to the Homeworld Armies."

Braïun gave Mala a serious look. "General Vallon turned it down. He is loyal to his men, and his men to him."

Mala smiled at that.

"And so you requested a transfer?" she inquired.

"No. It's quite rare, even for an officer, to be transferred at their own request. But your brother requested my unit. *He* requested the transfer."

Braïun looked almost emotional.

Mala knew of her brother as the passionate fighter, the brilliant strategist, and, secretly, the would-be rebel leader. She never knew he commanded such respect among other armies of The Vastness. She felt a pang of pride.

"All of us," the dwarf went on, "devote our lives to the Planewars. 'Tis a fool's errand to place thought into any other path. But when your brother requested my unit – I don't know – it felt as though I'd been chosen for a higher calling. It felt as though I had a more important role to play."

Mala nodded thoughtfully. "I believe you do, good Orgron."

"Well, whatever that may be," Braïun went on, "I admit a bit of pride at being chosen by the famous General Vallon for service, and so when he pulled me aside not two months ago and ask me if I would join him in his *true* cause, it made perfect sense to me. *This* is that calling that I answer.

"I've watched a thousand mortals die for the Wizards with my own eyes, and I was foolish enough to mask it in some noble concept of patriotism for my Dominance. When Artorus said I could leave of free will, even after he told me this most precious secret; when he said it was my choice… well, I didn't see any choice in it at all. It was duty."

Mala placed a hand on the commander's shoulder. "I can't thank you enough, Orgron. This rebellion will have need of people of such morals."

The two stayed in the training yard only a bit longer, as Mala had many things to do this day. In addition to her preparations for a rebellion against her Wizard-King, she still had magisterial duties to perform.

She thanked each of the men for being there, in her estate, and committing everything they had to a cause that they still only whispered about outside of these grounds. The day would come that Braïun, these other soldiers, Mala, and her brother would stand proudly together on the field of battle, but for now, Mala felt she had a mighty army right here, in this place.

But it still left one crucial detail burning in her mind: the enemy they intended to stand against. Her magisterial duties would have to wait some more.

Even shirking her timber management duties, Mala had desperate little time for her desired studies this day. The several dozen men that would arrive in only days now meant that the workers had to have those barracks complete.

Between the construction, the tallying of the ration stores, the orders for supplies, and her sparring with Braïun and the others, day had turned to evening before she even got the chance to reach for the dusty texts waiting for her in her library.

She finally entered her library to see Typhondrius sitting at her favorite studying table.

"My lady," Typhondrius said as he stood and bowed, "good morning."

Mala cocked her head to the side and smiled.

"Morning? I do believe the sunset is within the hour."

Looking quite shocked, Typhondrius opened a window. Outside, the sky had begun its darkening as the sun indeed fell toward the horizon.

"By the master, my lady!" Typhondrius exclaimed. "I'm quite sorry I've not been available all day. I simply must have lost track of time."

Mala laughed. She rarely saw the proper elf flustered as he was now.

"Typhondrius, I envy your day of study." She put a hand on his shoulder and guided him back to the table. "Please, tell me what you've found today."

Rubbing his eyes a bit to readjust from the outside light, he looked about at the various texts that were now organized across the table with elven meticulousness.

"Well," the elf began, "I did manage to find two more references to Wizard Dominances falling to one another. It seems that one 'Magus Ordon' and his Dominance 'the Everlasting Empire' was destroyed by Vith within the last century, and one 'High King Forrius,' who once ruled Eternity, was slain by Quirian about one hundred years ago on the other side of the worldgate from us, on Mortis – something to do with his alliance with Lord Brakken, it seems. Though neither is detailed quite so much as our account of Jazaan…"

He rubbed his eyes once more.

"Jazaan…" Mala muttered in thought. "So the other texts make mention of Dominances falling, but not so much of the Wizards' demises specifically."

Her brow furled.

"What if this talk of Wizard Dominances falling to one another is truly the *Wizard-Kings themselves* battling just as Jazaan fell to Kaladrius? A Wizard killing another Wizard…" Here eyes began to widen. "What if it was *only* the Wizards that could harm each other? What if that is *the* way to kill a Wizard?"

Typhondrius nodded slowly. "It does seem like that would be possible, my lady. Nothing about it is contradicted by the Sage's text. The books all tell of the Wizards falling in battle with another Dominance. They could be meaning that the Wizards themselves fall in these duels as Jazaan did..."

Mala thought a moment and then looked up to her elven friend.

"If you could, Typhondrius, catch some fresh air and call Artorus back here for the three of us to meet. I do believe it is high time we finish our discussion on how to kill Lord Brakken."

Typhondrius had left for a time. Mala had only just finished reorganizing her varied tomes and other materials into the wide scattering that she found much more productive when he returned with her half brother.

After Mala and Artorus finished a discussion from earlier in the day regarding the rations, a servant came with a late dinner for each of them; they ate as they talked.

"You see, Lord Vallon," Typhondrius stated as Artorus finished his cup of broth, "since the Wizards are immune to steel and at least one of these texts references the Wizard-Kings killing one another, we're fairly certain that the only way to kill the master – that is, to kill Lord Brakken – is to enlist or somehow otherwise persuade the help from another Wizard."

"Well," Artorus said in contemplation, "I'm still not entirely convinced they're impervious to our weapons, but... maybe we don't have to actually *kill* him..." He didn't look up from his cup as he spoke. "You both know I've seen Wizards come to battlefields and devastate entire ranks of men; I've seen them shirk off arrows like they were twigs and I've seen axes bounce off of them like children's toys. I've even heard a story of Brakken being run through completely by a spear, and he simply yanked it out with no effect whatsoever.

"But always the Wizards leave as quickly as they come. Usually they show up, hurl their wrath upon their enemies in a quick barrage, and then blink away in some flashy manner. Us lowly mortals can be entrenched in combats for days on end. Actual fighting can sometimes last hours. But I've never once seen a Wizard remain in a fight for longer than a few minutes...

"Either they exhaust extremely quickly, which would seem odd, or else... something more intricate... It's almost... *almost* as though it was *fear* that drove them. If a being were truly immortal – had nothing to worry about from all the ire man and elf and dwarf could muster – then what would he have to fear from battle? If a being never had to sleep, then why not stay for hours or *days*, wading through their enemies like a shallow pond?"

Artorus stroked his beard subconsciously.

Typhondrius spoke thoughtfully. "Well, Lord Vallon, I have wondered myself if there may be something to the thought that Wizards feel fear – however I do not think they fear mortal weaponry... But, just because they can't be *killed* by our weapons—"

"That we've seen," Artorus interjected.

"That we've seen, my lord. It does not mean they do not feel pain. Perhaps they merely avoid the pain of swords and arrows. I have once seen Lord Brakken pierced by an arrow, much like your story of the spear. It didn't seem to affect him any more than it would have had it bounced off. He didn't bleed after he pulled it out... But perhaps it caused him some pain."

All three pondered a moment.

"I like where you're both going with this," Mala chimed in as she still stared at the various books she'd laid out on the table, ignoring the exhaustion of a long day of working. "Perhaps we don't need to destroy him. If he always runs back to his fortress to hide from the battles of the Planewars, then if we strike directly at his home, he'll have nowhere to run."

Artorus nodded.

"Maybe," Mala wagered to guess, "if the creature truly is driven by fear, he'll submit to us if we display enough force while he is trapped in his last refuge, with nowhere else to run!"

The three were quiet another moment. Though the winter approached, it was still warm enough to let the windows breathe fresh air into the grand library chamber. The torches that stood guard in all the sconces had been changed often lately; many late nights of study and planning taxed their fuels.

"And if it is not us mortals and our weaponry that they fear," Artorus went on, "if they leave battles for some other reason, then it could still serve our purposes as well, whatever it is. Many battles proceed with some assumptions of your enemy's capabilities. But, when we burst into the very bedchamber of the War Maker with the entire Fifth Planar Army, whether he fears *us* or not, he cannot kill *us all*."

Typhondrius swallowed hard. He seemed perhaps unconvinced at that last statement.

"In fact," Artorus continued, "I hadn't really thought of it before, but perhaps they leave battles so quickly *because* their powers are limited; because the mighty magics they wield require so much of them that they cannot continue for long... This could bode just as well for us. Perhaps we burst in, lose some men to his fire, and then we simply capture and bind him that he may never harm another mortal again. Though the War Maker has immense strength, I don't think it's limitless." Artorus chuckled. "I did once see a troop of orcs pile themselves onto an ogre and subdue it! We still tell that story around the campfire..."

Looking down, Typhondrius spoke. "I prefer to think of him being destroyed... He is perfectly adept at simply teleporting away if he so wishes. I watched the master come and go from the fortress a thousand times, and he would teleport just as likely as he might have walked from room to room or taken his carriage on the road..."

The elf seemed to regret sounding so pessimistic.

"I find it hard to disagree with our elven friend," Mala admitted to her brother, "because every moment that creature draws breath is a moment the Planewars go unrecompensed. That Wizard owes a debt of blood to everyone in The Vastness, from the kings to the lumberjacks, and if he was to escape, our rebellion would face a great setback." Mala picked up the letter the Sage had sent them. "See, the Sage of Delemere told us that the Wizards of old were hunted down and destroyed in some sort of 'council of judgment.' It seems that the mortals held the knowledge of how to do this..."

Mala shifted in her seat. "And," she continued, reaching for one of the volumes in front of her, "like we said, both the histories and the Sage seem to agree with Typhondrius: that a Wizard can destroy another Wizard. Perhaps the *only* way to destroy a Wizard." She ran her fingers over the now familiar passages. "In fact, it sounds like it's quite a spectacular event... I do wish Brakken dead, but I also shiver at the thought of dealing with more than one Wizard at the same time... And what of these 'councils of judgment'? I still feel as though there is much we don't know. For one thing, we don't know how to convince another Wizard to come and kill Lord Brakken for us!"

Shaking his head, Typhondrius looked suddenly displeased with his own idea.

"But even then, what would we do, my lord and lady? Tread across the planes, getting each Wizard to destroy the last? Even if we were to succeed, I think that would still leave us with one in the end."

Artorus chuckled again.

"I'm glad to see your aspirations so high, good Typhondrius," he said to the elf, who shrunk sheepishly in his seat. "I think we can worry about all the other Wizards a bit more once we've got Brakken in chains at our feet. Besides, that's another thing I've been contemplating: hopefully *we* won't have to defeat *all* the Wizards."

Artorus grabbed his own copy of the Sages letter and read a single line in a hopeful voice, as Mala and Typhondrius listened intently.

"'It started with just one of their kind.'"

The general looked up with eyes alight. "It took just one Wizard to grab power from the mortals, and all the others realized they were not doomed to an eternity of servitude, right?" He grinned. "So maybe all we need is one band of mortals taking it *back* from the Wizards to get the twenty-seven worlds to realize *we mortals* are not doomed to this damned war for all eternity... Perhaps our actions will be merely the spark that ignites the great flame of mortal rebellion across the planes... Is this not the reason we sent letters to certain others across the other

Dominances? We sought help from many of them in our own rebellion, true, but even more so, we wanted to prepare them to take back *their* realms from *their* Wizards when the time came."

Mala pondered Artorus's words. What if that was all it took? What if defeating Brakken the Cruel was really the key to freeing the entire multiverse from these creatures? Mala had always thought of their task as the first step in an impossibly great labor, perhaps even to be completed by successive generations of freedom fighters. But Artorus was a brilliant tactician, and they might require fewer miracles than Mala thought.

If the rebels of The Vastness could *somehow* prove that Lord Brakken could be harmed by their mortal machinations, then this *just might* be the inspiration the multiverse needed to rise up.

After another moment of quiet thought, a cold wind rushed in through the open windows and blew out one of their torches. Typhondrius jumped a bit and they all looked to the window. With thoughts of Wizards swirling about the room, even the elements themselves took on a more sinister air.

"Well, my lords," Mala finally said with a sigh, "I suppose that is our cue that we should wrap this up for the evening. It is nearing time for bed."

The two men nodded.

Dinner was long finished, and the dark of night was upon the high plains. Mala and Typhondrius began the process of clearing the table, but Artorus still sat, with arms folded, staring thoughtfully at the table. His eyes were focused on the path ahead of them more than anything in the crowded library. He stroked his beard.

"I believe we have our plan, then," he concluded. "Riding high on the tails of dreams, I daresay it sounds like we can succeed at this after all..."

He broke his stare and looked up at Mala and Typhondrius.

"If all our swords and spears and arrows cannot slay him, then Lord Brakken shall be our prisoner – even if it takes all the chains in The Vastness. Or, if we find we can't even hold him, at least we shall drive him from his mighty fortress and remove him from his seat of power. One way or the other, we will have shown this multiverse that the immortals do not rule us any more than we *let* them."

Mala smiled to her brother.

"You're really starting to sound like your sister, General," she quipped. "All hopes and dreams."

At this, Typhondrius laughed heartily, and Artorus's grin widened.

The grand plan was crafted. They finished gathering up the things from the table and bade one another a good night.

Artorus awoke to a bright autumn morning on the high plains. Though frost had begun to cling in the early morning, by now it had melted, covering the estate in a thin sheet of water that glistened in the sun.

As he stepped out of the manor house, Artorus was pleased to see his dwarven commander already approaching.

"Ah, Commander Braïun," the general said. "I was just coming to find you."

"And I you, sir," replied the dwarf.

Braïun's beard was already braided neatly and hair parted perfectly. He bowed to Artorus and then saluted and then paused with a funny look on his dwarven face.

"You know, sir," the quizzical dwarf stated, "I'm no longer quite sure if I should be saluting or bowing to you. Are you still my general? Am I still *in* the Fifth Planar Army? Or are you now the lord and ruler of the rebellion? Some new class of nobility, perhaps?"

Artorus let out a hearty laugh.

"You, my crazy dwarven friend, are still a part of the Fifth Planar – perhaps more so now than ever – and I am not a lord or ruler of anything. Not a drop of noble blood in my veins."

Braïun did not seem to see the humor in his question, but he nodded in acknowledgement. "For what did you seek me, sir?"

"Walk with me," Artorus requested.

They began to walk toward the portion of the compound that had become the training grounds. It had been crowded of late, and the early morning time was when Artorus found he had the best opportunity to have some space.

"I needed you for a new training program," General Vallon said as he looked up into the clear morning skies. "I figure we'll have to know how to storm the fortress of a Wizard eventually – and hold it too. I have a few ideas, but nothing solid yet."

"Not a prospect that sounds particularly easy to accomplish, sir," Braïun stated in contemplation. "But I am honored to have the task. I shall call for a scribe so we can record the specifics."

Artorus nodded. "You recall the island fort on Learden," Artorus said. "That presented some unique challenges, didn't it? But your unit performed admirably once the fortress was breached."

"Thank you, sir," Braïun stated politely.

No army enjoyed a prolonged siege. Hopefully they could craft a strategy that would be as rapid as it was bold.

"And you sought me?" Artorus said.

"Ah, yes," Braïun said. "We received word that one Captain Keldon Horace shall be arriving a day or two ahead of schedule."

"This is good news!" Artorus exclaimed.

Braïun nodded. "Yes, I've had very few chances to meet the captain, but I hear he is a man of character."

Artorus nodded his agreement. "Precisely why I've selected him."

The two continued to walk in the pleasant morning. Braïun seemed to have a question on his mind still. He was lost in thought.

"What is it, Braïun? Something more about Horace? Something I should know?"

"Oh, no, sir," Braïun was quick to correct, "it is not Horace. I'm sure he is above reproach."

"What then?" Artorus peered at the dwarf.

"Well, sir," the commander said hesitantly. "Do I have permission to speak freely?"

Artorus simply gave his commander a look that he hoped would say *didn't we talk about this?*

The dwarf nodded and went on seriously. "I simply wonder why I was selected to come here first, sir, before any other officer in your army... Not any of your lieutenants or high commanders?"

Braïun was obviously uncomfortable even to ask the question. It was not a standard protocol of the armies of the War Maker for any soldier to question their general's decisions once they were made. But this army was no longer serving the Wizard-King. Protocols would have to change.

"Braïun, have you ever met Lieutenant Hakan?" Artorus laughed. "On the field of battle, I trust him with my life, but anywhere else and any other time... well, I'm still working that out." Artorus laughed again, though Braïun only nodded. "And then there's Highblade," Artorus went on. "It would probably be a little too noticeable to pull him from his leave in the sword tournaments of Jayce, don't you think? I can just picture the stampedes of women that would give us chase."

Artorus laughed once more, though the most he got was a polite smile from Braïun.

They had reached their destination and stopped outside. Artorus turned to his commander.

"But truthfully, Braïun, there is no other officer in the entire Fifth that is of greater character or resolve than yourself."

He looked into the gaze of the dwarf, who seemed to be guessing whether there was sarcasm under the general's tone.

"I mean that," the general added. "You remember the Battle of Lavon? You saved a hundred men from certain death when you ordered the withdrawal from the chokepoint. And when I promoted you to commander in the first place, you'll recall I applauded your will and your morality during the Battle of Ext. That was a hell storm.

"In all truth, the only reason you're not already a high commander is because I've had you in mind for this task for some time now. I apologize for any damage I may have caused to your career with the military, but it's far easier to whisk away a commander for a secret rebellion than a higher-ranking officer.

"Braïun, you are a mighty soldier, a reliable officer, and a dwarf of true quality. These are the sorts of people that will make this rebellion a success."

Artorus did not break his gaze with Braïun.

"Hm," Braïun contemplated, clearly searching for more words. His face had reddened some at the praise.

"Well," he managed, "I thank you for your kind words, General. I only hope to live up to them."

Artorus smiled at his commander. "I believe you will, Braïun."

They walked into the training grounds.

Chapter VII – Kratan Vythor

"Sir!" roared Captain Vythor in his broken orcish dialect. "There nothing left here, we must go!"

Nine years ago, Artorus was still a commander among the men of the Fifth Planar Army. He'd learned much of the famous General Hathey and his strange ideals – and he still had so much to learn. Now commanding over two thousand soldiers, several captains reported to him, and he had begun to gain a reputation as a leader.

"Sir!" the captain repeated in his gravelly voice. "I not let you die on us, Vallon!"

Artorus opened his mouth to ask what was happening, but all that came out was a cough. Where was he? He did remember something… He was on a world called Voryn: a place with four large moons, extreme tides, and a wild night/day cycle.

"He not doing well! We have to get back to army!"

Artorus could hear Captain Vythor yelling to somebody over the sounds of battle. Who was fighting exactly? Artorus did know his soldiers, though.

Kratan Vythor was an orc. There were very few orcs in Brakken's armies, and even less so in the Fifth Planar, as orcs were notoriously hard to control; bloodthirsty, savage, and possessing an unholy strength. Among men and dwarves, most simply called orcs *greens* in a sort of slur, even though most orcs were a lot more grayish than they were green.

Kratan Vythor, however, was unlike any orc Artorus had ever known. True, some might call him bloodthirsty by the number of enemies he had slain, but he did not lust for carnage like most of his race. True as well that some might call him savage, but in war one rarely had the need to cater to the demands of etiquette. And strength Vythor had in vast amounts. Artorus had once seen the orc lift a mountain wolf and hurl the still-living beast – with goblin rider – into its own ranks.

Vythor being an orc of unusual clarity and restraint, however, Commander Vallon had promoted him from sergeant to captain after many battles of brave acts and sound decisions. And the orc's broken speech was improving steadily, which helped things for those who served under him. Hathey had commended Vallon's eye for leadership after a few exemplary performances from Vythor in the battles that followed his promotion.

Artorus and Kratan had become quite the pair, between the two of them able to slay most any enemy.

In fact, that's how Artorus found himself in this predicament; it was beginning to get a bit clearer. The Fifth had been chosen for an exceedingly dangerous mission: a direct attack deep into the territory of Kaladrius. The goal was to sack a city that had been serving as the main supply depot for the front against Brakken.

Several armies had planned for many months to forge a path to the worldgate on Learden, and then hold it long enough for their secret mission.

This side of the worldgate, it was a two-army taskforce. The Second Planar Army, under an old general called Warin, was to distract the main forces of Kaladrius in the area while the Fifth would send a small unit to take the city as quietly as possible and hold the worldgate until they all could withdraw.

What happened?

"Wha—" coughed Commander Vallon.

His lungs didn't seem to be working quite right.

"What... happened?" he managed to spit out with great pain.

Something was very wrong with his body – with the mission.

An arrow flew just past the orc and his wounded superior.

"Arggh! Wizard save us... You fell down," replied the orc in exasperation, breathing hard. "Now be quiet."

Fell? pondered Vallon as he began to feel his body again.

If Artorus did fall, then he must have fallen off a cliff, because as quickly as he thought about it, pain filled every limb and burned in his chest like fire – terrible, throbbing fire.

"Do we have order to withdraw?" bellowed the orc to his commander.

Artorus nodded. He truly wasn't sure if it was the right decision at the moment, but he had learned to rely on Kratan's judgment in the past few years. He had a sound mind for tactics.

Another arrow whizzed past and then another. Artorus could hear the sounds of his men dying around them, but his senses still weren't at all clear.

There was motion – much motion. Artorus ached unbearably at being jostled so, but he doubted if the alternative would be better for him. The violent movement jerked his pained limbs. There must have been some bones broken. After a few minutes and many more arrows Artorus managed the strength to ask another question.

"A-ambush?" He sputtered the question at his orcish captain through his blurred vision.

"Yes, Vallon," the orc replied in his rough voice. "City not unguarded like Brakken think. Hathey try to tell him at last minute," the orc coughed, "but Wizard very dumb. Now you hurt and we running!"

Of course! Vallon began to recall.

His head seemed to form thoughts much more clearly – though the clarity of mind only seemed to make his body hurt more. The plan to sack the city was shaky, at best, but the fronts against Kaladrius were not going well. And so a risky maneuver was ordered from the very top. Lord General Kremaine didn't seem to have any qualms sending two of his armies to their doom, but Hathey and Warin both did.

Somebody must have tipped off Kaladrius, because the city that should have been undefended was not. Somehow Artorus's unit was attacked, driven back.

You're braver than this, Artorus thought to himself as his mind returned to him more with each labored breath. *You should be leading these men back to the main army. A few broken bones never stopped you.*

He struggled greatly against the throbbing pain in every part of his body, but he moved only barely. The pain was too much to bear, and the commander could only lie on the shoddily fashioned stretcher.

More arrows shot past as they hastened their retreat, and the commander could occasionally hear the clashing of swords around them, growing somewhat more seldom.

"H-how many?" Artorus coughed to his captain. "How many do we have left?"

"Plenty!" called the orc as he labored with something, grunting; the commander couldn't see what, but he imagined the orc's huge axe buried in some unfortunate enemy soldier. "That why we running, not staying and dying!"

Several more moments passed as the commander had little energy left to ask more questions, and the sounds of swords clashing and the clank of arrows falling upon them both subsided.

Staring up at the bright night, three of the four large moons in clear view, the ambush suddenly returned to his memory, like a flash of understanding.

The men all crept up under those bright moons, more than a thousand soldiers in all – most of Artorus's command. They had barely gotten within the city, but it was all too quiet. Artorus and Vythor had taken a small unit of their most elite fighters and moved ahead to better assess the situation.

They didn't hear it until it was too late. From a dark alley under the shadows of a tall building a terrible noise suddenly came – like the roaring of a dozen bears – and a huge log suddenly fell on Captain Vythor, crushing his right arm and probably much of his chest. Some sort of siege weapon, was it?

The details continued to return to Artorus. It was no log; it was a gigantic club. And wielding the club was a huge ogre – probably the biggest Artorus had ever seen. Kratan collapsed, and the ogre quickly swung his giant club directly at Artorus.

That was the last thing he remembered.

But... Kratan? Artorus's muddled mind wondered.

He must have recalled it incorrectly. With great effort, he managed the strength to sit up; he no longer cared about the pain. He *must* have remembered wrong.

With his mind returned to him and the vantage of sitting he now fully saw his orcish captain in the three-moon light.

Hanging from his shoulder by skin alone was the orc's massive right arm, now appearing more like a rack of uncooked meat than a limb; bones protruded awkwardly at several points. The orc's breathing was incredibly labored as much of his side was clearly crushed as well. From the captain's back jutted three arrows, each one dripping blood. The orc's legs now barely moved as he continued to shuffle forward. He had stopped talking some time ago.

"Stop!" Artorus yelled to his troops and the men ceased their hasty march.

The pain was either gone or it really didn't matter as the commander hoisted himself off of the stretcher onto unstable legs. He could feel blood coming from somewhere on his head or face.

"Why aren't you helping him?" Artorus demanded of his troops as the orc was still stumbling forward, seemingly unaware the men had stopped.

"Sir, I'm sorry," said Captain Matthias.

He was one of the soldiers already coming to Artorus's side to help him remain standing – a dwarf that Artorus had promoted recently.

"We tried to stop the stupid green more than once," said Captain Matthias, "but he pushed us away! Wouldn't take so much as a walking stick. We had you to carry among the other wounded."

There was a look of pain on the dwarf's face. He didn't hurt from his own wounds, but he too watched the still-shuffling orc.

"I'm sorry," Matthias repeated, more to the lumbering orc than to Artorus.

Pushing himself off of the soldier and walking painfully toward the orc, Artorus stopped directly in front of him.

"Captain Vythor!" Artorus yelled, summoning more strength than he thought he had left. "Halt!"

The distant eyes of the huge orc suddenly snapped to attention and he caught the sight of Artorus. He did stop. No longer stumbling along on whatever momentum he'd had, the huge orc suddenly collapsed with a thud to the rocky ground.

"Vythor!" Artorus called.

He rushed over to kneel beside the fallen captain. Perhaps falling more so than kneeling.

Kratan Vythor was looking at the commander, still breathing very heavily, and then a huge grin stretched across his fanged mouth. The orc's bright yellow eyes were still locked with Artorus's and his breathing slowed. Then he spoke.

"You look… terrible."

The labored breathing stopped, and the yellow eyes trailed off skyward.

Shouts came from the rear of the formation as arrows again began to fall on the unit; the noises all seemed distant to Artorus.

"We've gotta go, Commander!" called Captain Matthias beside Artorus, his voice reaching the Artorus's ears as strangely distant echoes. "Get back on the stretcher! Second Planar is not far now!"

Artorus still stared into those eyes that only moments before belonged to his brave friend. He sniffed back tears and laboriously stood on his own, the pain now searing through every inch of his body. With his senses mostly returned to him, the pain came through in clear, intense pulses. If he didn't move now, he'd likely fall back to the stony ground.

He nodded to his fallen friend and spoke in a stable voice. "Put Vythor on the stretcher."

"But, sir," the dwarf protested, "he's gone."

"I know he is," Vallon replied, "but I will walk, Captain."

Chapter VIII – A Trail of Tears, a Trail of Blood

Lord Landais Ormond sat once again in his administrative office. The crackle of the fire in his hearth was less friendly this evening. He had only just heard some rather distressing news. He still had the scroll unfurled in front of him on his desk:

SCS 343, 20th Day of 10th Month

To Lord Ormond of Manara,

It was confirmed the day before last that the mountainside town of Waterrun, in Central Province, has been razed.

The Imperial Legions marched to this place upon receiving their orders directly from our immortal Wizard-King, Lord Brakken.

Now we both know that our Wizard-King need not explain himself to any being in the twenty-seven worlds. It may in fact be treasonous simply to reference it, and I do not make a judgment of his action in any way, but it was said that rumors of rebellion had been surrounding the town.

> I only write you this because I know you would wish to know. Reports indicate there were no survivors.
>
> I know you had friends there, Landais. For that, I'm sorry, old friend.
>
> Laran Thames
Master of Post, Central Province, Eighth District

Landais sat in a deep silence, none but the sounds of the hearth to perturb it.

The mayor of Waterrun had been a friend for many years. Landais had known many people in the town. The children of the people that spared him and his mother, and children of theirs, lived peacefully in Waterrun.

One other person he'd known in Waterrun was a smithy by the name of Erick, who had been shipping weapons and supplies to the rebellion for about a year.

Every possible precaution had been taken for secrecy. How could Brakken's agents have known?

And regardless of any crime Erick had committed, what crime did the mayor and the women and the children of Waterrun commit? What wrath must live in the heart of Brakken the Cruel to spur him to such an act?

Waterrun was gone.

Landais could only sigh at the thought, heavy as it weighed on him.

And Landais cursed himself for one other thought that snuck its way into his mind: the thought that he should stop; the thought that he should burn all his correspondence with Lady Andrius and abandon his allies to their fates. It was a thought wracked by such cowardice that he nearly felt ill when it crossed his mind in a momentary flash.

This was the very reason he had cast himself in with this rebellious lot. *This* was the great crime that Wizard-kind committed *each and every day* upon the mortals of the multiverse.

... And this was why he had chosen to involve Erick with the rebellion...

Another quote from *On the Premise of War* came to mind.

In any war, it is not lord or noble that risks his flesh. It is not the king on his throne who bleeds for his country. Is it the farmers and porters, the craftsmen and tailors, who put down the tools of their trade in exchange for the spear. Though castles and forts may burn, so too shall towns and villages. The price of war is paid in the souls of the masses.

A knock came at the door.

Landais shoved the letter to the bottom of a nearby stack and wiped the corners of his eyes. He shuffled some other papers in front of him. There was always work to be done.

He took a deep breath.

"Yes?" he replied.

The door opened and a man stepped in. The man was a good-natured half-elf by the name of Haden. Haden was a member of a very small group of guards, servants, and other nobles who knew of the plans for rebellion.

Ormond had known the man since he was a small child. He had been a timid lad. He had not the capacity to follow his father into money changing, but he wanted to help the people of Manara. It was precisely because he didn't join the other boys when they started fights with one another that Landais knew he would fight for what was right.

"My lord," stated his servant.

Smiling up to the man, Landais finished scrawling out a note of summary for the city's production, year-to-date.

"Please – come in and shut the door."

Haden did so. "Thank you, sir." He moved to the desk, but did not take the chair.

"How are you, my friend?" Lord Ormond inquired.

"I am well, thank you, lord."

"And how may I be of assistance this day?" the noble inquired. Landais ran through all of the preparations in his head in an effort to preempt the servant's requests.

"The latest shipment," began the servant.

Of course, thought Ormond. *The storage buildings.*

"The expansion of the stores have not gone as quick as we'd hoped," the half-elf went on as Ormond nodded, "and so this shipment has filled the last of our space." The servant looked disappointed with his own words.

"I see," stated Ormond as he stroked his bare chin. "And tell me again the reason for our slowed construction."

Ormond already knew the reason, but he often preferred to hear a predicament more than once. It was a sort of tactic for him to think through dilemmas anew. Many times, it had helped him to come to a simple resolution to the more complicated troubles of running a city.

"Well, my lord," Haden said, "trying to maintain secrecy and stop the rumors that began to circulate, we were forced to use the new storehouse we'd built as an auction house. You recall the Master of Coin's complaints about the old auction space. We think this worked, but it has gotten in the way of the cause. And, of course, the old auction house was ill-suited for storage, besides, the smith's guild managed to successfully petition it for a guild house once they completed their repairs."

It did help.

Ormond nodded. "Very well, let us redouble our efforts to finish the new storehouse. In the meantime, I think we'd better hurry with our announcement."

Haden cocked his head in confusion.

"Yes," Landais continued, "our announcement that the benevolent Wizard-King, Lord Brakken, has appropriated additional foodstuffs to the good people of Manara, as thanks for the countless sons she has given to the war effort and another nearly flawless harvest."

Ormond smiled outwardly, but the words were bitter in his mouth. He had to throw the agents off the scent of rebellion. He had seen all over again the lengths to which Lord Brakken would go to quell even the slightest hints of disloyalty.

"Yes," he concluded, "each family will receive an extra ration, and we shall pay the able-bodied porters to deliver it, and the merchants who go regularly to Marton and Lendel to deliver portions to our neighbors."

Understanding, Haden smiled. "I see, sir," he nodded, "it will be done." He bowed and turned to leave.

"Haden," Landais called to the servant as he opened the large wooden door to the administrator's office. The half-elf turned back to the nobleman.

"Thank you," Ormond said sincerely, eyes locked with Haden's.

Haden smiled and responded, "You are welcome, Lord Ormond."

Exiting the office, Haden was nearly toppled by another servant scrambling to enter.

"My lord!" the other servant shouted from the doorway.

"What is it?" Ormond questioned hastily, standing.

"Imperial Legions!" the human servant huffed. "They come this way! Thousands of men!"

Ormond's heart sank in his chest as the feeling of panic began to grip his every fiber. His eyes met Haden's as he still stood in the doorway behind the huffing servant, and the emotion was all too clear: fear. They both knew what this meant.

Landais nodded intently to Haden. They had planned for this contingency, but it was a plan they hoped never to implement. He would save who they could. In Manara, there were nineteen people who knew of the plans for the rebellion. All of them must be alerted at once to scatter.

"I will need some time to myself," Landais called hastily, and the soldier closed the door.

Ormond hastily gathered secret ledgers, banned books, and illicit letters, casting them into his fireplace. Sweat beaded on his brow.

He paused only a second on the note that had been opened on his desk but moments earlier. Waterrun was razed. What fate would become of his well-kept secret of Manara?

Gnarrl, High Justicar of Lord Brakken, rode many days and through nearly as many nights – several weeks on the roads. The autumn storms had come and gone, and even the colder rains of winter would not stop him or his assassins from exacting the will of the Wizard-King. No downpour or thunder could sway a Midnight Linium.

It would be a short while later that they reached the province known as Chilton. In Chilton, intelligence had shown, rested many of the off-duty men of the Fifth Planar Army. Their leader was the well-regarded General Vallon.

Gnarrl had only met Vallon on one occasion, and they did not interact extensively, but the strategists all spoke of Vallon's superior tactics on the field and his exemplary performance in the armies of the War Maker. They said he was handy with that fine blade of his, as well. Gnarrl guessed such a man would be severely disappointed to find out these rumors of rebellion could be traced to his ranks. Though, perhaps he would get the opportunity to cross blades with him if his cooperation was less than complete.

But Vallon himself was not here. Just one particular unit. Just the men Gnarrl hunted.

Gnarrl and his assassins had arrived at the safe house of the half-elf that they had captured weeks ago, and the justicar was happy to have been proven wrong: not all of the vermin had scattered fast enough, it seemed, and two of these "rebels" were captured by his agents.

One was utterly useless, one of those types that would die before giving information; he kept praying to a dead god called Koth. It certainly made for great torture, but it gave the justicar very poor information. The other one, however, talked quite easily before he died. He did not seem to know who it was that led this resistance, but twice he made mention of the Fifth Planar Army and one "Captain Mallison."

And so Gnarrl had his next goal.

The cold wind and the dark winter night both suited Gnarrl fine. He rather preferred them over the bright, hot days of summer. Not so much heat to exhaust him, not so much brightness to blind him, and not so much insufferable cheer. The night brought concealment, fear, and despair. It was the truest home the assassin could have.

As an icy wind swept through the town of Maybend, just inside the border of Chilton, men huddled in the warm places, the conversation and the ale of taverns letting them forget their long tour of duty and the bitter cold outside. The door swung open, and the High Justicar with his two companions entered from the howling cold.

It was doubtful that most of the people in this tavern knew who he and his men were, they bore no imperial insignia, but whispers swept through the crowd as conversations hushed; their image alone would suffice to invoke fear. These were three of the most skilled killers in The Vastness. Gnarrl scanned over the patrons of the tavern and immediately spotted his targets, but for the moment he ignored them.

While several tables in the tavern held obvious soldier-types, only one person in the hall had the demeanor of an officer. He sat at a table of five army men, though they all wore plain clothes. The weapons they kept on them gave them away plainly, even if their actions wouldn't have.

Gnarrl walked straight up to the bar, where the innkeeper also served the ales to his guests. The human had a suspicious look as he eyed the three dark figures approaching, grime still dripping from the ends of their cloaks. He flicked out a small wooden badge – a marker indicating his position – and displayed it to the innkeeper. The suspicious look turned to dread. The innkeeper nodded slowly as he met Gnarrl's eyes.

Gnarrl grinned. He had grown to enjoy his position within the Wizard-King's dominion; it was a position of fear, and fear was the only reliable form of respect. For a few brief moments, the three stood at the bar, not drinking or eating, but listening. The barkeep cowed away, but caused no commotion to disrupt his unwanted guests.

Low conversations again began to creep back into the large room. Once the ambiance was loud enough, Gnarrl turned to his assassins and whispered.

"Far table," his voice eked through the thick tavern air, only barely loud enough for the two to hear, "likely hostile, you know what to do."

This was all the instruction they required. His two assassins swiftly headed for the indicated table, where five soldiers of the Fifth Planar Army sat speaking to one another in hushed tones. The High Justicar then slowly began to walk toward the same table.

In a flash of speed, as the two cloaked men got within striking distance, they each leapt to action. Their cloaks fluttered, spraying small droplets of mud as two glimmers of steel blurred through the air. Each assassin picked their own target, adjacent to each other at the table and opposite from the officer. The soldiers, who were already suspicious of the three dark figures, each quickly reached for weapons, but they weren't nearly fast enough, as two of their number were punctured by long daggers above the collar bone, right against the bone. Each of the men shouted in surprise as their weapon arms were swiftly and completely disabled by a crippling pain.

Gnarrl still walked slowly toward the table.

Chairs clamored to the floor. As the other three soldiers finished drawing their weapons, the seven men now at the table were in a stalemate. Each of the wounded men now also had a dagger at his throat.

A short moment of suspense filled the tavern as sudden gasps and the clanking of fallen cups turned quickly to painful silence. Only a few patrons were smart enough to scurry out the tavern door.

The High Justicar's boots thudded loudly in the strained silence. His pace was purposefully slow. Finally he reached the table, stopping between his two assassins and their captives. He slowly reached up and pulled back his hood, revealing his half-orc face, dark skin, and dark hair, which made a centerpiece of his yellow-specked eyes. Gnarrl knew his eyes held much of his power, as he stared intensely.

The soldiers at the table were still silent, but the other soldiers throughout the tavern, their companions, slowly began creeping to get in a position where they might just come to their friends' defense. This, of course, would be no surprise to Gnarrl, but he allowed the spectacle to play out.

The soldier who appeared to be the leader shook his head curtly and waved the other soldiers off with a hand motion. He was either nervous for the lives of his two threatened soldiers or he knew that Gnarrl and his assassins were not a fight they could win. By extension, this meant he was either a sap or he had some intelligence. Either way, this would be useful.

With a plink, Gnarrl threw his wooden signifier to the table before the lead soldier, allowing the thrown object to identify whom he was addressing, though he still scanned all of the men at the table.

"You. Who are you?" he demanded.

Seeing the insignia and recognizing it, the officer's expression grew very dark. "My name is Captain Mallison."

The soldier's words were measured, and he bowed his head slightly and continued. "How can we be of assistance... Master Justicar?"

At hearing the half-orc's title, many in the bar gasped and still more escaped through the doorway. Most of the soldiers who had drawn their weapons lowered them, knowing now what sinister force they faced. Some called the High Justicar *the Blade of the Wizard-King*. One does not cross blades with a Wizard-King.

Captain Mallison was clearly half-dwarf, having the thick, unkempt beard and sturdy stature of a dwarf, even if he had the height of a short human. Though he was not in his uniform, an officer always had a certain decorum. The half-dwarf wore a buttoning shirt and clean trousers.

Would these nice clothes be stained with blood this night?

Gnarrl smiled, showing slightly more of his fangs, and began to pace around the table, slowly inching toward the captain. His heavy boots continued to thud against the wood floor.

"Well, Captain Mallison," began Gnarrl in the same dark tone, "I'm glad to see we will have your full cooperation."

The assassins did not loosen their daggers' hold on their two captives.

"You see," the justicar continued, "there is talk of rebellion against your god; the immortal Wizard-King, Lord Brakken."

Gnarrl let the words sink into the people at the tavern like a poison. Every soul in The Vastness knew that rebellion was the greatest of treasons. Everybody knew it was dealt with harshly.

"Now, we both know that this is fruitless, and I am *certain* a man of such standing as yourself would not be involved with these rabble rousers." He paused a moment. "But I'm guessing you or your men know something about it."

He stopped his pacing, not quite next to the captain, and locked eyes once more with the uncomfortable half-dwarf. The justicar now towered over his captive audience menacingly.

The captain's eyes squinted slightly as tiny beads of sweat appeared on his brow, the slightest look of regret betraying that he did indeed know something.

Gnarrl smiled again. "So will we be doing this the easy way..." He inched one hand to his side and back onto the hilt of a dagger. "... or the hard way?"

For a brief moment, the captain hid his expressions as best he could, contemplating the justicar's words. Regret and anger both flashed on his face, and then Mallison turned to the man next to him, opposite where Gnarrl now stood.

"Soldier, tell them what you were telling us." The captain's voice was pained.

The human next to the captain had a sudden look of terror.

"No, Captain! It weren't nothing! Just rumors, it weren't nothing!"

Gnarrl's grin deepened. A low noise, rather like a growl, came from the half-orc as, with blinding speed, he leapt upon the table and lunged over cups of ale and plates of food to collide with the human across from him.

The soldier's sword was still drawn, and reflexively he raised it as the justicar flew toward him. With one heavy boot, he stomped the sword to the table, causing a great crash and pinning it between his weight and the hardwood tabletop. With the other heavy boot he kicked the man square in the face, and the sickening sound of a nose breaking – and likely a tooth or two with it – was heard in the tavern. The man immediately released his grip on the sword, stumbled on the chair that was still behind him, and then fell back onto the floor with a dull thud.

Not a split second passed and the High Justicar was on top on the fallen man, with the tip of one long, slightly curved blade pushing barely into his chest. The man gasped as blood began to trickle from his nose.

"Yes, 'soldier,'" snarled the half-orc, "tell us…"

"Please! It weren't nothing," the soldier pled in a nasally, gurgling voice through broken teeth as he continued to gasp. "Please! I don't know nothing!"

The soldier squirmed under the slowly descending knife pressed against his chest.

The High Justicar sighed. "This is not the place for torture, human. These people might still have finished their meals had you been quick about this…"

Scraping his long dagger down the soldier's squirming chest, he stopped low in the abdomen and then slid the blade deep into the soldier's stomach. It was a smooth motion, almost effortless. A grunting noise came from the unfortunate human, like the wind had been knocked from him. Then he began to whimper, tears streaking through the blood on his face.

Many of Gnarrl's victims would have been weeping openly by this point, with friends to look on at his pitiful demise. Bravery is a funny thing in the face of certain death – like bringing a parasol to the mouth of a volcano, that it might help you weather the heat. Gnarrl let the man whimper awhile yet, until the bravery bled away with his lifeblood.

"I don't want to die," the soldier finally cried softly.

The large tavern room was completely silent as all the people that remained watched the scene in horror.

"It's too late for that now, human," the half-orc said, his voice softer, "you are dead. A knife in the gut is a slow, painful way to die. Perhaps if you tell me what I need to know, I will end your suffering early."

Gnarrl could feel the discomfort of this man's friends, all staring on helplessly. The half-orc did not stop the torture, the blade still tight in his grip so that every slightest squirm from the soldier would grind the blade in more.

"Well?" Gnarrl asked after a brief pause, the human beneath him beginning to take shallow breaths.

A short, dreadfully quiet moment passed, broken only by the labored breathing and soft whimpering.

"S—" the soldier tried to speak.

Blood already flowing from his nose was joined by blood rising from the back of his throat.

"Sl-Slick," managed the human. "C-Commander S-Slick…"

It was just enough information.

Gnarrl pondered for a moment if he should end this man's suffering or not, as he peered curiously into those eyes, slowly growing more distant as the soldier began to slip into shock. He almost felt compelled to end his pain.

Odd, thought Gnarrl, *why should I? He is a soldier and a traitor…*

"Dammit!" yelled Captain Mallison from behind Gnarrl. "Just end it! You have what you want now."

Normally, such an outburst would elicit a rapid and vicious reprisal from the justicar for interrupting his work – crushed bones and blood and all that. Something stopped him from doing so, though. Something odd… what was it? Something in that captain's voice…

Gnarrl had heard the tone before. There was… *pain* in the captain's voice.

He'd likely heard it a thousand times from those under his knife, concerned for their own life. He'd heard it from lovers or mothers or sons when their family faced the justicar's knives, but from *a captain* for his soldier? This was odd indeed.

Why should an officer of war care for the death of his soldier? thought Gnarrl, confused.

There was no amity in soldiery; it was a relationship of superior to subordinate, like Brakken to Gnarrl. Why should he care?

At once, a vast and sharp pain shot through Gnarrl's chest. He almost recoiled from it; it was unlike anything he'd ever felt. No blade nor arrow had pierced him, yet it felt almost as though one had. His chest throbbed, the back of his neck burned, and his brow began instantly to sweat. Had he not had years of training controlling his breathing, he'd likely be gasping for air at this moment.

What is this? Gnarrl withheld his reaction as best he could, but his breathing did quicken barely.

It was like the cold hand of death herself gripping his heart; it was the touch of a Wizard's fire; it chilled him to the bone and brought him to a sweat in the same moment. Gnarrl wondered a moment if he was dying.

But, just then, quicker than it came, it was gone.

Gnarrl steadied his breathing. *What* was *that?*

He shook his head. If he hesitated any longer, the onlookers may start to wonder. His assassins probably already noticed this strange and brief affliction.

"Fine," Gnarrl growled back at the captain, not breaking his gaze from the dying man. "We've gotten what we came for. Where can we find this 'Slick'?"

"He was wounded in the Battle of Harmony Valley," replied the captain, gritting his teeth. "He is on leave. I think he lives in Juro – some town near the sea."

The captain forced himself to bow once more, nearly shaking with anger.

"That's all I know. I swear it, Lord Justicar. Forgive my outburst."

Still crouched over the pathetic dying human, Gnarrl drew his other dagger and in the same motion slit the quivering man's throat. The thankful look of embracing death stared back at Gnarrl from the soldier's beaten face.

He withdrew both his daggers and looked back to his assassins, still holding their two soldiers in place, and he nodded toward the door to the tavern. They both slid their daggers out of the men's shoulders then each concealed both daggers once more beneath their flowing black cloaks. The three assassins left the tavern, and reentered the cold night just as they'd come in.

Behind them, they left a bloody scene. Gnarrl had left perhaps hundreds of them before.

The blood spread slowly across the floor. Conversation and ale did not return to the large tavern hall that night. The blood takes time to clean.

Chapter IX – The Winter Cold

"I can barely believe it, Mal," Artorus said to his half sister. "It really feels like things are coming together for us. It feels like watching a battle as you notice the tides are turning in your favor…"

He chewed on a bite of bread, holding the rest in his hand in front of him, unconsciously rolling it back and forth in his fingers.

Moments earlier, a council consisting of the two of them as well as Typhondrius, Commander Braïun, a half-elf scribe called Renoir, and the Captain Keldon Horace – who had arrived that day with more troops – sat around the large library table away from the cold night.

The winter had found its way at last to the high plains of the Andrius estate and the snow flurried about, trying desperately to cling to the ground. The council met in the sanctuary of the library to discuss the recruiting stage of their rebellion. The plans had been laid – so carefully laid – for more than four years, and the time was fast approaching to stop the planning and begin to take action.

Changing a dozen times since its inception, the plan they currently acted upon was a complicated amalgamation of Artorus's war tactics, Mala's intelligence, Typhondrius's careful observation, and the input of half a dozen other trusted advisors. Logistics, communication, food, weapons: they were all accounted for, and if even half of the secret letters were received by their carefully selected recipient and had the intended effect, would all come together once the signal was given.

The signal: Artorus would soon be required to muster whatever members of the Fifth Planar Army would follow and boldly announce his intentions against the "immortal" Wizard-King. The strategy mostly revolved around some diversions, as a force would take up a defensible position in the mountain pathways of Delemere, with food stores enough to last perhaps a year, while a separate strikeforce, himself and Braïun included, would be ready and waiting to attack Brakken himself in the very heart of his Dominance.

Artorus felt the excitement coursing through him as he thought about it; it would not be long now at all, perhaps as soon as the onset of next winter, in order to make defensible positions that much better while they rallied support for their cause and readied for their strike.

It was materializing from dreams and discussions into commitments and actions.

"Well, I, for one, never doubted you, my dear brother," Mala said in her sisterly voice, her bright eyes beaming at Artorus.

The general really wasn't sure what he would do without his sister; she'd kept him going every time he thought the rebellion wouldn't work, she'd given them a place to stay and a base of operations... and she saved his life when they lost Elsa. There would be no rebellion without Mala.

Typhondrius came back through the foyer of the library building.

"They have all gone to their respective beds," he said in his precise elven voice, "I'd say that went rather well."

The elf remained standing while Mala and Artorus chewed lazily on some food he'd placed on the table before the end of the long meeting.

Artorus still thought it odd that his elven friend was so proper with Mala. Artorus had only so much time he got to spend at the compound with them, but Ty and Mala were here at all times. It had been nearly four years since Artorus found the elf wandering near the road to Lord Brakken's fortress and still the poor man felt he had to play servant to the lords and ladies. Typhondrius never did tell him his full story, and Artorus made it clear he didn't have to. It was quite obvious it had something to do with Brakken, himself – a very dark history, by Artorus's measure.

Artorus certainly didn't blame Ty for the way he acted. He felt bad for the elf – he was quite literally bred to serve. But that life was behind him now. He was no servant; he was a friend.

"I'm inclined to agree," Artorus said finally. "Please sit, Ty. Enjoy some food and drink. This is reason for us to celebrate."

He smiled up at the elf.

"There's nothing else the masters need?" the elf replied instinctively.

"Shut up and sit down," Mala said lovingly to the elf.

Ty smiled and did so. "You know, I did have one question that didn't really apply to our meeting…"

Artorus and Mala gave the elf their attention.

"Eventually," he stated thoughtfully, "the time will come to go to Lord Brakken. Just how do you plan to get into his fortress, once all the plans come to fruition? Won't a prolonged siege only allow for time to call the Imperial Legions down upon you?"

"You're right, Ty." Artorus nodded. "It is a task I have assigned to Commander Braïun. I had planned, at least in the preliminary stages, to rush the fortress quickly enough that they could not muster their defenses. But, in truth, that was always meant to be a placeholder until Braïun and I could fill in the details…"

"Well," began Typhondrius, "do you recall the old guard at the fortress? I've told a few stories of him. An old human named Granger."

Artorus nodded as he chewed on more bread.

"Well, he always used to say—"

The sound of shouting outside cut the elf off. The three shared a concerned look.

"Help!" a voice called from outside, and they could hear more clearly now that they were listening for it. "He's hurt badly!"

The three, with equal speed, each leapt up and rushed through the foyer, out the door of the library building. In the dark night, the few lamps that hadn't gone out from the wind barely illuminated the main courtyard of the compound. They could only just make out the shapes of three forms. Two of them appeared to be the guards posted at the front gate and one of those guards seemed to be helping a third form as it hobbled along through the cold night.

Rushing out from the warmth of the doorway, Artorus was first to reach the men in the night. It was an old man, and he was bleeding – heavily.

A moment later, Mala and the others managed to help the stranger into the library building and had one guard fetch the healers immediately.

Mala said a silent prayer of thanks to Koth that the healers had arrived at the estate with the last group of soldiers. After one fairly serious injury on the training grounds several weeks back, Mala had made sure to arrange it.

The old man was human. He had no facial hair and was well fed. It looked as though the clothing was of a fine quality before whatever it was that happened to him. He shivered violently. His garb was probably never adequate for travel in the winter night, and even less so in its torn state.

Mala's instincts were flaring, and she made every effort she could to care for the poor man before the healers arrived. Blankets that had been tossed in a corner of the library were needed to bring his frozen limbs back to life. Some additional cloth torn from Mala's own loose shirt to try to stem the major bleeding. What injuries did the man even have, exactly? There looked to be some blade wounds.

The old man, though dreadfully close to death, insisted on speaking.

"Please," he managed through the violent shivers, "I must find Lady Andrius."

Artorus and Typhondrius both turned to Mala.

"I am she," she said to the man, "but you need care, please do not try to speak just now."

"No!" the man shouted in desperation. "You don't understand, I am Landais Ormond of Manara!"

His shivering did not allow him to speak much more, but what he'd said was sufficient for each of the three faces surrounding him to grow suddenly grim.

Lord Ormond was the administrator of the city known as Manara, the City of Grains. Manara was an important city in the plans for rebellion; in fact, many resources had gone into preparing it to store much of the grain they would need for the forces.

Mala had been to the city on more than one occasion, and it was a peaceful place, quite out of the way, with very little disturbance from bandits or armies or war bands of orcs. And Lord Ormond had been one of their longest-standing allies in their secret resistance.

As many letters as they had exchanged, Mala had only seen Lord Ormond once. They made great effort so as not to raise suspicions. It was hard to see through the dirt and blood, but she realized with a start that this was indeed him. The man had clearly been through a battle. Mala did not like what that might mean for the rebellion or for the peaceful city he oversaw.

Ormond was also one of only three people outside of the compound that knew the location of the Andrius estate as their headquarters.

But right now, the man needed immediate attention or he would die, along with whatever news he came to deliver. Mala and Typhondrius had already begun stoking the dying fire in the fireplace, and her brother pulled one end of the large table closer to it. The guard and Artorus helped to place Lord Ormond on the end of the table now close to the fire. As they finished, the guards returned with the groggy healers, and they began hurriedly to heat water and prepare bandages.

Now, in the better lighting, as Ormond lay on the table, Mala cold see what state he was in. This nobleman was not doing well. If the biting cold did not claim him, it looked as though the three large gashes about his upper body might. Though he seemed to be in fair shape for his age, the man was older than anyone Mala had ever seen with wounds this serious.

Mala knelt beside the growing fire and prayed to Koth.

That night had passed, and the old man did not die. Indeed, another night came and went, and Lord Ormond's health seemed to improve some. He had yet to regain consciousness, though, and a vicious fever had taken hold.

The healers proved invaluable in seeing the man back to health, though he was still suffering pain. The healers told Mala that if Ormond could overcome the fever, he would survive. And so Mala now cared for him; horrid battle wounds and deep gashes Mala could do little for, but a fever Mala could defeat.

He had been given a real cot, though this library still served as the best spot to keep him. He had been propped slightly upward on cushions.

It was midday, but still quite cool; some snow was beginning to stick to the low grasses and the leafless trees. Artorus and the officers had called an emergency meeting to assess their current resources. They had sent many riders with many messages as swiftly as they could to gather information from their various safe houses across the plane, and spread word that their rebellion's secrecy was in no small way compromised.

Mala had a concern that she had shared with the officers: if there were forces of the Wizard-King that knew of the rebellion and they tracked that information to Ormond, with Ormond fleeing here, were the agents of Lord Brakken descending upon them now? Did they let him flee for just such a reason? Artorus had said he thought it likely. Preparations would need to be made for them to leave the compound. The thought made Mala's head spin.

And in the days they awaited Ormond's recovery, many preparations were made hastily. All eyes were fixed to the horizons.

"There were many."

Mala had been so lost in thought she'd barely noticed that the signs of the fever had all but disappeared. The old man looked weak – very weak – but he was no longer standing at death's door. And he had spoken!

"You're awake!" she said excitedly. Then, curious, she replied, "'There were many?'"

Coughing weakly, the man barely managed to speak a question in one more word.

"Food?"

"Of course!" Mala exclaimed.

She reached for the soup that had been brought in, set by the fire to stay warm. She fed him several spoonfuls of the steaming meal.

Agonizingly slow, he did manage to eat, coughing a bit more, until finally he sighed and thanked her.

She was ecstatic to see him awake and eating.

"You look concerned..." Ormond managed after another moment.

"Yes, of course," Mala replied. "We were worried you might not make it!"

He shook his head slightly, "For your safety... For the safety of those in your charge... I know that feeling all too well. Every noble should know that feeling."

His face became grim.

"... but I have failed my people..."

Mala blinked at the man. He barely had the strength to stay awake, he had escaped death by a matter of moments, and he was talking about *her* safety and the safety of the others?

"There were many of us," he continued through his obvious pain, "that escaped Manara. We each rode in separate directions so they could not follow us all, not with many troops anyway." Ormond managed a slight smile at Mala, wiping the melancholy from his face. "I am glad I made it; I had been wanting to see you again."

Though strained and weak, his manner of speaking was still practiced. Mala remembered being impressed with the man's poise and demeanor upon their meeting.

His brow again furled from pain and concern. "But they may have tracked me, nonetheless. I must sincerely apologize. I have endangered you and your people..."

Mala nodded respectfully and told the man, "You worry about regaining your health, I'll worry about the estate, noble Ormond."

She returned his smile and fed him some more soup.

The nobleman was perhaps older than sixty, and his facial hair had grown in the passing days, showing white, though it was stained by more than a bit of soup now. Aside from the scrapes and bruises, his skin was of an even, pale tone, betraying a lifetime of lordly duties. He was one of a distinct minority of men in the multiverse that was never in the army. In a new outfit of white, with most of the blood and dirt washed away, the elderly man looked really quite presentable, despite his ordeals.

And in all the years Mala had dealt with the nobles of The Vastness, it was rare indeed to find men or women of character. Landais Ormond had the character of a true noble. She always thought they would have been fast friends, if they'd had the opportunity to meet under less serious circumstances.

She remained by the nobleman's side, continuing to feed him soup as he was able to manage. But many other thoughts raced in her mind.

As soon as she was able, she had called for the healers to check in on Ormond and she found Artorus. There were many questions to be answered; Mala ran through their plan in her head – through hundreds of variables, trying to answer them. But she knew her brother would have a plan. They had been discussing the variables since that night Ormond had arrived.

As soon as she found him, Artorus quickly summoned Typhondrius, his two officers, and their scribe once more to the library.

Ormond, it seemed, already knew Captain Horace. The two men spoke briefly of Horace's late father. Mala had never realized that Horace was originally from Manara.

Once all the appropriate people were gathered, Mala asked Ormond once more, "You are sure you're up to this?"

"There is no time to waste, my lady," Ormond replied with a nod.

"Very well," she relented.

The room quieted immediately as Mala and the five men turned their attention to Ormond.

"As you all know, I am the administrator of Manara," Ormond began quietly. "However, I fear that Manara may be... no more..."

Tears welled in the man's eyes as his words hung in the silence of the library room.

Manara was a city of a population exceeding four thousand, and it was both a trade center and a waypoint for east-west travel from the area of the Winterlands where Mala's estate was to the more populous areas such as Marton and eventually, Keldt. To think of an entire city, all the people and their livelihoods, as being simply *no more* was a sickening thought.

Mala tried hard to ignore the chill creeping up the back of her neck.

"The Imperial Legions," Ormond continued morosely, "they descended upon our city. We are peaceful, we have only a small police force. We had no reason to suspect that Lord Brakken's men would assault one of their own cities – an *assault* as though they waged war on their own people...

"The commander told us that rumors of rebellion pointed to our city. They told us Lord Brakken does not suffer rebels... They told us our city shall fall before the almighty will of the Wizard-King. I barely had a moment to request a parley before arrows were already raining down around us..."

The pale, bruised man paused, distraught as he recalled the events to the group. The tears now were streaming down his cheeks.

"I..." He struggled for the words. "I should have stayed there and faced the same fate I've brought upon my city... But, I didn't... I barely escaped with several of my guard. I had to bring the news; I know that Manara was important to your plans, and I know that Manara was not the only place to suffer this fate.

"I do not know if they left any of my people alive; they started burning buildings, and they killed women and children as swiftly as they killed the men that tried to fight back. It was horrific. I'd not seen this kind of violence since Phax invaded in 338. Not here... Not within the borders of The Vastness...

"I had burned all our correspondence and there were nineteen in my city who knew of the rebellion. We had agreed to scatter if it ever came to something like this. But only I knew of the Andrius estate, I never told any of the others. I went south first, then back northward. My guards each split off in different directions as we went, until only I came here to this compound...

"But, my city..." He trembled slightly. "I don't know how many survived..."

"Ormond," Mala finally interjected, "you don't have to continue."

But the others had a different idea.

"How many were there?" asked Captain Horace hurriedly.

"Yes, and were you able to tell which legion? What did the banners look like?" Commander Braïun inquired.

"Please..." Mala pled. "It is difficult for him, can't you see?"

"No," the elderly man said, regaining his posture and looking Mala in the eyes, "what my people might have suffered... I owe it to them to do everything I can to see this rebellion to its intended end."

Lord Ormond looked back to the officers as the scribe hastily scrawled text on one of many scrolls.

"There were perhaps two thousand men of the Sixteenth Imperial Legion, a Commander Trallock leading them, I believe."

Both of the officers opened their mouths to ask more questions, but they halted as Artorus raised a hand.

"This means that our plan is compromised." Artorus spoke the words plainly.

His words struck each person around the table, a nearly palpable feeling of dread descending upon the room.

Compromised? thought Mala. *Is Artorus saying what I think he's saying?*

"With the food stores of Manara destroyed or captured," he continued, "we cannot support our army in the mountains of Delemere through a winter assault as we'd planned. Without food, we have no army – not in the winter, not in the mountains."

Braïun nodded slowly and Horace stared down at the table in thought.

"So, what is our contingency?" asked the dwarf. "Do we abandon the current plan? Return to our ranks until we can reassess the situation?"

All looked to the general.

"It's an option," Artorus replied, deep in thought.

"At this stage of the plan, only select people know who is behind the rebellion," Typhondrius added from the side, sounding defeated. "We did plan for this possibility. We were careful."

Mala could feel her cheeks flushing and her chest welled with anxiety.

Ormond nodded. "Only a close retinue of guards and administrators knew of the plans in my city, and even they were never told of Lady Andrius or General Vallon, nor the estate, as I mentioned."

Artorus looked thoughtful, mulling all of the information over in his mind.

Mala, however, was a maelstrom of emotion. She could feel tears welling in her eyes.

"I—" began Artorus.

"*Give up!?*" Mala's tone was harsher than she intended. All of the heads turned to her. "We can't give up because some of our people lost their lives! *Hundreds of thousands* die *every* year in the endless wars of those tyrants. This is *exactly* what we aim to stop!"

She looked back to Ormond, her voice quivering as she tried to soften her tone. "Please don't take offense, I don't wish to demean the lives of your people..."

She turned back to the others. "But we knew all along that blood would be spilled. We knew that this rebellion would cost many lives."

"Artorus." She took a step toward her brother. "Of course our armies need food, but what if we aren't hidden away in a mountain fortress? What if we change our entire approach? Didn't you say there were two generals you had already discussed the rebellion with in your travels?

Men with armies at their disposal, armies already mobilized? Supply chains established?"

There had to be a way. When the fox was driven from its den, it had to either run... or it had to fight for its life. Mala could not stomach the thought of receding from the precipice of their rebellion.

Artorus thought a moment as the others were silent.

"You're referring to Warin and Magron?" Artorus replied. "Yes, they both seemed eager enough to carry on the discussions..."

Horace seemed to recognize these names and Braïun spoke contemplatively.

"The Second Planar and the Thirty-Third Homeworld?" He pondered. "Two mighty armies, to be sure."

There was another brief pause. The small crowd seemed unconvinced.

Mala felt her chest was about to burst. This was a time for action. This was the moment that would alter the fate of their rebellion.

"We must not abandon our plans," Mala went on. "We must act! *Anything* is better than waiting for years more while people are slaughtered and children are torn from their families. We could still retain the initiative if we act cleverly enough."

Mala wanted to say so much more. She wanted to scream into the night that this only *strengthened* their cause. This only made *more* important what they wanted to accomplish. But in negotiation, it was sometimes wiser to reserve your thoughts than to continue. In the end, the other party would make their decision in their minds, not in Mala's words. She withheld.

Another pause gripped the room as everyone thought on the noblewoman's words.

Artorus finally spoke. "My sister is right."

Mala breathed a sigh of relief as the general scanned the men in the room.

"I too am sorry for Ormond's losses and for the people of Manara, but this only means we will have to adjust our timetable and tactics. It is not yet time to sound the retreat. This fight is only getting started."

Ormond nodded to Artorus. "I accept your condolences," he said, "and I agree. I have little to offer without a city at my command, the people who swore to serve me... or even the use of my old body, but you still have my services for the rebellion; I will do anything I can. I will do it for them..."

Both of the officers nodded as well, though Horace still had a look of concern furling his brow. Renoir continued to write at his furious pace.

Artorus went on, "Just short days ago, we were discussing the plausibility of moving up our schedule... It seems we now get our wish; we have not the time to wait any longer. We've wasted some days already. With our grain stockpile lost, the plan can no longer center on a defensive tactic; we will have to move now and move fast.

"My sister continues to remind me of the importance of initiative. Well, if we can hit fast and hit hard, then we will at least have the initiative on our side. She's right." He was stroking his beard again. He addressed his two officers. "You men remember the Battle of Ext? When we tried in vain to hold the pass, and prevent Ziov's forces from rendezvousing? It became clear our defenses wouldn't hold, so what did we do? We charged. The manuals of tactics back at academy used to tell that, on occasion, the best defense is a swift offense..."

Artorus's tone took on an edge that she'd heard him use sometimes when addressing the soldiers in practice.

"Commander Braïun, you will accompany me back to the Fifth Planar Army, we will seek deployment ahead of schedule and then we will attempt to rally the officers and then the men to the cause – fallen gods help us. I will also hasten letters to Warin and Magron and see what resolve they have to act on their words.

"Captain Horace, you will take our men here and begin your charge as captain of the guard; this is still headquarters for our rebellion until the time comes to change it. But we *will* be ready to change it at a moment's notice. Your first task is to backtrack Ormond to make sure that none of the Sixteenth Legion's men have followed, then send whatever scouts we have left to investigate Manara. I will send men as I can to reinforce your numbers. But you already have some of the most trustworthy and capable of the Fifth Planar here now in our guard."

Artorus looked to the wounded Lord Ormond, as his tone softened slightly.

"I believe we will still have much use of your skills, Lord Ormond, but for now, please rest and recover your strength."

Finally, Artorus looked to Typhondrius.

"And I need you to look after my sister, Ty."

Typhondrius nodded solemnly. The air in the room was charged with a nervous energy.

Artorus nodded to the scribe.

"I believe were done here for now," he concluded. He turned back to the group, his eyes shining in the torchlight.

"That's all for now, gentlemen. More orders will follow soon. From this point out, we are battle-ready at all times."

The soldiers each saluted and then jumped into action, exiting the room into the cold night. The general hurriedly began collecting some of the scrolls and maps that he'd brought in for the meeting. Typhondrius assisted.

As he was about to leave the table, Artorus stopped, papers in hand, and looked to his half sister.

"Be careful while I'm gone, Mala. We're in a more dangerous phase of our plan now... But..." He hesitated. "Well, you know what to do, Mal. I might be the general of our troops, but you're leading this rebellion. I'll send troops here as I can. One day before long, you'll be the beacon for all the people who wish to join us. Soldiers, I can manage, but I have no clue what to do with the nobles and the merchants and the rest of The Vastness; that's your arena."

He smiled at her with that confidence that only Artorus could muster at a time like this.

At once, Mala remembered the past four years: the planning, the letters, the secret meetings, and the debates. She remembered encouraging her brother, telling him to think of *this* moment; the moment when it would all come to action. Just when it seemed their fragile plan might topple, it turned out this was the impetus they needed to act.

She remembered Elsa, too... It was as much for her as it was for anyone.

But no matter the positive energy in the room, the thought of Artorus marching off to deal with generals and armies in an act of rebellion worried her immensely.

Overwhelmed at the emotion of it all, as a single tear fell from her eye, Mala found the strength to say exactly what she needed to say to her brother.

"I love you, Artorus. Go start this rebellion."

Typhondrius finished the last preparations for Lord Vallon to depart. He had grown used to the general's company in the weeks that he'd stayed at the estate again.

He recalled when he first met the human; it was the night that Typhondrius lost his right ear. When the Wizard placed his hand upon Typhondrius's head, he knew to his very marrow that he would be killed; he'd never seen the Wizard spare a life. So when he did not die, Typhondrius found himself running. He escaped the chamber, he escaped the fortress, and he ran into the night. Typhondrius was astounded at his strength that night; he knew not where it came from.

Despite it all, he probably would have been killed by the wilds if General Vallon hadn't passed by. Most any other noble or any other general would have trampled Typhondrius under his horses just as quickly as he'd have stopped for him – or worse yet, returned him to Brakken for judgment – but Artorus was not like the other men in the Wizard-King's empire. And now General Vallon was leaving to start a rebellion.

But Artorus was often away with his army. Typhondrius's charge these years was truly the Lady Andrius.

Mala... She was a being of true compassion. Her kindness knew no limits and, in many ways, her bravery outmatched even her half brother's. In the years of serving her, Typhondrius had never once seen her compromise her morals. In traveling to the large cities on quests of finding the people this rebellion would need, she encountered many of the corrupt nobility – almost certainly the majority of nobles. She stood in front of kings, in their castles, and scolded them for immoral words. Even if only in the way she carried herself, she called for action from peasants and nobles alike, in every place she went, against the tyranny of evil.

It was nearly as though, for her, there was no secrecy to the resistance against Brakken at all; it had always been an open rebellion. She and her brother were people unlike any Typhondrius had met.

General Vallon said his goodbyes to his friends and his family, and then departed with Commander Braïun and a few soldiers into the cold evening air. It was a dangerous task he had, and none of them expected it to happen so soon. Only time would reveal just how the next events would unfold.

And Mala was always nervous when Artorus left to return to the Fifth Planar Army. This day, his task would be infinitely more dangerous.

"My lady," Typhondrius said to Mala as she turned to watch Captain Horace preparing the remaining soldiers for their various tasks. "What can I do for you?"

"Nothing this evening, Typhondrius," she said, defiant to her anxiety, "besides pray to Koth and get some rest. Tomorrow, though, we have much work to do."

Typhondrius followed Mala inside to the large manor house, and snow began to fall lightly on the estate once more.

Part One End

Part Two:

<u>In the Face of the Impossible</u>

Chapter X – Paxon Gorthös

Twenty-five years ago, Artorus was a boy. He lived on the large estate that became his home when his mother married the nobleman named Andrius, but nobody could replace his father. Lord Thorton Andrius was not a bad man; he cared for Artorus's mother, he provided for her; he provided for Artorus's young sister; he even seemed to care for Artorus. But the Lord Thorton Andrius was not Horus Vallon.

Artorus never truly could understand why – no, *how* – his mother could join with another man. It seemed the news that his father had been killed on the front had barely arrived when she began to entertain the nobleman and his courtly advances. Artorus's childhood was spent mostly just waiting for the day that the army recruiters would come for him. Sure, he liked his little sister well enough, but all too often, she stood as another reminder of all that his mother did to try to replace his father.

There was one actual benefit to life among the nobles; Paxon Gorthös was a young dwarven noble, not quite thirteen years old – which for a dwarf was probably even younger than Artorus's nine human years. Pax was a rambunctious, rowdy, and incorrigible young dwarf. His father was always away for one ambassadorial effort or another and his mother drank far too much of the dwarven ales to care much about what her son did or didn't do, so that left all the time in the world for Pax and Artorus to get into all manner of trouble.

"You're lucky, Art," Pax huffed over at his partner in crime as they hid on the far side of an irrigation ditch.

The sounds of the squealing pigs played like a song in the air of the summer afternoon. But the cursing of the pig farmer chasing them down was the centerpiece. The man had to wonder at this point how the pigs had managed to escape once each week for the past six weeks.

Also huffing, Artorus looked over at his friend.

They had to pause to enjoy the creativity of the enraged farmer as he howled all-new curses at his escapees. They had heard *Wizard's fire* perhaps a hundred times, but *Wizards eat them* and *shite of the fallen gods* were both completely new. Both boys stifled their laughter.

"What do you mean, lucky?" Artorus responded quietly.

"Well, you know," the dwarf managed between glances back to ensure no farmers bore down on the pair with pitchforks or hounds or the like, "in another month or two, you'll be off running around the planes having battles and adventures and all that."

Artorus thought about it. "Yeah, I guess."

A few short minutes later, the two were sauntering down the familiar pathway back to the Andrius estate. The summer sky stretched forever in front of them, and the tufts of dust that crawled up into that bright sky from the fields being tilled sprawled out behind them. The short trees that lined most of the roads in noble towns blotted out the sun in an orderly pattern as the two boys made their way back to their homes.

"Hey Pax," Artorus asked as they walked, "when you said that earlier – about the army?"

"Yeah?"

"Well…" the young human hesitated, "well what if you joined too? What if we both went on adventures across the planes – or whatever you said?"

"Art, you know I can't do that." The noble boy looked down. "My father would never let me."

"Yeah." Artorus shook his head. "I know; it was a stupid idea."

The two walked in silence awhile longer.

"You know," Artorus said as their homes appeared over the small hill ahead, "I've never told anyone, but..."

The dwarf looked at Artorus curiously.

"But I don't really even know if I want to go into the army."

Artorus paused and the two boys stopped atop the hill. Artorus looked down as he kicked a pebble to go tumbling away.

"It's how my father died."

"That's crazy, Art," Pax said. "I'm sure your father was great, but to die in the service of the Wizard-King is – well, it's the best thing any of us can do."

"What?" Artorus's brow furled. "How can you say that? I'd rather have my father than have some dead hero on some battlefield three gates away!"

"Art," Paxon pled, "I'm going to be stuck in some office of some magistrate for my whole life. I'll never learn to fight or see a single battle. The Wizard-King blesses those he sends to battle – the blessings of glory!"

"The Wizard-King can go to war, then, and bless himself."

"Hey, Art," Pax pled, hands raised defensively, "this kind of talk could really get you in trouble, you know..."

The dwarf threw his hands up and started to walk down the hillside, away from the conversation.

Artorus went on anyway, with more than enough volume for Pax to hear.

"You don't understand! I never had a choice. My father never had a choice! We've been a part of the army since we were born, and if I ever had kids, it'd be the same for them. Everybody in the army dies, Pax. How could you possibly understand? You're just another spoiled noble kid!"

Pax stopped, spinning around, hands balled into fists.

"You know what? Fine! You can't change it anyway! Go ahead and go die with your father, Artorus! And see if I even care! See if any of us *nobles* care."

And then the dwarven boy ran home.

Artorus did not see Pax for some time after that conversation.

In The Vastness, under the immortal rule of Lord Brakken the War Maker, every boy is registered at birth. Failure to do so would always result in the death of the boy, should he ever be discovered unregistered, and usually the mother too. A small mark on the inside of the right wrist signified approximate date of birth and the province of the empire to which the boy owed their allegiance. Regional magistrates had the task of assigning clerks to keep general track of the boys in their area. Families had the choice to send their girls too. Many women in The Vastness served in the various support roles of the military, and many were even warriors if they were stout enough. But every boy knew that upon their tenth birthday the recruiters would come for them. Some got lucky and were spared for a few months or even a year or two in the better times, but every boy past ten knew they were living on the Wizard-King's time. And these days, the recruiters weren't always even waiting for the tenth birthday…

It was true that not every single boy was selected for military service, since craftsmen, laborers, farmers, sailors, and engineers were all needed for The Vastness, but Artorus was a strong lad and fit for service in the wars. He would be selected.

He often looked to his mark and thought on the topic when he was younger. Most boys dreaded their mark. Artorus always thought of his mark as a reminder of his father.

Artorus was only four years old when his father died. His memories of the man were scattered and weakened by time, but Artorus still remembered the huge, strong hands and the deep, comforting voice. His father taught him how to swing a practice sword and told him he should keep practicing hard, because one day he would need it. Even though he had maybe half a dozen memories of him, it felt like his father gave Artorus so much in their short time.

The day the man came to the door of their house to tell them… Artorus could never forget it. His mother had been showing him the different plants in the garden when a dwarven-looking man dressed in uniform came to the house. Artorus didn't know how he knew, but he did indeed know what the man had come to say. His mother immediately began to weep when the soldier looked at her with sorry eyes. That day, Artorus lost his father, his teacher, and his best friend.

Until Artorus met Pax, he'd been mostly distant to mostly everyone. At least his baby sister never expected things from him or asked him things like "why don't you cheer up?" or "why don't you help out?"

But the only person that Artorus actually felt he could have a conversation with – laugh with – was Paxon.

And had he just thrown that away by yelling at his only friend? It didn't matter; Artorus would be gone soon anyway. Pax would be off to train in his father's profession not long after that.

"Please, would you just talk to us, Artorus," his mother pleaded one morning, as he reluctantly helped with collecting vegetables from the garden.

Artorus glanced at his mother. Balia Andrius really was a beautiful woman. Too many nights of crying for her husband away at war had left her aged beyond her years, but a certain brightness shone through her features nonetheless. She was hardly ever angry with Artorus, and even Artorus himself knew what that must take of her. She loved him dearly – and his little sister too – so why wasn't that enough to Artorus?

"Why, Mother?" he asked. "I'll just be in the hands of the recruiters soon..."

He could always tell when he hurt his mother's feelings. Sometimes he felt bad about it. But he'd been trying to force every conversation to the topic of the recruiters lately. It seemed like it was the only thought left in his mind these days.

One time too many maybe... he thought. *Oh well.*

"Artorus," she pled through the tears that began to well in her eyes, "please don't do this, not now."

Artorus left the yard to go inside, but he was stopped. His mother grabbed his arm – she'd never done that before. It was a firm grip. It got his attention.

"Artorus," his mother said sternly, "I know we can't bring back your father, but we have a new life now, we have to make the best of it."

She was breathing heavily now in the bright summery morning. "And maybe the recruiter won't come... Maybe he won't... Maybe you can stay with us. Things will get better!"

"No, Mother. They'll come for me, and I'll go with them."

His words were poison to his mother, and she began to cry as she knelt in the mist-dampened dirt and embraced her only son – and her only remaining piece of Horus. She loved them both dearly.

Artorus struggled slightly against the embrace, but it was not heartfelt. In truth, he was tired of being angry; it exhausted him. Maybe he could try to give it another chance. Maybe he could try being a little nicer to his stepfather.

Maybe tomorrow.

"My lady," an elven lady servant called from further down the yard, "my lady! They are here! They are coming!"

The servant ran up the manor road as she yelled, and behind her could be seen several riders, two bearing great banners of the Wizard-King and his armies, the foremost holding only a large bundle of scrolls. All three of the riders in front were armed and armored in the unmistakable uniform of the soldiery of The Vastness. Behind the three riders were three more pack mules loaded with supplies, satchels, and young boys – already five of them.

Artorus froze.

This is really it, he thought with disbelief.

All the years of expecting it, all the days of talking about it, and somehow it came as a complete shock to him now. His chest felt tight and his breathing ceased as he tried to think of what he could say to his mother.

The soldiers seemed to come up the hill in slow motion, each thunderous hoof beat shaking the earth of the noble estate.

Will this bring me closer to my father? Artorus thought and then turned toward his mother, *or only further from my mother?*

All of a sudden it seemed so soon; if Artorus could just have a little more time...

No. No more time. It was time to go now.

"You there!" the lead rider called as the three came to a stop in front of Artorus and his mother. "Let me see your wrist, boy."

His mother was shaking her head – not at the recruiter nor at Artorus, but in simple disbelief. Artorus raised his arm high into the air and his sleeve slowly fell past the mark that he'd borne all his life, revealing the boy's fate.

The recruiter turned back to his two soldiers.

"Army for this one."

"No!" his mother suddenly shouted.

"Quiet, wench," barked the recruiter bitterly back at Artorus's mother, as both soldiers behind him moved hands to the hilts of their swords.

"You knew this day would come and yet you stand here and insult the Wizard-King? Your *god*?" The recruiter spat on the ground. "I should slay you for such impudence!"

Artorus's numbness turned immediately to anger at the words this man spoke toward his mother. Luckily for Artorus, he didn't have the chance to respond.

"Please!" called a new voice.

Lord Thorton Andrius came from his house, hearing the commotion. He still held the quill with which he'd been writing, and ink stained his fingertips.

"Let us be civil about things," he went on. "Our loyalty to the Wizard-King is without question." He bowed with noble poise to the mounted recruiter. "I am Lord Thorton Andrius of this estate."

"Yes, I'm aware of who you are Lord Andrius," the recruiter stated, calming somewhat.

Thorton Andrius was a large man, with a posture the likes in which Artorus had only seen rich men carry themselves. His beard was not long and scraggly, but it was not as trim as most noblemen and he was beginning to bald on the top of his head. The smiles of many pleasant conversations over many nights creased his eyes on the sides. His clothing was fine and he usually wore different insignia and mantles that indicated his place in the society of the Wizard-King. Artorus never really knew the details of Lord Andrius's work, but he knew he was some kind of magistrate in charge of the provincial roads or transport or something.

Thorton glanced somewhat nervously at his wife, sweat beading on his forehead. She looked back to him with desperate eyes still wet with tears.

"Perhaps," the nobleman began, speaking carefully, "we can reach an understanding. You see, I am a nobleman, and this is my son. We both know that a nobleman need not send his sons to the war if he does not so choose. I can elect a noble life for him."

It seemed this was the wrong thing to say.

"What is this?" the recruiter roared, Thorton's respectful tone lost on the man, "You know that the boy has the mark. Clearly he is not your blood, nobleman. He is to join the army and fight for the glory of Lord Brakken the Eternal. This is the greatest honor of all families in The Vastness." He paused, a slight, sinister grin crossing his thin lips as he shifted in his saddle. "You would dishonor the Wizard-King and refuse to give up this half son of yours, Lord Andrius?" His question slithered through the air like a snake through grass. "Because my uncle, the king, would likely be quite interested in such news... Your relationship is a little strained with him, is it not? He seems to think you a bit troublesome."

Another look to his wife and then Lord Andrius looked down. Balia kept shaking her head in disbelief and clutching Artorus's hand.

"No..." Lord Andrius finally said quietly.

Taking his time to let the distraught family writhe under his control, servants all gathered around now, the recruiter slowly prodded.

"No *what*?"

Another pause as Balia began to sob, falling again to her knees.

"No, *sir*, I do not wish to dishonor the Wizard-King," the nobleman continued slowly, pain in his voice, eyes now shut. "... The boy is his."

Amid the screaming and crying of his mother, the two soldiers slid their banners into holsters beside their saddles and dismounted. They stepped up to Artorus and his mother, each still with one hand on their sword hilts.

"You can take one satchel with you, boy," one of the gruff soldiers spoke down to Artorus, "the rest you leave behind. You'll get clothing, food, and lodging."

So many emotions now swirled inside Artorus. Suddenly, his possessions meant little to him. He thought about all of the things he'd amassed in this nobleman's home: the toys, the dice games, the practice weapons, and the charcoal drawings.

What if all he really had of this place were his family and his friends? Had he just spent years spurning them? Had he just told his mother he didn't care? Had he shown the man who took his mother in and gave her a life of comfort no respect whatsoever?

Had he told his only friend in the world that he wanted nothing to do with him?

He shook his head. No, this was always the plan; this is how it is supposed to be. His life was the property of the Wizard-King.

"And make it quick," the soldier added.

He pried his hand from his mother's without meeting her eyes. She still sobbed openly.

Artorus went inside the large manor house. He searched through all of his things as quickly as he could, but there wasn't really anything he wanted to bring.

Then he found it: the training sword his father gave him. It was probably too small for him to get much practice with anymore, but it was clear to Artorus that it would help him more than any of these things.

As Artorus headed quickly back out to the front, his sister found him in the main entryway.

"Where you going Atowus?" the little Mala asked, staring up at the boy with those bright, interested eyes.

"I have to leave, Mala," he said, looking down to her. "I won't be back. Not for a long time."

Even his sister was suddenly a sad sight to him. Was it really true that he wanted to stay here so badly? When had his heart changed?

"But I don't want you to go," she said, pouting.

Artorus could only smile at his beautiful little sister, glowing there in the light of the entryway. He hugged her.

"Take care of Mother, okay little Mala?"

She nodded dutifully.

He proceeded out the door. His smile faded quickly as he walked solemnly into the yard. By now his stepfather was holding his mother in his embrace.

"That's it, boy?" the recruiter was looking incredulously at Artorus who held only an undersized, splintered wooden sword in his hand.

The other five boys were now standing about and watching as well; one laughed.

"This is all I need," Artorus said, not much caring what the other boys thought.

With a sigh, the recruiter started to turn back to his horse. "Very well, boy, let's get—"

A loud noise stopped him. Not simply a noise, it was a *battle cry*.

Rushing up from the side of the road was a small dwarf wielding a short sword. It was Pax and he was furious.

Just as he reached the surprised recruiter, he cried, "You won't take him! He doesn't want to go!"

The soldiers both stepped into action, but before they could reach the charging child, the recruiter had already sidestepped and tripped the boy into the soft dirt. A thud and the muffled shout of a dwarven boy sounded the failure of his brave assault.

The two soldiers then disarmed and held the dirtied boy who was still screaming at them. Pax fought to resist the soldiers. They beat him, lightly at first, but then harder as it became clear the boy would not give in.

"Please!" called Thorton.

But the beating continued.

"Stop it," cried Balia.

But the soldiers did not.

The beating was escalating; Artorus wondered if the young dwarf would die, but still he would not stop fighting them.

Finally, a shrill call rang into the clear morning.

"*Stop!*"

Artorus had never yelled so loud in his life, and it stunned all of the people there watching the spectacle. The soldiers did indeed halt their beating, breathing heavily. Pax struggled to breathe through his severely bloodied face.

"I'm going," Artorus finished, more quietly. "Just leave Pax alone."

"Well," the recruiter finally said, shaking his head and brushing the dirt from his pants, "we've had quite enough of a delay at this place already. If you two are quite finished… he's not one of ours, is he?"

The soldiers checked Pax's wrist but found the symbol indicating his noble blood and shook their heads. The recruiter nodded disdainfully, and they threw the battered dwarven child back to the fresh earth, where his short sword was now broken. They began to round up the other boys, still catching their breath from their morning exercise.

Artorus was lifted onto one of the mules and he looked at his family, little Mala having stepped out to her mother and father. He saw that Paxon, the tough little dwarf he was, stirred and even began to rise to his knees, still very bloodied. Artorus breathed a sigh of relief. His family's sad faces stared at him as his young friend forced himself up.

I really will miss them, Artorus came to realize as the soldiers all mounted as well.

In turn, he met the eyes of each of his family members.

His stepfather, the nobleman, nodded to Artorus as if to lend him some small bit of strength. His eyes were indeed strong, but Artorus sensed caring behind his noble poise, tugging at his heart. How had he never seen that before now?

Little Mala smiled at her brother, already seeming to have forgotten she was sad. Artorus was filled with warmth at the sight, and it somehow did give him courage for his coming trials.

His mother's eyes still held tearful sorrow at the sight of her only son being carried away, and Artorus found her hardest to look at. He thought about the last words they shared, and he looked away. In his worst moments, he had been an awful son to her, and that was a dishonor to his father's memory.

As the horses and mules treaded onward, he caught a glimpse of the kneeling Pax, still huffing and bleeding about his head. His eyes were locked on Artorus's though, and through the grisly sight, Artorus saw a very distinct grin from the dwarf.

He finally got that heroic fight he was looking for, Artorus guessed.

Artorus smiled back.

"Thanks, Pax," he said, now too far away for him to hear, but the dwarf nodded a response nonetheless as the view began to disappear over the crest of the hill.

Paxon's grinning face was the last sight of his home Artorus saw as a civilian. He would not return to the place until nine years had passed, now more a man than a boy. His squiring was complete and his soldiering was to begin as a regular of the Twenty-Fifth Homeworld Army.

It was common for boys from Myrus to start their careers in the Homeworld Armies, before entering the planar arena, as Artorus would with the Third Planar and eventually the Fifth Planar.

As it turned out, his first deployment with the Twenty-Fifth Homeworld was to the very area that he had once lived.

His unit was tasked with cleaning up the dead.

Artorus was completely silent as he moved about the area that was once his township. Two of his fellow soldiers, though, did talk as they swept debris into piles and identified bodies to pull apart from the other charred things.

"You know," the first soldier said to the other, "I never got why a Wizard brings his armies through a place and cleans out the nobles like this."

"I dunno," replied the second soldier. "Heard it had something to do with taking down the leaders, so's they can put in their own. Sumthin' like that."

Blood, bones, and flesh were all strewn about on hills Artorus once walked; the trees along the road were burned to husks; the animals had fled, and the irrigations dried.

The Wizard-King Krakus had burst through the worldgate with huge masses of his troops and swept large areas of many provinces.

"Yeah, but it doesn't do much if they can't hold the land," protested the first soldier. "Right now, Krakus is getting beaten back to the worldgate! And we're here, cleaning up the mess."

The other soldier shrugged lazily, "Dunno. I guess it's just in case they manage to keep the spot."

"I don't see no enemy nobles, neither. They don't bring 'em along with the armies and set 'em in these pretty houses, do they?"

The first soldier was trying to pry some metal bit from a pile of rubble.

The Andrius estate was nothing more than ash. Only bones survived the heat of the flames. Artorus's family and his friends were almost certainly dead. The attack had been quick, and Brakken's armies were far away when it happened.

But this was supposedly quite common in the Planewars: surprise raids through worldgates with hundreds of thousands of troops, and a quick retreat to follow. Artorus's instructors at academy always called them "inroads." Some sort of effort to disrupt a Dominance's infrastructure. Obviously, his fellow soldiers hadn't been paying attention to those lectures.

"You know," thought the first soldier aloud, "I'll bet it makes it darned tough to get the place back up an' runnin' – no nobles to boss the folk around and get things done, eh?" He chuckled a bit. "Damn nobles..."

This only got another shrug from the other soldier as they decided this vicinity was clear enough and began to move on.

"Whatever it is," the second soldier finally admitted, "I'm glad we're here with the dead rather than out in battle *becomin'* dead."

The first soldier chuckled once more.

"I got no plans to become dead," he agreed in earnest.

Finally, Artorus wiped the tears from his eyes, hoping the others wouldn't notice. They had found some bodies around where the Andrius estate had been, but there was no way to tell from the burned ones who might have been a servant and who might have been a member of his family.

He would later come to learn that Mala was sent away before the attack, but here, in this moment, he had suddenly lost everything he had ever known before the army. He expected to be the one in danger's way, deployed to other worlds where war raged hotly, not his family nestled safely on his home plane.

But no place was truly safe from the Planewars. That day he was taken would be the last time he saw his family alive.

And his last time seeing Paxon Gorthös was burying him alongside the remains of his own family in shallow graves as the battle still raged mere miles away.

They never talked about this part of war as children. They only talked about far-off adventures of untold glory – not burying friends, not burying family, not losing the things you only realized you treasured once they lay smoking among the rubble.

Chapter XI – Fates

The darkness of night and the gore of murder both saturated the fine house that sat beside the sea, sounds of waves in the far distance. The town was called Juro.

Gnarrl had not yet cleaned the blood of the Braïun family from his blades when one of his assassins approached. It was rare that the justicar encountered so many that were unwilling to talk before they died. Even the dwarven children seemed to hold some notion that their honor would not permit them to talk. No matter, dead informants were usually about as useful as living ones if one knew where to apply leverage. The silent form moved up behind the justicar.

"What?" he spoke from under his heavy, deep gray hood as he continued cleaning his blades of the ruddy dwarven blood.

"My Lord Justicar," the assassin hissed in a low voice, "we found exactly what you'd hoped for." The assassin held out a folded piece of parchment.

Taking it into a bloodied hand, he unfolded it. He read all he needed to read: "Andrius estate," the document read. "Rebellion," it went on, with pleas of secrecy scrawled throughout the calligraphic text.

"Good..." the justicar said smoothly, handing the parchment back. "Send for the town herald. We will find this Andrius estate."

Bowing low in the darkness of the blood-splattered room, the second assassin spoke. "It will be done. Shall we prepare to leave?"

Grinning, the half orc replied, "Yes, and it is time to call in the cavalry..."

Artorus wiped sweat from his brow. He shook his head, curious at how the snow could collect on the plains above and the mountains afar, and yet walking here he could sweat. Then again, it was not so surprising. Some of the coldest worlds were hot in battle; entire valleys could become cauldrons of steam from the furor of combat.

But the winter really is somewhat warm this year, Artorus pondered.

Artorus's letters and secret meetings had been going this way and that and hiding in the shadowy places of Myrus and other worlds for years. At different times, Artorus was both thrilled and terrified for the events that would soon come to pass; great personal peril and likely much death awaited his rebellion.

He was often most concerned for Mala. A soldier lives his life on the field of battle and expects death at every turn; Artorus did not fear for his life, but his half sister he feared for.

It wasn't as though she was helpless, of course. Mala was actually quite skilled with a sword. And she was not at all unfamiliar with battle tactics – Artorus had always been impressed with her ability to pick these things up from their discussions. What took him years of training seemed to take her a few days to grasp more often than not.

And, truthfully, she was as much a leader of this rebellion as he was. He would have to purge from his mind his brotherly instinct to protect his sister from all harm. She would now be protected from harm only if they finished their task.

Mala's strategic mind had come up with the idea for their rallying point, toward which Artorus now traveled, and where he would one day soon determine which generals would lend their aid to the rebellion.

Mala and Artorus had both always known this would be a critical juncture in their plans. They would need armies to follow them in their task, but they could hardly go about the countryside openly advertising their intentions. And so, with their accelerated timetable, what they had hoped would have been small, personal meetings across the course of months had now become a mass invitation to generals and their staffs, to occur in this fateful meeting place.

Of all the generals Artorus knew, that he'd hoped might be crazy enough to join him, many were currently stationed in the lowland provinces. They would meet in a designated area, far from any of their important strategic targets. They had picked a broad valley in the hill country of Chilton Province, a bit more than a hundred miles east-by-northeast of the Lakewoods that would eventually play a vital role in his strategy.

The generals with the greatest distance to travel had already been sent an invite to the rally point, while most of the remaining invitations were ready to send. They would surely think it strange to be summoned to a strategic meeting by a general of the Planar Armies, but hopefully, none would go so far as to suspect open rebellion. And here is where Artorus would rely on his reputation among The Vastness to at least pique the curiosity of these generals.

This meant that they could select a location that was ultimately unimportant in exchange for a screen to know truly whether each general would help them or not.

But there were two in whom Artorus had more faith than any: the generals Magron and Warin. These, he'd forgone secrecy with. Such was his faith in these that he had sent them directly to the estate to meet with Mala.

Any of the armies that would join the rebellion would be committing to an early deployment. The Fifth Planar was already doing so.

In Lord Brakken's armies, a general could request a shortened leave for his men, thereby initiating an early deployment. In exchange, a general would earn his men more leave later. This was all, of course, at the whim of the Wizard-King, who could suspend any and all leave orders. But for now, it served Artorus's exact purpose. At this moment, his army of almost ninety thousand men, dwarves, and others assembled to his command in the low plains of the Chilton Province.

The Fifth Planar... His brothers-in-arms now for more than a decade. Which, if any, of these ninety thousand souls would join him on his quest to kill the invincible ruler of worlds? It was a question that had burned inside of him for years now.

Fortunately, Artorus's full plans still seemed to be unknown to the Wizard-King as of yet. There would likely be no way to know which letter fell into the wrong hands or which mortal had betrayed their secrecy to the agents of Lord Brakken. Perhaps one day, Artorus would have them to thank. His hand was now forced to act.

Already it had been almost four weeks since he'd left the estate.

About time to send more men, thought Artorus.

"General," Commander Braïun reported to his superior, "I believe the lieutenants and high commanders are all assembled. We did have some trouble with Hakan, as you suspected, but he came. He was the last."

The proper dwarf smiled that polite smile of his at his general.

Both of the men looked rather immaculate, each wearing newly cleaned and repaired armor, with bright new cloaks draped about them. Though Artorus's armor was still scraped and cut from uncounted battles, it had been polished back to its grayish-silver color and it shone in the high sun above. As he often did before deployment, Artorus had his hair and beard trimmed short and neat.

Braïun, however, always had his armor buffed and polished to a high sheen after each deployment, to the point that few would guess it had seen as many battles as it had. The commander always wore his military decorations, unless he was on the very field of battle, and his cloak was a rich blue color that matched several tassels and painted segments of his armor. He had some different style in which he braided his beard when he dressed in armor, though Artorus could hardly pinpoint the differences and it was still tucked neatly into his belt. The dwarf's hair was parted off-center and combed carefully to the side, as always. Artorus was also happy to note that the dwarf was no longer limping; his leg had improved markedly in the last weeks.

Artorus grinned at his respectable officer standing next to him.

"You know" – he paused as they were headed toward the flap of a large tent – "I sense a big promotion in your future."

"Sir, if we find time between rallying insane men against an unbeatable enemy with superior forces and godly powers of destruction, I will accept such a promotion with great honor."

He bowed slightly and Artorus chuckled.

Was Braïun learning some humor at long last? Had it always been there, hiding just beneath that slick veneer? Or was this the Braïun that had left the armies of the War Maker and become a rebel to the empire – a new dwarf standing before him?

"On the topic of your military achievements... any of those captains of yours here yet?" the general prodded.

The two men were outside the tent flap, where the hum of many voices could be heard inside.

"Not yet, sir, and I'll be certain to chide them for their untimeliness just as soon as they arrive. Now stop stalling. You'll do fine, sir."

Artorus *was* stalling, wasn't he? He and his commander had grown to know one another quite well in the recent weeks.

General Vallon grinned and said under his breath as the two walked in, "I'd better do fine..."

Sat around a large table were the eight highest-ranking men in the Fifth Planar Army, aside from Vallon himself. The table rested in the middle of a very large tent, hastily erected by the general's host of troops, which was growing by the day. Food and various maps were strewn around on side tables. Several other aides, guards, and scribes were about the tent as well – all staff of the Fifth Planar Army which were already a part of the plans.

But each of these high commanders and lieutenants in the center knew that this was a meeting of special interest; they all knew that it was very much unlike their general to cut leave short and request his men be redeployed. The small crowd silenced almost immediately at Vallon's entrance.

Artorus tried hard not to show his nervousness as he breathed deeply and took in the sight of the men that – possibly for the last time – called him general. These men would normally obey his command to the letter – through storms, through fire, all the way to death's door if he asked it. Yet, he had managed to dream up a request that even these loyal officers would surely balk at.

The next few moments would speak volumes about the loyalty of these men, one way or the other.

"What took you so long?" a booming voice called from near the back of the table.

Braennor Hakan was an impressive form, a few inches taller than Vallon. He was wrapped in the thick layer of muscle that most people born in the intense gravity of Ebbea shared.

He was known to be fire-blooded; a *fireblood* was the title people gave to men of more than two racial ancestries. Though Hakan appeared largely human, he proudly spoke of his dwarven ancestors who drank liquor by the gallon and elven ancestors who supposedly led the infamous Elvish Insurrection of 188.

But Hakan's orcish features were the only ones that showed themselves with any prominence at all, as he had a slight grayish tinge to his skin tone, and though none of his teeth protruded as an orc tusk would, his grin definitely showed a few fang-like teeth. Those soldiers brave enough to call him a *green-blood* would either get a hearty laugh or a swift punch to the gut, and more than one soldier of the Fifth Planar had his nose broken for claiming Hakan a *gob-blood*.

It was said that a fireblood was so named because the varied races that coursed through their veins were never at peace with one another. One thing was quite difficult to deny: Hakan was very hot-blooded. He was known to speak his mind without any need of an invitation, and where most lieutenants would break up fights between the troops, fights seldom broke out with Hakan around because he would join them. Many a soldier of the Fifth Planar had spent time in the infirmary because of Hakan's hand-to-hand talents.

But, all his many talents aside, it was Hakan's brutal honesty that Vallon had come to depend on over the years. Also true, this blunt honesty meant that he would spit insults at his general nearly as quickly as he would acknowledge orders. Vallon was *fairly* certain that after the three years he'd spent as lieutenant, the man did understand the chain of command... In truth, he was a man that could be trusted. There was not an inkling of deception in his bones.

In the last four years, Artorus had stopped promoting based on skills alone. He had judged the worthiness of his troops on an entirely different level. Skills *were* important, yes, but they could be taught. Intellect, creativity, and perseverance were all vital to warfare, it was true. But what Artorus had come to know as the single most valuable trait in his army was trust. That could not be trained any more than it could be purchased. In fact, he had transferred away entire units of men when it became clear their trustworthiness as men of the Fifth was in question.

And so, this was how the very vocal Hakan, along with the rest of the most trusted men in the Fifth Planar, came to be in this tent on this day.

"What took *me* so long?" Artorus echoed back playfully.

Hakan grinned devilishly at his own question, since he, of course, was the reason for the delay. The other officers had been at least a day ahead of Hakan.

"We've all been waiting – and what's Slick doing here?" the lieutenant questioned.

"You're a fool, Hakan," a half-elf spoke up from the side of the table in a smooth voice. "I'd say this is no time to have the general make a mockery of you again, but I think we all know that truly anytime is good for that."

He winked at Hakan.

The only other lieutenant in Vallon's Fifth Planar was named Gregory Highblade; promoted from high commander only months prior, after the death of Lieutenant Rreth, Highblade was a man of unbelievable skill with a blade. He was, in truth, an interplanar celebrity from his time in the sword tournaments, and most believed he'd never been defeated in single combat. The man made the battlefield a work of art when he loosed steel. His elven blood gave him grace and his human blood, determination. But, just as with Hakan, this skill was not what Artorus valued most in his other lieutenant; he could trust Highblade with his life.

The man's thinly haired face usually displayed a confident smirk. His dress was impeccable as he leaned back in his chair, with his sheathed blade point-down on the ground beside him serving as a sort of arm rest.

He was an honest man – more honest than most men Artorus had met. He always said that honesty was like a sword: bare steel. If it was sheathed in lies or deception, then it could no longer cut. And so, he lived his life as he wielded his blade.

But no one bore more of Highblade's honesty than Lieutenant Hakan. The half-elf beamed happily at the other lieutenant.

Artorus smiled at the sight of his two lieutenants getting ready for another verbal bout.

"Gentlemen," Artorus interrupted as he trod the remaining steps to the table, "I brought you here not for us all to make fun of Hakan, as good a reason as that is, but to discuss our next deployment."

The men quieted again, Hakan sniffing nonchalantly. He would bide his time to return fire at Highblade and Vallon both. He rarely let anyone else have the last word.

"You know that it is not often that I pull the men from leave," he said, looking at each of his men in turn, "but the timing for which I'd hoped is no longer possible."

He allowed the men to ponder his statement for a moment. Each of these men present would be keeping up on the movements of Brakken's major rivals in the Planewars as best they could.

Kaladrius, the snake of a Wizard with whom they'd had the most recent interactions, had exhausted all of his tricks recently and could only rebuild his armies for the next assault; Phax, though distracted with offensives against other Wizard-Kings in recent years, held quite a base of power that could be tilted toward Brakken at any moment; Kraken rarely ventured out of his borders except on the most massive of campaigns or surprise attacks which couldn't be accounted for until after they were sprung; Vith seemed to have enough enemies besides Brakken to keep him occupied. These were the most immediate external threats to The Vastness.

There were more gates to more worlds across the planes of The Vastness and so there was always the chance that another Wizard, maddened with power, might burst through a worldgate on some interplanar gambit. Even Quirian, on the other side of the Oldgate, was a threat only chained by the strength of the Hundred Years Truce – a Wizard's truce... whatever that may be worth.

Artorus smirked. It was, of course, none of these threats that caused him to muster the Fifth Planar Army.

None of these enemies were nearly so prevalent as the Wizard-King that readily sent hundreds of thousands of the young men of The Vastness to their certain deaths...

"Every man in here has fought with me for years now," the general went on, quietly at first, "and seen many of our best men die on the blades of other mortals. You are, of course, aware that to be an officer in my army you must know that *war is death – nothing more*." He began to raise his voice slightly. "But each of you are in the position you're in because we can be more than simple warfare – more than just instruments of death. We are men; we are sons, we are fathers; we are husbands and brothers; we are soldiers, too, because there is no other way. This is something we have all accepted."

He walked slowly toward the map table a few dozen feet away from the table where his men sat, his voice now at its most commanding. "These scrolls – these countless maps – each represent a battlefield where *thousands* of ours died, and for what? For change in this endless war? I think not..."

His expression grew dark as his voice lowered almost to a growl. "Not change, but simply more blood at the foot of the altar – an altar to one who would have you call him a *god*. But he is no god; he is a simple warlord."

Now there was complete silence in the tent before him. Treason was afoot, from their very leader. His high command listened seriously to these grave words he was speaking. Some of his officers looked to him, and others simply looked down nervously.

"This next deployment that we make will be my last as your general," Artorus continued loudly, filling the tent again with his voice, "and I shall not command anything further from you. In fact, I ask the greatest thing of you *before* this deployment. I ask that any man here who does not trust my judgment – not as an officer of war, but as a mortal man – leave this tent and this army. I will grant you a transfer to whichever army you desire."

The briefest flash of fear swelled in Artorus's gut as he paused. This was the moment of truth, where he would come to know if the men he needed most for this rebellion would stand beside him.

He allowed sufficient time for men to leave or, at the least, question him, but each of the eight faces at the table – indeed, all of the faces in the tent – now looked to him in silence. He knew each of the faces, some for decades, and it filled him with the courage he needed. He breathed in sharply.

Artorus drew his beautiful blade from its scabbard with such quickness that it sang in the silence of the tent. With a flourish, he then thrust it into the earth in front of him and the singing faded slowly in the quiet.

"From this day forth, this sword will kill *no* more beings in the name of the War Maker. From this day on, this sword is my own and it shall be hefted only against those *I* deem worthy of its wrath. From this day on, this sword shall be a tool of *peace*, not of war; a tool of *progress*, not of *perpetual* strife; and it shall be a tool of *mortals*, not a tool of the despicable creatures we call *Wizards*.

"Any man at this table that wishes to join me in what will almost certainly be the greatest task you have ever faced; in what will probably amount to more killing than we've done in a thousand battles; in what could cost your lives… as well as the lives of your families… in what must be done – may each man draw his sword and place it here in this dirt.

"This moment, I swear to you that I will fight the hardest I have ever fought, and I will give my life if necessary to free you from the rule of Immortals. Place your sword beside mine and swear that you will fight to end the rule of Wizards, beginning with Brakken the Cruel. I ask you to tie your fates with a rebellion against the Wizard-King, Lord Brakken."

Artorus was breathing heavily, more from exhilaration that from windedness. His eyes saw more clearly, and his hands tingled with sensation.

He raised one hand back toward the entry to the tent.

"And may each man who wishes to return to the Wizards and their unending war leave through this door... and pray that we do not have to face one another on the field of battle."

He awaited the response from the eight men in front of him with an almost painful silence as each face stared soberly back at him.

Lieutenant Highblade stood from the table, grabbing his sword as he stood. He drew the fine blade – likely matching the general's in its quality – and thrust it into the ground next to the Vallon's.

"I swear it," said Highblade confidently.

Braïun's blade was next. "I swear it."

One by one, each of the high commanders came and placed their swords beside his, each man looking into Artorus's eyes as he did and swearing their service. The other men in the tent, too, came and swore their allegiance. Those that had them placed their swords in the ground too, a large collection of blades sprawling before Artorus.

This continued until just one man remained sitting outside of the circle of people, looking up at the standing crowd.

Slowly, all attention in the room turned to the sole remaining man; it was Lieutenant Hakan as he still sat with his arms folded in the exact same spot he'd been when the general entered the tent.

Artorus felt something at the sight of the large man; it may just have been fear; fear that one of the men he would count on most might not be moved by saving the lives of soldiers and ending the Planewars. He was trustworthy, yes, but was he compassionate enough? How could he not have thought of it? A lack of solidarity now could be deadly, but here and now, he could only wait.

"General," Hakan finally responded in the quiet of the tent, "we all knew this day would come."

He rose from his seat, slowly.

"We knew that you were different from other generals – strange." He walked around the large table toward the other men, grasping the scabbard at his belt. "You got no loyalty to the Wizard-King."

He stopped amongst the blades standing in the earthen floor and then he drew his own sword, largest of all the blades in the tent. It was a heavy weapon, meant to be wielded two-handed. In his one hand, arm outstretched, it nearly spanned the gap between him and Artorus.

At once, a dozen men grabbed for their swords and held them to the lumbering lieutenant. Hakan's own sword was pointing lazily toward Artorus in the same unconcerned manner with which the lieutenant spoke.

He went on, completely unfazed by the dozen swords pointing at him.

"And all I got to say to you is what I said already."

A huge grin drew across his face, showing his oversized incisors. "What took you so long?"

Sighing, a nervous chuckle escaped Artorus. The swords all eventually lowered. Hakan flipped his great sword around and thrust it into the ground in front of him with a rumbling laugh.

Highblade shook his head at the other lieutenant, but couldn't help a laugh as well. All the men in the tent joined.

"So, what now, then, General?" Highblade asked, turning his attention back to Artorus. "How do we act against the Wizard-King?"

Artorus also withdrew his sword from the ground. He looked to his most loyal men, with pride in his chest and anticipation filling his every muscle.

"The multiverse will thank you one day for these oaths you have made… But we start first by assembling the troops and mobilizing.

"We have a meeting to attend."

Mala considered the man across the table from her. General Warin was an older gentleman, with a bushy white mustache, whose eyes told many tales. The general had traveled to the Winterlands from unknown deployment on an unknown world, traveling far at Artorus's request, which would hopefully bode well for his intentions regarding the rebellion.

Mala had also received a letter that one General Magron of the Thirty-Third Homeworld Army would be arriving soon, and the compound would get even more crowded. Only these two were the most trusted in her brother's assessment, and due to their shortened timeframe, they could not afford to establish secret locations and hidden meeting places. For at least these two, the estate would have to do. They were at the point at which some safety had to be sacrificed for an advantage in timing.

By now, the Andrius estate was buzzing with activity, many soldiers having come from Artorus to aid in the resistance, each one for his own reasons.

"I must thank you again," Mala said to the aged man, "for risking so much to come here."

"Do hush up about that, young lady," Warin said. "If I bothered to come here, I think you know that means that no thanks are needed; it's an ideological similarity that draws us together." He smiled from under his white mustache. "We both wish to see that devil, Brakken, deposed."

General Leon Warin spoke with a slight rasp to his voice, but it certainly held the weight of both a general and a very wise man. His moustache was the same color as his hair and both only barely hid a well-tanned, wrinkled face. For being as old as he was, he was still in great shape, thick arms and broad chest filling his armor well. He was, in fact, quite well regarded among Brakken's military, and rumors that he was being considered for lord general had circulated for over a year now, as Artorus had relayed.

"Very well, good general," replied Mala. "Then if we're already in agreement on the task at hand, I wish to take questions from you.

What must you know about our operation or my half brother, General Vallon?"

"So, he *is* to lead this rebellion?" Warin asked. Mala nodded. "I daresay that bodes well for us... I suspected the letter was truly from the man, but one can never know what careful measures might have been taken to conceal or deceive... Even on Learden, words of Vallon's tactics have spread; he is supposed to be quite the general. Indeed, I have met him once when his army and mine co-opted a mission some years back. He was a commander then, but I can recall the face."

The general pondered another moment. "What, exactly is his plan, madam?"

Mala bowed her head slightly. "You'll forgive me if I do not reveal too much. Suffice it to say he has a strategy that we feel confident can give us a chance at victory. But I'm afraid details could only follow an affirmative from you."

General Warin pondered again.

"Very well, what are the terms of General Vallon and his rebellion?"

"Artorus Vallon shall have final say concerning military matters of the rebellion and, as such, your armies shall be pledged to him. I shall have final say on all other matters of the rebellion, not strictly military in nature. Now this is, of course, not to say that we do not wish for your considerable skill and leadership to aid him in the task to come, and we will look to you for both guidance and action. And, once the War Maker is dethroned, a new government will be established."

Mala paused, holding the general's gaze. When it was said aloud, the whole idea they had been working toward so desperately these last few years sounded almost like fantasy. But what would General Warin think?

He breathed deeply and then nodded.

"Then I humbly accept the offer to join your mighty rebellion on behalf of myself and any of my army foolish enough to follow."

Mala strained not to lose her composure. Every last fiber of her being wanted to jump up and down and scream for joy.

Warin shifted in his seat. "...with a request as well."

The general waited for the Lady Andrius to nod for him to proceed. She did so.

"That I be special advisor on interplanar affairs for such time as it is required. I have had many years of experience fighting each of Lord Brakken's adversaries across the planes and I believe I may be able to preempt some of their moves during and – Koth willing – after our rebellion is acted upon."

Mala's face lit up at the mention of Koth – General Warin was a fellow believer.

"You seek the Lord of Truth?" Mala asked, a little more excited than she meant to sound.

"Of course, my lady," Warin replied with a slight bow of his head. "All the worlds are fogged by deception and misdirection, and Koth shows us the one true path, if we can open ourselves to it."

"This is most excellent! Well, we will have many more opportunities to discuss The Light, but I should greatly look forward to your counsel in the matters of the rebellion as well. Of course, there will be many meetings to come..."

"My lady," Typhondrius interrupted, "my apologies, Master General."

Mala hadn't even noticed him enter. It was quite rare for him to interrupt a meeting.

"What is it, Typhondrius?" Mala asked, concerned.

"It looks as though we have another visitor," Typhondrius said uncertainly.

The general looked to Mala, sharing her concern. He nodded to her as if to give permission to end their meeting early, and she got up and followed.

Typhondrius explained little more as they walked, but as they exited into the courtyard he spoke again.

"I don't believe we were expecting *him*."

Standing in the middle of the courtyard, among the small piles of snow amid the slush and mud, was a very tall figure. He was cloaked in a rather thin robe of dark brown fabric with complex patterning in golden thread, wearing no hair on his head and only simple sandals on his feet, despite the inclement conditions.

Beside him were two more figures robed in the same cloth, though wearing boots somewhat more appropriate for the weather, at least. They also had heads completely shaved of hair. One looked to be an elf, and the other, human.

The central figure appeared like a human, though perhaps not quite... He was impossibly tall – perhaps seven feet? But there was more about him that somehow differentiated him; it was as though he were the tallest and, Mala found it odd to admit, most handsome human that walked the twenty-seven worlds. He was almost too human to *be* human – there were no scars, no pockmarks, no wrinkles to blemish his strangely beautiful face. His deep, sparkling eyes seemed to hold such wisdom it was, at once, both astounding and terrifying.

"Hello, Lady Andrius." His voice was booming – commanding, even – but not exactly harsh. "This is Brother Hereditus," he said, gesturing to the elf, who bowed. "And this is Brother Orion," he said, gesturing to the human, who bowed in the same fashion.

"And I am Kellos, Sage of Delemere."

Mala could not help gasping.

All her life she'd heard the tales of the Sage of Delemere, but she'd never dreamed of meeting him – some scarcely even believed Sages existed. She'd written many letters to the man, in hopes he could satisfy her curiosities, but until he'd responded to Artorus, she had never even read anything he'd written. She pored over that letter, but even then, it was the closest she ever imagined she'd get to the man.

And that voice gave her a feeling at the base of her skull, like it somehow held a power that no mortal could ever wield. This was indeed an immortal Sage.

A glance and the slightest look of consternation from Typhondrius made her close her mouth. Snapping out of her befuddlement, she managed a greeting.

"Hi."

Hi? Was that all she could muster? Her countless hours of tutorship under all manner of noble educators throughout her youth all flashed through her mind, as even still, she stood stupidly staring at the Sage.

Typhondrius cleared his throat a bit.

"And welcome to the Andrius estate, honored Sage and companions," he finished for Mala, glancing at her as he rose from his polite bow.

"Um, yes," she finally said, "welcome indeed, noble Sage. Please forgive my being forthcoming, but to what do we owe this honor?"

"There is much to discuss, I believe," the Sage said in his deep voice. "Perhaps indoors would be better?"

After several apologies and an introduction to Captain Horace and General Warin, Typhondrius and Mala served the monks and the Sage a small meal inside the main meeting hall of the estate, and they talked.

"You see, I took your letter to mean that you would not partake in such a rebellion," Mala said curiously.

Both monks were eerily silent, but not at all impolite as the Sage and Mala spoke.

"Yes. 'I cannot endorse any actions which I surmise to be planned behind these questions. As a Sage, it is not my place nor my desire to interfere with the activity of mortals,' were my exact words."

Those were indeed his *exact* words. She nearly had all the words of that letter memorized by this point.

"It is clear how this would cause confusion given my current presence here," the very tall man continued. "I do indeed corroborate that sentiment. That notwithstanding, I believe the operative term here is 'the activity of mortals.' You fight to end these Planewars that have been ongoing for more than three centuries, involving countless millions of mortals, I have no doubt. I have contemplated this situation for some months since receiving and responding to your half brother's letter. I have resolved that the Planewars are not the activity of mortals; they are the affairs of Wizards – quite different."

"As such, I graciously accepted the offers for brothers Hereditus and Orion to accompany me and I came to aid you in your activity in the affairs of immortals, however my services may do so."

Offering his assistance to the rebellion? Mala thought in disbelief.

And that way he spoke... it did indeed feel like touching the immortal knowledge of a Sage. Mala wasn't entirely sure she followed it all. It was overwhelming.

"Pardon, Master Sage," Typhondrius stated hesitantly, before the silence turned awkward. "But may I interject?"

The Sage gestured for him to do so.

"I can't say I completely see what you mean," he went on. "The affairs of Immortals seem like an even *more* dangerous place to interfere..."

Mala could see something on Typhondrius's face; some tiny flash of concern when his gaze fell upon the Sage. Had he encountered a Sage before? He certainly had mentioned no such experience to her. She thought she had noticed it in the courtyard earlier, but now she was sure of it.

She would have to approach him about it later.

"It may be so," was the Sage's only reply to that thought.

Mala had to shake her head to clear away the utter surprise at the Sage being here at her estate.

He is offering his assistance, she thought. *The assistance of an immortal Sage...*

Mala suddenly felt an urge to be forward with Kellos. Questions had burned on her mind to ask the Sage of Delemere for decades now. If the Sage was offering his assistance, then the least he could do is answer questions. She decided on one question that had been on her mind since one of her earliest readings of the letter.

"A question then, Master Sage," Mala proposed. He gestured for her to proceed, much as he had Typhondrius. "We read through the letter you sent us quite a few times..." Mala began. "Would it suit you to discuss it with us at some point?"

"Lady Andrius, please do not qualify your questions of me. I have brought my services to you that you may gain what you will from my knowledge. It is true that you did not receive a response to any of the prior four letters you addressed to me. You have my apologies that I did not make the time to respond."

He remembers those? As though Mala hadn't given herself enough reasons to be embarrassed since the Sage's arrival. Mala could hardly even recall how long ago she had written those. *I was a girl.*

"You see," he continued, seemingly oblivious to Mala's steadily warming cheeks, "we are keepers of knowledge, and so too are we sharers of knowledge. It is my belief that permeation is indeed the very purpose of knowledge; a thing to grow and to metamorphose through its being shared and multiplied. And, as I have stated, I offer my assistance in your actions with Immortals. So please simply ask what questions you have without the hindrances of presuppositions of indignities or the propriety of etiquette."

The Sage's manner of speech was off-putting, to say the least. She had spent so much of her life wishing for but a trickle of the knowledge he commanded, and now it was as though he poured it upon her like a raging waterfall.

Mala attempted to gather her thoughts. "I— You're right... Presuppositions... Um..."

She shook her head in disbelief. She sat before a Sage; the entire multiverse was practically at her fingertips. She shoved aside her embarrassment in exchange for her burning curiosity.

"Well," she mustered, "I am curious if you really remember the letters I wrote you as a girl?"

"I do," was his only response.

Hm, she thought, *may as well start with a big one, then...*

"I recall asking you about what makes the worldgates work..." she tested. As a girl, she asked the sort of questions only a child could come up with – the kind that exasperated her parents. "Care to elaborate on that?"

"Yes," the Sage responded earnestly, much to Mala's surprise, "you inquired on the connections between the planes, and the nature of the space that must separate the worlds, commonly called 'the æther.' Verily, this is the subject of much discourse among the Sages. Generally, two competing schools of thought prevail: one theory states that the worldgates are essentially holes punched through the very fabric that makes up the worlds, operating very much like a needle piercing two layers of clothing and carrying thread through; the other school posits that the fabric of our multiverse operates more like the surface of a pond, and worldgates are more like vortices." He paused for half a second. "I will cease at this summary for the moment, as full disclosure would require more hours than you have to spare, I believe."

That made almost no sense to Mala. She blinked.

She would have to ask for a repeat of that incredible exposé, but now she was alight with excitement. The Sage's unmeasurable knowledge really was at their disposal... Perhaps a more relevant topic, then.

"I have another question," she began. "In your letter, you mention the number of Wizards in the known worlds. If there were previously two hundred seventy Wizards, and they were far less powerful than the Wizards of today, and now that there are only seventeen of the creatures they are significantly more powerful..." She licked her lips as she paused.

The Sage peered at her with his mighty gaze, interested.

"Could we possibly assume that they increase in power, the fewer there are? Do they somehow steal the powers of each other? We read through all the texts we could find. We saw a reference of one Wizard killing another." Mala shifted in her seat, excited to present these questions to one who may just have the answers. "Could we possibly assume that this is the *entire reason* for the Planewars? They fight to become more powerful? Until, maybe, just one of them holds the power of all Wizard-kind?"

In an expression that likely outmatched all the emotion he had yet shown, the Sage raised an eyebrow and breathed deeply. He collected his thoughts before responding.

"Lady Mala, I do believe yours is a superior intellect." He sharpened his gaze at the noblewoman, nearly piercing through her. "This is a hypothesis that I myself have held for some time, and I have not shared it with any mortal – not even my monks. I have not so much as written a word of it down."

The slightest looks of surprise on the two monks seemed to confirm the Sage's words.

"It has been ninety years, four months, and days counting now have I kept my theory most private from mortal ears. Please do not mistake my meaning when I say: this is the kind of information I do not recommend discussing. Exploring the motivations of immortal warlords is not the kind of thing one should do lightly."

The two monks each shifted uncomfortably. It seemed this was indeed a topic that Mala should not be broaching.

Somewhat crestfallen, Mala nodded. "I see, noble Sage. I'm sorry, I just got rather excited. We've read your letter over and over again since we received it. We dug out all the histories this compound contained."

"Knowledge," the Sage continued after a brief moment, "is a powerful thing in this multiverse of ours. I do not know that even the Wizards themselves comprehend entirely why they continue to fight. It certainly seems to me that the Wizard-Kings would kill just as many just as quickly for knowledge that may help them in this conflict as they would for control of entire planes. The Sages are now spread throughout the twenty-seven known worlds, and we have, each of us, taken a vow to exclude ourselves from the affairs of mortals in our effort to collect and maintain immortal knowledge.

"All the same, there are those of our number that would work with the Wizard-Kings, given the right motivations. So, while my presence here is intended solely as teacher, please know that talk such as this, with beings such as we, is indeed dangerous."

The Sage's stare was very intense, and Mala found herself looking away.

Have I done something wrong? she thought. *Perhaps I need to practice a little more restraint. The Sage may be risking his own life to be here, and I should not do anything that might bring him greater jeopardy.*

Still, Mala found it quite difficult not to dwell on the fact that she seemed to have formed the same hypothesis as *a Sage*.

Mala's mind raced. *Have I really stumbled upon the very reason behind the hundreds of years of war between these awful Wizards? They are so powerful, and yet they crave nothing more than to increase that power? And what if they could only do so by destroying others of their kind?*

It all cast a certain desperation over the Planewars that Mala had never broadened her perspective enough to see before. It was a dark contemplation – *the motivations of immortal warlords*, as the Sage had put it.

And here stood the mortals, pawns in this interplanar game of life and death played by Wizards. Countless mortals had died, and, unless the actions of Mala and her brother and their friends could change something, the mortals would never stop dying for the power plays of these crazed monsters.

A moment passed, the two monks ever silent, and Mala was quieted in thought.

"Well," Typhondrius stated to the three robed figures, "I'm certain your travels have drained you. I believe I know which building in this compound you would most prefer." He smiled to Mala as he finished. "I'll have the library made up with all the proper sleeping arrangements for you."

Their three guests nodded in unison – quite unsettlingly, in truth – and all of them got up from the table.

After Typhondrius had arranged for the Sage and his companions to take up lodging in the library and Mala bade a good night to General Warin, Typhondrius finally walked with Mala back toward the manor house.

As they walked, her elven friend was lost in thought. His expression seemed to have returned to that same look upon his face that she'd noticed earlier. His brow was furled, and he almost seemed... fretful.

"What is it, Typhondrius?" Mala asked her friend. "I noticed that you act strangely around the Sage. Are you concerned? Is something we should know about this Sage?"

"Well, perhaps not so strange as yourself, my lady," Typhondrius retorted.

Mala blushed again. It was just that all her training in the life as a noblewoman had not prepared her for encountering her childhood muse. She had spoken with dukes and counts and kings in her magisterial duties, but she had only dreamed of being able to have a conversation with the Sage of Delemere.

Thankfully, Typhondrius had returned to his contemplations, saving her from responding.

"It's just that..." Typhondrius hesitated.

"What?" Mala encouraged softly.

"That man," Typhondrius went on seriously, "has an appearance that I tried desperately to ignore from the moment I saw him. But once I heard him talk, I couldn't possibly..." Typhondrius stopped walking and looked Mala in the eye. "The Sage of Delemere... he looks just like the master. He looks just like Lord Brakken."

"*What?*" Mala couldn't hide her concern. "What are you implying, Typhondrius?"

"Nothing... Just what I said – a simple likeness of appearance and voice. They are even about the same height."

"They look and sound similar?" Mala prodded, hardly believing it.

"They look and sound *exactly the same*," Typhondrius replied intensely, "aside from Lord Brakken's hair and tattoos. And perhaps Lord Brakken is more thickly muscled... But they could be twin-born, were they mortals."

"I..." Mala wasn't sure what to make of that. "I'll have to think on that."

"I can't imagine what it means, but it is quite striking..." Typhondrius said contemplatively. He shook his head as they stood in silence.

But after a moment, they both decided it best to bid each other a good evening. There were stacks of missives Mala had been ignoring more and more in recent days. And the whole of the Andrius estate was in a rather hectic state these days. It took all her powers of organization just to keep things together.

And despite all her work, her mind still raced with questions.

Despite the many quandaries, one thing was certain: the Sage of Delemere was no longer sitting atop his mountain in contemplation; he was taking action in this conflict. What exactly that would mean, only time could tell.

Chapter XII – Thy Home, But Not Thy Castle

"It is just as we feared, my lady," Captain Keldon Horace said to the Lady Andrius. "More killings from the Imperial Legions, and more assassinations all across the plane. We now have reports from Northrealm to Sandis to Myral, and everywhere between. I believe this is the time, my lady…

"It is true that our greatest advantage is likely that, by all accounts, Lord Ormond was not tracked here from Manara, but I'm afraid that luck has likely only purchased a few extra days here. I'd not wager lives that we remain unknown much longer. It is not safe here, Lady Andrius."

The human was not overly tall, but he had the build of a soldier. His chivalry was apparent in the way he took great care to protect Mala. His disheveled brown hair lay across his head in whichever manner befit it for the moment, and his green eyes stared out of his oft-stoic face, but Mala always felt a warmth from the captain. He was a good man, and her half brother had carefully selected him to lead the guard at the estate; it was only too bad that they had to enact their plan so early. It was beginning to feel like every move they made was put on an accelerated timetable, taken before they were fully ready.

She had made a career of careful calculations in her duties as a magistrate of timber management. Cities often requested more than their share of resources, and Mala had cultivated a measured way of managing so many requests at once. So, making decisions quickly, sometimes with more intuition than information, was foreign to her. It was one of many changes she'd have to manage from here on.

Mala was concerned, not for her own safety, but for the safety of those who now called the Andrius estate home: the still wounded Lord Ormond, who could walk a bit more each day, but was not ready for any trouble that might find its way here; the mysterious Sage of Delemere, though far from helpless, she suspected, who had only just dedicated his efforts to their cause and barely knew any of the soldiers or servants; the wise General Warin who was preparing to depart; the unknown General Magron who would be arriving shortly; the kind, patient Typhondrius, and the many dozens more.

"Very well, Captain," she finally said with a sigh, "I agree we should complete the preparations to leave. Take a letter to my brother to inform him that we're moving up our plan and send scouts to try to find Magron before he arrives. We shall have to set a new meeting place before they ride... That is all for now, Captain."

Horace nodded and then left to carry out his orders.

There was likely only two or three more weeks' snow for the Winterlands, based on how mild the winter had been thus far. Only light snow had clung to the grasslands. Still, Mala was not looking forward to traveling in winter on the high plains, and this climate could take a turn for the worse.

In Mala's younger years, she had coined the term "false spring" for weather such as this, when some years, a ferocious few days of snow would punctuate the end of winter.

This estate had been her home for decades now. The library, carefully cultivated by her own hand; the manor house, comfortable and safe; the beautiful fall trees and spring flowers, so tenderly cared for by the staff; all these things brought an ache to Mala's chest now that she thought of leaving it.

They had only just completed the new buildings to make this the base of operations for the rebellion. None of this was supposed to be happening so soon. But they had known all along that plans would have to change. In no small way, *this* was what the preparations had been for.

A few more servants had walked with Mala to the estate library, and she continued to issue orders; what must come with them and what must be destroyed. They would travel light, in the interest of mobility, but she had to make sure the wounded Lord Ormond and the Sage and his monks had at least some accommodations for their travels.

"I understand," Kellos, the Sage of Delemere, declared to Typhondrius.

Standing in his usual upright posture, the Sage was in the middle of the warmed library that now held three simple bedrolls and several more candelabras – all the accommodations the travelers had requested.

"You have our apologies for the short notice, but you are welcome to take any and all of the books you like, since, unfortunately, we'll be leaving any others behind."

"That won't be necessary," the Sage replied. "I have committed all of them to memory."

Typhondrius's brow furled.

"You *memorized* them? *All* of them?"

The library was not the most impressive, but packed into the large room were almost a hundred books, along with perhaps several hundred more scrolls and manuscripts of various types.

"Yes," the Sage replied matter-of-factly. Then, seeing the look of confusion on Typhondrius's face, he went on. "Apologies, my good elf, I do not mean to say that I read all of the volumes in these few short weeks – though that is possible, I believe. I have read most of these books already. With the help of the brothers Hereditus and Orion, we located the volumes I had not yet read and completed those."

"And you have them *memorized*?" Typhondrius asked.

"Yes."

This time, the Sage did not follow with a more detailed explanation, seeming to think that his answer sufficed. He then turned around and began to pack what few belongings he'd brought with him in his satchel.

Typhondrius could only shake his head.

Perhaps they looked alike, but this Sage and his old master certainly had their differences. Typhondrius had never seen Lord Brakken so much as look at a book, let alone memorize one… Their manner of speaking, too, was quite different. Lord Brakken was concerned only with lording his might over those who served him. Typhondrius was rather certain that Lord Brakken did not know the meaning of many of these complicated words the Sage liked to use.

There was much to do. And apparently, the Sage and his monks had what they needed.

Mala finished her instructions for the servants, each of them seeing to their tasks, and she turned to head into the library to see to it that the news be delivered to the Sage.

She was happy to see Typhondrius already there, likely for that same purpose. He had a very strange look on his face.

"What?" she asked.

"Nothing," Typhondrius replied, blinking and shaking his head.

Mala would have to try to bring it up again some other time. She put the scrolls she was holding onto the shelves near the entryway.

"Kellos has been informed, then?"

A simple nod of his head gave her her answer.

Moments later, Mala, Typhondrius, the Sage, and the two monks were heading through the soft snowfall to the barracks where most of the others had assembled.

"Ah, my lady," Captain Horace nodded as they entered. "As I was saying, we've sent word to all the riders we thought we could reach not to return here."

He referred to several maps and battle charts that were strewn about on the tables and walls around the mess hall of their new barracks building, where most every person in the compound now gathered.

"We'll be sending General Warin out at first light tomorrow, but unfortunately, we still have more preparations to make, and I doubt if we'll be able to effect a proper departure until the day after. So long as this weather holds, it should make for relatively easy travels, but just enough snow to cover some of our tracks." He scanned all the faces looking toward him, stopping on Mala's. "So let us hope the weather holds, my lady."

General Warin raised a finger, and the group turned to him.

"Might I suggest," he began, "small groups of soldiers can manage to make way through weather like this in a single file formation when snow is not falling, and fan out as wide as possible when it is falling. They will remain relatively difficult to track. At a distance, our trail might be missed. A skilled tracker will find the trail, no doubt, but it is worth consideration."

It seemed like a good idea to Mala.

"And," the general went on, "in the cold, blankets and warm wear have more value even than an excess of food or weapons, when considering the weight capacity of the pack animals and wagons."

Horace nodded and made sure his soldiers in the room would accommodate.

"Also," said Lord Ormond to the group, "Greenford is just a few days north of our destination, should we need to find another location." He took a deep breath, pain still obviously affecting him. "Or Brightspring could prove a possible alternative as well, but I think we should otherwise avoid Polm and the other larger towns to minimize innocent involvement."

Mala thought of the people of Manara, just as she knew Ormond was. A horror she would avoid repeating at all costs short of abandoning the rebellion.

"I agree," stated Mala.

"Sir?" a large soldier voiced from the side of Captain Horace.

If Mala recalled correctly, the man's name was Jarl. Horace nodded for him to continue, and he addressed the group.

"I've seen non-combatants rushed here and there during battles – nobles and the sort. They usually end up stumbling into the way of a blade." The large soldier gestured toward the various non-combatants about the hall. "I recommend we put guards to each of them and make sure they know each others' names. If battle comes and it gets messy, it might make the difference between life and death."

The man was huge and thickly muscled, but he was obviously more than a simple brute. It was good advice, and the group agreed to do so.

"What else?" Mala asked Horace.

"I believe we have our plans," Horace stated after a moment of thought. "My charge is your protection, my lady. I only ask that, once we are under way, you treat me as a soldier would their superior. Orders may be called out frantically and must be followed strictly." He looked to the others and added, "That goes for all in the room."

"You will have our compliance, Captain," Mala assured him. "And thank you."

The plans seemed to suffice for the time being, the group dispersed, and it felt to Mala like their fledgling rebellion might soon take flight.

The Sage and his monks elected to remain in this room until the time of departure, their few possessions already packed on them. Mala wondered if those three ever slept, as they each took a seat near a pile of maps and began to look over them. She was sure she had not yet seen any of them sleep one moment since arriving. Despite the weeks of conversations with the wise man at every opportunity, she still had so many questions. Apparently, they would have to wait somewhat longer.

The following day passed all too quickly. Nearly every last waking moment was spent packing, and the estate had begun to change in Mala's eyes. Mala had piled her ledgers of timber with all of her stationery and quills she used for her work in a corner; they'd not be needed again, unless perhaps, once their task was done, they remained here to be picked up by a new magistrate.

The estate she was preparing to leave was, in fact, not the estate she had spent so many years in. Not if she were being honest with herself, really. Gone was a peaceful haven of work, study, and residence, and in its place was a mostly-completed military camp. Change had a funny way of occurring before Mala ever even took notice of it.

As the evening approached, General Warin was well on his way with his escort of troops. The weather did indeed hold, with a thick blanket of clouds hanging over the estate, but no downpour of snow to disrupt their fragile plans. As suspected, after much sweat in the dark winter day, the group would be ready to leave at first light.

This compound was the home of Mala for so many years, and now it would be abandoned, only a few servants left to keep up the appearance of a noblewoman away on holiday. As they had wrapped up their work for the day, she had taken spare moments to walk through the trees and pathways where she often spent time as an adolescent.

Her thoughts dwelt on her fallen parents. What would they have thought of all this? Surely, they'd claim Mala and Artorus foolish for acting against the Wizard-King. Likely a sentiment shared by most in the multiverse.

One last meal graced the warm halls of the Andrius estate, song and drink both lingering late into the chilled night. The Sage and his monks observed as Mala, Typhondrius, and the many others enjoyed what might be their last night by the warmth of a hearth for some time.

Mala took the time to thank the various staff for their hard work before finally retiring to her bedchambers, which were now largely empty of the scrolls and tomes that normally occupied it. Aside from her magisterial work in the corner, they had all either been packed up or placed in the library to remain here.

In the night, Mala dreamt, which had scarcely happened in recent years. She dreamt of Artorus and Elsa, long, long ago – almost a past life to her now. But in her dream, the child had been born; a beautiful girl with Elsa's long, golden hair and Artorus's deep brown eyes.

Lush green grass stretched for miles on rolling green hills, and it must have been midsummer, for the air was warm, like a caress on Mala's cheeks. The little girl squealed with the sheer joy that only a child can experience, that beautiful shining smile on her perfect little face.

Mala opened her mouth to say something, but she could not. It was not for disbelief – in her dream, this was right and this was normal. Simply, nothing she could contribute could possibly improve this moment. This was perfect.

Her brother and Elsa both sat on the bright green grass as their little girl twirled about them with flowers in her hand. They both faced away from Mala and they were nearly invisible within the rays of the bright sun, but she knew it was them.

Suddenly, the sky darkened, though no clouds could be seen, and a cold wind whipped through the meadow they sat in. Both Artorus and Elsa looked back to Mala, with their faces twisted into a grim and dark expression.

Once more Mala tried to speak, but a booming voice interrupted her thoughts.

"Lady Andrius!" the voice called from somewhere unseen. It echoed off of hills afar. Though her brother and his wife looked distraught, their daughter kept laughing and playing. The sound now was distant, and the sight became distorted.

"Lady Andrius!" the voice called again, this time louder, more frantic.

Mala looked around for the sound, but could not find it, then when she turned back, her brother, her sister-by-law, and her beautiful niece were all gone, replaced only by an endless field of snow – dark, windy, frightening. The howling wind, in fact, was growing rapidly louder and fiercer, until Mala thought it might rip her apart.

Mala awoke with a start to see that the window across from her bed had blown open at some point in the night. The large stack of books that had long since replaced the loose latch was now gone and packed away. The cold air swirled with snow in her room.

Turning, she saw in the doorway beside her a large figure looming over her in the dark. Already jarred from her dream, the huge frame seemed almost sinister to Mala in the black of night, until she realized she knew this man.

"My lady, please! We must leave *now*!" It was the soldier, Jarl, a look of dread on his face. "We are being surrounded. The Wizard-King's men have come for you."

Mala's heart sank to the pit of her stomach.

In a rush, she collected her things; a heavy robe for the winter cold, the scrolls of strategies she'd kept beside her bed, and her sword – recently excavated from a stack of scrolls.

Even without having felt its weight in some time, the heft of the blade was comforting. She hoped dearly not to need it.

As she was taken outside, Typhondrius immediately found her. His was a look of terror.

Mala could see torches flickering in the deep of the night, slowly surrounding the estate. In the courtyard, recently wakened soldiers either gathered the packs and horses for travel, or else they hastily donned armor.

A few brief moments passed as shouting could be heard – both from the soldiers outside the compound, carrying through the winds, and from the men rushing to take up defensive positions. Despite all of her planning for and training toward this very moment, Mala found herself frozen, unable to move or speak, then something caught her eye.

Across the courtyard, very out of place amid the chaos, was the Sage and his two monk companions, all calmly looking to her, expectant.

This was indeed her time to act. Like a rush of blood, her head was cleared, and her lungs filled with the cold night air.

"Take only the most essential things!" she shouted to the servants who were collecting the baggage. "Burn the rest!"

She turned to a disheveled Typhondrius beside her. "Oversee the estate staff, see that they all come with, and make it *fast*."

He nodded and disappeared into the night.

Scanning the estate grounds, she saw Lord Ormond as he was being helped onto his horse, extra clothing to keep his wounded form warm.

"Stay close to me Ormond," she called through the chaos, keeping his eyes just long enough to catch his nod.

Then she scanned for the captain and found him shouting to a group of soldiers to hasten their equipping. She approached quickly.

"What is our plan, Captain?" she asked hurriedly. "You're still in charge of our defense."

"My lady," he shouted between orders to his men, "you and the other important persons will be escorted by two dozen of my best men, while Jarl and I keep the rest here to allow you time to escape."

"*What*? Captain, this is no time for heroics! You'll be killed, sure as Koth. No, you and the rest of the men will gather what weapons you can carry and—" He stopped her.

"My lady," Horace said, more calmly now, "I do wish there were another way, but look around you. These are surely Imperial Legion troops of the Wizard-King himself – elite among the armies of the planes. They do not allow for second chances, and they will surely kill you... and the Sage."

He called some more orders to men who had assembled before him, then went on, stepping slightly closer.

"Lady Andrius, it has truly been a great honor to serve you and your brother in this rebellion, if even for a very short time." Torchlight glimmered in the captain's eyes. "In this time, I have known freedom, and for that I'm thankful."

He took a knee before Mala and bowed his head to her. Then he stood once more, briefly held her stare, and sped off into the night.

Though she so badly wanted to contradict the captain, her strategist's mind knew he was right. Though she so badly wished to stand or to fall with the noble soldiers, this was quite plainly the reason they'd been sent here: to shield her from sinister forces, that she may continue to lead the rebellion with Artorus. Though she so badly wanted to weep at the thought, she hadn't the time to spare.

"Thank you, noble captain," she whispered after him.

Turning, she saw to it that the essential materials were packed, and the rest set aflame. There was no longer anything to come back to. Everyone was coming with now or staying here to fight. She helped to lead the horses out into the night.

The bulk of the forces coming for the estate seemed to be coming from the northeast, so she and her three dozen riders rode directly southwest into the night. The snow had stopped falling and the now-cloudless sky revealed a bright full moon, lighting their way but also marking them for their enemies.

I can only hope the captain's sacrifice even has its intended effect, she thought surreally as she pushed her steed ahead, torchless.

No amount of clothing could fully block the chilled night air as it rushed past. It seemed to claw at Mala as she and her riders sped through the night.

Keldon Horace stared into the deep winter night. The full moon made dark forms barely visible beside their torches in the distance, rapidly closing the distance to the estate.

He breathed deeply. As a soldier, he knew his end would likely come on the field of battle. He took pride in the thought that his death would serve something other than the War Maker, something nobler.

He looked over to Jarl, who stood beside him, a lumbering giant in the moonlight. Jarl looked back to his captain, and Horace saw fear in the large man's eyes.

"This is the rebellion, soldier," he said plainly to the man, "this is what we came for." He grinned. "Let's give them hell, shall we?"

Jarl returned the grin and nodded to his officer. In his hand was a massive sword, the sort greens often used, with spikes and jagged bits across the huge blade. He raised it in front of him and tightened his grip.

"I'll take a few of those imperial bastards with us, sir," Jarl said proudly.

Whether or not he feared for his life, he was confident in his fighting abilities.

"Good," Captain Horace replied.

He hollered a couple of orders to the other soldiers, who stood gazing at the dancing lights as they approached steadily.

Then the lights stopped a moment, eerily motionless in the cold night, until a whirring noise was heard: a volley of arrows to precede their charge.

And then the Imperial Legions sent another and another. Horace and Jarl each took cover on opposite sides of the main gateway; the vast majority of his men were able to take cover amid the buildings and the small wall that protected the compound.

After perhaps half a dozen volleys, there was another moment of silence, until new orders were called out. With a tremendous roar, the armies of Brakken the Cruel charged the Andrius estate.

Horace and Jarl, as well as six other men, guarded the front entrance, and, as expected, this is where the greatest concentration of troops seemed to be heading. Horace guessed that their total force likely exceeded three hundred – not even close to an entire legion, but more likely one commander and those in his charge. It could have been worse odds, but not quite hopeful compared to the rebellion's numbers of less than sixty. Aside from him and Jarl, the best two dozen fighters had been sent to safeguard the escape of Lady Andrius and the Sage.

The charging army reached the estate.

The first blood spilled as a legionnaire charged and one of Horace's troops stepped up and thrust a short spear into the man's gut. This was not enough to stop the momentum of the man's charging, however, and his sword was buried into the defending soldier's neck. Both men fell to blood-splattered snow.

The man's name was Karlsson; he was a good soldier, and he'd had a good nature. Horace would miss him.

Horace took the opportunity he saw in front of him, stepped deftly out from the gateway, and ducked under a sidetracked legionnaire's spear, sending it upward with his small shield. Before the surprised attacker could recover, Horace's sword found the man's chest with a sturdy thrust, and he fell.

Horace saw Jarl's massive sword cut clear through another legionnaire in the light of the full moon, and more blood splashed to the white snow.

The true mass of the attackers now arriving, each of the defenders gave ground as they fought against the charging men. Another of Horace's men fell to an axe and bled on the snowy ground of the entryway to the compound.

This soldier's name was Varron – a wry dwarf with a heavy limp, whom he'd feared would not last long in the fray. He would be missed as well.

Two more legionnaires singled out the captain, both wielding swords and shields. Some of the arrows that had rained into the Andrius estate had been alight, and buildings were starting to catch, further illuminating Horace's two attackers in a flickering, ghostly light.

They each lunged forward, and Horace was able to repel one sword with his shield and the other with his own blade, quickly counterattacking, but his sword finding only the metal of a shield. Knowing that he did not have good odds against two men, he rammed into one of the assailants with his shield, throwing his weight fully against him.

The soldier, it would seem, expected something like this, and he quickly sidestepped so that Horace fell.

Curses, thought the captain, but as he went down he noticed a clear opening.

Landing hard and striking out with his sword once more, Horace hoped to find flesh. The soldier screamed into the night and fell back. Horace's blade had sliced through his knee – an ugly wound.

Imperial soldiers rushed past, further into the compound, parting for the three combatants.

The still-standing soldier now barraged the prone captain with rapid sword strikes, hoping to break the guard of his shield, while the captain attempted to regain his footing. Finally, unable to get back up, the captain kicked hard for the attacker's groin, landing a solid blow and sending this legionnaire down to his back as well.

Scrambling to his feet, he did not have the time to deal with the two downed soldiers as two more charged from the darkness. He lurched backward in an attempt to gain proper footing enough to withstand the two new attackers.

In the night, he could see that another of his men had fallen to the Imperial Legion.

The man's name was Kardon, a half-elf of a serious nature, who was rather competent at leadership. He'd seen a place for him as an officer someday, but no longer. His blood was added to the trampled snow in the compound.

Suddenly a blur of dark fabric rushed out of the night and past Captain Horace to his left. He tried not to let himself be distracted from the two charging soldiers, but suddenly a searing pain in his leg dropped him once more to the ground. He could easily guess what this pain was; his hamstring had been partially severed.

I hope it was enough time, the captain thought in pain as he awaited the inevitable descent of at least three weapons.

His racing thoughts dwelt momentarily on the fleeing noblewoman whom he had come to know well in these short months. Mala Andrius had a quality she shared with her brother: the ability to build trust and to gain understanding, to feel at one with the people around them – the ability to lead.

Hopeful, Horace prepared to embrace oblivion.

Suddenly, a huge crashing noise came from his left, and he saw around his shield the hulking form of a familiar soldier.

Charging to his officer's relief, bloodied from several cuts across his arms and chest, Jarl screamed, "Captain!" as he hacked down and trampled a screaming legionnaire like he was no more than a shrub.

Horace noticed that the other legionnaires that he'd expected to be on top of him were holding back, fearful of something. Who was this new assailant that had flanked him? Looking up from the ground, he saw a very tall figure – possibly as tall as Jarl – looming over him. He looked to be of some green-ish descent, and he was cloaked fully in deep grays and black, two wicked curved daggers in his hands, each already dripping with blood. That couldn't have been just his blood; this killer had been busy already.

Distracted from his fallen prey by the new combatant, the robed figure turned to face Jarl in an easy sort of fashion. Jarl swung his massive sword as he reached the mysterious figure, but the cloaked man was fast – very fast – and he ducked to the side, stabbing Jarl three times in his side before the hulk could whirl about and swing once more. Easily ducking under the next swing, he stabbed Jarl twice more in his opposite side.

"No!" the captain cried as he struggled to gain his feet again.

Any one of these might be a mortal wound, given time, but Jarl was still on his feet.

The legionnaires were still holding back; that couldn't possibly be a good sign for Horace, but he took advantage nonetheless and struggled onto his one good leg, hobbling toward the two combatants.

Jarl stumbled back a bit, bleeding from five deep new punctures in his abdomen, struggling for breath. Horace stumbled up beside him, lacking the use of his left leg, but still in far better shape than his friend.

The cloaked assailant – which Horace figured was half-orc – grinned widely at the two men in the moonlight. Legionnaires had killed all of the other rebels nearby and were now gathered around, watching the spectacle play out. This killer apparently did not like his fighting to be interfered with.

Well, thought Horace, *just maybe we can take this bastard out with us.*

Horace lunged at him, swinging a feigned strike from the left, but pulling back just as the half-orc moved to avoid the cut. His feint working, he quickly jabbed his sword at the man's chest instead. But still the green-blood was too quick; even as Jarl's huge sword also came toward the man, he deflected Horace's stab and then stepped inside of Jarl's arc, now squarely between the two fighters.

Horace felt the sting of steel in his gut and saw the half-orc's well-placed strike had gone around his shield and into his left side. Horace dropped to one knee, unable to support his left side any longer. It was a mortal wound, but not immediately.

Wizard's fire, Horace swore to himself, *infernal green-blood's toying with us.*

The captain had fallen to both knees now. As Jarl turned to strike at the cloaked figure one more time, blood still pouring quickly from his many wounds, the assassin had already spun around to Horace's back and removed his helmet. His wound sapped everything from Horace, and his every motion was slowed. His body failed him.

Horace felt his hair grabbed, and then he felt cold steel slide across his throat.

Warmth washed over his chest. All was quickly fading, but he could see the look of horror on Jarl's face as his head was still being held upright by its scalp.

The last sight Captain Horace saw as the blackness took him was that of Jarl, slowed greatly by his deep wounds, pounced upon by the cloaked man in the cold winter night. Then, all was dark.

Keldon Horace died in the entryway of the Andrius estate.

More blood soaked the snow.

Somehow, even over the thundering of the horses, Mala could hear the sounds of battle behind in the compound as they sped away. Fear had been driving her muscles. Fear had been pounding in her chest.

Then utter terror gripped her as they topped a small hill just outside the estate.

In front of them were at least fifty soldiers of the Imperial Legions, mounted with torches, bows, and armor. She'd heard the captain estimating two or three hundred soldiers surrounding them, it was clearly more than that as she saw a patrol of equal size far to the west and another far to the east. They had planned for escape attempts, of course.

No! was the solitary thought that rang in Mala's mind.

Spotting the fleeing group in the clear night, the troop of Imperial Legion soldiers fanned out. They began knocking arrows and leveling lances at Mala's group as the two bands of riders quickly closed distances.

"We will charge them, my lady!" called one of the soldiers – a human named Hazzin – over the thundering of hooves. "We will punch a hole, and you and the others try to break through!"

The dozens of riders seemed to have paused. Their lances were raised up, and no arrows had yet been loosed. It looked as though their captain was halting them.

What? thought Mala.

"No, Hazzin!" she shouted back at the soldier. "Look, they do not attack! Perhaps there is a way to talk to them."

She raised her hand, slowing her horse, and all of the other riders slowed as well. They were now surrounded by the superior force, as all the menacing faces stared down the small group.

Mala swallowed hard. *I hope I'm right.*

The captain of the Legion, along with two of his guard, came forward after all the riders had stopped. Mala also rode forward, and, though she had not commanded it, she noticed two figures also followed her. She knew Typhondrius was still back with Ormond and the others, so she spared a glance. One rider was Hazzin, which was understandable.

The other was Kellos. She was surprised, but she did not have the time nor the attention to devote to him – a dire task was right ahead of her.

The imperial captain was a human with some dwarven blood in him, and he held his head high, as if to look down on Mala. He scowled as they drew closer, but the slightest curl of his lip seemed to betray some undertone. Mala waited for him to speak, but he seemed strained by something.

"Who— who are you?" he finally spat in a loud voice.

His two accompanying guards glanced at one another.

"I am Lady Mala Andrius," Mala said, putting forth her best scornful noblewoman appearance, "we are on official business, and you shall let us pass."

She stared directly at the captain's gaze, but he seemed to be glancing between her and something behind her... the Sage? She held her gaze, not daring to look away.

"You do not give orders here, girl! I act under the command of Lord Brakken himself!"

Wrong choice, Mala thought to herself, but she fought hard not to cow away.

"Luckily for you," the captain went on with a hint of resignation as he cleared his throat, "you are not the ones we seek. You may pass, but if I see your impudent face again, I might just have to teach you a lesson."

His face was still strained, and he still glanced behind Mala. He twitched nervously. It was as though he was in some great pain or fighting against some unseen poison. His guards kept glancing incredulously at one another.

In disbelief at what she was hearing, Mala finally allowed herself to break his gaze. She looked back to where the captain kept glancing. She met the Sage's eyes. He did not glance at Mala, instead staring steadily at the imperial captain ahead.

What is this? Mala thought in amazement.

Hazzin finally spoke up.

"Very well, then, honorable captain," he cautiously called back toward the imperial soldier, "we shall be on our way."

With a poorly masked expression of surprise on his face, Hazzin motioned for Mala and the others to proceed.

"Captain?" one of the soldiers beside the imperial officer questioned. "We're letting them pass?"

Other troops began to shift uneasily, and some also rode closer to hear what was going on. Bows were let down as troops looked on in confusion.

"Yes, soldier!" the captain suddenly yelled, loud enough to ring out in the clear night. "Do you disobey your captain? Do any of you disobey me?"

He pulled his broad sword from its scabbard.

Sharing perplexed glances with Mala and her group, the soldiers reluctantly parted way to allow them to pass. None of the soldiers seemed willing to give their captain more opposition than that.

Do I know *that man?* Mala thought, bewildered. *Is he a part of the rebellion? Or an ally to Artorus?* Despite her best efforts, she could not think of any reason why he would help them. *Does he know* Kellos *somehow? This makes no sense!*

She dared not speak and ruin the moment. The riders passed awkwardly through the midst of the Imperial Legion detachment, an uncomfortable silence gripping both factions.

The group hastily trotted on as each of them worked hard not to bolt into a gallop. It took strength not to turn and look back every few seconds as well.

After what seemed to Mala like a torturously long time, the imperial forces finally disappeared into the darkness behind them. Carefully, steadily, the rebellious group picked up their pace.

As though speaking of it would somehow shatter the illusion of what had just occurred, the group was silent, but for the tramping of the horse hooves.

Dark clouds began to intermittently envelope the moon, a light snow starting to fall as the rebels made their way from the embattled estate into the cold night ahead.

Gnarrl walked out of the blazing building empty handed. His black armor was still slick with blood, somehow darker in the flickering mix of sparse white light from the moon and the brilliant orange of the flames.

He breathed heavily, rage boiling under his unrevealing exterior.

These people had burned everything. There were no caches of illicit weaponry, no stacks of secret correspondence, and there was no Commander Slick and no Lady Andrius.

What truly vast incompetence these Imperial Legions commanded. He never should have involved them. He and his assassins could have easily extracted information or personnel from this place without them. There were no mighty rebel armies waiting to face them in a clash of weapons – just a thin line of guards to hold them at bay while everything important burned. A complete waste.

"How many did we capture?" he hissed to the commander who was still getting reports from his men in the courtyard of the large compound.

The commander was a human of slight stature, with a dark moustache on his face and a wiry frame. Clearly, he feared the justicar – as all men should. His eyes were sinister, though; he was likely a cruel and efficient leader on the field of battle. But night fighting and subterfuge were outside his area of expertise.

"Eight, sir," he replied over the roar of the fires.

"That will do just fine," the half-orc said. "A true artist needs only two for a masterful session."

He felt the rage subside a bit at the thought of the blissful torture to come.

His two assassins approached from opposite directions of the compound, each having searched a different building, and they both shook their heads slowly, holding nothing in their hands.

The rage returned, and he locked on the commander's once more, bloodlust showing in his gaze.

"Still no word on those that fled, Commander?" Gnarrl wanted the answer to be *no*. Gnarrl wanted to rend flesh. One of his hands was already on his dagger.

As the commander opened his mouth to make some excuse for his incompetence, a commotion behind him gave him pause.

Coming into the clearing between two flaming buildings, a unit of soldiers was escorting a man, hands bound. As he got closer, it became clear that he was an officer of the Imperial Legion.

Shoving him in front of Gnarrl, the two foremost soldiers kneeled to the justicar.

"Lord High Justicar, sir," one began, "this man let the noblewoman and her escort escape."

Blood already boiling in his veins, Gnarrl had to consciously stop his twitching muscles from carving all of the soldiers before him to bloody pieces.

"Explain," he managed to growl slowly.

"They approached and we surrounded them, as ordered, but the captain halted us to parlay. He said they weren't the ones we were looking for."

He looked to the other soldier next to him to somehow mitigate his story's absurdity.

The other soldier nodded, and the first soldier continued. "After they were gone, the captain began shouting, asking us why we let them go – why *he'd* let them go." He shook his head. "He finally attacked Sergeant Anvers. Clearly, he's lost his mind. So we bound him and brought him to you, my Lord Justicar."

As every living thing should, the soldier looked terrified in the presence of Gnarrl. The soldier's eyes darted about as Gnarrl's menace grew more palpable.

"I'm sorry, my lord," he sputtered.

This captain stood bound between the two soldiers that had delivered him. He was beaten slightly about the face, but he attempted bravery to cover his terror. He breathed heavily as the justicar walked slowly up to him.

Gnarrl did not have fits of rage – not externally. His motions were smooth and deliberate, even if wrath filled his every fiber at the moment.

Impressively, the captain did not run when Gnarrl slid his dagger from its sheath, nor when he slowly, carefully raised it to the captain's throat.

Gnarrl did not ask any questions of the man, he simply cocked his head slightly to the side, taking in the mixture of terror, bravery, and perhaps a bit of confusion on the man's face. Then, slowly, Gnarrl slid his dagger into the captain's throat. The man remained standing even as his blood and his life drained from him. The way a man dies says much about him.

"Have these men tortured to death," Gnarrl said to the commander as he waved his hand at the two soldiers that brought him.

The commander quickly nodded to several other legionnaires, and they dragged the screaming soldiers into the night amid the flames as the two assassins slowly followed them.

The captain finally crumpled into the light snow cover, blood pouring from his neck. The look on his face was sick, sweet terror in the flashing light of the flames as he finally came into death's grasp and saw his end. Gnarrl felt his rage drain away into elation at the sight, if only for a moment.

"This was a horrific waste," Gnarrl said aloud, though not to anyone. "We gained almost nothing, where we could have gained much."

"Pardon my obtuse question, lord," the commander said after a short moment, "but won't they be crippled now? Haven't we just destroyed their base of operations – these rebels, these heretics? What could a band of fleeing miscreants do to the Dominance now?"

"No, Commander," Gnarrl spoke calmly in the cold night air as he stared into the growing pool of blood, "these people have lost some buildings, but they will find a new nest from which to pester our Wizard-King. We must eradicate them as we would any rodents..."

He finally looked up to the commander with his deathly stare.

"To the last."

Chapter XIII – The Hunted

"Our next step must be to meet with Magron and his troops of the Thirty-Third Homeworld Army," Mala insisted. "His support is vital to our rebellion."

"But your safety is the primary concern," replied Hazzin. "General Vallon gave us this charge specifically."

"Death does not frighten me, Hazzin, only failure. We meet with Magron and that is final."

Hazzin bowed to Mala and trudged back through the snow to inform the other soldiers. He was a sergeant, and thereby the highest-ranking member they had with them.

The winter did not turn out to be mild after all – in fact, it might well have been the harshest Mala had seen in years. It was a "false spring," indeed... Blizzards had been frequenting in the past two nights and the land was now blanketed in thick snow. The clothing they'd brought in their rushed escape was barely adequate. And incredibly, the monks and their Sage still wore just those thin brown robes.

The Sage... what happened back there? Mala pondered.

Many whispers had been shared, but none had discussed the events openly. Soldiers, servants, and nobles alike are not quick to question the fates when they spare their lives.

Approaching the three robed men who sat around a small fire, Mala bowed to the Sage and addressed him.

"Noble Sage," she said politely, "may I have a word?"

"Of course, Lady Andrius," Kellos replied, not moving from his spot, but looking up to her from the scroll he'd been reading.

"Um," she hesitated, "perhaps in private?"

"You may hold a conversation here without restraint, my lady," the Sage said in his commanding voice, still stoic and unmoving.

"Very well," she acceded.

Mala gathered up her courage; she wasn't sure why, but she still found conversations with Kellos to be difficult. Truthfully, nothing Mala was ever taught on etiquette and propriety had ever addressed precisely how mortals and immortals were supposed to interact, outside of groveling to Wizard-Kings.

"When we were escaping from the estate the night before last," she began, and the Sage nodded, "that imperial captain – he was... affected by something. Do you know what happened?"

"I do, my lady," the Sage replied, "and I am afraid this is one topic that I will not be discussing with you now. Please do not take it as an offense."

For some reason, Mala had half expected an answer like that. She almost turned to walk away.

No, she thought, *this could be quite important.*

If this Sage had some ancient, lost knowledge that could somehow change the minds of men, what could that mean for the rebellion?

Again, she built up her courage, the Sage still looking at her with his emotionless face.

"Good Sage, you say that you are here to share knowledge with us, knowing our purpose for such knowledge, and yet you do not wish to discuss this topic with me, when it could possibly affect the outcome?"

"That is an accurate assessment, Lady Andrius. More accurate than you know, I believe. I can understand the appearance of contradiction here."

He thought for a moment before continuing.

"Perhaps a metaphor: just as with a stream, a flow of water is important, necessary for a stream to be what it is – life giving, even – and yet when the rains become too harsh, just as is in water's nature, even a simple creek can overrun its banks and cause destruction – death, even. Knowledge can be like the stream."

He paused, peering into Mala's eyes, looking for understanding.

She was not entirely sure she understood. But, still feeling brave, she guessed, "So it is that this information I seek would be like the torrential rain – dangerous in some way to me downstream?"

"Indeed, it might," the Sage said, nodding. "I believe there will be a time for me to reveal this to you; my senses tell me it may not even be long from now. I do not see that time as now."

Finally rebuffed, Mala nodded.

"I think I understand, noble Kellos. Then I shall trust your wisdom and await such a time."

The Sage smiled to her again – the third time he'd done so since he had arrived with the group. He had an awkward smile – somewhat cocked to the side and bearing too much of his teeth, like it was not something with which he had practice. It was a rather odd sight on that statuesque face of his. Mala could not recall him smiling to anyone else; perhaps she was not so bad at communicating with him as she thought.

She smiled back and then returned to her various maps and charts.

Later that morning, they were traveling again, riding single file and designating the last in the line to brush the snow behind them. They covered their camp well, though the heavy snows would likely do that for them before long. The brief morning respite of blue sky ended, and the clouds returned to pour their snow on the travelers once more.

The High Justicar trod back through the dense snowfall, his two assassins waiting up ahead as he approached the commander of the imperial soldiers. They had been trailing the escaped group for a full day now and covered pitifully little ground.

The Imperial Legion had outlived its usefulness to him and three master assassins and their Liniums could travel much more quickly without a few hundred brutes in tow. They served little use to Gnarrl in the first place. He should have dismissed them much sooner.

The commander stood at attention and saluted the justicar.

"You are no longer of use to me, Commander," the justicar said as he reached within earshot of the officer.

There were still twenty paces between the two, but the commander's hand reflexively moved to the hilt of his sword at the statement. Gnarrl huffed in amusement, a puff of white coming out in the frosty air of morning. If he'd had reason to kill the commander he'd have done it long before now. Gnarrl turned and unceremoniously left the Imperial Legion behind.

The commander stood, dumbfounded, as his hand still gripped his sword hilt with whitened knuckles.

"We can now resume at a proper pace," Gnarrl called to his assassins.

He leapt onto his Midnight Linium in a flourish of fluttering cloak and immediately began to gallop ahead. The huge black steed plowed through the snow.

The two assassins followed deftly on their own stallions.

Having discovered the abandoned camp just within the borders of the Winterlands, they were almost a full day behind, but they had the scent of blood. Gnarrl had tracked far more cunning prey through far more difficult terrain, with a far greater lead. It was only a matter of time now; he would have his blood.

Landais Ormond rubbed his side, where scars were still fresh, but his thoughts were not on his own wounds. His thoughts were on the city he'd lost and the people he'd failed. He wondered whence they may have scattered... those that still had their lives... He dared to hope that the servant girl Chara had escaped the bloodshed, and the romantic in him even imagined her fleeing with his master chef, having each other, even if they had nothing else. He wondered if his guard, Haden, might have been able to escape to Polm, as was his direction should they need to scatter. He fought not to imagine all of the people he once knew and called friend lying in ashes in the place that was once his well-kept secret of Manara...

He shook the somber contemplations from his mind once more. They would remain with him, likely forever, and so they need not demand his attentions now. He'd have whatever time was left in his life to consider his failures. He returned his attentions to what was in front of him, to what could still be a success.

The meager band of rebels had been fleeing for several days, wounded and cold, from what were now the ruins of the Andrius estate. They were preparing to strike camp under the bright blue skies of another frosty morning on the high plains of the Winterlands. Though Landais's limbs served the rebellion very little at the moment, he intended to use what tools he had left.

He was thankful for the object that lay open in front of him on a small collapsible seat, which for now was serving as his desk. Opened before him, protected from the snowfall by a small canopy that had been erected for his studies as the able-bodied struck camp, was a book.

He'd heard one of the soldiers comment quietly to another at the wounded man lugging a book, of all things, in their desperate attempt to flee the Andrius estate and now in their frigid ride through the snowy landscape. But this book was of incredible importance to Ormond, and, he hoped, to the people of the multiverse in the future they intended to build.

The History of Morto-Myrian Politics sat in the dreary scene, ignored likely by all here but Landais himself. He had been pleasantly surprised to find that Lady Andrius had a copy in her collection. It was, perhaps, the most solace he'd found in his first days of painful recovery in the lady's library.

Though he had read this book more times than he could count, so replete was it with knowledge, that he never felt as though his understanding was complete.

While he'd be shocked to find this forbidden tome in most any other library, it seemed so very appropriate in the estate of Lady Andrius. And in these rough days of fleeing from the agents of the very same Wizard that had sent a legion to destroy his own city, Landais found every moment he could to read from its pages.

Though not from the author whom he read presently, Landais could not help but recall another piece of wisdom from Akrenemous's *On the Premise of War*.

A people can be oppressed. A people can be slaughtered by the thousands. A people can be forged into an army for the whim of warlords. But a people remains undefeated so long as they have hope. Hope is the most dangerous weapon against an enemy so powerful as a Wizard, for not spears nor arrows nor swords may pierce his flesh, but hope can render him low, defeated by those he intends to rule.

Landais smiled to himself. He'd always thought the passage a little poetical, perhaps even foolishly so. But, here on this snowy plain, chased by murderous forces, Landais could find it nothing short of inspirational.

"My lord," Sergeant Hazzin addressed Landais politely, though in a hurry.

Landais closed his tome and smiled up to the sergeant.

"We've finished striking the rest of the camp. Your setup is the last."

"Of course, good sergeant," Landais replied as he strained even at the weight of the tome he picked up from his makeshift table. "I thank you once more for the opportunity to study while you toil away."

The soldiers had already begun to quickly pack away Ormond's tiny mobile study, even as the sergeant had addressed him. The rebels were still on the run. They could not afford any second that wasn't absolutely necessary. Ormond knew this and reveled in his briefest moments of reading.

Hazzin bowed politely and concluded, "Lord Ormond," before picking up the two seats and folding them.

They mounted up for another day of hard riding. Landais checked his bandages and tightened them where he could. Then he wrapped his large cloak around him once more.

Stopping only briefly to regain their bearings, the group of rebels was well on track toward the small town called Weathering. Mala's familiarity with the surroundings helped them stay on course through the extremely poor conditions – or at least she hoped they did.

Though, as a girl, Mala had always treated her riding lessons as a respite from the more arduous lessons, she found herself thanking her riding teachers more now than ever in her life. Her experience on the saddle not only kept her on top of the horse, but it staved off the exhaustion that extended riding would cause and kept her from driving her horse too hard.

In Weathering, the plan, as it stood, was to await General Magron and his small host of men, but there were two problems with this: the first being that stopping for any amount of time, let alone in a village, would only make the fleeing group easier to track and catch; the second being that they were a day ahead of the schedule they'd set with Magron, meaning that unless the rider they'd sent into the snowy yesternight could accomplish his goal, and the general could quicken his pace enough to make up the time, they would have to wait a day for the general to arrive – a day in which the Imperial Legions could find and destroy their small group.

Night fell and camp was being set again. Sergeant Hazzin and the others were good soldiers. Captain Horace was not lying when he told Mala he was sending his best with her. Occasionally, Mala wanted desperately to think that the honorable captain might still be alive – captured or maybe even escaped from the clutches of the evil warlords – but she knew it was not true, and if he were alive he would be all the worse for it.

The Wizard-King would not let criminals so egregious as rebels live, except long enough to be subjected to untold tortures. Things would change soon, though, and the Wizard-King's reign of terror would end – for Horace, for Elsa, for all the fallen mortals. It all would change.

The relentless snowfall was both a blessing and a curse. It had the power to obscure their tracks for as long as it kept falling, but it made their travel both slow and miserable.

Mala worried for the still-wounded Ormond, but he gave continual assurances that he was fine. Lord Ormond carried himself with poise regardless of the biting cold or the aching wounds.

As they settled into camp for the evening, Mala wanted to accomplish some more cerebral tasks while her body and her steed rested as best they could. Ormond had requested a council if they could manage the time.

With Typhondrius in tow, Mala found the Sage and requested his presence. The monks seemed busy toiling away over some scrolls, but the Sage agreed to a discussion. So, Kellos, the elf, and Mala all went to where Ormond was bundled and seated near a fire in the cold evening.

"Ah, we're all here," Ormond smiled up to the three visitors. "I take it you considered my proposal, then, Lady Andrius?"

"Indeed I did," she said, returning his smile, "and I'm quite sure we'll want to hear anything Kellos has to tell us on the subject. Let us discuss your topic, Landais."

"Excellent," the nobleman said, "then let us not delay. Perhaps this night we can even find some sleep a bit later." Straining some to stand up, he nodded to each of his three visitors, and then he went on. "I thank each of you beforehand for your consideration."

But, as soon as he'd started, Lord Ormond's brow fell and his tone grew sullen.

"Seeing firsthand the sickening destruction of my city and my people – everything I am as a nobleman or a friend – has kept me up nights with countless visions of the lost lives..." He paused and closed his eyes, washing away the sorrow for the moment. "But so too has it helped me to see things," he said looking back up to the three.

Ormond started to pace slowly, still with a slight hobble to his step.

"My city was not nearly the first to be destroyed under Lord Brakken's rule and it will not be the last. You see, for hundreds of years the Wizard-King has ruled these lands much the way he does now – as I'm sure the noble Sage could attest to. For all its faults, for all his unspeakable evils, I think one must admit the Wizard's form of government is effective – brutally so. Beyond his personal might, beyond the unquestioning loyalty of his hounds, and beyond even the belief by many that he is a god, this extremely long tenure presents other less immediately apparent problems for us and our rebellion...

"I have devoted some study to this topic in the past years, since receiving the first letters from Lord Vallon and Lady Andrius. Indeed, the Lady Andrius has contributed to my continued studies."

He smiled and gestured to the copy of *The History of Morto-Myrian Politics* which he had saved from Mala's library in their escape.

She was glad the stuffy old tome found somebody more suited to it. She had attempted to read the forbidden script more than once, but she found its authoring to be complex and dry. It reminded her of the worst tutors she'd had as a girl. But Landais seemed to be immune to its shortcomings.

Ormond continued. "With his style of governance, nearly everything that happens in The Vastness is inexorably tied to the Wizard-King by now. Indeed, for hundreds of years the people of The Vastness have lived their lives much the same, generation after generation, and always under the immortal Wizard-King.

"So my proposal is that we set a serious effort toward the discussion of *our* government – after our rebellion succeeds."

He smiled to each of the three – a confident smile, like he was not worried about the plan, about the freezing snow, or about the killers at their heel.

"I think we would all agree," Lord Ormond continued, "that Artorus Vallon is to become king when all is said and done; he has the incalculable ability to lead and to inspire greatness in those around him."

Mala and Typhondrius both nodded. It surely seemed logical, though she could hardly imagine Artorus liking the idea. Perhaps that was why he would be best.

"But there are forms of government other than a strictly monarchical system," Ormond added. "I've read of ancient city-states on Ebbea and even the far kingdoms here on Myrus that once had councils of men, elves, or dwarves, called parliaments – among other names – that ruled as much or more than did the king. I even once read of something called a 'republic' which had no monarch, though that seems a bit of a stretch to me..."

Pieces of what Ormond said did seem familiar to Mala from her attempts at *The History of Morto-Myrian Politics*.

Finally chiming in, Typhondrius pondered, "Pardon, masters, but it is true that Lord Brakken holds much power. He wished to know of all the goings on across the Dominance, though it was an impossible task to know *all* of it.

"So it is that there are many others who contribute to ruling The Vastness. There are the ministers which we all know about – the High Ministers of military and coin, the bishop of his religion, and most have heard the horrible tales of the High Justicar and his ranks of assassins – but he also has men of less prominence who nonetheless hold *very* important jobs in the empire; there are the Wizard-King's Priests of Light with their secret 'academies,' and entire guilds of spies and saboteurs, likely on every world that spins... In fact, the master had spies assigned to spy upon his own agents... But even more mundane ministers, like the Minister of Cities, who plans roads and city development for The Vastness, and magistrates devoted to all aspects of the Dominance, such as the Lady Andrius here, are all critical to the operations of The Vastness."

"Yes," Mala added, "I've had many dealings with the Minister of Cities and his organization. They are the ones that send the requisitions for lumber. There is a whole bureaucracy surrounding that simple task alone... I have to agree that a king alone cannot rule – especially not a nation state so great in scale as The Vastness. Not even a Wizard can do so."

"Agreed, good lady," Ormond replied, "and well mentioned, Typhondrius. This is indeed the point of my proposal, since I'm quite certain we will have numerous problems, even beyond overpowering the Wizard-King and his armies. The rule of such a large empire sounds especially daunting when I compare it to the small city that I once had the honor of ruling. Financial troubles, famines, diseases, and crime were all balanced delicately with the merchants of power and the voice of the people – an extremely delicate balance, I assure you."

"So, do you propose yourself for the role of 'Supreme High Minister of Everything,' then?" Mala asked Ormond with a grin.

"I vote for you," Typhondrius inserted before Ormond could reply, much to Mala's delight.

"And I second," Mala added hastily. "Is our rebellion at all democratic? Do we get votes?"

Ormond laughed heartily. "My friends," he pled, hands up in front of him, "I would not volunteer for such a task for all the gold in The Vastness." He shook his head. "But we must prepare for these things, nonetheless, because I'm sure that none of us wish for Artorus to be subject to such a fate either."

They all stood in thought for a moment.

Turning to the Sage, who had observed quietly for the whole conversation, Mala asked him, "What are your thoughts on the subject, Kellos?"

After the usual pause, he replied, "My thoughts on the subject are… numerous. The topic of the governance of mortal masses is one that has intrigued me for many ages. It seems doubtful that we have time for me to fully divulge my musings, with present circumstances; perhaps you could specify the question."

He held Mala's eyes in the firelight with his usual stoic gaze. Mala smiled; she was starting to get used to the Sage and his peculiar way of conversing – and she was starting to see perhaps why the monks didn't talk.

"A fair request, good Sage…"

She thought for a moment as to how she would specify. It was quite a topic, indeed. She and Artorus truly hadn't given much thought to the aftereffects of their rebellion in all their years of planning. It seemed such a daunting task to kill an immortal warlord that the thought of thereafter seemed trivial, but now the gravity of the topic was beginning to reveal itself.

"If I may?" Ormond asked Mala, who nodded. "Perhaps then, noble Kellos, you could expand upon the topic of parliamentary government?" Catching himself, he added with a finger up, "To further clarify: how they operate, an overview of their strengths and weaknesses? Will that be a sufficiently specific question?"

Ormond smiled to the Sage.

"Yes, it will," the Sage replied. "The author of your work there, a Master Koûrum Onton, was likely one of the foremost experts on the topic, prior to the coming to power of Wizard-kind. To begin with an overview, a parliament – or other such co-ruling body – is an elected group of beings that serve generally under the pretense that they represent a larger body, such as an aristocracy or an entire populace. As such, they act to balance the methodology and ethical dispositions of their represented body with those of the monarch."

The Sage paused, as he saw his audience straining to pay attention.

Ormond chuckled after glancing at the others. "Good Sage, I daresay we're not quite following. You have more information than we can comprehend… I suppose we should ask to be *taught* these things more than we should simply ask for your thoughts."

Ormond raised a questioning eyebrow to Mala and Typhondrius. Mala laughed as she nodded to Landais. It was a dangerous game to go asking the Sage for his thoughts. She had discovered this for herself just recently.

"So please," Ormond concluded, "*teach* us about this concept. We lack even a basic understanding."

Nodding, the Sage rephrased. "A parliament is in place to balance the power of a king with the will of the populace. Often has history produced tyrants from kings that attempted to bend a country to their will too harshly, regardless of how noble their intentions might have been. A parliament would have certain powers a king has not, and the opposite would be true as well."

As the other three pondered the Sage's statement, he met Mala's gaze again.

"I feel you should know too that there is a disadvantage. No such system has long held a place in our histories. Republics have also come and gone with little longevity. Furthermore, every example of such a government was limited to a small city or city-state.

"The monarchy is the most stable government, historically, because the power is held fast by the ruler, not dispersed amongst many, prone to dissolution and decay. In addition, the monarchy, through feudalistic mechanisms, can extend his or her reach great distances."

Mala felt concern creep into her thoughts at the notion of their rebellion toppling the immortal tyrant, only to fall to politics of men.

"Why do you think this is?" she inquired. "If all the people suffer together under a vast war, why couldn't they cooperate to find peace?"

The Sage nodded, as though he had studied this question already. He probably had.

"Just as traveling with many reduces the speed of the group to its slowest member's pace, a government of many can only be as efficient and powerful as its least efficient, least powerful ruling member. A lone ruler will succeed or he will fall to the next being that thinks they can rule better, as the pre-wars histories tell again and again – and a truly immortal king falls to no one and rules forever."

That last comment did not inspire many great feelings of courage in the group.

"Well," Mala said in playful defiance, "if you say a Wizard falls to no one, then I suppose we will have the distinction of being the first people to disprove a Sage, no?"

Ormond smiled at her.

"I do believe," Ormond stated, "given what little I know of the histories, that a parliament would be our best approach once the

Wizard-King has fallen. This is a government that can best act on the will of the people, I think. Though we may have to consider splitting up The Vastness into significantly smaller nation states..."

"This is the theory," the Sage added with a nod. "Although a republic also has this goal. They each have assigned members through an elective process; each voting member of the populace makes their selection for a prespecified term. Typically, these systems also have a precondition for citizenship, such as only those who have served in the military or only those who own lands. The definition of a voting system implies responsibility to vote wisely, and ruling bodies have attempted different such ways of determining this wisdom."

"Votes..." Ormond said ponderously. "Can you imagine a voting system to elect leaders in The Vastness?"

Mala thought on the idea of people having a say in who rules over them and how they do it. It was such a foreign concept, and yet, it held the ring of truth. Why shouldn't a citizen have a say in who leads their empire? But if the many millions across the twenty-seven worlds were to have this choice, then the Wizards must first be removed from power...

"Well," Mala began, "we are all exhausted. Or at least the mortals among us... Shall we retire for the evening and keep these matters in our thoughts?"

The three men nodded.

"Until we can discuss it again, then," Ormond agreed.

She thanked the nobleman for his thoughtfulness and the Sage for his knowledge, and they all went to their tents in the cold wind. A gentle snow fell steadily upon the camp as guards watched carefully into the blackness. If the weather was mild tomorrow and Mala's navigations were correct, they may be able to make Weathering by day's end; and with a fair amount of luck, so too would Magron.

No stops tomorrow, she thought as she lay down, *we are close.*

We are close, Gnarrl thought as he rode through the night.

Gnarrl breathed deeply of the night air, snow aflutter in front of his eyes. Greens have long been known to retain some vestige of night vision – indeed most orcs not marshaled into the armies of the multiverse still reside deep within caves and only exit at night to raid or plunder. Gnarrl's orcish blood allowed him some of this sight, but the winter night was very dark, and he was able to see little beyond his immediate fore. A slight trough in the snowy blanket before him, however, indicated exactly which path to follow.

His assassins each held a length of rope that was tied to the justicar's saddle, allowing them to follow in the pitch black. The three Midnight Liniums would gallop through the high snow in the black of night nearly endlessly. It seemed even these impressive steeds did finally have some complaint after the days and days of galloping, though, as their mighty lungs pumped furiously. But onward still they pressed.

The hours droned ever on. The conditions improved little when daylight barely brightened the dark sky. Dawn came and went, and it was soon fully morning.

Suddenly, Gnarrl stopped his winded horse, his assassins also stopping immediately behind him. Each of the beasts let out a whinny, as their breaths came out in heavy clouds of vapor in the cold air. Ahead was something in the snow – a campfire, still smoldering. He rode up a bit further and then leapt from his horse into the snow cover. Just before him was a full campsite, at least three dozen people, matching the count that the now-mutilated soldiers had given him back at the Andrius estate.

He knelt at the smoking firepit, feeling the heat, and he inspected the tracks as they all left the camp; one horse was frozen to death and left behind.

"We're close," Gnarrl said softly to the assassins, who were also inspecting things. "Very close…"

Each of the assassins sped back to their massive Linium and sprang to a gallop, into the falling snow of morning.

Gnarrl's prey was no longer bothering with trying to hide their numbers in their tracks or carefully covering their trail; they were panicked, hurried. Gnarrl grinned deeply as the snow flew past his face.

For nearly an hour, they galloped at full speed through the deluge of snow. The clouds began to part by mid-morning, and only a frosty mist and a fresh blanket of snow covered the land into early afternoon.

Then the mist broke.

Ahead of the assassins, not four miles away, was the group of criminals – weak, exposed, and fragile. Gnarrl was nearly salivating at the thought of slaughtering them. They clearly spotted their pursuers as well, for they hastened their pace over the sloping hills of the lowlands.

Before long, the pitiful group of rebels found a road with much less snow and hastened further. But they were no match for the Midnight Liniums and the three assassins steadily gained ground.

"Ha!" called Gnarrl as he whipped his steed faster still.

This is bad, thought Mala, as she pushed her horse and pushed it again.

Only light snow covered the slightly elevated roadway, which perhaps increased their speed, but it would surely increase the assassins' as well. A feeling of panic now grasped tight her chest, already fighting to take in cold air as they raced along the path.

We are close, she thought desperately, *I know we are. Hold on, Ormond!*

Mala glanced back to see Ormond grimacing against the pain of his not fully healed wounds as he managed to keep his horse moving. The servants all pressed their horses as well, but none of them were adroit riders – and the assassins closed on them. Kellos, Mala realized, was a surprisingly able rider, and he kept up quite well.

"Weathering is just up ahead!" Mala called out to those close enough to hear, more hope than fact.

Then they crested the last hill and saw the small town in the distance.

Thank you, Koth!! she rejoiced. But suddenly, her panic only worsened. *What* now? *How will this help? These assassins will not stop simply because we've reached a peaceful town.*

At first Mala had been relieved to see that there was not an entire Imperial Legion at their heels any longer, but as they approached the town, she couldn't help the sickening fear that these assassins were worse than any legion could be. She hoped she was wrong.

We will have to make it to the village, she thought desperately, *and then we will think of something. Maybe the buildings can hide us, maybe the people can aid us... something!*

"To me!" she called and she whipped her steed again, racing faster down the hillside toward the unsuspecting village. The other riders followed with the same swiftness.

The three assassins were now a hundred feet from the rear of the riders. Gnarrl could see the servants, weakest of the riders, at the rear of the group just waiting to feel his blade.

The three dark riders reached the flat stretch on which the town rested, and their horses flew over the snowy road at impossible speeds. As the criminals started to reach the town, two of the soldiers nearer the rear of the group suddenly stopped, rearing around to face the assassins and drawing their steel. Other soldiers began to follow suit.

Gnarrl could only laugh at the carnage soon to be spilled. He motioned for his two cohorts to deal with these soldiers and with blinding speed he blew past them, betwixt the swings of their swords as the other two assassins slammed into the soldiers, daggers slashing and blood flying.

By now several of the foremost riders had entered the village. The justicar spurred his horse onward, catching up to a servant of some kind and dispatching him with a quick slash to the side of the neck as he passed.

Perfect, he thought as four soldiers stopped and turned about on their exhausted horses to face him.

They dismounted and grabbed spears from beside their saddles, only just before the justicar was upon them.

Slowing his massive black horse some, he raised his feet, planted them upon his sturdy saddle, and launched himself well over the four soldiers. He landed in the trampled snow behind them, rolling to absorb the fall. He came up quickly, flicking his second dagger from the sheaths crossed behind his lower back.

Each of the four soldiers whirled about with his own look of fear on his face, and the justicar could only smile as the soldier now farthest away from him was slammed into by the Midnight Linium, still traveling rather quickly.

The man died horribly as more than two thousand pounds of muscle and iron-hard hooves crushed a dozen bones and then a skull. The cacophony of snapping and screaming, of course, distracting each of the other three soldiers just enough for Gnarrl to slip well within the striking range of the lead soldier's spear, easily dispatching him with several raking slashes from his long daggers.

Gnarrl looked past the remaining two of his combatants who now moved to strike at him with their spears and saw his assassins in a beautiful dance of death with several more soldiers of their own – but there was something else, something farther off.

What? he suddenly thought as, looking past them, he saw troops – dozens of them – bearing banners, arms, and armor. *The Thirty-Third Homeworld Army?*

They bore down from the east, looking to have also only just arrived at the village, and began to join the fray outside of town.

Here to help, perhaps? His brow furled. *Dispatched by whom?*

He did not have time to dwell on the matter, as he twisted between the two spear thrusts, bringing both his daggers down on the base of the closer shoulder's neck and dropping him to the packed snow in a splatter of blood.

The last soldier retracted his spear fast enough for another quick strike at the half-orc, but he fell to a very similar maneuver, Gnarrl's daggers now thoroughly bloodied.

Damn! he thought has he finally had a moment to see that the new forces were engaging his assassins. *More rebels!?*

The disciples of the High Justicar were extremely skilled killers, but they were quickly being surrounded by dozens of soldiers, armored and determined.

This will require more killing than I had planned for. His brow twitched in frustration and his fangs showed as more soldiers joined the bloody scene on the main street of the village. *If I must slay all of the Fifth Planar and all of the Thirty-Third Homeworld with my own blades, I shall...*

Another three soldiers from the original group rode their mounts back from within the village, and Gnarrl quickly whirled about to face them.

"No time for this," the justicar growled as he crouched low, ducked underneath the swings of two swords and an axe from the mounted soldiers, and dashed between them further into the village, where he could still see his true prey.

This Andrius woman clearly thought of herself as some sort of rebel leader. A special death awaited her at Gnarrl's bloodied hands. But he would make her talk first; this one would give him answers before he would let her die.

The frustrated soldiers each came about again, only too slow on their exhausted horses to give chase to the agile assassin. He raced into the village, his thick legs pumping with muscles, launching him toward the noblewoman. Other riders unwilling or unable to fight scattered before the charging justicar. The noble had with her three more soldiers, one other noble, and two servants.

The soldiers, who were watching the action closely as they desperately tried to usher the nobles further into the village, quickly came to the front of the group and dismounted to engage the rapidly approaching justicar.

Not breaking his stride, he directed his charge for the foremost soldier, who wielded a long sword and shield. A dagger, braced against the outside of Gnarrl's thick bracer, deflected a downward strike of the sword as he got close and, in fluid motion, the half-orc brought his other dagger about for a stab into the soldier's chest. The shield quickly moved to block and he only connected with a glancing blow, having to use his dagger once more to block a counterattack with the sword. Gnarrl leapt back to avoid getting caught in the striking range of two or three combatants as the other soldiers moved to attack.

Interesting, thought Gnarrl.

The number of beings in the multiverse with quickness of action and clarity of mind enough to block a blow from the justicar, let alone counterattack with any skill, was depressingly few.

This is no time for sport, though, the justicar thought.

It had been quite some time since any prey had given him so much trouble. He felt a rage growing within him. The Andrius woman would die slowly, indeed. He bared his fangs and bellowed at the soldier he had struck, bleeding some from the light wound in his side, but determined nonetheless.

"Die!" he shouted as he launched himself once more toward the same soldier.

The other two soldiers now stood by the first soldier's side, forming a defensive line of sorts. The lead soldier was still quite quick, moving this time to block first, before striking.

Perfect, mused the assassin.

The half-orc dropped to the ground, abandoning his feint strike in the last second of his charge, rolling and slamming into the knees of the soldier; a long dagger stabbed upward and deep into the man's groin. A shocked scream reverberated from the buildings lining this street of the town.

Before two more blades could come down upon him, as the soldier fell to the ground, he rolled back, and the swords only hit packed snow and frozen dirt. He could now hear the galloping of the three soldiers he had darted past earlier coming up behind him. His frustration built further.

The grip on his daggers tightening with rage, the justicar shouted once more and charged back up toward the next soldier still in front of him. A flurry of slashes fell upon the soldier; the first one was blocked by his sword, the second and third by a spinning shield, and the fourth and fifth cutting through the man's light armor and deep into his chest; he too fell.

The three soldiers behind him were forced now to dismount to enter the foot battle.

Now will be my chance, he thought.

He lunged forward once more at the last remaining soldier between himself and the nobles, who was now backing up in hopes of protecting them against Gnarrl's inevitable blades. He planted his left foot well as he got within striking distance, using his left dagger to block a solid blow from the man's sword and kicking high with his right leg into the man's hefty shield. Even the sturdy wood shield and readied shoulder could not stop the full power of the justicar's kick, and the shield flew up enough for a stab deep into the man's stomach.

The three soldiers were now upon him, so Gnarrl ripped his dagger out, allowing the last soldier to fall and then rolling forward to avoid yet more sword swings. He sprang from his tumble and launched his predatory form directly at the noblewoman, once again darting away from the three horsemen.

"Hazzin!!" the noblewoman screamed as she charged right back at Gnarrl.

This was a surprise. Fully expecting her to be scurrying off, this move caught the justicar somewhat off guard, and he was forced to block a quick succession of three strikes from the noblewoman's own sword. She was not without skill and there was passion in her eyes.

For a brief moment he thought he felt that feeling from the night in the tavern: a twisting, burning feeling that gripped his chest and neck. Why do these people care for each other like mothers and sons? Like blood brothers? They are soldiers – superiors and subordinates, not friends and not family.

Thankfully, the feeling dissipated quickly as there were weapons at his back. Adrenaline was able to drown out whatever this creeping sensation had been.

The three soldiers behind him moved in to fully surround the justicar, and he heard the telltale sound of more thunderous galloping as the dozens of soldiers from the Thirty-Third charged down the main street toward the combat.

Despite the noblewoman and her deft assault, despite the soldiers at his flanks, despite the riders bearing down on him, the High Justicar was surprised to see one more thing he truly did not expect.

Gnarrl recognized not one, but both of the men whom he had presumed to be servants to Lady Andrius. One was an extremely tall man in brown robes with a shaved head and the other was an elven man missing most of an ear.

Just once, Gnarrl had met the Sage of Delemere. He was a creature of very little interest to the High Justicar's tasks, since he rarely involved himself in the goings on of mortals and, despite untold knowledge, would not share information with the justicar. But in their meeting, Gnarrl, a man who spent his entire life reading people, could tell this Sage had no love for Lord Brakken or The Vastness. He feigned his disinterest well, but Gnarrl could see that hint of disdain in this creature's expressions. And now to conspire with these rebels? This was a shocking move.

The elf, however, Gnarrl knew well. It was going on four years ago that Gnarrl had interrupted his Wizard-King just before the elf was to die. He ran from the fortress. Gnarrl even assigned an assassin to track and kill the escaped servant, but nothing came of it; the assassin told of how the target was likely washed away with the Brannus River. It seems the elf found his way somewhere else entirely...

Everything about this tiny group of rebels was counter to Gnarrl's thinking. The thrill of the hunt was being replaced, through a vexing succession of setbacks, by disdain.

Another rapid succession of strikes from the surprisingly apt noblewoman regained his attention and forced him to block. The justicar was, however, unable to dodge two of the strikes from behind. Thick leather and a heavy cloak absorbed much of the strikes, but the half-orc felt steel bite his flesh on the back of his right arm and the back of his left calf.

Shouting in frustration, he had little choice but to duck low, sweeping the feet from under the noblewoman, and leaving himself with two options: he could either take her life and sacrifice any chance at the information she could spill under his tortures, or he could let his prey live this day.

Gnarrl felt rage spilling over him as every inch of the long chase of these past days stung in his eyes and his arms and his lungs and his legs.

He didn't know how the elf survived his assassin, he didn't know why the Sage of Delemere traveled with the noblewoman, and he didn't know why this prey gave him such trouble. His assassins were both now dead and he'd managed only to kill some useless soldiers. There was certainly more to this rebellion than Lady Andrius. Why would the Thirty-Third Homeworld wish the wrath of their Wizard-King and how far had this insurrection spread? He spat hate as he hissed at the various combatants surrounding him.

His choice was made. He let the noblewoman live for now.

Barely escaping several more strikes from the three soldiers, he lunged over the fallen woman, a look of sheer terror on her face. As he sailed over her, he lashed out with one dagger to give her something to remember him by. He hoped to take an eye at least, but a short cut across the cheek was the best he could manage while flying over. He landed and rolled into a run directly to the east, toward the edge of town where a gnarled grove of woods stood guard.

He would leave his dead assassins, his quarry, and his Linium behind. He would abandon his plans for the time being. Such rage filled his chest.

Another howl escaped him and it echoed from the woods as he leapt into and was embraced by them, leaving the soldiers behind in the bloodstained streets of the town to count their dead.

Chapter XIV – Hazeus Nightstar

Twenty-four years ago, Artorus Vallon was a ten-year-old boy. He missed his mother and his home and his little sister. He missed Paxon and he missed his freedom.

Life in the military was difficult, but not more so than expected. He awoke early, trained all day, and was beaten when he failed to perform. Already, though, he was displaying some promise to his masters. He grew physically and he grew mentally.

One particular master, the sword master of the Twenty-Fifth Homeworld Army, had taken a particular interest in the lad.

Master Hazeus Nightstar was an ancient elf who likely surpassed one hundred sixty years of age, though young Artorus was inclined to believe the tales of the other children that he was as old as the Wizard-King and twice as wise. His elven frame was slight, but not without the muscle of a soldier – if tempered much by the many decades. Like all elves, he was rather short and bore no facial hair, but his long, silver hair seemed to flow like an argent waterfall as he moved with a grace that only a master swordsman could command. He smiled rarely and spoke to few at much length, but Master Nightstar seemed friendly in comparison to most of the other masters.

"Young Vallon," Nightstar called through the thin mist of morning as he held his wooden practice sword at his side, "I do not believe you are prepared for training this morning."

Every so often Artorus did not like the fact that Master Nightstar spoke to him far more than any of the other children. He seemed content to point out any and every flaw the young boy had.

"Sir?" the boy replied.

He'd come wearing his standard sword training uniform, and he bore his practice sword, held in its proper position.

"Yes, I believe you heard me..."

Artorus looked at his clothing and his sword. Everything seemed in order. He looked around him.

Suddenly, like a whirlwind, air rushed nearby, and a terrible force collided with his left shoulder, behind the shoulder blade.

Losing his breath and shouting in pain, Artorus fell to the ground.

"You see?" the old elf said from where he'd been standing just before, about six feet in front of Artorus.

Attempting to catch his breath, Artorus looked up from the ground at his master.

"That's not fair," he gasped.

"Oh? So the lad wishes another lesson about fairness on the battlefield?"

Artorus managed to get onto his feet. He looked around to see if any of the other boys had noticed, but the training yard was mostly empty. At least there was that.

For the past three months now, Master Nightstar had been getting Artorus up early so that they could practice together before the day's lessons with all the other boys. It was a peaceful setting... some days.

"No, Master," he replied in a defeated tone, once on his feet, "I do not require another lesson on fairness."

Knowing now what today's lesson was, Artorus's sword was already raised in a combat stance.

Nightstar's sword still hung lazily at his side – or at least that's how it appeared. In truth, the master did nothing without a careful, practiced hand.

"Very well," the master replied, beginning his slow pacing – as he often did while he lectured, "then today's lesson is about preparedness.

A soldier – a *true* soldier – is never unprepared for a battle. A skilled swordsman expects ambush at every turn and sees a sword in the hand of every being before him. No sleep is ever completely restful, as the true soldier expects a surprise attack each and every night."

Artorus nodded; his brow was already beginning to glisten from perspiration in the cool morning after fighting to regain his breath. This did not inhibit his attentions.

The old elf had an easy tone, even if he could scare some of the pupils. Artorus always guessed this was a practiced mixture, learned through unknown decades of training groups of noisy boys.

"For instance, even a friend or a mentor can attack at any mo—" The master stopped abruptly as he lunged forward, easily clearing the distance between them in a single bound.

With impossible speed, Nightstar's wooden sword blurred and headed straight for Artorus's chest. Still somewhat shaken from the blow earlier, Artorus strained to react in time. With all of his strength, he brought his wooden blade up and he heard the satisfying sound of wood clacking against wood.

He had blocked the strike.

"—ment," completed the elf, again in the position where he'd started.

Artorus couldn't help but smile.

"You've nothing to smile about, young Vallon," the old master said plainly to Artorus. "You lost that engagement, just as clearly as the first."

"But, Master, I blocked it! I was ready!"

"No," Nightstar shook his head. "And tell me why."

Artorus fought the urge to protest, as it was never successful with Master Nightstar. Instead, he thought hard. He had blocked the elf's blow, so how had he lost?

"I did not strike back?" Artorus guessed.

This elicited only a shake of the head from his master.

He thought longer, until moments had passed.

"What then, Master? I do not know."

Sighing lightly, Nightstar spoke.

"Where shall we start, young Vallon?" He began his pacing once more. "The stance lacked strength and the grip had far too much of it. When you learn the true path of the sword, you can kill your opponent at any time; it was not in the lack of counterattack that lost you that engagement, but the overabundance of reaction."

Nightstar waited for understanding to show on Artorus's face. It arrived.

"I see, Master. That is why my hands still sting from the blow."

Nodding, the master added, "Yes, and had you swung your sword to block with less might, you'd not have been completely susceptible to my next strike – had I chosen to bruise you again."

"Yes, I remember, Master. You told me how you so easily block my strikes. Most swings require only a small amount of force to deflect. I should have strengthened my stance and loosened my grip some."

Nightstar nodded.

Artorus looked down at his hands as they gripped his wooden sword. Lighter grip. He could do that.

"Good," his master said.

Then, Artorus heard another crack of the wooden sword and found himself on the ground again with a throbbing arm.

"Not yet a complete lesson, it would seem," the old master said ponderously.

He began walking through the mists toward the buildings. Artorus groaned on the ground, his arm searing with pain.

"I shall see you for today's lesson with the group, young Vallon," called Master Nightstar without looking back. "Good work," he added softly.

The boy couldn't help but smile at that, lying in the soft mists.

In Lord Brakken's armies, training was held in high virtue. Brakken and most other Wizards, it was said, had lost too many battles early in the Planewars to nothing more than superior preparation. So it was that military training and technologies were always advancing, Wizard-Kings locked in an eternal race for that elusive secret that would one day tip the balance of these perpetual wars.

The training regimen for boys was four years in length and included about three dozen topics, ranging from tactics and historical battles to various weapons training and maneuvers. Training concluded with a further five years of squiring in the armies of The Vastness.

The years in training passed quickly for Artorus, but he was fortunate not to be transferred to another sword class. From beginning swordsmanship, Artorus stood out; in intermediate swordsmanship, he was superior; and now, in advanced swordsmanship, Artorus was beginning to gain the notice of officers, with whispers of a future sword master circulating. Master Nightstar made a point to never seem impressed with Artorus, though.

For several days each week, for three years, Artorus continued the morning sessions before starting his day. Though there were months here and there that the master was called to fighting, there weren't many other reasons to miss their meetings. Artorus got used to the lack of sleep after just a few months, but even now he still found new blisters to tear and new muscles to ache.

"Ah, young Vallon," the old master Nightstar sighed, as Artorus arrived through the morning mists for his lesson, "today is a special day for you."

Gone was the boy and now standing before the elven master was an awkward creature – not a boy and not a man, but what the humans called an adolescent. His arms and legs had become long and lanky. His height was one and a half times what it had been three years ago, and he now towered over the elf before him and many of the other children at the college.

Artorus nodded to his old master, careful not to show too much excitement – betraying one's emotions was only another way to give your enemies knowledge to use against you.

Artorus had been asking, though, for years now, about one particular topic. It was a topic that Nightstar had avoided each time – often with a surprise attack of his sword. But Artorus had noticed that his elven master did not have his practice sword this morning.

"You wish to know about this," the elf said. "Every young soldier does."

From behind his back, he revealed a wondrous thing.

The mighty blade of Hazeus Nightstar was more a work of art than a sword. Even from within its fine leather sheath, studded with golden clasps to affix it to the belt, the sword nearly shone in the light of dawn. The hilt, crafted of ancient metal that was still as lustrously polished as the day it was forged, had a pommel of solid steel embedded with a single shining ruby. The leather wrapped around the grip was well cured and well used, probably changed a hundred times since the blade first saw battle. The guard of the sword was of simple design and flat, extending sturdily a few inches beyond the handle in both directions along the broad side of the blade. It had smaller twin rubies embedded at either end, one set on each side of the guard.

"This sword has been passed down through the family of Nightstar for four generations. My father received it from his father, like he had his father before him."

Artorus listened attentively as the light mist swirled about. All the children in training had stories about Nightstar's blade. Some said he killed a Wizard and took it from him, some said he forged it in the fires of the deepest volcanic caverns, and others said it was crafted by the elven kings who ruled long before the Wizards ever took power. Artorus truly didn't know where the blade came from, but he had caught precious few glimpses of it when Master Nightstar was dressed for battle.

"The blade was crafted nearly a thousand years ago, in the kingdom of men, when mortals ruled over themselves, before the Wizards fought across the planes."

Despite telling his tale, Nightstar did not pace; he did not move at all, still holding the blade sheathed horizontally in front of him.

"A king named Thordrin had the blade created; it was to be a gift. You see, Thordrin had long since fought a war with his rivals for land and for power. His daughter was to be wed to the son of his greatest rival in an attempt to garner peace between the two large nations. Their warfare had nearly destroyed the world of Myrus, they say.

"But the blade, it would seem, was not meant for peace. Thordrin's daughter was brutally murdered in her bedchambers the night before the wedding. Thordrin suspected her betrothed, despite his pleas of innocence. The youngest son of Thordrin's rival, you see, had always wanted war – it was no secret. He saw glory and pride where death and mayhem were all to be had.

"The wrath of the mournful father was complete. Using the very sword he'd forged for a peace offering, he led his armies in one of the greatest campaigns the world of those forgotten ages had ever seen. At his armies' forefront, Thordrin wielded this blade."

Holding the sheath in his right hand, slowly, Nightstar reached up with his left and grasped the sturdy handle. With the soft singing of the blade scraping out of the hardened leather sheath, Nightstar slowly drew the sword.

All of the splendor of the gold-encrusted sheath and the bejeweled hilt were made suddenly plain by the sheer magnificence of the blade. A pure steel that shone bright even in the mist-shaded sunlight of dawn comprised the broad sword that looked sharp enough to pierce an ogre's hide. All of the countless nicks and divots in the ancient steel did little to dim its luster, as Nightstar maintained the blade with elven meticulousness.

"This," Nightstar said once the sword was fully drawn, "is known simply as Thordrin's Blade. You will find its name in tomes of history, the records of ancient battles, and in the songs of wizened bards."

Artorus stood in awe of the mighty weapon before him. He could feel it – its history, its power, and its majesty emanating through the mists and into his body. This was so much more than a sword; it was *history*. Artorus knew this morning's lesson.

"History," whispered the young man. "You have spoken often of the power of history on the battlefield and in the minds and hearts of soldiers." Bringing one of his master's lessons to his recollection, Artorus recounted. "Just as the rain and snow are inextricable to the rivers they produce, a battlefield is simply an empty swatch of land without the countless factors that have led armies to face each other there. Knowing *why* a soldier stands and fights is significantly more valuable than knowing *how* to fight him, if one is able to watch closely, and apply the right leverage."

Smiling, Master Nightstar nodded to his pupil.

"Yes, young Vallon. I am impressed."

"Please Master," Artorus began, "tell me how you came to own it."

"I do not," his master replied plainly.

Artorus thought a moment.

"Please explain, Master."

"Well, you are not an elf, so I do not expect you to understand fully, but beings do not 'own' any object – especially not something so very replete with history and life as this. Orcs and dwarves and especially humans like to think that objects somehow owe them allegiance. A thing such as Thordrin's Blade is no more owned by me at this moment than it is still owned by King Thordrin himself."

Finally, flipping the sheath about to hold it under his right arm and deftly swinging the naked blade behind his back with his left, Nightstar began his characteristic pacing. Artorus dare not display earnest emotion on the training ground, but inwardly, he smiled wryly. He'd grown quite comforted by the pacing of his elven mentor.

"Someday I too shall pass from these worlds and the sword will continue on. I am its custodian, its carrier, perhaps even its servant, but surely not its owner." Pausing a moment, Nightstar took several deliberate practice swings. The blade sang as it sliced the mists. Then he flipped it back behind him as he resumed his pacing.

"I see, master," Artorus said. "Then please tell me how you came to be the holder of this blade."

The master took a breath of the cool morning air. "For many, many generations – *elven* generations – my family resided on the coast of the Raging Sea. We were always soldiers. The elven kingdom of Taerlas was our home, and we fought bravely against the forces of the Wizards when they arose. But, as the fates often do, they turned tides, and when the Wizards had conquered all, we were some of the very few true-blooded elves that remained as soldiers for the Wizard-Kings.

"But one day, amidst a fierce storm, my great-great-grandfather saw a man on the shores outside of the family home. Quickly, he rushed to the aid of the half-submerged man, but found him merely meditating, while violent waves crashed upon him. He dragged the man from the frothing seas and into the house, amazed that he was still meditating. It was not until he got the man inside and dried him and wrapped him in blankets that they realized something was very different about this man.

"As it turned out, he was no man at all. One of the timeless Sages had been brought into our family home; he was the Sage of Moriad. Eventually, the Sage awoke from his meditation and was surprised to find himself in the home of an elven family. He told of how he had been traveling by boat from the island nation of Ama, which you call now Aman, but the storm had come and overturned his craft. All of the monks and sailors had died at sea, but the Sage was immortal.

"After sinking to the bottom of the sea, the Sage walked for forty-one days to finally reach the shore, where my family had found him. The Sage, intrigued by the actions of this family, decided to stay briefly at our estate. He said that he heard wisdom in my ancestors' words and saw knowledge in their eyes.

"And so for several months the Sage of Moriad stayed, and he shared his knowledge with the men and the women and the children. He observed how my family practiced their swordplay and meditated on their destinies. Finally, deciding it was time he left, the Sage told my family he had something for them.

"Telling them he would return, in time, the Sage walked back onto the beach where he'd first come into their lives and then tread straight into the ocean. My family waited and waited until hours had passed, and then days, and then months. But my family did not doubt the Sage's word and every day they looked for him. Finally, almost seventy days later, the Sage returned from the ocean with something in his hands."

Nightstar held up Thordrin's Blade.

"This."

Artorus was fixated on his master's tale. He could almost feel the story, see the events as they had been.

"You see," Nightstar continued, "the Sage told my family of how he'd become the custodian of this mighty piece of history, and he taught them its great tale – its lesson. He told them that he intended to simply leave it at the bottom of the sea, in peace. But, having spent time with my family, he saw our history still very much alive, and knew the blade had more to teach – to them, their descendants, and to many more beyond that.

"The Sage of Moriad left, but since that day, my family was no longer simply soldiers; we are teachers. The knowledge of this multiverse lies in everything around us and the Sage of Moriad simply showed us how to listen for it. And so, we have ever since passed on this lesson."

The elven master stopped his pacing directly in front of Artorus. With the sheath still grasped under his right arm, he carefully swung the blade around to lightly rest in both hands, and he maneuvered it so that the hilt faced Artorus.

With a hesitant hand and a nod of encouragement from his master, Artorus grasped the handle and then lifted the sword in front of him. It almost vibrated with power and with elegance; it spoke to Artorus in a wordless language and without sound.

Master Nightstar looked into the young Artorus's eyes with seriousness.

"If you listen carefully enough, all things have a lesson – some in their history, some in their present, and some in their future, but *all* things teach." Cocking his head slightly to the side, Nightstar continued, "You know something of this, I think, young Vallon."

He nodded to the barracks behind Artorus.

"You keep a child's practice sword at your bunk – all these years you have. What lesson does it teach you?"

Artorus had to force his attention away from the feeling of power coursing through him from the sword to think on that question. Thoughts of his father then flooded his mind and he met the gaze of his master.

"It teaches me to remember."

Nodding, the elf said, "Yes, your father."

He paced once more in thought. "I see something in you, young Vallon – almost desperation. I feel another lesson is worth knowing. Just as my forefathers were dutiful soldiers before the great Sage came to us and they became teachers, you too have the power to change the fate of your bloodline.

"To remember a fallen father as a mighty warrior or a loving man is honorable, but to respect and to follow are two different things, my young swordsman. I believe that, if you have heard the lesson of that wooden sword, then you can remember your father thusly and you can choose your own path without fear of losing those memories."

"But Master," asked the boy earnestly, "are not we all born into soldiery?"

"Are we?" the Elf asked intently, but without searching for an immediate answer.

A moment passed. Not fully understanding, Artorus simply nodded and let his attentions fall back to the exquisite blade in his hands once more.

After a moment more, he returned the weapon to his master. Their lesson was complete for the morning, but his master's words remained burned in the mind of the young student; from that day Artorus saw everything in a new light.

The tamped training yards, to which Artorus never gave a second thought before, now told him their stories of many generations of trainees past, present, and future. The austere buildings in which every student spent their days spoke to Artorus of the thousands upon thousands of brilliant minds they had housed over the years. And the hardened instructors of the academy each carried a thousand tales of battles and glory, whether they told them aloud or not.

One more year of the morning lessons passed and Artorus, quickly changing into a young man, was nearly done with his years at the college of war. His graduation would mean he would leave this place to squire with one of the many armies of Brakken's Dominance. He no longer even had a class with Master Nightstar, having completed his sword training in his first three years.

Still they met in the morning mists, though.

One morning, just months before he was to graduate, Nightstar was late for their morning session. This was a *very* rare occurrence. Artorus waited patiently, nonetheless.

Finally arriving, looking somehow older than he had ever looked before, Master Nightstar walked up to Artorus. He stopped, looking over the boy before him. Artorus waited patiently for his lesson and then his master smiled.

"I believe there is little else I can teach you," Nightstar said to his pupil. "Your sword skills accelerated beyond what I teach in your first two years here – a feat that many students never achieve... You are combat ready and you act intelligently. More importantly, you now listen carefully to the history and drink in the knowledge of the world with eagerness – and there is no greater lesson I can teach. Besides, I am old and I am tired of beating young boys with sticks."

He smiled again. He so rarely smiled, and already twice this morning.

Artorus waited nervously for a surprise attack or a hidden lesson to show itself. None came.

"I am to be deployed again," he said as he began to look out into the swirling mists. "To Ebbea; you know this place?"

"Yes." Artorus nodded. "It was learned long ago, Master Nightstar." He just barely allowed a smile to escape at the ridiculous question. "Ebbea is one of the first lessons in planar geography and planar physics. We had a field lesson there in year two."

With a wave of the hand, Nightstar dismissed any thoughts that his was a frivolous question. "Well, I depart on the morrow and I hear the battles are pitched. It could be dangerous for an old man such as myself."

Artorus thought for a moment that some deep seriousness was hiding somewhere in the tone of the old elf, but the conversation ended quickly as he bade Artorus farewell.

"Be well, young Vallon," he said, and he headed back toward the masters' buildings from whence he came.

"Thank you," Artorus said after his old master.

The weeks passed into months and Artorus let the strange words of his master pass into memories. The news came four months later, as Artorus was preparing for his graduation ceremonies in the coming weeks.

Sword master Hazeus Nightstar had been killed in battle.

The funeral service of the old elf was cold and unfeeling, done in all the military style that couldn't quite capture the greatness that was Hazeus Nightstar. But it allowed each of the students and each of the staff to pay their respects to the esteemed master. He had even taught some of the eldest officers of the college when they were just boys, and he was a respected figure to all the varied crowd.

After the service, the crowd parted and Artorus heard the headmaster call his name. An odd occurrence, but Artorus stood at attention for the man and saluted.

"Here," the gruff man said, holding out a letter. "Nightstar left instructions to give this to you."

He paused, a commanding figure in his full uniform and scars from untold battles tracing their way over parts of his head and neck.

"I'm very impressed, Vallon," he finally said. "Your time in the college has been exemplary, and we are looking forward to your ceremonies. You deserve this."

His tone was far from warm, but the message was endearing. He saluted and left.

A short while later, Artorus opened the letter there, still in the courtyard where the service was held, the courtyard where he'd trained with Nightstar for four years. Most of the people had gone by now, but the lone adolescent stood and read a short letter written in impeccable elven penmanship.

To my greatest pupil,
To my only pupil,

For many moons now, I have foreseen my death on the field of battle. I am very old. The bureaucracy and politics of the college have won over the many years of wisdom that also reside on the masters' council, and so I am still deployed like any other soldier. An Academy Swordmaster must always be an active-duty officer.

I have left instructions that this letter be delivered to you in the event I do not survive this battle.

I did not take Thordrin's Blade with me, for fear that such a priceless thing would fall to the mud of the battlefield and be a rotting prize for a wretched goblin.

Please take up the Blade. Be its holder and caretaker.

And, as always, I know your every move. You'll say: "But I cannot accept this." And, as always, I have anticipated your moves, young warrior.

Please read these next words carefully:

I never had a son. I have told you of how the blade has been passed down within my family, and so, who would take it now that I am gone? The college where its lesson will not be heard? A museum where it would collect dust? Or with you: one who will continue to make history with Thordrin's Blade at your side?

Yes, you hear the lesson that Thordrin's Blade has for you. Indeed, you will craft some of your own.

I will miss our morning lessons, but I thank the fallen gods that you came to my college these short years ago, that we might have ever had them.

Never stop learning, young Vallon. It is your greatest asset in all the worlds, the ability to learn and to grow and to become better than you are. And, perhaps when you are old and gray, a young child will come along and teach you a thing or two about the multiverse.

> Sword Master Hazeus Nightstar,
> Twelfth Planar Army Reserve

Artorus graduated from his training and the years of squiring went quickly. Officers consistently recognized him for his swordsmanship, his intuition, his leadership, and – perhaps what he had valued most – his wisdom.

In this way, Hazeus Nightstar lived on.

Chapter XV – Rebellion

General Loren Magron of the Thirty-Third Homeworld Army was a thick man; he clearly had some dwarven blood in him, though he kept clean shaven. His armor was such that his meaty arms were exposed, despite the winter cold, and his cloak was of thick animal fur. He seemed to rarely take his heavy blade off his belt. His hazel eyes were rather intense as they looked at Mala.

"You see," he said, continuing to eat sloppily from his bowl of porridge as he spoke, "we got the letter from Vallon before we ever got your request for assistance, so we'd already taken a large detachment and made haste to arrive at your estate." He shoveled another load of porridge into his mouth and chewed as he spoke. "If we hadn't found you there, we'd have gone looking. I'd say General Vallon saved your life, lass."

"So, you've mobilized the *entire* Thirty-Third Homeworld Army?" Mala asked, surprised.

"Well," Magron explained, "we weren't terribly far away on our last deployment – had training maneuvers outside the Quarry Towns in Greenstone Province." He shoveled one more spoonful of porridge and continued. "I basically told the high commanders I had a surprise for them, had 'em keep the army mobile, and then I gathered up my lieutenants and a few thousand troops I could trust most. I took these here to you and sent the rest of the Thirty-Third marching northeast."

He slurped up the last of his porridge and laughed through an overly full mouth.

"I told 'em over a night of heavy drinking I'll be joining Artorus Vallon in a rebellion against The Vastness and we came on over here as quick as we could." Magron let out a belch. "I'm just glad we decided to take South Delemere Pass. Hoped that if you fled north, you'd encounter the Thirty-Third. If you fled south... Well... Here we are in Weathering."

Magron stretched his arms out as if to present himself as a gift, his grin wide, food still clinging to his beard.

"Incredible, General," Mala exclaimed with reverence. "We've rallied a few dozen trusted troops here and there, along with some noblemen working in secret, and you say you recruited several thousand to the cause over some drinks. Then you went ahead and preempted the tactics of the most sinister agents of Lord Brakken!"

Magron burst out in laughter as he finished off his mug of ale. Mala couldn't help but laugh with him.

"Hells," Magron continued jovially, "half of 'tactics' is just dumb luck, and most of my troops would probably leave me in a second if they got to join on with Vallon, rebellion or no. He's got more stories 'bout him than can hold a two-bit tavern in a seaside town. Him and his godsbedamned sword!"

"Well," Mala replied, "we are very thankful for your timing and for the Thirty-Third Homeworld Army."

Around her sat Typhondrius, Ormond, and Kellos as well as two of Magron's officers. Their rebellious band was growing quickly, indeed. As it turned out, the village population was likely outnumbered just by the detachment Magron had brought from the Thirty-Third.

The people of the village were quite jostled by the commotion that suddenly came upon their small town, but their chief – an older half-elf named Gennet – allowed the noblewoman and the general to stay temporarily, and made arrangements for them to have access to several of the larger buildings in town to house many of their men.

Those quiet monks of Delemere that seemed so awkward before were now showing what the great knowledge of the Delemere monastery could do; they treated the wounded men with more skill than any healer Mala had ever seen. Among those wounded, Hazzin had been on death's door. The monks had done what they could, but he had a puncture deep into his chest cavity. He lived, for now, but Mala had never heard of a soldier surviving such a grave wound.

"What of those assassins?" asked Typhondrius with concern.

General Magron looked troubled. "Well, we managed to put down those two that were outside the edge of town – at the cost of many lives – but I fear for the consequences of that last one escaping. It confounds me how that godsbedamned thing can hide from the whole of our troops, wounded and without aid." He had stopped gnawing on a piece of bread he'd found. He pointed it at Mala. "I'm rather certain that that beast you fought with, lady, was none other than the Wizard-King's High Justicar."

Ormond and Mala shared a look of concern. She couldn't resist placing a hand on her cheek where the slash the assassin had left her still stung.

Everyone had heard the many stories about the High Justicar, said to be an inhuman killing machine for the sadistic whims of Lord Brakken – unfeeling, unstoppable. He was the Blade of the Wizard-King. She felt a shiver at the thought that she crossed swords with the creature. He did indeed move with a speed that she hadn't seen before; a blinding speed that made even Artorus look slow; a frightening speed that had meant the deaths of at least five of her best men, perhaps more if the monks could not save the wounded; a terrible speed that would surely have consumed her if not for Magron's timely arrival...

Typhondrius looked down. "I thought I recognized him. His name is 'Gnarrl,' I believe. Always like a ghost did he slip in and out of the fortress to meet with the master. He is a very twisted man and an extremely talented killer. I never once heard of him failing to kill his target in all my time serving the Wizard-King, not since he first attained his position... I am quite certain we would all be dead now if you hadn't intervened, General."

Mala's elven friend was paler now than she'd ever seen him.

"I see, then, why the Legion was no longer pursuing us..." Ormond said. "This justicar wanted us for himself. And he would have been capable of it."

Typhondrius nodded in silence.

Magron's eyes hardened as he looked back up to the others. "We'll keep trying to smoke out that godsbedamned justicar from the woods, but it is for exactly this reason that we should fight and destroy this rotten empire. The War Maker deserves death for the crimes he's committed on these people. Even when he's not marching us to war against the other Wizards, he's sending his assassins to murder his own subjects...

"And I'd like to be the one to deliver that justice... I only wish Vallon had contacted me sooner; I could never have planned a rebellion on my own, but Vallon – Vallon is brilliant."

At that, Mala nodded her agreement.

"Very well," she said finally, "then I suppose it is time for a change in plans. With the deadliest assassin in the multiverse stalking our every move and the brave General Magron and his armies at our side, it comes time to consolidate our forces."

She looked to Magron. "General, how are your supplies for the Thirty-Third?"

"They're good enough, my lady," the stout man replied. "We've stocked much for the winter, packed on the mules and carts. But we've also stored caches and pulled in a favor I got with the mayor of Amberdale. The Thirty-Third's a lot of bellies to fill! But we're supplied for now."

Magron laughed and the others joined, but Mala found herself lost in the moment.

From the earliest stages of Mala's planning with her brother, the very inception of their schemes against the Wizard-King, they knew that any generals crazy enough to follow them down their foolish path would have to rally quickly. They had decided on a meeting place long ago. It was time to get Magron back together with his Thirty-Third Homeworld Army and get to this meeting. It was time to see Artorus.

"Good," Mala said with newfound confidence at the thought of meeting with her brother again – at the thought of this rebellion beginning in earnest.

"We march tomorrow then."

It had been three short months since Artorus had left the home estate of his sister. It wasn't nearly the longest he'd been away, but somehow on the cusp of history, it seemed far too long. The departing winter, which at first seemed so mild this year, was now much colder to him: the chilling death throes of a season that was robbed of its purpose.

The discovery of Commander Braïun's family had been a horrible shock. The Fifth Planar Army's march toward the meeting grounds passed them near the dwarf's homeland, and he made the time to go visit them. What he found, no words could describe.

It had been only two weeks ago. Because Artorus knew that pain he did not attempt to console the dwarf; words failed. They spoke of supplies, of troops, of many things; but they did not speak of what Braïun found that day. The commander had been completely quiet other than tending to his military duties.

As soon as Braïun brought back the news, Artorus knew that the agents of the Wizard-King would have followed the trail to the estate – much sooner than they had planned for. Artorus had immediately drafted two letters and sent them with his fastest riders. The first was a letter to warn Mala of the impending danger. The second was for General Magron if the first did not arrive in time – which Artorus was all too certain of. He could only hope that Magron received his message and was able to free Mala and the others from whatever trouble the Wizard had beset upon them.

It was two weeks of torturous suspense. Artorus could only focus on the more immediate tasks and lead his troops until he heard back.

The Fifth Planar Army had been marching at a manageable pace through the harsh winter, but their meeting place was fast approaching, and with it, hopefully, the news of his sister's safety.

"General," Lieutenant Highblade called. "The word has just arrived, the messenger was delayed by some trouble with the Legions, but your sister sent word that the good General Warin has joined our cause."

Relief washed over Artorus all at once. Mala was alive. Artorus liked nothing less than the thought of Brakken's assassins pursuing his sister. But she was safe for at least a brief time.

In a moment, though, Artorus's demeanor brightened even farther.

"Excellent!" he exclaimed. "Completely wonderful news. And this will mean good things for our strategy; Warin has long been a cornerstone of Lord Brakken's tactical might here on Myrus. This rebellion will do well to have him amongst our command."

The half-elf nodded. "I agree. And it seems that all the other generals have accepted your summons, since nearly all of them have been accounted for. I'm quite certain we've earned the suspicions of the lord generals by now, but we knew this would happen, yes?"

Their careful plans of having Mala screen the different generals and send them to the rally point had been cast aside. With the Wizard-King's assassins on their scent, they no longer had time or need to be so secretive and careful. They were entering the deadlier stage of this rebellion.

And it would only get more deadly from here.

"We did, Lieutenant," Artorus replied, still in thought. "Things now will have to move quickly."

He breathed deeply. He looked out to the open sky that brought the most sun these lands had seen in a month. The plains and rolling hills beyond soaked in the warmth and snow was melting. Spring was nearly upon them.

"This will be a meeting to remember, I think, Highblade."

The two looked out to the landscape a short while and then the peace of the moment was broken.

"What are you two doing?" called a gruff voice from behind, his very tone insulting. "No time for painting pictures."

They both turned to see Lieutenant Hakan with a disdainful look on his face.

Artorus smiled back at his other lieutenant. "We thought you might enjoy a moment of meditation, Hakan."

"No, we didn't," Highblade inserted quickly, returning Hakan's scowl.

The fireblood snorted. "You meditate. I'd rather get to killing." Hakan smiled wide. "Got to admit, General: I'm impressed with this rebellion idea. Not only do we get to take charge of this empire, but we'll beat the snot out of all these piss pots that put us through the ringer. Them Imperial Legions're supposed to be tough, but *I've* never seen them fight an army. Seems they prefer burning down villages and killing women and children. Happy to put 'em to the test, sir."

Hakan laughed lowly – almost a growl – as his hand unconsciously gripped the hilt of his sword.

A casual observer might think the man lived for violence, but Artorus knew it was not quite so simple. He was indeed violent, but beneath that hardened exterior, there truly was an honorable man. And his methods might not always make it clear, but his was a just heart. Artorus doubted anyone who was raised on Ebbea, among the orc- and goblin-kind, would have a softer exterior than Hakan.

"Listen," the general stated to his two lieutenants, more serious in tone, "if this meeting should go poorly, this rebellion may end much sooner than we think. We will need the support of at least three of these generals, but four or five or more would be much better."

He squinted up into the bright sky as he continued.

"I've heard counts that Lord Brakken's total armies across The Vastness number something the likes of three million – *three million* troops, loyal to this Wizard-King whose Dominance we mean to topple. And that's just actual fighting men, with many times that in auxiliary forces." He glanced back to his two lieutenants. "Our Fifth Planar is ninety thousand at full strength, and, aside from the Ninth Planar, most of the generals we will meet this week command no more than one hundred thousand. Magron has perhaps one hundred twenty thousand, if we're lucky.

"These are large armies, to be sure, but we will need every man we can muster; I've been thinking on this. Even if our plan succeeds to the letter and we slay the evil Lord Brakken and his most loyal dogs in all swiftness, we will face an even greater threat: while we would struggle to control The Vastness – or what's left of it – we would be beset by maybe half a dozen more Wizard-Kings. Kaladrius, Phax, and Krakus will surely smell the blood and strike before the War Maker's body is cold. Quirian will undoubtedly break the pact between the twin worlds at some point. I'll be attempting to hold him at bay with diplomacy, once we're in a position to do so, but he is a Wizard.

"I believe we can hole up on this world, pulling in all the people we can from the outer worlds of the empire and guarding the worldgates with all of our forces, but for how long?"

The general paused a moment.

"I believe we may have to deal with the other Wizard-Kings for a time… but if the dead gods smile upon us, then these other Wizards should start dealing with rebellions of their own before long. We're trying to make an example here."

He glanced back over the plains toward where they marched and thought on the future. The future thoughts led him to memories of the past.

"Either of you serve in the Battle of the Boils?" Artorus asked, his gaze still cast afar.

Highblade shook his head, but Hakan nodded.

"Was just a sergeant then," the larger lieutenant said, "but I remember it."

"Remember the earliest stages?" Artorus reminisced. "Those days when the Lord Generals thought it might be a brief engagement? It was then and there that we lost our chance to make it quick. I recall the Twelfth Planar had skirmished with Kaladrius's Expeditionary Forces. We thought we might be able to encircle them or at least force a withdrawal, but Kaladrius wouldn't have that. He charged his armies straight in, suffered terrible losses, but strategically, it was a smart move. The engagement became a much wider affair, and it gave him the chance to rally his other armies to the battle..."

Artorus breathed deeply and turned back to his men.

"We may just rally enough forces to give them a hell of a skirmish, but we won't win a drawn-out battle. So, our beginning must go well for us to stand any chance in the end. If it does not, we may resort to a simple charge of the fortress, and likely die upon its walls."

Neither of the two lieutenants flinched at the thought; they were both intelligent enough to know that this quest would likely end in death.

Another soldier came.

Commander Braïun approached the three, walking slowly up the small hill they stood atop. His beard was braided lazily and swung free from the belt in which it was usually tucked. His hair had not seen a comb in a day or two, but he still wore his proper uniform. He stopped and saluted.

The general returned his salute and spoke.

"Commander?"

"Sir, I believe the army is ready to move again," the commander stated to his general. "The towns in the area have given all the supplies and men they could spare."

Not surprisingly, his eyes still held pain in them as he looked up to Artorus, and his tone was somber as he spoke.

"Thank you Braïun," Artorus nodded to his friend, a hand on his shoulder. "Then we march."

Typhondrius sat with Mala and Kellos. He still felt a deep unease when his gaze fell upon the Sage. It was, perhaps, simply an effect all immortals had on the peoples of the multiverse.

Mala had inquired on the history of The Vastness. Typhondrius was not well versed in the histories, and so he was glad she had posed the question.

"Well, this is an interesting question, Lady Andrius," the Sage replied to Mala. "Wizards often work to destroy the records that tell of anything beyond their own rule, and so information is sparse. I will tell you that Lord Brakken was not the first Wizard-King of this political Dominance – this, along with Mortis, being one of the original twin worlds. At first, the Wizards cooperated and expanded. At a point, there were treaties drawn to rezone lands on these worlds, granting each Wizard their own kingdom on the twin worlds, as well as lands on one or more of the new worlds as they were being discovered. Once the discoveries ended with the plane of Turm and records of Fadrus, who led the efforts to open new planes, stopped, tensions mounted almost immediately.

"This is when the Wizards turned on each other. Control of the plane of Myrus went from the many to the few, as most of the Wizards made haste to claim Dominance over the newer planes, where resistance was sparser. Eventually, Myrus was split between three known as Jolus, Youv, and Warrok for a time. Jolus was replaced by one called Kaspin, who was previously his lieutenant, but Kaspin fell to the other two shortly after. Brakken did not become a force on this plane until about two hundred years ago. Having originally gained power off-world, on the core world you know as Zeeaf, he struck at this world and destroyed, first Youv, and then eventually Warrok.

"This bold move was likely calculated for some time, as Brakken shifted his center of power and brought with him his many armies and conquered peoples from Zeeaf. He eventually lost Zeeaf to Quirian, who still controls much of it today. With his power consolidated on a highly populous world, Brakken continued to remain a powerful force in the interplanar theater. Some strategists argue that he could have defeated several more Wizards if he had not focused so much on our world here, but others contend that, like so many Wizard-Kings, he would have spread his dominion too thin and fallen to outside forces and, therefore, his consolidation of Myrus is one of the better strategies yet deployed in the Planewars. No other Wizard for more than a century has had such a stable hold on large portions of four core worlds."

Typhondrius still wondered at how the Sage could simply contain all of this information in his head. The more time he spent with the Sage the more he was interested by his duality; much more relatable than Typhondrius had first thought and yet much more foreign and intriguing with each thing Typhondrius learned.

Perhaps most importantly, the more time he saw the Sage spend with Mala, the more it seemed his intentions were honest. Typhondrius had developed what he thought was a healthy distrust of all Immortals, but this Kellos might change his opinion yet.

Still, it was impossible to settle his stomach when he let his thoughts return to just how much the Sage looked and sounded like Lord Brakken... He tried as best he could to ignore it.

The group consisted of sadly fewer members from the Andrius estate now. However, they were now escorted by several thousand men of the Thirty-Third Homeworld Army. The cadre was only a couple days from their meeting now.

They had left many of the wounded behind in the village, Sergeant Hazzin included. Whatever those monks had done for him, it must have worked. Typhondrius had never seen a man survive a wicked stomach wound like that, and yet, incredibly, the sergeant seemed to be stabilizing by the time they had departed.

General Magron was an interesting man. He was rather blunt, but he did indeed have passion for his soldiers. Typhondrius could see why Artorus and Mala chose him for their rebellion. It seemed what he was most passionate about was beating Lord Brakken. Great effort must have gone into hiding his feelings about Brakken, as Magron didn't seem to be one to avoid speaking his mind.

The last days of travel passed quickly, even if Typhondrius's legs ached for every waking moment, and spring was definitely about them. The snow was all but melted in the lowlands, not so many miles from the eastern coasts.

The animals emerged from their winter hidings, making for great hunting for the humans and dwarves – the Thirty-Third Homeworld Army even had several units of orcs, which, as best Typhondrius could tell, were completely carnivorous. Typhondrius could not imagine how the other races ate animal flesh. An elf could not do so if they wanted to, or so he assumed. Typhondrius was thankful to stick to his diet of berries, tubers, leafy greens, and whatever nuts they still had in their stores.

Then they arrived, coming over a low hill into a broad, flat valley. They came upon what could well be one of the more amazing sights Typhondrius had ever seen.

Sprawling ahead of them in the huge valley, nearly to the hills at the north end, was a vast collection of tents, larger than any of the cities Typhondrius had visited. The elf had seen small armies, even one or two of intermediate size, but nothing like this. In front of him was what he could only guess as three or four different armies. He was awestruck.

Though there was one familiar sight: the colors of the Fifth Planar, near the center of the gathering. This visage was comforting.

Typhondrius thought he also recognized the banners of the Second Planar Army in addition to the colors of the Thirty-Third Homeworld with which he'd become familiar in recent weeks. From what he had known of the meeting previously, it was supposed to contain only generals and command staff, but it would seem both General Magron and General Warin were able to accelerate their plans and muster most or all of their armies to this meeting in the recent weeks.

Their party trickled into the huge valley as scouts of the Fifth Planar approached, saluted, and immediately recognized Mala.

Their small troupe sped ahead of the bulk of their detachment. The meeting was already in session.

History will be made this day, thought Typhondrius excitedly. *And, through some twist of the fates, I shall be a part of it...*

Artorus looked over the large group of men mustered in the giant assembly tent. There were thirteen other generals here, and each had at least two of his officers with him. A low roar filled the tent, and many guards of the Fifth Planar stood at each exit. Tensions were high.

Artorus had very much wanted to wait longer, in case the Thirty-Third might arrive, but time was not a luxury they had. The generals had traveled far and wide to be here now and hear his proposal and it was impossible to say how near the agents of Lord Brakken might be. He would not allow this nervous energy to transform into restlessness or hesitation. Generals of the Planewars were men of action.

At either side of the general sat his two lieutenants: Highblade at his left who surveyed the room keenly, watching the various generals and hearing what they said with his half-elven ears, and Hakan at his right, looking unimpressed as he too surveyed the generals.

It had been nearly an hour since they'd gathered, and Artorus had already announced his intention to stand against the Wizard-King; most had surmised it by then. There were discussions, there were debates, there were arguments, and there were pleas, as the many minds – likely over a thousand battles' worth of experience – whirred in the huge tent.

Everything was in place – everything that could be. He'd promised the crowd that there were already entire armies willing to stand for justice, he'd talked at length about the evils that Wizards beset upon mortals, he'd made it personal to each man, and he'd made it about all mortals across the twenty-seven worlds.

The stakes had now been raised. From this point, secrecy was a thing of the past; there was no returning now, no retreating back into the shadows – not for Artorus and not for those closest to him.

General Vallon had entertained questions, concerns, challenges, and requests from generals, but mostly they argued back and forth amongst each other. Some argued it couldn't be done, while others argued how it might be done, and still others argued simply that it must be done.

The lack of anything resembling solidarity concerned Artorus as he watched the arguing mass of military men.

Artorus rose to gain the attention of the many generals once more. It took quite a time, but eventually most of the varied leaders quieted their staff and turned their attentions to Artorus. The roar slowly turned to a murmur.

But before Artorus could address the crowd again, a scout burst through one of the large entrances at the south end of the tent, catching more than a few glances. Rushing around the large assembly, the soldier headed toward Artorus, attracting more attention from the generals as he went.

"General Vallon!" the scout called, once he was close enough, "They are here! The Thirty-Third Homeworld has arrived – with your sister."

She's safe! Artorus thought.

Though she'd gained the protection of the Thirty-Third Homeworld, until Artorus had his sights on her, he would not believe Mala was completely safe.

But it seemed not even the greatest assassins and most sinister agents of the Wizard-King were a match for the indomitable determination of his noble sister. Weeks of worrying bled away as Artorus reveled in the news.

"And with someone else," the soldier continued.

Suddenly realizing that all eyes in the tent were on him, he began to flush, clearly not as practiced at speaking as he was at scouting. "Eh – uh, there's... a Sage with them, sir," he said to Artorus, having no way to say it at this point without all the others hearing.

Yes! Artorus thought as the concept hit him, *The Sage!*

A quick murmur shot through the tent. This scout, it would seem, did a better job of gathering the attention of the assembly than Artorus could, as dissenting voices hushed.

Ever since the news had arrived that the Sage of Delemere had actually come to the Andrius compound, Artorus had greatly hoped for a chance to talk with him about this rebellion. The timing of his arrival would not allow for such a thing just yet, of course, but it was quite timely in its own way...

This rebellion has the assistance of a Sage, mused Artorus. *That's not a thing easily disregarded.*

His half sister, their good friend Typhondrius, and Lord Ormond – looking much better than when Artorus saw him last – entered the tent as the eyes turned now to them. Artorus smiled intently at them. He couldn't help but dwell on the sight of his sister, undefeated by the agents of Brakken.

Behind them, a very tall man with an impressive physique, a dark brown robe, and a bald head entered, followed by two shorter men of the same garb. This Sage of Delemere was quite a sight to behold. His figure was, even from this distance, commanding. These three entered and each nodded to the crowd before them, curiously unaffected by the gazes of a hundred people.

Magron and one of his lieutenants followed. The general finished discussing something with one of his officers that had been camped, waiting for him with the bulk of his army at the meeting. He frowned at missing a large portion.

"Good generals," Artorus called out, his voice booming in the quiet of the latest news. "You now see the full extent of the minds behind this proposal."

He held the room with his voice, as most still looked at the Sage; his image was truly striking. Already, servants rushed to set a new table for the Sage, his sister, and their party, while others showed Magron to where his other lieutenants were already seated.

"What we will ask of you in the coming months – or even years," Artorus went on, "may result in your death or your dishonor, but it is the way of change. Each of us has been designated a soldier since birth, our lives committed to this war of immortals, and we should have no fear of death. And those who are deemed honorable in their deaths will only be determined by those who write the histories."

Artorus motioned to the towering form of the Sage and threw his voice to every edge of the tent.

"I now offer you a choice: a choice to make your life your own, if *just* for a brief time, your own! We have discussed things enough. I expect each general here to speak for the greater will of his soldiers, as is expected of each of us at war."

Artorus locked eyes with several of the generals, each seated at their table with their entourage, in a wide circle in the center of the tent.

"It is time for each of us to announce our intentions, true and clear. Let now your destiny in the coming war be known."

Artorus looked to his left, allowing the order to proceed clockwise. Now the crowd was silent and attentive. One by one the generals would announce their will, and by doing so, announce the fate of this rebellion.

The general to his immediate left, a human named DiBeris, first thought on Artorus's words.

Eventually, General DiBeris spoke. "The Forty-First Homeworld Army cannot commit to your rebellion, honorable General Vallon, though neither shall we oppose it. I cannot doom all the lives at my command to martyrdom... I shall do everything I can to simply... stay out of your way."

DiBeris looked down, shaking his head.

Artorus's heart froze in the silence after this general's words. Was this going to be it? Would his rebellion end before it even began? It took all his courage to remain straight faced as he allowed the order to proceed.

The next general in the circle was a human with some distinctions of elven blood, called Tennian.

He rose and spoke. "The Ninth Learden Army shall do the same, General Vallon."

General Tennian sat back down. He didn't avoid Artorus's gaze, but some hint of shame did show on his features.

Fear gripped Artorus and his heartbeat seemed to be suspended. He had faced countless battles, charging ogres, and Wizard's fire, and none had tested his resolve as it was being tested in this moment.

But then he caught a glance from Mala, those strong eyes of his sister almost whispering *Elsa is watching*. His sister was the strongest person he knew. His fear washed away, and only determination remained.

A meaty dwarf named Däruth Orrogen was next in the circle, and he rose from his seat and spoke loudly.

"The Seventeenth Planar Army will commit to the rebellion against the bastard Wizard, Lord Brakken! We will give our lives, if we must – not to continue this godsbedamned war, but to finally end it."

A few scattered whispers rippled through the tent.

General Orrogen gave the salute of the Seventeenth, the clenched right fist over the heart, and his officers followed suit. He nodded slowly to Artorus as the murmurs continued, and sat back down.

The Seventeenth Planar, thought Artorus. *A fine army under a fine general.* He nodded his thanks back to Orrogen.

The intentions of the next two generals in the circle, Artorus knew already.

"I think," spoke General Warin as his turn came, "that the good General Vallon has what most of us do not, what few in the planes have... He has vision. I have seen a hundred thousand men die fighting the wars of the Wizards. We accept it as a way of life. Not Artorus Vallon. The Second Planar Army pledges its valor to this rebellion. General Vallon will be the torch that guides our way."

He nodded respectfully to Artorus.

Without much pause, Magron slammed his tankard to the table.

"Ha!" he bellowed. "The old man is wise! He's seen many more battles than me and he's learned things I'll never know. But me? I only know one craft: war."

Magron drew a dagger and stabbed it into the table in front of him with another loud thud.

"I will use all my skills at this craft to bleed that Wizard dry! And I'll gut any of his dogs that rise to stop us! The Thirty-Third Homeworld Army – all one-hundred-twenty-bloody-thousand of us – have pledged our arms to Vallon!!"

At this his three lieutenants drew weaponry of their own, raised it to the air, and shouted cries of support.

Fear had given way to pride in Vallon's chest. These two generals would prove invaluable in the coming weeks.

However, as the moments progressed, the generals continued in turn to announce their intentions regarding the rebellion, and the majority gave similar answers to the first two.

Artorus knew well a general's concern for the safety of their men. It was an incredible thing for him to ask these men around the circle to risk the lives of their men so brazenly. It was one thing to follow the orders of a Wizard, sending your men to their death, but entirely separate to request it of your own volition.

Artorus mentally tallied his numbers. In the circle of what was now fourteen other generals, he had affirmative replies from Orrogen, Warin, and Magron, and negative replies from another six generals beyond them. Five remained to give their answers.

The speeches proceeded, and two more generals were unswayed by the motivations of Artorus, the wisdom of Warin, or the passion of Magron. They each replied much as the first two had.

There was little way Artorus could put a number of lives to what his rebellion might require, but as the speeches went on, he fought the feeling that what he had wasn't enough.

He shook the pessimism from his mind. These men represented hundreds of thousands of souls who were now pledged to fight in his rebellion. It would be enough to show the War Maker what he needed to see. Three generals now remained to give their answers.

The third-to-last general in the circle was a human by the name of Hakim Ayedd. He was a sleek man who wore tattoos across his sun-darkened skin, and his speech, like his every action, seemed careful and deliberate.

"The Nineteenth Homeworld Army," Ayedd proclaimed seriously, "has long valued their moral character over their might in combat... or even... their loyalty to the War Maker. We will fight for the rebellion, Lord Vallon. You champion a moral cause which cannot be ignored."

One more for the cause, thought Artorus as he bowed his head respectfully to Ayedd, *only two more to speak now...*

The penultimate general was another human called Antonius Brakson. He was a true soldier and he bore the scars to prove it.

"General Vallon," Brakson began in his rough voice, "I will command that my army follow your orders on one condition."

Artorus listened.

"That each man has the option to choose for himself if he will remain and fight this rebellion or if he will take his leave now and forever hold his peace. As a soldier myself, I know all too well the woes of fighting a battle I don't believe in. If this truly is the dawning of a new age for The Vastness, then let me show this to my men by giving them this choice."

Artorus could only smile. "I would have it no other way, noble Brakson. I made that very same offer to my Fifth Planar."

"Then the Twelfth Learden Army tentatively commits to your rebellion, General Vallon," the scarred man finished with a quick nod.

The last general in the circle, immediately to Artorus's right was another human named Symon Evvet. Evvet was general to the single largest army represented here this day, and a force of renowned might: the Ninth Planar Army.

The Ninth Planar was a force that children told stories about; it was they that defeated the Army of the Night at the battle of Bloody Pass, it was they that defended the construction of Castle Blackwell against all odds, eventually turning the tides in the struggle for Learden, and it was they that bore the unmistakable golden banner of the eagle and bear, which nearly every last soul in The Vastness could recognize.

Taking a moment after the last general had spoken and then rising slowly in front of the other generals, Evvet began in a calm voice.

"You are all fools."

Evvet's eyes were cold. After the harshness of those words sank into the room, General Evvet turned his icy stare to Artorus. "Every rebellion that has ever been assembled against the *immortal* Wizard-King has failed. Every last one the history books tell of. I do not wish his rule any more than you, but he is a *god*. It is not a matter of mortal wishes that determines his rule or his demise." He looked out to the rest of the generals. "And the Ninth Planar Army *will* oppose you on the field of battle *when* the Wizard-King commands it – just as each of these armies will." He waved toward some of the generals that pledged moments earlier not to interfere.

General Evvet let his stern and hawkish face punctuate his statement.

An eruption of noise sprung from the circle of tables. Some of the generals agreed with the human, while others spat insults across the circle.

"Please!" Artorus roared to gain the attention of the crowd.

Some quieted at the mighty shout of the general until a dwarven voice roared out, made louder in the half silence.

"Kill him before he sets them upon us!" Orrogen howled. "He knows much!"

The shouting redoubled and a flurry of yelling turned quickly to threats, until Orrogen, Magron, and several others drew steel and entered the middle of the circle, making for Evvet.

Artorus burst to action, stepping onto his table, jumping from it into the circle, and his lieutenants quickly followed. He moved directly over to Evvet's table, where the man, who had been watching wearily, finally drew his sword at General Vallon, expecting an attack. His several officers already had their weapons drawn and they each held the points toward Artorus and his two lieutenants from behind the sturdy table.

Artorus halted, looked Evvet in the eye, and then turned about to face the approaching men. He drew Thordrin's Blade, and his two lieutenants fell in behind him, drawing steel as well. Artorus Vallon faced down the several dozen warriors, and they all stopped at the sight of the three determined men.

There, staring at these many men who had just pledged their lives and the lives of their men to his own cause, defending one who just admitted he would oppose them, Artorus learned something of himself.

"This is the first order of a new kingdom, a kingdom of mortals!" he shouted to the silenced room in a stern voice. "Any council in which I ask the opinions of others, they shall have free rein to share it.

"This *ruthlessness*, this fear and death," Artorus hissed, "this is the stuff of *Wizards*; of madmen and of warlords." He scanned the men arrayed before him with a serious glare. "This man shall go free from this meeting, and, if he so wishes it, we will meet him again on the field of battle so he can fight on for his Wizard-King, but none shall be set upon in this meeting tent where I invited men to share with me their thoughts. If we are to face Evvet, it will be on the field of battle, should it come to that."

Silence held the huge tent for a tense moment as many men stared seriously across the short distance. Then slowly, one at a time, each man before him lowered and then sheathed his weapon. After they did so, Artorus heard weapons being sheathed behind him as well.

After one more brief moment, Artorus returned Thordrin's Blade to its scabbard and turned to Evvet behind him.

With a look of cautious reverence, many thoughts obviously racing through his mind, Evvet bowed his head ever so slightly to Artorus and then left the tent with his entourage.

Turning back to the crowd of men before him, Artorus spoke once more, clearly and with determination.

"And I admire your passions, good people of The Vastness. Let us take this fire and let us have the Wizard-King taste it." Artorus paused and then smirked. "And until that time, let's try to avoid drawing weapons on one another – at least for another meeting or two."

Orrogen laughed loudly and the others seemed to relax some.

As the generals who would not commit to the rebellion left with their staffs, discussion returned to the crowd.

Artorus took the time to approach and thank each of his new generals sincerely as he advised them that this day's meeting was done. Those staying with the rebellion would share the news with their men, and then reconvene at dawn tomorrow to discuss strategy.

Slowly, the assembly dissolved and the tent became emptier.

This rebellion now has armies, thought Artorus as there remained only a few people now in the tent with him, *It is only a matter of time now... But I have far more pressing matters for the moment.*

Chapter XVI – Reunion

Moments after the huge tent cleared, siblings embraced.

"Mala!" Artorus exclaimed. "I'm so glad you're safe. I feared the worst after we found out about Braïun's family... I..."

It was still troublesome to talk of it. Braïun had loved his family truly, and now through no fault of their own, they were dead. Artorus could not help but feel the pain of old wounds at these thoughts.

"What of Braïun's family?" Mala asked in a distraught tone, as she stepped back.

Her face showed that she knew what had happened even before she heard the words. Artorus simply nodded to her and looked down. Tears welled within her eyes, but she said nothing for the moment.

"I know you sent Magron to find us," Mala finally said, wiping the tears from her eyes. "That was not a part of the plan, good brother..."

She continued as she shook the thoughts of death from her mind. "And you saved all of our lives... Thank you."

Mala smiled sweetly to her brother – it was the kind of smile that Artorus had thought he just might never see again.

"Of course, Mal," Artorus replied, shaking his own sullen thoughts. "What is a leader of a rebellion without his ragtag band of rebels?" He thumbed her wounded cheek lightly. "And I must say that I think I like this battle damage on you. It seems somehow fitting. Even the blades of the Wizard-King's worst cannot stop you."

Mala and Artorus both smiled, and they each put an arm around one other. This was a time to celebrate the lives they still had, not the lives that had left them.

Typhondrius bowed to the general. "It is a pleasure to—" he began in his best noble voice, but he was quickly cut off as Artorus pulled him into the embrace.

Everyone shared a laugh.

Artorus broke the embrace to shake Lord Ormond's hand carefully. "And I am very happy to see you doing so much better, my lord."

"Please, sir," he responded, enthused, "the honor is mine at being in the presence of the mighty leader of the rebellion. Congratulations on your meeting, General."

Artorus had to pause at the thought of congratulations. He had been somewhat crestfallen that so many generals would not commit to the cause.

Still, when Artorus thought back to all the years he'd spent planning this day, he did have trouble feeling anything other than pride. There were indeed five generals that pledged their armies to their cause; this boded well for their fledgling rebellion. Five mighty armies to stand against Lord Brakken and make him see mortals would no longer follow his whims.

But the thoughts of tactics faded quickly. Artorus now saw clearly the immensely tall and impressive form of the Sage of Delemere. The man was clearly not quite human, now that he saw him from up close; his muscles formed perfectly over his frame, leanly marking his shape. The man's eyes were piercing and Artorus could almost see the wisdom of a thousand years in them as they peered at him.

"Greetings, General Vallon," the Sage said.

His voice boomed through the huge tent and surrounded Artorus. But, despite the sheer volume, the tone was far from harsh. Somehow, it was comforting like the roar of raucous tavern conversations on a cold night or inspiring like the blaring of trumpets at march.

"Greetings to you, honorable Kellos," the general returned. "This rebellion has in you a treasure that cannot be valued. We are humbled by your presence." He nodded to each of the monks who stood behind the Sage. "And this rebellion welcomes the assistance of brothers Hereditus and Orion."

They each bowed in return.

"My sister has told me that you three offered your talents to our cause," Artorus went on, "but it nearly defies belief. I simply can't thank you enough. I've mentioned to my compatriots before that I think information is likely the most powerful tool in warfare. I doubt seriously that many mortals could say they were offered assistance from a timeless Sage."

"Divine providence, brother," Mala replied, half joking. "Koth has made it so."

She always did like to prod Artorus about Kythianism. He gave her a light-hearted chuckle in return.

But, as Artorus glanced over at Kellos, a question came to him. There were so many religions among the planes, and he wasn't entirely sure which, if any, a Sage might prescribe to.

"You know, not everyone's beliefs are the same as yours, Mal," Artorus admitted cordially. "I'll bet the Sage could tell us about a thousand religions across the multiverse."

And it certainly was no lie that Artorus did not share Mala's belief in Koth. There wasn't yet a thing in the twenty-seven worlds that had convinced him of his sister's *truths*. For that matter, his travels through the gates had exposed him to all manner of different peoples with different customs and different religions.

"They don't have to be believers, good brother," Mala replied. "Koth will guide skeptics to his Light just as he guides his most fervent followers."

"I have studied Kythianism some," Ormond chimed in. "It is one of many belief systems that intrigues me."

"I'm happy to tell you anything you want to know," Mala replied. "I just may turn you to a believer," she added playfully. "I'm still working on my dear brother, as you can see."

"Belief," the Sage interjected, "is a choice – perhaps even a skill. This is one topic that I have studied in great depth. Mortal belief systems are a topic with nearly limitless intrigue."

Artorus raised an eyebrow. He'd had many days of pondering strategies and guessing at the politics of kings; he was fairly certain he would enjoy a dose of the Sage's company. Perhaps he would share with this audience just what might cause intrigue for a Sage...

Artorus called for food and more comfortable furniture to be brought into the massive assembly tent. He did not intend to leave the tent this day; he had everything he could want for the moment here and now.

"Belief?" Artorus pondered aloud after he finished with the servants. "I figure it is a pretty basic part of mortal existence. How is it that a man or an elf could exist without believing *certain* things? That does not seem like a choice or a skill to me. My sister, for instance – belief is one her greatest strengths. I always figured she was born with that as it is not something I am capable of."

"And I would agree, good general," Kellos said, "that a child chooses their beliefs no more so, say, than he or she chooses their language. And once they become cognizant of that choice, they choose either to continue that belief or to discard it for something they find more suitable or relevant. In no small way, this is one of the most prevalent ways for knowledge to progress beyond what one's ancestors taught in ages past."

"So, you're saying that my sister's attempts to convert me are fruitless?" Artorus prodded jovially. "It's a simple choice and I've chosen? It's not about changing my heart of hearts or touching my soul in some manner?"

"Desire, alone, for another to choose as one might wish," the Sage replied, "has seemingly little effect, though I would hesitate to call it futile. It is your choice though, General Vallon, to believe what you will, subject perhaps, to your skill at doing so."

Mala frowned, a skeptic eye cast to the Sage. None of the mortals here, in fact, aside from the stoic-faced monks, seemed entirely convinced by the Sage's theorem.

"Now," Mala added, "I know that not everyone shares my belief in Kythianism, but if Koth was to one day come before my brother and show him the Truth, I don't believe there would be a choice in the matter whatsoever. I speak from experience, as a matter of fact."

Kellos seemed to change tack, and he turned back to Artorus. "A demonstration of my findings: tell me something that you do believe, good general."

By now furniture had started to arrive and food behind it. They each took seats on padded benches, though the Sage and his monks seemed no more comfortable for it.

"Well," Artorus replied, picking up a grape from the plate in front of him, "I suppose I *believe* we will succeed – that this rebellion will topple the rule of the mighty Wizard-King." He tossed the grape into his mouth and looked expectantly at the Sage for his evaluation.

"And why do you believe that?" asked the Sage.

Artorus thought. The others watched, seemingly bemused by seeing the immortal Sage engage Artorus in the debate. Artorus had certainly never faced a Sage in a duel of wits before. This would probably get embarrassing.

"Why..." Artorus repeated, "that is difficult to say at once... I suppose it would have to be because it *must* be true; this multiverse cannot continue this strife – this unmitigated destruction across the many worlds... It *has to* end."

The Sage nodded at Artorus's response. "So, because you feel it is mandatory, this is enough to base your belief structure upon?"

Artorus smiled as he chewed another grape. Several of the others slowly began on the fruits, cheeses, and bread the servants had laid before them.

"Well, all right, Sage," the general admitted through his smile, "you've got me there. Desire does not define truth, nor do ethics define what is or what is not... I suppose that's not something I *believe*; not the right term..."

The Sage asked, "So what *do* you believe? Something a little more elementary, perhaps."

"All right," Artorus replied more quickly, beginning to catch on, "I believe the sun is out today."

He punctuated his statement by tossing another grape into his mouth. Artorus was a little surprised to see that the Sage and his monks did not partake in the food, as they sat stiff-backed on their bench.

The Sage asked, "So, General, *why* do you believe that?"

Mala chuckled through her bite of cheese and bread, obviously having seen that coming.

Artorus, who thought he might have provided an unquestionable answer, had to think on his response yet again. Why did he believe that?

"Well," he replied, "is it not common knowledge that the sun rises and falls each day? Is it not eternal? Is it not *believable*?"

"Three questions, good general," the Sage replied, "do not make an answer."

Mala snickered at seeing her brother the tactician so aptly out-maneuvered.

Chuckling, Artorus responded, "You are right. Then I suppose I believe it *because* it is common knowledge; *because* it is the way of nature; because it is constant."

"And do you see the sun now?" the Sage asked calmly.

"Of course not, we're in a tent."

"And so, do you *know* the sun is out today?"

"Well..." Artorus hesitated; he was certain he could argue the point further, but he could see where the Sage was going with this. "No, you're right. For all I know, the sun has burst and extinguished. Though I should think that would cause something of a commotion outside..." He stroked his stubbled chin. "I cannot *know* until I see it," he admitted. "So maybe I don't *believe* that either? Mm."

He pondered a moment.

"But I *do* believe that you and I are sitting here now!"

Perhaps Artorus could catch the Sage here. This fact was irrefutable, but Artorus knew the Sage would ask about *why* he believed it, nonetheless.

"I can see that we are here," he expounded, "you respond when I speak, and I hear your words. I *believe it*."

Mala had to laugh again at Artorus as he struggled through his logic. He smiled as well.

The Sage thought another moment. "And when you sleep, good sir, do you dream?"

Although he didn't exactly like where this was going, Artorus replied, playing along. "Yes, Sage. I sometimes dream..."

"And when you dream, do you not see things, hear things, and interact with things?"

It was a fun conversation, and the Sage was quite skilled at logic. Artorus shuddered at the thought of a game of strategy with the immortal.

"Well, but I *know* when I'm dreaming and when I'm not!" Artorus professed.

"After you awaken, I suppose," the Sage presented. "Though, I estimate it certainly feels real while dreaming it."

Artorus thought on the dreams he would often have after days of battle. They did seem real enough within the dream. He'd often awake with his heart racing. "All right, Sage! You win! I suppose I cannot believe any of these things; perhaps I believe nothing."

Defeat was wiped from his face, though, as Artorus could not help but laugh heartily. Did he actually believe nothing at all? Where was the Sage going with this?

Mala chimed in at this; some of her levity had faded. "So, Kellos, you seem to imply that we cannot truly believe anything, but there are many things in Kythia that I know in my heart, that I *believe*, and I shouldn't think you'll ever convince me otherwise... Every being I've ever met has had beliefs of some sort. In fact, I seem to recall hearing *you* state what you 'believe' more than once."

She looked to the Sage expectantly. Perhaps she had trapped him – or perhaps not – but Artorus was glad to have help at least.

"Yes," Kellos admitted, "I have many times. It is as I said: belief is a *choice*. I choose to believe certain things."

"But you don't truly *know* anything, right? You don't know the sun is out and you don't know we're sitting here talking," Artorus retorted, using the Sage's logic against him, "How can you *believe* something you don't *know*?"

"It is precisely because I don't *know* it that I must *choose* to believe it."

The large and statuesque Sage sat calmly on his bench, the two monks flanking him silently throughout the conversation. It was almost surreal to be here, having this discussion with the immortal.

Perhaps I am *dreaming,* Artorus mused.

"Truth, knowledge, fact, even our senses – in the many centuries of watching these worlds, these things only ever seem to amount to one level of conjecture or another. It is the choice, perhaps even the skill, to *believe* that which I will that separates what I shall take for truth and what I shall reserve as dubious or discard as frivolous."

Artorus had noticed already that the Sage had an interesting manner of speaking. He never seemed to second guess himself or stumble over his words. Everything he said was deliberate and precise, even when he seemed to string together complex sentences of intricate words.

"Hm," was all Artorus could respond with.

It was an intriguing concept. Artorus thought on the things he held as trusted beliefs, and he was all but certain the Sage might be able to poke holes in any of them. Maybe it was all really just one level of conjecture or another.

There was a moment of silence as all present thought on the wise words of the Sage until the silence broke with a laugh from Artorus.

It was a hearty laugh. It seemed like it had been far too long since Artorus had laughed in earnest.

"Good Kellos," he said, "most people tend to bore quickly when I wander into my more philosophical moments... I do *believe* that I shall enjoy your company!"

"And I, yours," the Sage replied.

"And what of the brothers?" Artorus asked. "Do they not partake in the conversation?"

The Sage spoke. "They converse freely, good human, when they so wish."

Hereditus nodded to Artorus. "Yes, good general," spoke the elf in a soft voice, "we simply devote much time to books and little to discourse. You have our apologies if this offends."

"Oh, not at all," replied Artorus quickly. "I was simply curious."

The human, Orion, nodded to Artorus and spoke as well. "Good general, we find that Kellos has more than enough wisdom to express any of the thoughts we have, so we are most often content with observing."

"They might hardly talk, but at least they *do* sleep some," quipped Typhondrius toward Artorus, "unlike the Sage. I've not seen him sleep a single moment since he came to the compound."

This was a surprise to Artorus.

"Do they?" questioned Mala. "I haven't seen it!"

"Yes," replied Typhondrius with a finger raised, "I witnessed it not two weeks ago. They're crafty, but I caught Brother Hereditus in the act."

Artorus smiled broadly at the interaction. Typhondrius, normally perfectly servile, seemed quite content to speak his mind now, playfully so. What had changed since Artorus left the Andrius estate?

The Sage nodded in admittance to Typhondrius's comment. "Yes, sleep is something I do not share in. Though the monks of Delemere practice the meditations and metabolic control of the Sages, they do require some sleep – something on the order of five or six hours each week."

Five or six hours a week? This was a shock to Artorus.

"Yes," replied Hereditus, "though we aspire to better ourselves each day."

Artorus looked in disbelief at the two monks and then to his sister, who nodded.

"It's true," Mala said to her brother, "I'm sure even you couldn't keep up with them."

Smiling, she turned to the others.

"I seem to recall a *younger* Artorus staying up all night the day he got home on leave, and then, the next day, he *actually* fell asleep while driving the carriage to Polm."

Ormond and Typhondrius chuckled at the thought.

"Did he fall?" asked Lord Ormond.

"Yes!" Mala said through her laughter. "He survived the battle on Ebbea nearly unscathed, but he looked like he scrapped with an ogre from his wagon adventures!"

Laughter filled the tent as Artorus couldn't help but join in.

"And to be fair," he managed over the uproar, "the *reason* I stayed up all the night was because of a *certain* sister's incessant requests to hear my tales of battle and strategy. I can't be held completely accountable!"

Mala began to tell another story of one of Artorus's youthful adventures, but Artorus was only half listening, as his thoughts dwelt on the Sage.

While the rest of the group laughed, the Sage and the two monks sat patiently. Though they seemed unamused, they were not rude; they merely paid careful attention to the others. The Sage even had this awkward sort of smile. Artorus doubted the endless studies in the stuffy monastery of Delemere gave the Sage all too many reasons to smile. Perhaps that was something he could help with in the coming weeks...

But how will he help our rebellion? thought Artorus. *The infinite knowledge inside that brain of his must hold the key to defeating Brakken...*

Artorus didn't know what secret knowledge might swing the odds in his favor, but he couldn't help but feeling there was *something* out there – some great secret that would one day be revealed and *might* one day seal the fate of Wizard-kind. He foresaw many more discussions with Kellos in the coming weeks.

"... And that's when things *really* got interesting!" Mala proclaimed loudly.

Artorus knew the story: it was of the briar bush and her father. It always surprised him she could remember it so well. It helped that they recounted it often.

"Since he had to pull the weeds from the yard," Mala told the group excitedly, "my brother, the strategist, figured the proper place to dispose of them was the master bedroom!"

More laughter erupted.

"Needless to say, my father gave him just about the best thrashing he'd ever had..."

The group had continued to eat the food laid out for them, and by now, a large portion had disappeared.

"Well," stated Ormond, grasping his side where wounds were not entirely healed, "though it quite literally pains me to say so, I am glad to see brother and sister reunited; I daresay neither of you is whole without the other."

"It is quite so, if I may speak plainly," Typhondrius said with a fondness in his voice and a smile on his face. "The Lady Andrius never shares the warmth of her smile quite so much as when the good general is back on leave."

"You flatter me, Typhondrius," admitted Mala.

"And you both speak the truth," Artorus added, "though I doubt if that is quite what Kellos would call it."

He smiled to the Sage, who then nodded and returned the smile – that funny expression that didn't quite seem to fit him.

Something caught Artorus's eye to his left. Though he hadn't noticed at first, another person had quietly entered the large tent and was standing to the side. As Artorus looked to the figure, Mala noticed as well.

"Braïun!" called Mala.

She stood immediately, rushed to the dwarf, and embraced him. The prim and proper soldier seemed more than a little surprised at the enthused greeting. The others couldn't help but smile at the display, as he finally returned the embrace.

"It is good to see you," Mala said softly.

"Say," recalled Artorus as Braïun came to the group with his sister, "didn't I threaten to promote you some time back?"

Braïun, who was already looking uncomfortable, began to redden about the face.

"Um..." was all he could manage.

"Yes," Artorus said more surely. "I can think of no commander more deserving of the title. And besides, '*High* Commander Slick' has a great ring to it, don't you think?"

He grinned at his officer, but then his tone became more serious.

"But truly, Braïun, I would be honored to have you as such."

Finally smiling, Braïun couldn't help but laugh some.

"Very well, sir." He bowed slightly. "Then, with humble thanks, I accept this charge."

"Well, that's another thing—" Artorus retorted, putting a leg up onto his seat with a few more grapes in hand, "high commanders aren't usually humble. We'll have to work on that."

The group laughed as Braïun's face returned to its previous shade of red.

Now, with Mala around, Artorus could see it clearly: it was time to bring Braïun out of his mourning – or at least time to start the process. He hadn't seen the dwarf smile in far too long. It was a welcome sight.

The afternoon moved on and topics ranged; the conversation of siblings, the laughter of friends, and the wisdom of the Sage and his monks filled the center of the large tent for the remainder of the day.

Lord Ormond dragged the group into his theories on politics and the Sage added some of his depthless knowledge. Artorus and Braïun tried their best to steer the conversation back to military strategies. Mala seemed to enjoy it all.

And, as evening arrived all too quickly, the valley cooled and fires were lit inside the main assembly tent and others among the camp, so the cold night of early spring was kept out of the warm interiors.

It was comforting to have this bubble for just a moment in time. Artorus knew that outside, in that cold night, awaited a rebellion. Out there, the agents of Lord Brakken likely hunted them in these very moments as they sat and talked. Out there, the problems of the twenty-seven worlds awaited, but in here for this moment of reunion between brother and sister and friends, for now, they were forgotten ever so briefly.

Chapter XVII – The Spring's Breeze

"Surprise," General Vallon stated plainly to his audience. "Surprise will be our greatest tool. The Wizard-King knows of the many whispers of rebellion that have circulated the land for these past years. Indeed, they are not the first, but we will be the first to rise and face him, we will be the first to strike him just where it hurts, and our tactics must be both unconventional enough and swift enough to accomplish this."

The audience listened closely.

Though only five other generals sat in this assembly, now even more officers were with each of them in the large tent, making the total number of people only slightly less than it was one day prior. The tables, which were probably too large for each general's small entourage the prior day, now seemed crowded as they'd been moved in to form a tighter circle and were packed with lieutenants, tacticians, officers, and scribes. Six tables held generals with their accompaniment and a seventh completed the circle with several more scribes, as well as Mala, Typhondrius, Ormond, the Sage, and his two monks.

In the attentive silence, the birds could be heard chirping their morning song outside, as the sun was rising on the broad valley, and a morning mist still clung to the grasslands that harbored a desperate last few patches of snow.

Vallon then looked up to each of the other generals arrayed before him.

General Warin sat patiently observant, his intellect always showing in his thoughtful eyes, and he nodded to Artorus. Opposite from Warin in the circle, General Magron had fire in his eyes, eager to take action in this plot.

Now seated to Artorus's immediate left, General Orrogen was an impressively built dwarf, with muscles bulging from his stocky frame and a bushy beard that could make other dwarves envious. He wore his heavy armor in each meeting Artorus had ever seen him attend. He and Artorus had, in fact, shared the same lord general – a relatively cold, calculating, and heartless man called Kremaine. Orrogen had always seemed to be a man of action to Artorus, and he was happy to have him and the Seventeenth Planar Army with the rebellion.

The general of the Twelfth Learden Army, between Warin and Magron, was the human named Brakson. General Brakson had a long scar running the length of the left side of his face. It was well known that this was his constant reminder of death, since the wound nearly killed him and left him slightly paralyzed on his right side. He carried his long, sheathed sword with him always, doubling as a cane. He was not an old man, but the years of warfare had not treated the human well, and he carried more scars than the obvious one; it was said that his two children were lost in a raid from Kaladrius some years back. Artorus knew that sort of pain too well.

The last in the circle was the tattooed General Ayedd of the Nineteenth Homeworld Army. He was a relatively young human who had fast earned himself distinction as an officer through acts of valor and strategic intelligence alike. He came from a relatively small continent on Myrus known as the Sayedlands – a large island chain of blistering sandstorms and rocky mountain chains as far as the eye could see – though he'd long since been stationed on the mainland. His ability to lead with both passion and clarity would be something Artorus would likely come to rely on.

As Artorus went on, he motioned for servants to follow along with his descriptions on the large map of Myrus laid out on the floor; blocks of wood with flags represented different armies.

"Each of us will have a very specific task to perform here, each with different objectives. Warin, Magron, and myself will have the unfortunate objective of drawing the direct attentions of the Wizard-King and his bulk forces, but keep in mind that our ultimate goal is for the Fifth Planar, with the help of some deceptive maneuvering, to get a clear shot at Brakken's fortress in the Central Province.

"I'll be looking for Brakson and Ayedd to split each of their armies into two main taskforces," Artorus went on. "The goal for each will be to hit several strategic points in the outer provinces and rally people to our cause. We must always remember that we are doing this as much for the people of these lands as we are for the soldiers enslaved in Brakken's armies – indeed, in Wizards' armies across the multiverse.

"I've got a couple targets in mind, but I'll look to the two of you for some thoughts on that. You generals know your armies and their capabilities better than I ever could."

A moment of thought occurred.

"I see," pointed out Ayedd, "where the forges of Finrel might make for a good target. Not only do they have military importance, but Finrel has long been called 'the City of Sweat' for its treatment of the laboring class, has it not? We may have some sway here. My taskforces can stay in this general area."

Artorus nodded, and the servants added and moved blocks as indicated.

"Excellent," replied Artorus. "And you, Brakson? Where do you see your forces having the most effect?"

"Well," the scarred man eventually replied, "I believe the open country of the Chilton Lowlands would provide ample opportunity for my taskforces."

"Hm," thought Artorus aloud, "not heavily populated..."

"No, but heavily traveled, General Vallon," Brakson replied. "The supply caravans of nearly two dozen armies pass through these highways to and from the worldgate, the last count I heard. That would get some attention, would it not? Perhaps we could even appropriate some supplies for our forces."

Artorus laughed at the thought; plenty of open space, plenty of targets, and plenty of lord generals to infuriate. "Indeed it would get some attention, General Brakson."

Both the accompaniments of Brakson and Ayedd began to speak amongst themselves, and further strategize on their tasks. They quieted after only a moment, as Artorus continued the overview.

"Orrogen," Artorus continued, looking to the thick dwarf, "I'll need the Seventeenth Planar nearby our main forces, but doing the same general thing. Our goal here is to spread out and occupy the massive numbers of Imperial Legions, hopefully drawing them away from the most inner parts of Central Province, but should things turn ugly with our battle, I'd like to have your help, Orrogen."

"Of course, Vallon," the dwarf replied in his deep voice, "you will have it. I know the many mining villages below the Feathertop Mountains. Gemmet is a large city, and it is the hub of the mining towns nearby. We could get some attention on the roads betwixt Gemmet and Anleth. At a forced march, that shouldn't put us more than a few days from the Lakewoods."

Artorus nodded to the servants once more, and more blocks were added appropriately.

"Good," he proceeded, "now our main objectives for all the outer forces will be to harry the Legions, not engage them. I don't need to remind the people in this tent that the Imperial Legions are comprised of the most elite forces in The Vastness. In fact, I always imagined that they were groomed for just such a reason as what we're concocting now. I don't want any of our outer forces engaging them in an extended battle. Likewise, I don't want any more of those Legions coming out of the woodwork and surrounding our main forces."

Artorus motioned broadly to all the blocks on the map that represented the known locations of the twenty-five Imperial Legions, many of which were about the Central Province.

Orrogen, Ayedd, and Brakson all nodded in agreement to the sentiment.

"Oh, and speaking of the main force, we have the vast majority of the troops we need here now, so once we announce our rebellion to the Wizard-King, we will meet whatever forces he musters here, as mentioned earlier."

Artorus motioned to a servant, who then moved the wooden blocks representing the three armies to a spot on the map. All the generals present would likely recognize it as the Lakewoods Plain.

"Yes," inserted Magron, "I think it is a supreme spot for our first engagement! From our last reports of the Central Legions, they'd have to come at us from the small paths in the crags, or else waste perhaps a week of marching to go around. If we're able to beat their forces, they'll have little option for retreat. We could maybe have ourselves a rout!"

Magron laughed at the thought and Orrogen seemed pleased with the idea as well.

"Agreed," added Warin, "and if the battle should go poorly for us, we have the Lakewoods themselves as a defense. We could even prepare some fortifications and other measures to guard a potential retreat."

"I don't plan to need it, Warin," General Vallon replied confidently to the old man. "But I agree with you. And yes, Magron, this is precisely why I've selected this spot – along with its relative proximity to our main target."

Artorus took a deep breath.

"So," he summarized, "in short, the plan is this: Brakson, Ayedd, and Orrogen will raid and plunder military targets, and recruit from among the populace where we can, with Orrogen being close enough to assist our main forces as needed. Magron and Warin will accompany me to present a large force to fully engage the bulk of the Wizard-King's forces at the Lakewoods. In our battle, we will be keeping the Fifth Planar largely in reserve.

"Once victory is secured at the Lakewoods Plain, or even slightly before, the Fifth Planar will split off of the main taskforce. In a matter of perhaps five weeks, the Fifth Planar will make their way up the Brannus River and along the woodlands at its flank, directly to the fortress of the War Maker himself. There, we will take the grounds, fight our way into the throne room, and I plan to prove to the multiverse just how mortal Lord Brakken – indeed, all the Wizards – truly are. In the least, he will flee from our assault, proving his weakness and toppling Brakken's empire forever. And any way our plans play out, we will make certain that Wizards will never again forget what mortals are capable of."

At this, the hum of discussion once again filled the tent, as all the various staff spoke with their generals and looked over the large map in their center.

Artorus watched the generals and related personnel in the assembly tent. He found it hard to keep a wide grin off his face. He had spent years imagining this moment, and yet now it seemed unreal to him. Mortals plotted to overthrow their Wizard-King on a scale that, to Artorus's knowledge, had never before been attempted.

Artorus waited for the discussion to quiet back down and then addressed the crowd again.

"What questions? What are we missing?"

A moment of silence ensued. A thousand thoughts whirled about the assembly.

"Well," spoke General Warin, "I do believe there is one item to discuss."

"Please, General Warin," Artorus invited.

"We have six generals here," Warin stated plainly. "But I believe we should instead have five generals and one *lord general*."

"Hear, hear!" interrupted Magron. "Artorus Vallon, the 'Lord General of the Rebellion!'"

Artorus had to fight a small round of applause to complain. "No, no, gentlemen! I'm not looking for any glory here; we are equally important to the success of this task."

"It's not about glory, young general," Warin replied. "It's a simple fact; we are military men, and we have a chain of command. Just as your troops follow theirs, I think these generals would do well to agree on a leader. And I'm sure we all agree that leader would be you, Lord General Vallon."

Another short cheer of approval followed.

Artorus shook his head. This wasn't exactly his purpose for calling the meeting, but Warin's point was hard to argue. "Very well, then," he finally submitted. "I shall take the task until we need to establish a more robust leadership for our new world."

The assembly broke once more into discussions of the various tasks until a booming voice broke the murmur. It was the Sage of Delemere.

"Lord Vallon, may I provide input at this juncture?" requested Kellos in his typical, monotone fashion.

All other voices ceased at the sound of the Sage, and the assembly turned its attention to Kellos.

"Of course, noble Sage, I would welcome it enthusiastically," replied Vallon.

"I understand that mobility and speed are cornerstones of your presented strategy. Conversely, might I also recommend creating a base of operations?"

"Well..." Artorus pondered the idea.

Until now, he had specifically planned to avoid any one location getting too much attention; it hadn't seemed prudent. True, in their original plans, they did plan to fortify a position in the mountains, but much had changed since then.

Or course, he didn't exactly feel confident contradicting the immortal Sage.

"I believe," Kellos continued, "the benefit to your cause will be three-fold, if properly selected. Firstly, a base of operations allows for people to come to you once you announce this rebellion and intend to rally supporters; secondly, a base of operations will improve the communications and logistics of the rebellion as a whole; and thirdly, if properly selected and prepared, a base of operations will be a location that the Wizard-King would not conquer easily, thereby bolstering your claims that the rebellion is mighty and that Lord Brakken is not all-powerful."

Slowly nodding as the Sage spoke, Artorus searched for any counter-points to the proposal. He found none.

"Agreed on all counts, Kellos," he replied. "May I presume you have a location in mind, then?"

"I do," Kellos replied. "The monastery of Delemere would be suitable for all of these things. It is well enough known to serve the first purpose; numerous hidden passes and watersheds from the mountain mean that it would be accessible to those who learn the environs, thereby serving the second purpose; and the monastery is nearly a fortress already: high walls edging on steep cliffs, protecting a self-sustained community, guarded by monks who devote their entire lives to perfection of both mind and body."

The Sage's face was stoic, but his words were impressive nonetheless.

"Noble Kellos," Mala interjected, "you do us a great honor to offer such a thing to us, but we cannot endanger the centuries of knowledge contained in that ancient place. We had long had a plan to hold our armies up in the mountains surrounding Delemere, but the monastery itself is a location too precious to be risked. And I would dread the implications for you... possibly for all Sages."

"Lady Andrius," the Sage replied, smiling that strange smile at her, "perhaps you forget that we Sages are, like the knowledge itself, immortal. I do not fear destruction by armies, nor do my monks."

Hereditus and Orion both nodded in unison to the Sage's comments.

"And please trust me, mortals," he continued to the entire assembly, "when I say that I can speak for all of the Sages of this multiverse in telling you there is a time for contemplation and there is a time for action. I have contemplated on one form of this idea or another for eons. It is true that it will doubtlessly garner some form of discontent from the others of my order. This, too, I have contemplated and accepted."

Artorus thought on the Sage's comments for a moment. "You truly wish to make your home a banner of the rebellion?"

The Sage nodded.

"And you're willing to risk all of the scripts and all of the people within for this task?" Artorus added.

"It is not so precarious as you might think," Kellos replied. "Each monk in every monastery and every Sage makes it their life's work to transcribe knowledge; so too is their calling to spread this knowledge among the many worlds. Nearly every script within the walls of

Delemere is copied at least thrice and kept elsewhere among the twenty-seven worlds."

Artorus thought another moment.

"Very well," he stated cautiously, "I accept your gracious offer and I agree that Delemere will serve each purpose for our headquarters – at least, in the immediate future." Back to the other generals assembled, he went on. "Are we in agreement on our battle plan, then – high level?"

One by one, each general glanced back at his staff and then nodded to Artorus.

"Excellent," he stated, "then let us begin the preparations for our armies."

Many officers and staff unseated at this, but Artorus halted the generals as they arose.

"Gentlemen," he advised the leaders, "there is one last task that I shall require of you five, along with my personal council here."

He motioned to Mala and the Sage's table with a smile.

Shortly the tent was occupied only by the generals and Mala's table.

"Our last order of business," Artorus announced once the others were gone, "is our declaration of rebellion. It's time to decide just exactly how we're going to inform Lord Brakken that his empire is no longer his…"

He grinned wickedly at the others who were present, and Mala produced the draft of a document which had been in development for the better part of two years now.

Some discussion followed as each general moved their chair to Mala's table and they began to read.

The first draft gave way to a second, and then a third and a fourth, until each general felt they'd provided adequate input. Kellos and his monks were mostly silent for this, though Mala and even Typhondrius added their own thoughts.

Within two hours, the group was in agreement.

Sighing deeply with satisfaction, Artorus sat back. "Then it is done."

Slowly, each person around the large table nodded.

General Vallon called for a servant.

"Let's see... Last count I heard, I believe we shall need twenty-six copies of this, to be sent to the many kings of The Vastness and one to the Wizard-King himself."

Then back to the group around the table, Artorus went on, "Mala and I will draft a letter to accompany our declaration, inviting all of the kings of mortals in this empire to our cause and explaining just briefly our planned operations – enough to inspire, not enough for them to hang us with it."

"Good general," Kellos interjected, surprising some of the people with whom he'd sat in silence for the last two hours. "Please allow my monks to make those copies. And it would be twenty-nine copies, if you intend to include the island provinces and the provincial leaders off-world."

The servant – a young human boy, not likely past seventeen – who was still standing, holding the original draft of their declaration, looked suddenly embarrassed. This effect was doubled when the Sage turned and spoke to him directly.

"Would I be correct in assuming it would take you and your scribes the better part of a day to create these copies – longer if attention is given to calligraphy?"

"Um," the boy hesitated. "Y-yes, sir. I think so."

Artorus smiled as the scene played out next to him.

The Sage nodded and concluded, "We will have it done this afternoon in perfect calligraphy."

The monk Orion stood, bowed slightly to the servant – which also seemed to be something the young man was not used to – and took the large scroll from him.

"Um," Artorus said through his smile to the boy, "I suppose you're dismissed then."

The group laughed lightly as he scurried away.

"That is quite impressive, Kellos," Artorus said glancing between the monks and the Sage.

"While your reaction is understandable, General," the Sage replied, "do remember that the monks of Delemere have had centuries of technique, practice, and training from Sages for just such a thing."

Artorus nodded and smiled to the monks. "Thank you, brothers."

"We are dismissed, then, gentlemen," Artorus then said to the group. "I thank you for your time this morning." He paused, looking around the huge tent. "If it is still morning... Mala and I will be meeting to discuss further details with each general individually – with necessary staff, of course. Preparations should be made to leave by tomorrow morning – even tonight, if you think your men can do it. Until then, please break and eat, and we will see you soon."

The various generals each stood, saluted, and left the assembly tent.

The sunny spring afternoon shone all too brightly as Mala exited the huge tent. Her eyes hurt, her bones ached, her head was fogged by lack of sleep, and her scabbed-over cheek burned from all the smiling with her brother and friends over the past day. And, somehow, none of it much mattered; now their rebellion had an army; now thousands upon thousands of men were pledged to Artorus and their noble cause... To *Lord General* Artorus...

This was the stage of the plan she and Artorus had barely dared to dream about a short year ago.

Now the rebellion moved. Now the Wizard-King would know fear.

Artorus was up ahead, meeting several of Warin's high command. She watched as he interacted with the officers. Mala had spent much of her adult life carefully observing how people interacted with one another. It was a matter of survival as a magistrate of The Vastness.

These officers each looked to him with a certain respect, a certain admiration. He was quickly becoming more than a mere military superior.

Artorus always had that charisma – even when they were young, when he lived with them on the Andrius estate. Some of her earliest memories were of him organizing games among the noble children, leading them on expeditions into the thicket outside of the estates and, often enough, getting in trouble doing it.

Mala laughed quietly at how perfectly it all fit together now. In retrospect, she couldn't see any other way for things to turn out. He was still that child – still leading the others into the thicket, and still heading for trouble.

Typhondrius came up beside her as she watched her half brother.

"My lady," the elf said softly in the bright afternoon, "it is good to see you do that again."

She looked to him, confusion on her face.

"Smile. It is good to see you smile like that again, my lady."

Her smile widened at his sweet remark.

"It's just so wonderful to see it all coming together, Typhondrius," she said, still watching the general speak with the officers. "The wait was long enough on its own, but to have seen that pain in his eyes every time we would speak of Elsa… It just ate away at me."

She paused for a moment as the elf stood patiently.

"Mourning is a funny thing, my friend," she contemplated. "Even an open rebellion against Lord Brakken won't mask his pain. It won't mask mine either… But it's as though every day seized by sorrow, every late night conversation by the fire, every dream of Elsa's memory… every tear… was a step in the journey that has led us here…"

Mala breathed deeply of the spring air.

"I know that Elsa is with Koth," she continued. "She is a part of the Greater Truth now, and when this rebellion succeeds, she will see us and Artorus will know peace. He has fought wars for the Wizard his whole life – those very wars that claimed his wife and unborn child – but no more. He is now a free man, after all these years. And no longer shall her death be for naught."

She turned back to her friend. "That is why I smile, Typhondrius."

He watched the scene for a moment as well.

"You know, my lady," he started, "I believe what you say about your brother, but if I may be so bold, I think your smile means more than just that."

She eyed him once more.

"I believe that, in some way, it represents your greatest place in this revolution," he went on. "If your half brother is the brain of this movement, then you are its heart. Even if now it is just a hint of what will be, I'm quite certain that the people of our new world will look to you for that good nature – that positivism that you wear so easily. I don't know if you've noticed, but it is not a common thing in The Vastness. All my life in the fortress, I scarcely saw it at all. It was more like a rumor than an emotion."

She felt her cheeks blush slightly.

"You are too kind," she said, shaking her head. "Let's get that new world first, and then I'll try to refute your claims, shall we?"

She paused. "'Positivism?' I think you've been spending too much time with our wordy Sage friend lately."

They both laughed. It really was great to see Typhondrius, her elven friend with such a carefully cultivated submissive personality, developed in a lifetime of serving the Wizard-King, finally feeling comfortable to express himself. She had always cared for him, but this newer Typhondrius was decidedly her favorite.

They both walked a short distance to where Lord Ormond was stretching his stiff muscles and surveying the forces which were busy breaking most of their camp. He had been talking with a small group of soldiers as they moved food barrels from nearby him.

"Greetings, good noblewoman," he said, nodding to Mala. "And good elf," he nodded to Typhondrius.

They each stopped next to the nobleman, taking in the same view.

Bustling soldiers stretched for about as far as the eye could see in the broad valley and the bright sun. Foodstuffs, horse feed, fresh water, and other such supplies had been amassed – meant to be a part of the Planewars, but now appropriated for the opposite goal.

"I've been thinking about one of the last things Lord Vallon said in there," Ormond said to the two of them as they watched. "'The many kings of The Vastness,'" he quoted. "I would much appreciate being included in that process to write those letters." He looked to Mala. "I think we have much potential in those kings."

She forced a smile as she eyed the nobleman.

"I don't know, Ormond. I don't expect much to come of those letters, truthfully. The kings of men are some of the most loyal hounds of the Wizard. Pointedly so. Brakken allows only the most depraved men the opportunity."

"Well," Landais replied, "having had the opportunity to speak just briefly with some of the good soldiers of Warin's Second Planar Army, it seems that as retribution for some of our rebels being caught in the Kaluk Province, Lord Brakken has publicly executed King Perrinor – a bloody show from the sound of it."

Ormond's eyes held pain in them. Typhondrius and Mala listened, both somewhat stunned by this news.

"I had met Perrinor once," Ormond continued, "and he was not without his faults, but he did care for his people, if my impressions were correct. If not even the kings of men earn a reprieve from the slaughter of the Wizard-King in his rage, then perhaps we could make an ally out of one or more of them yet."

He turned to Mala. "I know that the kings and other high nobility are seen merely as voiceless puppets of Lord Brakken, and for some, it is surely true. But many of them are like you and I, Lady Andrius; they are simply nobles that wish the best for the people in their charge..." Ormond cast his gaze downward. "Or what's left of them..."

Mala nodded and placed a soothing hand on Ormond's shoulder.

"You may be right, Ormond. I would welcome your assistance." She then smirked. "But you might just be happy to know that a couple of those hounds I'm so quick to judge, King Antioch and the High Count Mastus, have both already pledged some small assistance to Artorus in these past years. I think they are not unlike you, noble lord; they actually care for the people of their lands more than the coffers of their castles or that long and bloody ladder up to the feet of Lord Brakken."

Mala shook her head. "In all my travels about this corner of Myrus, I've seen so many terrible things that noblemen and noblewomen can do... I tend to think of my fellow nobles as a lost cause, but there are a precious few that still value life. I need to remind myself of it."

Ormond raised an eyebrow.

"So, Antioch and Mastus are sympathizers?" He smiled inwardly. "Yes, I think that there is indeed hope for many of these kings, if we can only appeal to them."

"And..." Mala replied contemplatively, "I always felt like something of an outcast among the nobility. I didn't have people to oversee as a low-ranking noble or a magistrate of timber management. My charge was clerical in nature. But I came to a realization that I hope might have value to you, Landais. In taking up this cup of rebellion, we've vastly expanded the people in our charge.

"*All* the people of The Vastness, perhaps all the people of the multiverse, are our charge now. That compassion we have for those we serve must apply to every mortal who has been oppressed by Wizard-kind. All of them."

He nodded thankfully at her assessment.

"So," she finished, "I can think of no other that would have better insight on these letters than yourself. If you have the time now, then we can begin a draft immediately. What say we serve the people in our charge?"

Not an hour later, the two nobles had worked up a draft, and then within an hour more, they had shown it to Artorus, personalized each letter to each king as best they could, and written final copies.

Within the day, the declarations were sent to each of their places, the swiftest and noblest riders to deliver their missives in secret and hasten back to report of their responses – or die with pride when they were executed for their crimes, if it came to that. They departed with heroic honors from the rebellion.

To the surprise of Mala, the Sage and his monks not only completed each calligraphic declaration in perfect form, but they had also produced duplicate copies to be sent back to the records at Delemere.

The armies that were once settled comfortably into the huge flat valley were to be ready to move in the morning. In fact, Magron and his Thirty-Third Homeworld Army had already struck camp and marched ahead that night. The headstrong general was clearly looking forward to his role at the forefront of the large battle to come.

That evening, there were more to depart than just Magron and the messengers. Kellos had determined he would be staying with Artorus and Mala and would send Hereditus and Orion with several units of troops back to Delemere to establish the headquarters and deposit their copies of the letters in the libraries. It had seemed a good plan, but mostly, Mala was happy to have the Sage staying on.

As the soldiers all prepared for their journey back into the mountains above the Winterlands, Mala and her brother paused as the Sage of Delemere prepared his monks for departure – no speeches, no instructions, no farewells even, but something else entirely.

The two monks entered some kind of meditative trance, there to the side of the large assembly tent – with no better place to do it, Mala supposed. Kellos approached each of them, one at a time. While they meditated, he reached one long arm down, hand closed, and pressed his thumb to the center of their forehead, closing his eyes momentarily. Each of their eyes snapped open immediately after Kellos released his thumb. And then they both nodded to him and departed.

"What do you suppose that's all about?" Artorus asked Mala quietly as they watched.

"I wonder myself," she said, eyes suspicious, "but I have a theory…"

The night passed too quickly, and Mala's sleep was again inadequate. Everyone at the camp awoke before the sun and they struck the last of the tents and packed the last of the supplies in the half light of pre-dawn. Brakson, Ayedd, and Orrogen each went their directed ways to meet with their own armies, and the two massive armies still present began to march for the huge, snaking river that led directly toward the

Lakewoods. The valley was several days' march from the river, and then the river would guide them for at least two weeks toward the plain, where destiny awaited.

A brief shower met them as morning came, leaving inland as swiftly as it came, as the herds of buffalo trotted in the distance. This part of Myrus had always impressed Mala with its rugged and open beauty.

And now, in this beautiful land, the armies of the rebellion were under way.

The first weeks of travel passed rapidly as the armies marched toward the Lakewoods Plain. Showers continued sporadically during their journey, but neither food nor water was of any difficulty to obtain as they marched up the road beside the great Lower Brannus River. This river was, in fact, an extension of the very river that eventually led to the Central Province that was their ultimate destination. Many tributaries converged at the two great lakes that flanked the Lakewoods and they all flowed into the massive river now beside them. It was likely still a few more weeks of travel upriver before they reached the edge of the Lakewoods, but likely only a few more days to the plains from that point.

Artorus could see the frightening prospect of battle press on Mala's mind like a stone as they traveled. Despite her affinity for tactics and despite her knowledge of soldiery – indeed, despite her skill with a blade – she'd never been in a battle. It likely scared Artorus more than it scared Mala though. During their travels, Artorus practiced swordplay with her most days, and it was not her skill with the blade that concerned him so much as her presence of mind, when the battle would finally come. More good soldiers fell to the overwhelming spectacle of being amid the fighting than those who fell from a lack of swordsmanship.

Currently, he and Mala practiced with wooden swords beside the sparkling river.

"So," Artorus started, sword at the ready, "are you ever going to tell me your theory?"

Typhondrius watched, along with Highblade, who was giving Artorus pointers, despite the general's best insistence that he didn't need it.

"Is it time for a break?" his sister asked him.

They were both sweating in the heat of midday, though it was mitigated significantly by the cool breeze from the river that periodically rushed through the surrounding trees in a soft song.

"No, what's that got to do with it?" the general replied as he tested her guard with a quick stab and a couple wide swings.

"Nothing at all," she grunted as she attempted several attacks in succession, all blocked by Artorus's deft movements. "I guess it's just not time for you to hear my theory then, either."

She smiled as she jumped back to avoid Artorus's return swing.

Highblade laughed loudly from the side, whether from hearing their conversation or perhaps from his offense at the sluggish maneuvers.

"Fine, Mal," Artorus relented, "I suppose it's time for a break before my lieutenant says something that gets him demoted anyway."

He shot a glance to Highblade in mock scorn, which only solicited more laughter. The two of them handed off their practice swords and went to the water where they could walk quietly.

They had procured rags and they each wiped sweat from their brows.

"So," he began, "perhaps I should specify which theory I'm requesting from my philosopher-strategist-warrior-diplomat of a sister." Artorus grinned to Mala as they walked. "You recall when the monks were—"

"Yes," Mala interrupted, "it's actually been on my mind since that day; truthfully, since before that day." She stopped and looked out over the river. "There was something else that happened, Artorus – when we were on the run from the estate."

Artorus stopped beside her and listened.

"One of the captains of the Imperial Legion," she went on, "had surrounded us with several dozen men; he was ready to bring us to that justicar, I'm sure of it."

A hand went to her scarred cheek, and she shook her head.

"But he didn't."

He didn't? thought Artorus, perplexed. Mala turned to him.

"They had you surrounded?" Artorus confirmed.

Mala nodded. "Something stopped him; something affected his mind, like he didn't even know who we were – or he did, but he was forced to pretend we weren't the ones he wanted."

She obviously had trouble believing her own story. "He called off his men." Mala shook her head as she recalled the events.

This perplexed Artorus. "I'm not sure I follow..."

"I know, it still doesn't make much sense to me either, but I know what I saw. The man was fighting with himself, somehow. He kept glancing from me back to Kellos. I'm fairly certain Kellos was doing something to him... I think the Sage uses magic, Artorus."

Artorus could not help his face growing skeptical and he shook his head. "Look, Mala, I'm not saying you didn't see what you saw, but everyone knows that only Wizards have magic, and Kellos is no Wizard."

"I know," Mala refuted, "but I don't have any other way to explain it. We should have died that night. My home burned behind me, Ormond was still deathly weak, and those troops had a hundred lances pointed at us."

She shook her head again. "I'm sure you know more than I do about Wizards and magic, but truthfully, if he does know how to use magic, I don't know what that might mean. What if Kellos is somehow connected to the Wizards? He couldn't possibly be in league with them, could he?"

Mala could not hide her concern at such a concept. It had clearly been eating at her for some time by now.

"Why didn't you ask him about it?" Artorus questioned.

"I did, but it's another one of his topics that he doesn't wish to discuss." She frowned. "Sometimes his decision to withhold information gives me pause. I don't wish to be distrustful... but..."

"Listen, Mala," Artorus admitted, "when battle rages all around you, you can't control the forces of chaos that ebb and flow; you can control only what you do... You can't control the actions of forces greater than yourself. It's a lesson I learned long ago."

He thought another moment, stroking his beard. "So, I... I don't know if a Sage could control magic, but if there's one thing I *do* know about Kellos, it is that he is a much wiser and more powerful man than I. So perhaps we should trust that wisdom and that power?"

Artorus's statement was meant to invoke thought in his own mind as much as it was in his sister's. He really didn't know what to think of his sister's theory about the Sage. But he too had seen the strange ritual beside the tent with the monks. There was certainly a thing or two the Sage was not telling them.

Mala nodded, "I suppose you're right. He says he will tell us when the time is right to do so."

The two eventually continued their walk, returning to the camp for the armies to depart once more.

The Second Planar and the Fifth Planar had traveled more or less together, but marshaling nearly two hundred thousand troops was no easy task. Some days, being a general was as simple as trying to know where all your men were. Often groups would separate by numerous miles and travel separately. The rough roadways, wooded paths, and shaky bridges were hardly built to accommodate massive interplanar armies.

Artorus imagined Magron farther ahead, pushing the Thirty-Third Homeworld hard through the countryside, eager to taste the blood of those who would oppose their rebellion. Artorus was not quite so eager to spill blood again.

The faces of the families that had cottages by the river and the innkeepers and shopkeepers in this sparse part of the Great Continent would always appear at their doorways to watch as the huge armies trudged past. Children would play at sword fighting with sticks and look on with wonder at the fluttering banners marching through.

Surely, they assumed these armies marched on the orders of the Wizard-King and his Ministers of Military. They couldn't possibly imagine the truth of their cause. Not yet, anyway.

Precious few days remained now between the two armies and the place where battle would be drawn, if all went to plan.

Artorus trusted each of his new generals in earnest and he trusted his men unendingly, but none of these things ever stopped him from the thoughts that he was *causing* more strife, more death, for the people of The Vastness that he marched past. What if that were all that came of his rebellion? What if it was all the history books told of Artorus Vallon? Many would die, that was for certain, but would they accomplish their goal? If they could, by the hands of fate or Koth or any other power, accomplish their goal, then wouldn't it be worth any price?

But to fail would only amount to a colossal waste of life. Just as Elsa and their child were collateral in the Planewars. A waste of the most precious lives...

Can't think like that, he told himself as he sat, reviewing the battle charts once more by candlelight, another long day of marching behind him, *it will work. It has to.*

Chapter XVIII – Storms on the Horizon

Hinthus was a servant; he had been one all his life. He'd always considered himself honored to be one of the elite few elves who were blessed to serve the Wizard-King directly.

But Hinthus wasn't unobservant; he knew that someday he would die by the Wizard's hand. It happened all the time; countless servants were said to have been slain by Lord Brakken and exceedingly few lived to an age of retirement. Unlike the less faithful servants, however, Hinthus looked forward to this moment – to be touched by a god was a great honor, even if that touch was the touch that brought death.

He slowly rose from his bowed position in front of the supremely tall Wizard-King. Somehow, despite the hundreds upon hundreds of times he'd seen the immortal, his presence never stopped inspiring awe.

"Who has sent this?" demanded Lord Brakken of the lowly servant, his incredible voice filling the entire chamber with its magnificent power.

"My lord, a messenger who identified himself as 'Jerion' delivered it to the fortress entrance," the meek elf said in a soft voice, maintaining his half-bowed posture, eyes on the table.

"And why is this messenger not here before me?" Lord Brakken asked, anger welling beneath the booming voice.

"My lord, the gate guards slew him where he stood for daring to utter the word 'rebellion,' as per your almighty orders."

Hinthus bowed as he finished his statement. He prepared himself; he had read the document, his sharp elven mind memorizing well the message. Hinthus had heard the whispers, even in the Wizard-King's own fortress, that there were a vagrant few who, in all lack of faith in their lord, thought to rebel against his greatness and claim The Vastness for themselves. He now had proof that such lunacy existed. Of course, they would fail; Lord Brakken was supreme, but the message was disturbing enough.

In front of him, Lord Brakken unrolled the large piece of parchment. Hinthus had to concentrate very hard to slow his breathing as his heart began to race. He kept his eyes fixed on the table in front of him.

Lord Brakken snorted disdainfully, and his breathing became heavy as he read the document. The ire of the Wizard-King would come very soon now. Hinthus reminded himself of the words on the scroll.

SCS 344, 1st Day of 3rd Month

To the Wizard-King, Lord Brakken,
and all else whom it must concern:

>The Vastness and her many peoples have long been under the stranglehold of eternal strife. It is the belief of this party that this is invariably and inexorably tied to the Planewars. The Planewars are exclusively a product of Wizard-Kings, including yourself, and do not represent the will or the interest of the people. They have enslaved, oppressed, and destroyed mortal lives for centuries and are a plague on the many worlds of this multiverse. There is no benefit to be gained from the Planewars and no end to come.
>
>~
>
>It is for this reason that the signatories of this document, in full representation of all others who seek our

political or military asylum, hereby declare our independence from, and if needed, rebellion against, your rule.

~

Though we prefer peace, as it is the ultimate goal of this declaration, we are fully prepared to fight on any and all terms to secure a long-lasting independence from your rule and the rule of any Wizard. Under the assumption that you will respond in kind, we hereby declare war on you and any mortals that choose still to align themselves to you.

~

It is our intention that you pay for the many crimes to which you have subjected the peoples of our races these past centuries.

If you should find the courage to submit to the people of The Vastness for their judgment, then inform your armies to cooperate with us and a trial will be held publicly.

If you should not find the courage to rise to our request, if it is war you desire, then meet us on the plain of the Lakewoods. We shall let destiny decide the more righteous party.

Signed:
Lord General Artorus Vallon, Fifth Planar Army
Lady Mala Andrius of the Winterlands
General Leon Warin, Second Planar Army
General Loren Magron, Thirty-Third Homeworld Army
General Däruth Orrogen, Seventeenth Planar Army
General Antonius Brakson, Twelfth Learden Army
General Hakim Ayedd, Nineteenth Homeworld Army
and all the peoples of The Vastness who seek freedom

A low noise came from the depth of Lord Brakken's lungs, welling within him like the roar of a lion. His hands clenched on the paper and it immediately erupted into flames.

Hinthus could no longer contain himself; he was now breathing heavily, and he began to feel the air around him move, rushing inward, pressing against him.

This is the moment! he thought excitedly. *To be touched by a god!*

For the first time in an entire life of serving him, Hinthus looked up into the Wizard-King's eyes: sweet beauty, terrible power, almighty wrath – the single greatest sight Hinthus had ever seen and also the last.

The air became crushing, he felt blood rushing to his head and the elf's vision blurred rapidly. As the Wizard-King raised his left hand slightly, palm down, his fingers slowly closed into a fist. Hinthus could never have imagined the pressure he felt under the might of his Wizard-King's magic. He required only air to crush his being into oblivion, but the air felt more like a raging waterfall now.

As all went black, Hinthus could no longer speak, but one thought rang true in his mind: *Thank you, my lord.*

Thunder rolled through the hills and woods ahead, echoing from distant cliffs, telling two mighty tales: the great size of the huge plain ahead of the travelers and the great power nature holds – even in her voice. Stalwart lakes stood guard at either side of the vast plain, somehow enhancing the ability of the cloud cover to dominate the landscape, looming over all. There was an intense beauty overarching the gloomy scene.

Mala's conversation had paused momentarily to take in the impressive sights and sounds. Rain could be seen creeping into the lowlands ahead, clashing against the faraway crags, as closer to the armies spots of sunlight burst into life, moved across the plain short distances, and disappeared again.

Mala resumed the discussion they had been having with the Sage, clarifying her inquiry. "Have the people of The Vastness rebelled against Wizards before?"

Kellos replied, "One's definition of 'rebellion' would be prudent to discuss, I believe, since there have been many actions of various magnitude acted out against the Wizard-Kings of Myrus since the Planewars began."

He looked expectantly to Artorus and Mala.

Mala elaborated, "What of action at this magnitude? Against Lord Brakken?"

"Ah," the Sage responded, "then 'none' would be your answer – not since The Vastness became a solidified Dominance of Lord Brakken. Indeed, even the infamous Elvish Insurrection of 188 was confined to a few small towns on the far continents of Myrus."

The Sage spoke, as always, in his commanding tone, without much emphasis, but his words certainly gave Mala and her brother a sense of accomplishment.

Never has Lord Brakken faced a rebellion of this magnitude, thought Mala.

"Of course," the Sage added, "in a partial answer to your foremost question, Lord Brakken has made his sole occupation for the last three centuries warfare."

The question that had begun this particular conversation was whether or not they had the numbers to accomplish their goal, to scatter and beat the Imperial Legions and eventually dethrone the Wizard-King.

Slightly crestfallen, Mala and Artorus glanced at one another as the Sage went on.

"This notwithstanding, I do not believe the Wizard-King himself is of much strategic aptitude; his successes are built largely upon the planning of his military staffs, such as the reputed strategy of yours, Lord General Vallon. So, his ability to respond to this rebellion would be in question to the outside observer, I believe."

"'Lord General Vallon...'" Artorus quoted, shaking his head. "That will still take a bit more getting used to... Very well, I believe I have some more preparations to do before Magron and Warin arrive for the meeting. I thank you for your wisdom, Kellos."

Artorus rose, bowed his head to the Sage and to Mala and headed off through the multitude of tents. The Fifth Planar and the Second Planar's encampment sprawled into the light woods on the sloping hillsides, a city of cloth and trees before the vast plain.

"So," Mala began, once Artorus was out of earshot, "can I ask your opinion on something, Kellos?"

The Sage nodded to her.

"Do you think we can do it?" she asked.

He thought a moment. "I'm not sure, Lady Andrius."

He didn't appear to have the intention of elaborating on his answer, but Mala's expectant look prodded him.

"One must weigh all of the factors at hand," he said, "of which there are many, and one must also consider what exactly one defines as success. One must discuss the period of time in which one is framing this question. The factors are numerous."

"Do you think Artorus and I can kill Lord Brakken and maintain rulership of at least the plane of Myrus for a time?" she asked intently.

The Sage thought another moment.

"Still, my lady, I am not sure, though your clarification does aid me in balancing the possibilities."

The Sage thought one more moment on his words.

"In the centuries of Wizards fighting each other for power, I have neither witnessed nor heard account of a mortal overcoming a Wizard. Many mortals, such as your half brother, have met their end in such an attempt. Any critical mind would know that histories and perceptions do not tell entireties, and so this does not necessarily preclude victory for your rebellion."

He looked to Mala for a moment.

"It does cast a troubling light on your task. You will face great tribulation."

Mala looked now more seriously at the Sage, as she pondered her words. "So, you don't think we can do it," Mala guessed quietly, looking down.

He did not respond to this statement immediately either.

"No, my lady," the Sage admitted, finally. After another moment he seemed almost regretful. "You did ask for my opinion."

His words stung fiercely, and Mala felt her frustration getting the better of her.

"Why would the Sage of Delemere even lend us his assistance," she said to the Immortal, "if he saw no possibility for victory? Why give us ineffective information and insubstantial hope?"

There was more sharpness in Mala's voice than she would have liked, but there was no fallacy in her words.

"I suppose it falls on me, then, to prove you wrong," she finished.

She got up, not looking at Kellos, and left in the same direction as her brother.

Inspecting the weapons and shields of one of his units of men, Artorus nodded to their sergeant.

"These are well kept, sergeant," he stated to the man – a short human who kept a beard and rather long hair.

Artorus continued on through his camp. There was a difference – *something* different – in the way these men held themselves. Before, there was pride in their unit and their army; before, there was confidence in their general; but never before were these men... free.

When he'd informed the men of the rebellion, he spoke to most all of them at once, much as he did his high command – the same impassioned speech, knowing well how much he needed these brave men and women. Always had Artorus taken great pains to earn the respect of his army and it would seem this had paid off. The General Vallon had offered each and every man the opportunity to leave the Fifth Planar Army without judgment or reprisal.

None had – not a single man or woman of the Fifth Planar. This was, quite plainly, one of the greatest moments of the rebellion for Artorus. It taught him much about the mortals of this multiverse.

"Lord General, sir," a voice came from nearby, "could I have a moment?"

Artorus looked to his side and saw a man – he appeared to be half-dwarven – standing in armor, wearing a captain's insignia, and looking respectfully to the general. He knew this man, but the name escaped him at the moment.

"Yes, Captain," he replied, "what is it?"

"I know you are busy, sir," the man stated, "perhaps I can walk with you."

Artorus nodded and the two men began walking through the huge encampment.

"Sir, do I have permission to speak freely?" the man asked his general.

"Always," he said, "Captain…" allowing for the man remind him of his name.

"Mallison, sir," the man said, "Captain Mallison of the Fifty-Fifth infantry battalion."

Captain Mallison was taller than most dwarves and perhaps not as stocky, but neither was he scrawny, and a large bushy beard jutted from his face. His eyes were serious and his shoulders hung slightly low.

Artorus nodded.

"You always have permission to speak freely with me, Captain Mallison – so long as you do so with tact. You wouldn't be an officer if I didn't intend to have your input."

He smiled at the man. The half-dwarf looked to be somewhat calmed by this.

The officer went on, "Well, you see, sir, it's about this rebellion." He paused, as if he expected this to be a closed topic, but Artorus listened patiently. "Well, I…"

He paused again, obviously searching for the words. Until finally, he stopped walking and turned toward the general with sorrow in his eyes.

"After the Battle of Harmony Valley, many of the men in my unit and I took retreat to a town that we've grown fond of, by the name of Maybend – in the Chilton Province. It had become something of a pastime... It was just getting to be winter, when we took food and drink in the tavern. Out of the cold winds..."

He locked eyes with Artorus, a very serious tone to his words.

"But the cold found us anyway. That creature that the Wizard-King calls his High Justicar came to that tavern, and he was looking for us."

Artorus felt a chill at those words.

Mallison looked away. "Nero was a soldier of mine; a good human... never disobeyed a single order, and he was liked by the other men. Nero died to the long daggers of that monster – truly I thought we were all going to die."

The captain was now subconsciously gripping the hilt of his sword as he spoke.

"That beast is no man... The justicar is a creature of pure hate, and he kills without a thought."

"I've met the creature just once..." Artorus said ponderously. "'The Blade of the Wizard-King'..."

It was a fitting title for the justicar: an instrument of death. *How can we fight this shadow?* Artorus thought as he slowly began to walk again, the captain keeping pace.

"Well, you see, my reason for mentioning, sir," the captain finally continued, "is that he sought information about the rebellion. None of us even knew of it then, but he killed Nero anyway. Nero told him of Commander Slick before he died..."

He looked down again.

"We're the reason that poor dwarven family died..."

Artorus felt a pain burst to life immediately in his chest as he thought of Braïun. "There I shall have to respectfully disagree with you, soldier," Artorus responded ruefully. "*I* am the reason they are dead."

Artorus let those words echo in his mind a moment, painful as they were.

"And they will not be the last to die for my cause either... Many shall die in the name of this rebellion, and I ask more of my soldiers than I have any right to."

He could only shake his head at the thought of what a terrible cost he asked his men to pay. Artorus felt sorrow and pride and regret and determination all at once.

"No, sir," the captain continued, "it's not that we blame you, sir. When you told us about the rebellion, my thoughts were ablaze with that bloody night in that Maybend tavern. My decision was made even before you finished your words. I knew Nero and all the others who tasted the justicar's steel needed a chance at justice."

The captain hesitated again. "It's just... Well, I've got a family of my own..."

"It is for their very lives that we fight," Artorus assured. "It is for the lives of all mortals that we fight this rebellion. These Planewars have claimed *so many* lives, and I truly wish for the lives of High Commander Braïun's family to be the last... They will not be, but if we can just make the multiverse see that there is another way, perhaps these Planewars can end, and people can one day simply *live* again."

The captain nodded. "And that is exactly why all of your men stayed with you when you told us we could leave, sir; it's *exactly* why we follow you, sir. It *is* a cause worth dying for..."

The captain paused again as he sighed.

"The only reason I mention the justicar, sir, is that I do not think he can be stopped; I do not think the Wizard-King can be stopped."

The captain retained his serious eyes, looking through the trees to the large plain below, as he spoke his fateful words.

"They are dark forces, beyond our mortal comprehension or action, by my figuring."

"We will show them our might, Captain," Artorus said encouragingly. "We will prove the people wrong. He *can* be killed. He *can* be stopped."

Mallison shook his head apologetically. "Please forgive me, Lord General. I don't wish to contradict you, but you should have seen the ease with which the justicar killed... I still feel his stare when I lay down in my bedroll to sleep each night... and he follows Lord Brakken with the darkest loyalty. The Wizard-King is powerful enough to command this creature at his whim...

"I..." Mallison paused. "I just... I'm sorry, sir. I don't wish to disparage."

This man thinks we will lose this battle? Fail at this rebellion? Artorus's mind raced, *Then why does he follow me?*

"So," Artorus asked the man seriously, "you do not think we can win?"

The captain waited a moment, and then shook his head solemnly.

"And, you know that the repercussions of our actions might very well claim the lives of our families if we should fail?"

The captain nodded with the same solemnity.

"Then why do you follow me, Captain?" the general asked in earnest, almost exasperated. "If you do not mind *my* speaking freely. Why in the twenty-seven worlds are you here? I would've granted you a transfer to any other army you wished."

The captain stopped walking once more and looked to his lord general. No more was his gaze sullen, but stern. His shoulders rose up and he breathed in deeply.

"Because, sir, I would rather fight and die for what is right than kill even one more mortal in the name of Brakken the Cruel... It is just as you told us: we may choose to live free, or we may choose to remain a slave to the Wizard-King. We have chosen, sir. And if that choice means an early death, then so be it."

Artorus stood in awe of the resolve of this soldier before him. *Is this truly how the men of the Fifth Planar feel?*

It was one thing to follow their general because he issued them orders, it was something else to follow their general on a rebellion they thought they would *lose*.

Mallison had spoken his peace. Bowing, he concluded, "Thank you for letting me speak, sir, and thank you for being the only man I have ever met who is brave enough to stand up to the Wizard-King and his justicar. For that we owe you everything – our lives, the lives of our families, everything. Please excuse me, sir."

He left the general standing there and went off to continue the preparations for the coming battle.

Artorus stood awhile longer as he looked over the field beyond the woods – the field where many men would likely be giving their lives in a few short days – and pondered the captain's words.

He was right.

Whether they won or lost this rebellion, the effect would be the same for many of these men; they would die free. It was more than they ever had before.

I shall have to show them that it is more than just an ideal, though, he thought with renewed resolve. *I'll show them we can win.*

The meeting with Magron and Warin came and went, and each general knew their task. While some of the Fifth Planar Army would partake in the combat to come to prove they were there, most would remain in reserve among the woods, hidden. Magron and Warin would take on the bulk of the fighting.

It had been several weeks now since Brakken should have received their declaration. Artorus smirked when he thought of the wrath this must have caused in the Wizard-King's fortress on that day.

They had scouts all about the region, and reports poured constantly into the command tents. There were corroborated accounts of major imperial troop movement coming toward the Lakewoods, assembling for a massive engagement. Things seemed to be going as planned, as, from the other reports, the other armies of the rebellion were getting equally satisfactory results from Brakken's legions.

Once the rebels had – hopefully – scored their first victory against the mighty Wizard-King's armies, Warin would put into place the careful deceptions that would leave the impression that the Fifth Planar Army remained at the site of the battle with the other two armies.

This is when Artorus and his men would carefully use all of their distractions to creep up beside the woods of the Brannus River and strike directly at the Wizard-King's fortress, all of his armies in disarray.

Somehow, having everything in place made Artorus nervous – it always had. He could deal with catastrophic events, he could deal with the tides of battle as they changed around him, he could deal with a need to improvise, but when everything went just as he planned, it put him on edge.

As Artorus exited the meeting tent, propped among the sparse trees, he saw Mala.

"Hello, brother," she said to him as he approached. "I think we should talk."

She had a look of concern on her face, but her voice was as even as ever.

"I do have many things to grapple with my attention at the moment, Mal," Artorus half joked.

The words were true, but he would make time to listen to his sister if they were in the very heat of battle, and she knew it.

Mala did not laugh.

"I fear that there is too much despair in this camp," she stated. "How are we to win if our troops are not hopeful? Even the Sage does not think we can win – Koth guide us."

Artorus did furl his brow at this. As he was about to reply, a strange sound caught his ear from the far side of the tent. It was a noise like a tiny squeak.

Likely some animal in the brush. And even more likely, he did not want to have this conversation at the moment. He had only just shaken his sullen thoughts from the conversation with the captain earlier.

But, of course, he shook the distractions, and looked to Mala. "What makes you say that?"

"I asked his opinion on the matter just after you left our conversation this morning. He said it plainly."

Artorus thought a moment and replied in earnest to his sister. "I do fear that Elsa may have to watch me die before this is through. I think we've known this since we began planning – that it might not work, that it may end in death."

Mala was getting upset, her even voice becoming impassioned. "I'll not allow countless thousands to die after all your inspiring speeches about freedom, and after what we've lost, just to be a martyr for a lost cause, Artorus."

"Look, Mala," he replied, trying to help her see reason, "we've set this in motion now, we can't stop it. And there is a short list of possible outcomes in what we've started – in what *we've* caused. A *very* short list: victory and death; there are no other options."

Mala shook her head.

"How can you be so disparaging? After all we've done, after all we've been through to get to this point?"

Artorus could feel his temperature rising, he could feel a deep sorrow welling in his chest. Why would Mala press this issue? Didn't she know these risks all along?

"I don't think even you understand all I've been through to get to this point."

Mala looked to her half brother with hurt eyes. His words had wounded her.

"How could you say that? How could you say I don't know? Elsa was not my wife, and she did not carry my child in her belly, but she was my sister and *I'll* never have a child; you know I am barren, whether by the plan of Koth or by the poison of Wizards' magic."

Tears began to well in her eyes as she continued.

"When *we* lost Elsa, I lost my best friend and the only chance I would ever have at anything like a child of my own. *How can you say I don't know?*"

Artorus looked down. "I didn't mean Elsa. I know you share that pain." He looked back up to his half sister. "I meant my father."

"Yes, Artorus," she said quickly, now somewhat cold, "your father is dead." Mala's words cut like a blade. Tears were now streaming from her eyes, running over the fresh scar on her cheek. "So is mine. Countless fathers have died in the Planewars – *countless*. It is natural to mourn for your father, but what makes your pain different from mine or Braïun's or Ormond's or *anyone's*?"

Artorus could not contain his anger any longer. For all her compassion, his own sister could not understand his pain.

"You weren't there. You weren't even born yet. You didn't see how our mother changed when my father died. She vowed never to love another when she married Horus Vallon – *never*."

"So, what would you have, Artorus?" Mala's voice was sharp.

Their conversation was now drawing the attention of the many soldiers and other staff who moved about, trying to ignore them.

"Would you that I had never been born!?" she shouted.

"No, Mala!" Artorus raised his voice in return. "You know that's not what I meant! I just couldn't bear it, all those long years with a man who married our mother just *months* after Horus died. How could she? It's as though my father – the man she *swore* to love – was nothing, just another nameless casualty of the Planewars!"

Mala suddenly looked down. She wiped the tears from her face. More softly now, she continued.

"Do you want to know why our mother married my father?" Her voice became almost distant. "She told me once. She was sitting by the hearth; I asked her why she was sad... I think she had partaken in some of my father's drink...

"It was not out of love that she married my father. She spoke it truly, if not by those words. I was not born from romance like you. I was simply a byproduct of a false marriage."

She looked back up to her half brother, now more tears in her eyes, voice stronger.

"The only reason she married Thorton Andrius was in desperate hope that they would not take you from her, that *you* would not become just another casualty of war. She did it for you."

Artorus stood shocked at what his sister was telling him; he shook his head slightly, but he could summon no words.

Everything changed in a single moment.

Is it true? he thought, his head aflame with memories. Memories of all the terrible ways he treated his mother in his youth after she remarried; they were flashing through his mind, his vision nearly spinning. *Is that why?*

Mala went on, "Our mother loved you *so* much; she couldn't bear the thought of Lord Brakken's armies coming for you too. The only chance was if she were *noble*. The noble boys don't get taken for the armies, Artorus. Her ploy failed and all she got from it was me – a consolatory reward for the loss of her beloved son."

Artorus was finding it hard to breathe. He looked upon his poor sister, standing in tears, in the shame of the knowledge she held in secret for so many years. There she stood, having finally borne all.

His mind raced. *How could I have been so concerned with myself, when my sister only gave of herself again and again, only loved me unconditionally? All those years by my side. How could I have been so* blind?

There was a long silence as Artorus stood dumbly and Mala cried softly in the late morning. Activity in the woods had halted around the siblings, and no disturbance came from the people nearby. It seemed as though even the chirping of the birds had ceased. The quiet was pierced only by Mala's weeping.

Slowly, Artorus took his sister into his arms.

"I'm sorry, Mala."

She sobbed openly now in his arms, wrapping hers around him as well.

"I'm so sorry... You are right; you're always right. My mother always loved me, and she never stopped loving my father."

His voice wavered with the words, but he could see it all clearly now.

"But there is *one* thing you are wrong about; Balia Andrius loved you dearly. And maybe she didn't love your father as you say, but since the news returned that my father had been slain, there was nothing – *nothing* in the twenty-seven worlds – that brought light to her eyes... until you were born, Mala..."

The two embraced for some time in the middle of the camp.

Artorus couldn't tell if it was a moment or an hour that they stood there, embracing one another. His thoughts, which had been racing all about, finally returned to what Mala had come here to say in the first place.

He finally broke the embrace and held his sister at arm's length, so that he could look her in the eye.

"So, if the Sage thinks it cannot be done," Artorus continued with resolve, "then maybe the Sages don't know *everything*... We will prove him wrong; we will win." He breathed deeply of the cool air. "If the men think it cannot be done, we shall have to *show* them."

The chirping of the birds returned to Artorus's ears, and the various staff slowly began to return to their tasks.

Gnarrl wrenched the neck of the rabbit, snapping it. The pitiful creature let out the tiniest of squeals. A death throe to end a meaningless life. There was apparently some small commotion in the enemy encampment, so none had taken notice of him and his prey in the bushes, not far from the command tent, as he fed his starved stomach.

He bit into the creature's side, his fangs piercing deeply into the flesh. He drank the blood first, so as not to waste it, and then ate the creature, small bones and all – no fire to cook it, nor seasoning to sweeten it.

His armor was blood-soaked, his daggers unclean, and his cloak saturated and heavy, but none of that mattered to him. He hadn't even cleaned or dressed the wounds from the village; he simply let them fester – all the better to remind him of his failure.

In the thicket of the woods, he could hide easily, despite his injuries. He had seen something in these past weeks: the human wench that he was trying to kill before was not the only leader of this rebellion. She would have to die too, but in fact, this man – this "Artorus Vallon" that was previously regarded so highly by the Wizard-King – was the very man that wished to undo him.

Gnarrl had seen thousands upon thousands of Brakken's soldiers commit to this man. This rebellion was not whispers in the dark corners of taverns, it was armies marching in broad daylight. How could these foolish mortals be so indignant? They acted against the very Wizard-King who trained them and fed them and equipped them.

Gnarrl could not return to Brakken – not unless he held the bloodied heart of this General Vallon in his hands. His failure was complete; he'd failed to kill his target and failed to stop this rebellion from forming. He could not return unless his failure was reversed – unless his success was complete.

He would taste the blood of Vallon, of Lady Andrius, and of every general that opposed the Wizard-King, and he would regain his worth to his master.

But there were too many in this encampment. Their patrols were tight.

In fact, the High Justicar had been shadowing the rebellious criminals throughout the many long weeks in travel, waiting for a moment to strike. He grinned at the thought that hundreds of thousands of troops could not detect him traveling alongside them.

Truly, he could strike at any moment. It was not that Gnarrl in any way doubted his ability to kill – rage and hunger fueled his muscles far better than good food or easy travel; his blades cut all the better dulled by rust and grime. Gnarrl knew he could kill one or two of his targets easily. All the guards in the world could not stop the determined half-orc from that. But he would almost certainly be overtaken in such a brazen assault. He needed for all his targets to be relatively close, and he needed something that could cause a distraction for him.

The generals of these other two armies would need to die as well, and Gnarrl had nearly decided to strike out as they had held a meeting moments ago. But Gnarrl found himself desiring the blood of the Lady Andrius perhaps most of all. He would not settle without her death at his hands.

The Sage, though, would be trouble. Gnarrl still didn't know quite what to make of it. And he remembered that scrawny elf with the burned ear; he was a servant to Brakken years ago. What secrets had the two of them already given these criminals? They too would have to die under his blades.

So, Gnarrl waited patiently and continued to stalk his prey from the shadowed woods. Only time separated the throats of his targets from his long daggers... only time...

Some sort of distraction, or some news that would gather all the leaders together at once would come, and then Gnarrl would have his payment in flesh. It may take some time.

A commotion caught Gnarrl's ear as he listened to the camp quieting for the evening.

"They are here!" yelled a scout as he ran into the camp. "Lord Vallon, they are here! The Imperial Legions march onto the plain this evening!"

Gnarrl grinned wickedly.

The time may not be so far off, after all.

Part Two End

Part Three:

<u>All Eternity, Unraveled in Time</u>

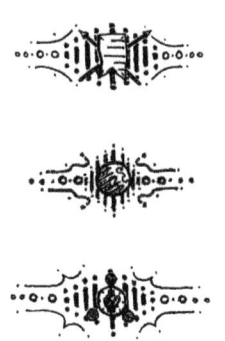

Chapter XIX – The Battle of the Lakewoods (pt. I)

"Still no word from any of the kings?" Artorus asked.

"None, Lord General," High Commander Braïun responded.

They both looked out over the vast plain, just being lit by dawn. Assembled before them were hundreds of thousands of men. They stretched well beyond what scenery the creeping light of dawn revealed. Only about one third of the Fifth Planar Army was assembled for battle – about thirty thousand men. The mainstay of their forces were the impressive ranks of the Thirty-Third Homeworld Army – more than one hundred thousand men under Magron. The Second Planar Army would also support a large portion of the fighting – at least seventy-five thousand men under General Warin.

But off in the darkness, through the morning mists coming off the mighty lakes at either side, somewhere between the rebel army and the cliffs beyond the Lakewoods Plain, were between one hundred fifty thousand and two hundred thousand men of some of the Wizard-King's elite Imperial Legions, augmented by likely an entire Homeworld Army.

Artorus had underestimated the Imperial Legions; he truly did not expect them to be able to muster such numbers in this time, especially given the numbers of theirs that were already dispersed throughout The Vastness, engaged in the skirmishes as planned. But Artorus had faced worse odds.

As the reports of their movements had come in, and as these armies amassed on the fields over the Lakewoods Plain, Artorus could only wait for them to engage. One army turned to many. His task was always going to be difficult, though. If all went according to plan, the greater the force Brakken chose to field here, the greater his shame would be in defeat.

"Well, I think that our resounding success afield will inspire more of a reaction." Artorus continued, "But, until then, I guess it's just us, friend."

He smiled to his high commander, who nodded in return. Braïun's hair and beard were back to their immaculate state and his demeanor had improved some, but his eyes still held pain – vast pain. Artorus knew that pain. It would not be gone anytime soon. Perhaps never.

"I could want no other beside me," the dwarf replied. He paused and then turned to his general. "You know that I mean that, don't you sir? It's not just politeness."

Artorus grinned and nodded to his dwarven friend.

"I do know, Braïun – you couldn't be saying it in hopes of another promotion; two in one month is just unheard of." His grin turned to a smile. "And I hope you know the feeling's mutual, my friend."

A soldier raced up the sloping hill on horseback, calling to the lord general in the early morning mist. "They wish to parley with the generals! They call for a parley!"

Both officers shared a glance. Parley could provide an invaluable opportunity, or it could prove an unimaginable catastrophe.

High Commander Braïun adjusted his beard somewhat nervously and stated the obvious. "It could very well be a trap, you know, sir."

"Yes," thought Artorus aloud, "but I can't help thinking it would be worth the risk..."

"What is worth walking into a trap, sir?"

"We are about to face Lord General Kremaine, friend," sighed Artorus. The scouts had long since identified each of the Imperial armies that drew down on the Lakewoods Plain. "I always prefer to see the face of my enemy before we clash armies, but I rarely have the opportunity.

You can learn a lot about the morale of an army, the constitution of their generals, and just how likely they are to make a mistake. The last parley I held was back on Learden. Remember when we first came to bear against Hemmet's Fourteenth Colonial? It was then and there I determined I'd break his flanks and push him into Harmony Valley for a decisive battle. So, we shall parley."

Artorus started off to gather his generals and turned back with a smile.

"Besides, we have to give them *a chance* to surrender."

Braïun only looked at his lord general with concern.

As reassuringly as he could smile at his high commander, in truth Artorus did think this trap could prove serious. But Kremaine had been his lord general for many years before Artorus became a lord general of his own sort. Even if the thought of facing him down as an equal now didn't drive Artorus's ambitious idea; it was undeniable that he owed every last opportunity he could muster to his men – and even to those of the Imperial armies – to let discussion replace bloodshed. Kremaine was a brilliant strategist and a ruthless general. He would not be surrendering to the rebels. But could they find *some* common ground? *Some* way to mitigate the coming bloodshed? What sort of new empire would he be forging if he didn't at least try for the sake of these mortals?

The sun rose, with time, but it was slow to burn off the mists from the plain. Artorus, the generals Magron and Warin, and a select guard rode slowly across the grasses through the swirling mist. Though not very thick, the remaining mists did obscure their enemy some, making the Imperial Legions seem to stretch on forever in the caliginous terrain. It was an unsettling effect.

A group of riders could be seen approaching. Artorus took a deep breath.

This is it, he thought, *it is time to face my enemy.*

All of the riders knew this could be a very deadly trap, and nerves were thin.

"I still say we kill them now," Magron grumbled from behind General Vallon.

Artorus was rather certain he was joking, since, despite his brashness, Magron did seem a man of honor. Either way, he didn't respond to the comment. Warin did a fine job of generally ignoring the larger man's posturing as well, as he rode quietly beside him peering thoughtfully into the mists.

Ahead, seven forms became clear, all riding very mighty steeds that trotted heavily in the dew-moistened earth. Slowly they became recognizable, and though he was familiar with the heraldry and banners of all, Artorus saw two faces he knew personally.

Once, some years back, at a council of generals convened to discuss the tactics of the villainous Kaladrius and his many armies, Artorus met a man – a particularly ruthless man – by the name of Victor Vayan. He was a dwarf with incorrigible loyalty to the Wizard-King – a bloodhound, of sorts, that specialized in stamping out activity perceived to be counterproductive to the war effort against Kaladrius. He'd found the man unsettling then, and he found him unsettling now that he faced him once more.

Victor Vayan rode a blackish steed of a height and build befitting a dwarf. His armor had been polished meticulously and his black hair and beard were knotted into perfect braids that hung about his square face.

The other face Artorus knew was the Lord General Gorrand Kremaine, an older human with a slim, leanly muscular build. He had a short-cut beard and combed-back hair, each turning from black to gray. He wore the fine armor and equipment of a lord general, which the blazons and decorations that clung to his excellent armor confirmed. Artorus was never too skilled at hippology, but he guessed Kremaine's steed was some variety of Linium.

For as long as Artorus had been a general, his direct superior was a uniquely uncaring man, devoted only to the victory of his Wizard-King over his rivals. Artorus supposed he shouldn't have been surprised to find out his old superior was the one to come here, and yet he'd hoped not to have to face him – at least not so soon in the conflict. Kremaine was promoted primarily because of his superior tactics in warfare. From what Artorus had witnessed, the lord general was easily worth any two other generals on the field this morning.

Artorus swallowed his discomfort. He had agreed to this parley so they could talk. This might prove one of the more important discussions of Artorus's life. Now was no time to get shaken.

The two groups of men stopped in front of one another in the cool morning as the sun continued its struggle to burn away the mist, grass reaching the knees of most of the steeds, though just touching the girth of Vayan's dwarf-sized mount.

Artorus stopped slightly in front his two generals.

"I am Artorus Vallon of the Fifth Planar Army and Lord General of the Rebellion against Brakken, the War Maker."

Kremaine scoffed at Artorus's title and seemed to have some words to interject, but Magron quickly followed Artorus in a booming voice. "General Loren Magron of the Thirty-Third Homeworld Army," he barked.

Warin added in short order, "The General Leon Warin of the Second Planar Army."

Chuckling some under his breath, Kremaine rode slightly forward from between Vayan and the other general that flanked him. "My, how far we've come, Vallon... a lord general now?"

Kremaine shook his head. He never had much liked Artorus, as far as Artorus could tell. He never had much liked anyone Artorus was aware of.

"Somehow," he went on, "I'm not quite as surprised as I ought to be; you always were a strange one." He turned to Warin. "But my own mentor? This is a saddening sight... I'd had truly hoped there was some misunderstanding."

He sighed, but straightened his shoulders and continued, now with at least some sense of propriety. "But if we pretend at some official capacity here, Vallon, then I am the Lord General Gorrand Kremaine of the Planar Armies, servant of *your* immortal Wizard-King, the mighty Lord Brakken."

His dark eyes glared at Artorus – sharp, unyielding.

Vayan, garbed in the distinct colors of the Imperial Legions, adjusting the long saber at his hip, spoke. "I am General Victor Vayan of the Ninth Imperial Legion."

The last general beside Kremaine, clearly marked of the Homeworld Armies, spoke. "I am General Marcus Ethos of the Thirtieth Homeworld Army."

Ethos seemed to have locked eyes with Magron, who then spat upon the ground beside his horse. Artorus would be interested to know the history these two shared.

Kremaine scanned the three generals before him, stopping on Vallon once more. "Why do you keep up this charade, Vallon?"

Artorus simply straightened his back and held his former lord general's eyes, not dignifying him with a response.

Kremaine shook his head once more. "I've been told to allow Vayan here to deliver Lord Brakken's terms."

Kremaine motioned to the imperial general, who rode slightly forward to come beside Kremaine again, and he unfurled a small scroll.

"The immortal Wizard-King, mighty Lord Brakken," he began in his curt manner of speaking, "has informed me to decree that, should you stand down and beg forgiveness for your brazen and foolish actions thus far…" he paused, obviously finding even his own words unbelievable, "then the mighty Lord Brakken *may* end your lives quickly, *he may* spare your families, and may even spare some of your men from the justice they, by all rights, deserve. However, if you should continue this pretense and insult his lordship, the Wizard-King, further by combat against his loyal men, you will never again be offered this mercy. It is so decreed."

The general of the Imperial Legion looked expectantly to the three rebellious generals before him. Artorus heard as a couple of his guards shuffled a bit in their saddles and one of the horses twitched reflexively. Indeed, all of the sounds and sights and smells of the moment flooded into his senses.

This is the moment, Artorus thought with singular clarity.

"Good generals," he started, "my fight is not so much with you – or even the Wizard that pretends to rule you – as it is with all of Wizard-kind." Artorus's horse trotted lightly in place. "You see, I find you each to be as much or more a victim as myself or any of my men, and we would welcome you to our cause if you chose to free yourselves."

Kremaine scoffed again, but Artorus went on. "We foolish few, we who are called 'general,' we think ourselves somehow privileged to serve the Wizard-Kings mightily in their endless war." He moved his mount a few steps to stop directly in front of Kremaine. "But war is only death, *nothing* more. We are but lords of death, serving the whims of these madmen that fight evermore for their own power."

Turning to Vayan, voice raised, he went on. "You tell your Wizard-King that *we* will accept *his* surrender, grant *him* leniency if he *begs* all mortals for forgiveness! If he apologizes to *every* fatherless child and widowed wife! Then we *may* let him live in shame rather than be destroyed in justice."

Kremaine continued shaking his head, laughing under his breath. "Vallon, you *are* mad. The Wizard-Kings are the most powerful beings the multiverse has ever known; it is only right that they rule – this is the way of things. Besides, even if you *wish* to change it, they are *immortal*."

Magron spoke up from beside Artorus. "We shall test that thought, Kremaine, by driving our swords through him. If it takes a thousand hacks of a thousand axes or ten thousand thrusts of ten thousand spears, we *will* kill that godsbedamned beast!"

"The fool speaks!" shouted General Ethos. "You always were brash, Magron, but this is insane. This pathetic power grab of yours will not end with anything other than your death!"

"Gentlemen," Kremaine interjected forcefully, "we did not march hundreds of thousands of soldiers here to share insults." His tone became darker as he continued. "I offer you one last chance to see reason before we crush you... Warin, at least you can see this madness for what it is."

The elderly general raised his head and met the gaze of the lord general. "No, it is not madness to open one's eyes to the way of things.

For all our lives we have fought for these Wizards, killed countless of our own kind. If Artorus Vallon is the only one willing to stop it, then I will choose to open my eyes and follow him, to victory or to death." His voice became softer. "Young Gorrand, did I not teach you of compassion for those that follow you? Of intellect over might, of the heart being the general's greatest tool?"

Kremaine's eyes now flared with hatred as he growled to the elder man. "I've surpassed your teachings long ago, old man. I'll have your heart on a platter."

"If it is to be battle, Kremaine," Artorus attempted, "then shall we agree to standard rules of warfare?"

"No." Kremaine's words dripped with poison. "Lord Brakken has told me that no quarter is to be given. Not one soul of your rebellious lot will leave this battlefield alive if I have any say. If you withdraw, I shall pursue. If you surrender, you will be executed summarily. In truth, I plan to skewer you upon my very own lance, Vallon."

Kremaine did not flinch as he stared directly at Artorus and spoke his hateful words.

While he could hardly claim to be surprised at the results of this conversation, Artorus had indeed learned a thing or two about what to expect in the coming fighting.

He did not honor Kremaine's disdain with a response. Artorus turned his steed about, away from his enemies, but he did not ride away just yet. He spoke over his shoulder.

"Then if you all wish to remain pawns of your Wizard-King, it is clear mere words will not dissuade you from this fight nor garner you any clemency from our wrath. Come gentlemen: let us fight one more battle against our brethren, that we may someday show others the light of reason."

Magron, Warin, and the guards all spun their mounts around, and they steadily trotted back toward their armies, now fully assembled on the field. The mist had burned away, and the bright spring sun shone down upon the place that would soon be littered with death.

Two of the guards, keeping their eyes behind them, suddenly shouted.

"It is as we feared!" one shouted.

"Arrows! *Ride*, Generals!" called the other, and all the men broke into a gallop.

Artorus glanced behind him to see Kremaine grinning at him, not turning away, as from behind them hundreds of arrows had been nocked. In a moment they launched and came soaring through the sky toward the rebels.

I knew we were too close to their ranks, Artorus thought in anger as the riders spurred their horses to a full gallop, desperately racing away from the coming hail of death.

It was only a moment before the arrows began to land, the telltale whistles and snapping sounds of arrows meeting with earth, armor, and flesh. Two arrows planted themselves into the back of the guard nearest Artorus, felling him; he felt one smack into his horse's hindquarters. He heard more grunts from those around him as arrows found their flesh.

The horses ran fast, and they were nearing their armies, hopefully out of range of those archers. Artorus turned to Magron and saw an arrow jutting from his back.

"Magron!" he shouted over the rush of the wind and the thunderous galloping.

"I'm fine, Vallon!" the general shouted before Artorus could say more.

Shaking his head, Artorus called out to him. "Order the men into lines, archers return fire. But remember, we will make them come to us!" Artorus could hear more arrows landing in the earth behind them as they rode. Magron nodded and broke off with his two remaining guards to make for the command of the Thirty-Third.

Looking over to Warin, he called, "Same orders!"

Warin nodded as well and broke off for his own army with his one remaining guard, bearing arrows in his mount and his flesh.

Artorus looked around and noticed that all of his guards were gone, only two horses still running beside him.

Gods bedamned! he thought. *Kremaine will pay for that.*

He rode onward to his lieutenants, not slowing his pace. He saw High Commander Braïun first.

"Braïun!" he shouted, finally slowing his steed as the dwarf nodded to him. "Form defensive lines in front, ready archers and catapults!"

"Of course, sir," the dwarf hollered back as Artorus began to ride onward. "And I told you so!" he added without levity.

Artorus couldn't stop shaking his head. This was not going according to plan. He rode on to find his lieutenants.

Men rushed about to form lines. Hundreds of thousands of them followed Artorus's command, unknown numbers likely to die in the upcoming battle. Archers were rushed to the front, and the armies under Kremaine did just as Artorus expected, marching forward to the attack.

He is overconfident, Artorus thought, *he is eager to please his Wizard-King, and he sees only the numbers we show him.*

The Imperial Legions and Thirtieth Homeworld Army rushed together, infantry in full attack, with cavalry moving to flank on either side.

"Give those infantry a couple volleys," Artorus shouted to the commander of his archers, "but if that cavalry gets in range, you give them hell!"

He turned to runners on either side, perhaps a dozen of them assembled – as was the practice for such large-scale battles involving so many armies.

"Same orders to the others!"

Two of the runners darted away.

Artorus had commanded his army of just under one hundred thousand for years now. It was a dizzying thought if one let so many men with so many families and so many fragile lives into one's mind all at once. This force was greater than any he'd commanded before, and he foresaw a possible need to call upon many more thousands of Orrogen's forces to the northeast before this battle might end. As the enemies charged at them, Artorus thought it important to take a moment to think about the new magnitude of his responsibility.

After waves of arrows rained on the attackers, dropping some, the archers retreated behind the front, and the mighty surge of charging men crashed into the steadfast lines.

Swords cut flesh, spears pierced armor, and shields beat back bodies. This carnage, Artorus had seen before, but somehow it was all different now. These men in front of him were not fighting for a Wizard's power; they were fighting for *their freedom*.

Despite that, bones were crushed, axes hewed limbs, and armor splintered in the steadily rising sun. The blood began to stain the high grasses red.

High Commander Braïun shouted orders as the waves of attackers surged against his lines like the sea in a storm. A wayward arrow flew just passed his head, causing him to duck reflexively.

"Archers, keep firing so long as you have a shot!" he shouted back to the lines of bowmen behind him who were steadily exhausting their supply of arrows, loosing them into the attacking droves.

Arrows never were Braïun's preferred mode of combat, though he understood their necessity. Without arrows to harry the forces into assault, the defensive lines could be ignored or outmaneuvered. Without arrows to bleed their enemies, the forces charging them would have the full might and momentum of the charge. But arrows were not noble. If a soldier must kill a man, Braïun always thought, he should kill him straight to his face. Swords, axes, hammers – these were the weapons of a true soldier.

And if an assassin wants a rebel dead, he should face him, not kill defenseless children out of cowardice and malice.

My children... thought Braïun. *My wife...* He shook his head. *I can't do this now.*

He shoved his braided beard back into its spot in his belt and adjusted the sword still in its scabbard at his hip.

Braïun spotted an enemy captain, bearing the uniform of the Imperial Legions and the long saber of their officers. He was probably a hundred fifty feet ahead of the high commander, charging atop his horse, spurring the beast and the men below him toward the defensive lines that still held fast against their assault.

With a powerful shout from the imperial captain, which spread quickly through his men, the surge pressed forward with renewed vigor. Slowly the lines wavered under the force of their attackers, then shook, and then broke. Many were trampled as dozens more were simply forced to fall back. The attacking legion spilled through like a raging river.

"Reserves! To me!" Braïun called as he tore his short sword from its sheath.

He quickly made for the many dozens of attackers that were pushing, slashing, and trampling the men of the Fifth Planar Army.

The dwarf, dressed in his usual fitted uniform, with highly polished armor over it, could not run at full speed. The armor weighed him down. His leg was still sore, but his many days of practicing on it since his recovery held fast. He ran at the front of his counter charge, as dozens of his own men fell in behind him.

Braïun thought of his family again.

The first soldier Braïun met with a high block as a sword came down toward his head; two blades clashed loudly. Planting on his good leg, Braïun kicked high to catch the man squarely in his stomach. The man crumpled at the force of the blow, and Braïun quickly sidestepped and brought his sword down onto the back of his neck, beneath the helmet line.

The man fell to the trodden earth. Two more charging soldiers quickly closed on the high commander, only to be met by two soldiers of the Fifth.

The men fought one another fiercely as the surging attackers were met with all the might of the reserves that had been waiting for just such a moment. The Fifth Planar Army was a proud group of men – loyal, honest, and mighty. Braïun was honored to be a part of such an army.

The high commander fought on, quickly felling two more soldiers in the deepest part of the melee. Two things worked to Braïun's advantage: his low center of gravity allowed him to move through the fray more freely than his taller compatriots, and thirty years' fighting gave him the experience he needed to stay alive.

Braïun caught sight of the mounted captain approaching through the massive throngs of embattled men.

Braïun scanned around for a pole arm, but found none. The captain had caught sight of him as well and now spurred his bleeding horse forward through the fighting men, hacking with his long saber as he went. He was most likely a full-blooded human, but his beard was longer and more tangled than some dwarves'. The man had a certain disdain in his eyes as he looked down upon the high commander; Braïun knew it was more than a simple animosity that comes with doing battle. This man thought he was truly better than Braïun, that the rebellion was a simple disease to be eradicated from The Vastness and purged with all the other infectious bile.

Was there no room in battle for respect between enemies? It seemed not.

As the distance between them closed, each officer slew another combatant that stood in their way. Braïun now bore several flesh wounds and his leg seared with an aching pain, but his determination was had not wavered. He would have to take care of that mount if he were to avoid becoming just another corpse beneath the feet of this captain. The poor horse was badly wounded already; it was time to put the beast out of its pain.

As the mount was just reaching him, Braïun stepped quickly to his right, onto his good leg, successfully getting the captain to rear his horse around leftward to allow for a clear strike. Springing off his good leg he dashed back to be in front of the mount and he slashed with his sword: once to cause the beast to rear back slightly and then again and catch the horse low in the throat with his steel. With a horrible noise and a short, silent apology from Braïun, the mighty steed reared and fell atop two corpses already lying in the reddened grass.

It was at this point, however, that Braïun realized he had not fully dodged the captain's long saber, as his right shoulder was now bleeding rather heavily from under the shoulder guard.

The imperial captain's reflexes were proven superior yet again as he launched himself well enough away from his tumbling steed to avoid having a leg pinned beneath the large beast. He rolled to the ground, somehow avoiding impalement on that long saber as well, and regained his stance.

Well, I guess I accomplished my goal, thought Braïun as the captain now crouched into an attack stance. *That long blade is going to be a problem though.*

He tightened his grip on his short sword. All around them, men were still fighting, but as was sometimes the case in such battles, they gave some berth to the dueling officers.

The captain pounced toward Braïun swinging his large blade from his right. Braïun blocked hard, hoping to throw his attacker off, but instead lost his footing, slipping on something – he didn't care to know what – in the slickened grass. Braïun stumbled back, barely blocking another strike from the same side, before he regained his footing to block yet one more.

The captain was swinging hard.

He'll tire soon, thought Braïun, *no matter how much he trains with that sword.*

Braïun continued to block the harsh swings of the captain's sword, attempting to deflect or dodge when he could to allow his opponent to wear himself down. Where a heavy blade and mighty swings were a deadly combination from a moving horse, now that he was on the ground, it only allowed Braïun a better opportunity to evade the attacks and tire out his opponent.

But apparently, Braïun did not have the luxury of time. All around, the attacking armies were surging further and further, pushing back whatever men remained from the lines along with the reserves that had come to bolster them.

And then the captain's blade barely caught Braïun's left forearm. It was not a debilitating wound, but with his right shoulder already weakening severely, it could very well cost him this fight.

No time! Braïun's mind seemed to shout.

His thoughts once again returned to his family.

Braïun took an opportunity between hefty swings to launch himself at the captain. He connected with a solid left shoulder into the man's torso. The imperial captain knew that these close quarters made his sword useless and he dropped it, instead punching Braïun hard in his face.

The blow disoriented Braïun only just enough. The battlefield was spinning around him as Braïun tried desperately to keep his guard up. Many images swam around the high commander in the fray, but he thought he could make out his enemy clearly enough. He reared back for a thrust of his sword.

Then it got even worse.

Braïun felt the undeniable pain of a dagger in his side. The imperial captain had stabbed him just behind his chest plate.

But the sharp and sudden pain cleared Braïun's senses. Though Braïun's breath escaped him, he could see his enemy quite clearly now.

Not wasting his opportunity and shouting with the last of the air in his chest, Braïun shoved his sword directly into the other man's neck, just above the armor.

The captain stared hatefully into Braïun's eyes for a moment and then fell lifeless to the ground as the dwarf ripped his sword free. Braïun noticed that his men were watching.

Raising his bloodied blade once more, Braïun found his breath as quickly as his punctured torso would allow. He roared with all the fury that a dwarf could and called for a renewed charge from his reserves.

The spectacle seemed to have its desired effect, and the reserves pushed mightily against the now leaderless attackers. Once more like a churning tide, the attackers were now pressed in on each other, as the defenders would not be trampled so easily, and the waves now rolled back into the sea.

This rebellion had spirit, indeed. Within a short time, the attackers were rebuffed, and the lines were reformed. Braïun still had a dagger protruding from his side and he bled heavily from his right shoulder, but he would not dare let his soldiers take him from the combat on the precipice of the day's victory. Men fought bravely all around him.

Shortly after, however, he found he had little choice in the matter. His knees weakened and he collapsed from the loss of blood. His men had their way after all and brought their officer to the medics at the rear of their formations, where hundreds of other wounded were being gathered.

Artorus watched as arrows flew forth over the tens of thousands of fighting men to land upon the enemy's rearward ranks and their quickly maneuvering cavalry at the edges of their formations.

No sight inspired more awe, terror, and sorrow than the sight of hundreds of thousands of men pitted against one another to slay or be slain. Nowhere in the multiverse could one find the hatred, the desperation, or the sheer wrath that is found on the field of battle.

Though the attackers punched through their lines at several points, they were being beaten back each time. The enemy had lost their momentum.

"Lieutenant Hakan!" Artorus shouted to the large soldier not far to his left. "Spread the word: we push back!"

Hakan grinned wide, showing his sharp teeth, and then nodded to his general. Runners were sent once more in each direction along the massive lines of the three armies.

Time for my horse, thought Artorus.

For many minutes now, Mala had watched as horribly wounded men missing hands, limbs, or eyes – maimed in the name of this rebellion she and her brother had started – came past her to the hospital tents behind the lines, protected only by the beginning of the trees of the Lakewoods.

For countless hours, Mala had listened to her brother describe the strategies of warfare and the tales of battle and conquest. Now, standing on the gentle slope up to the vast woods between the lakes, overlooking a large plain filled with dying men, she understood why Artorus had always skipped over the details like this. There was not so much glory in battle as there was in the tales of it. The truth of the vision she now witnessed was unyielding.

Horns began to sound over the large plain and battle drums followed. With great cries, entire regiments of the rebel armies began to move forward, crashing into the surge of attacking men with frightening strength.

Through the masses of men, Mala could barely see the personal banners of Artorus as he moved to lead the counterattack. She'd been keeping careful track of her brother. Once she spotted the banners, she could even make out his form now that he had mounted. The harshness of seeing with her own two eyes as Artorus waded into battle was unexpectedly intense; her muscles tightened and she could not turn away.

Her hand moved to the hilt of her sword, which she had worn despite Typhondrius's best protestations that she wouldn't need it. She had her armor on too. She was not some handmaiden to be kept from the fighting; not now, when it might mean the difference between success or failure for this rebellion.

As though her thoughts were written on her face, Typhondrius, standing next to her, spoke somewhat hastily. "My lady, your brother knows what he's doing."

Mala looked to the elf, slightly surprised at his intuition.

He held Mala's eyes for a moment. His face betrayed concern. "This," he urged, "is not the first time he has led his men in a valiant charge, nor will it be the last."

"Noble Typhondrius," Mala replied, "I know you mean to protect me – and truly, I appreciate it. You are a good friend." She looked out to the raging battle once more. "But this rebellion is as much mine as it is my brother's. I cannot resign myself to hide behind noble ideals and lofty goals forever. Sooner or later, I must face the harsh truth of what we're doing."

"Yes, my lady, of course. It's just... I do wish there were a way for you to face it that didn't involve lots of angry, muscled men pointing weapons at you."

She smiled at him.

"Besides, if I'm not mistaken," he added halfheartedly, "Master Artorus directed you to stay back here."

Mala gave Typhondrius a look of mock disdain. "And since when, good friend, have I followed orders from the lord general? I am no soldier of the Fifth Planar."

Typhondrius smiled and placed a hand on Mala's shoulder. "Please just be safe, my lady."

Mala kissed Typhondrius on the cheek, but left to find her horse before she could notice his pale complexion turn a bright shade of red.

Mala latched her sword to her side, donned a helm, grabbed a spear from a nearby page, and rode off down the slope toward the massive fray at a quickened pace.

Racing forward toward the dangerous melee, Mala scanned to find Artorus once more, but she had lost track of him. Soldiers pressed the counterattack from all sides. The cavalry of the Thirty-Third Homeworld Army and the Second Planar could be seen in the distance on either side, engaging the enemy riders to avoid their countercharge getting flanked.

Mala drove on through the rushing soldiers to the center of the counterattack, spear held tightly in her hand. An arrow flew just past her left arm and the danger of the situation, if ever there were a doubt, was now solidified in her mind. Mala had no intention of being skewered by arrows or blades or anything else in this battle.

Mala did wear armor, but it was lighter than the typical field plate of some riders – only chain link with some mail and a breastplate protected her flesh from the countless weapons before her. She was glad she'd had the helm put aside for her.

She quickly came upon the thick of the fighting and called out to the soldiers. "Press onward!"

She pointed the spear into the air above the men and spurred her horse forward.

"For victory! For freedom from this endless war!" she called as loudly as she could manage over the deafening sounds of fighting.

Men shouted a battle cry and fell in behind her and she formed a spearhead. Mala could feel blood rushing to her head and her lungs pumped to keep up with the adrenaline now coursing through her. No fireside story of warfare could ever describe this. It was truly exhilarating.

Then another stray arrow soared directly toward her. She felt as if in slow motion, and she tried to get out of the way, but it struck her left leg, just past where the chain shirt ended.

Biting pain slammed into her, a spasm gripped her leg under the immense pressure of the wound, and her breath left her. Mala had been bruised, she'd even been beaten rather badly in sparring matches, but she had never felt a pain like this in her life. She tried to ignore the pain as she drove her horse onward, but it was not possible.

Then she saw a soldier of the rebellion hacked down by an imperial soldier. All of a sudden, the pain was gone, replaced by passion. She snapped the shaft of the arrow off with a grunt and charged.

The soldiers of the rebellion parted at the thundering of her horse's hooves and the ringing of her battle cry. The imperial soldier she rode for was quickly reached, and though he attempted to parry her spear with his sword, the force of her mounted charge was too great and he caught the weapon in his right shoulder and fell. She had to clench the spear desperately to avoid it ripping from her grip.

Two more arrows whizzed past Mala.

I'm too great a target on this horse, she thought, and she hurriedly dismounted and sent the horse back as the men from behind her swelled forward to press the attack.

It was painful, but with a heavy limp Mala could still walk on her injured leg. The arrow hit true, splitting open the heavy leather pants which were intended to help deflect such attacks, but they did lessen the impact. Mala now gripped her spear in both hands as she waded into the combat.

At that moment, a large, half-orcish-looking man burst through the soldiers in front of her with a bellowing roar. He was quite big, and in his right hand he gripped a bloodied axe, while his left bore a spiked shield. He charged her.

Instinctually, Mala only wanted to run; this was certainly the largest opponent she had ever faced. And, here she stood, bleeding from an arrow to her leg and facing down death. Was she completely insane to charge into battle like this? Did she really think all her years of fighting Artorus with sticks would prepare her for this?

Well, she thought as time slowed to her senses and her body rushed with energy, *this will be my test.*

She jabbed the spear directly toward his stomach, but his shield blocked it. Mala heard the wood crack, but the spear did not break. The force of her attack, however, was turned against her and she stumbled back a bit. The half-orc kept coming; she thrust the spear once more at the beast, hoping a quicker strike could get through his defense. It did not. The half-orc blocked once more and, just as quickly, swung his large axe around, snapping the spear.

Mala hastily dropped the broken shaft and drew her sword as quick as she could, but the large man was already attacking.

Just as he lunged for her, a soldier cried out and attacked from the half-orc's left side. This paused the hulk's attack long enough for him to swing a massive arm and impale the soldier on the twisted wooden spikes. The man screamed, but the half-orc had to shake the shield to remove the injured soldier from the spikes.

Mala had no time to think; she launched herself at the half-orc and drove her sword deep into his abdomen with a shout. A grunt and then a hiss escaped the half-orc as he dropped both the shield and the axe, Mala's long sword protruding out of his back.

This was a mortal wound. There was no doubting it.

Unless the shoulder strike earlier was more severe than she realized, Mala had never killed a man. She truly wasn't sure how to feel. Even in the heat of battle, it was shocking to have killed someone.

But as huge meaty hands grabbed Mala's neck, it became apparent that she still hadn't yet killed anyone, so the feeling could wait.

The half-orc growled in an unearthly voice, after glancing down to the sword impaling him. "You will die with me, woman..."

Massive hands crushed her neck. Mala had never felt a force so great in all her life, and the entire world seemed to fade into red as her vision blurred. The pain in her leg was completely forgotten, and she could feel her very spine straining under the strength of the man's gnarled hands.

Mala was certain she lost consciousness for at least a moment, but the next thing she saw, as the red faded and brought the world to her eyes again, was the sight of three soldiers hacking the half-orc to a gruesome heap right in front of her. Blood splattered onto her face in a sickening scene. For a moment, she wished her sight had not returned.

Battle still surged all around her. Mala didn't have the time to be shocked by the bloody spectacle, and so swallowed her disgust and grabbed her sword from the corpse as the men helped her up.

She continued to fight to regain her breath, coughing and wiping the splattered blood from her eyes. Unable to speak at the moment, she simply pointed her sword forward and continued moving as best she could. The soldiers got her message, and they pressed the counterattack still further.

Several moments passed and the melee became more spread out as the forces that were once on the assault were now beginning to steadily back away from the defenders. Mala limped and rubbed her throat, but she remained with the soldiers on the front.

More officers of the Fifth Planar Army led the charge on ahead as the imperials steadily withdrew. At first following the countercharge, Mala then noticed something that gave her pause.

Two men were crossing blades well behind where the fighting had now passed. It seemed like none of the other troops noticed, or perhaps for some reason they couldn't lend their ally help. She left the progressing forces and approached the lone soldier from the Fifth Planar to provide him assistance.

Each man appeared to have some elven blood as they exchanged blow after blow with two sabers. The opposing soldier wore the garb of an imperial sergeant, if Mala recalled correctly. They appeared to be evenly matched until Mala was able to reach them and take up a position beside the desperate Fifth Planar soldier.

Breathing heavily, the soldier beside her spoke to Mala. "You are the Lady Andrius?"

She nodded, still staring down the imperial sergeant.

"Please, my lady," her ally said from beneath his light helmet, "do not aid me in this fight."

She took her eyes off the other combatant, who was also gasping from their drawn-out duel, as he seemed to be waiting for this conversation to play out. She looked to the soldier in confusion.

"He is my cousin," he concluded, not breaking his gaze with the other man. "Only he or I can end this."

The words struck Mala with great force. *His cousin...* She looked from the dueling men to the battlefield around them. *What fate have we forced upon these men?*

The dead and dying were interspersed with still-fighting men.

How many have we pitted against each other this day? Mala thought morosely, *How many cousins and brothers and fathers and sons?*

Nodding solemnly to both men, she backed away from the fight on her bleeding leg, and they finished their fated duel.

The enemy sergeant, after some skillful, if tired, swordsmanship, finally landed a solid blow across the other man's chest, cutting through the leather armor and dropping him to the earth.

The victorious sergeant stared at Mala, breathing heavily, but he was done fighting for this day – indeed, most of the fighting had now subsided as the Imperial Legion and other loyalist forces withdrew back to their side of the great plain. The man nodded his thanks to her, still breathing heavily, looked back to his fallen cousin. With tears welling in his eyes, he turned and walked back to his withdrawing army. Soldiers of both sides parted to allow the wounded that were capable to return to their lines.

Mala's throat felt like it had been crushed by a boulder. Her leg was still bleeding somewhat steadily. She was pained, but by more than just her wounds.

Mala stood amongst the carnage. *War is death.* Her brother's words never held truth to her like they did in this moment. The scene was truly horrific.

Mala knew, logically, that this would be the road to their ultimate goal. The grisly imagery held more intensity than she ever could have guessed.

Artorus scanned the massive armies as he saw the Kremaine's forces withdrawing. The imperial cavalry raced back across the flat lands, and the soldiers made a steady, protected retreat.

This day is ours, he thought as he squinted into the high sun.

At least three hours of fighting had passed, Artorus guessed by the sun's height; there would be many dead.

Artorus ordered his forces to return and regroup, and then called a halt to the few archers that were still firing as he made his way back toward his command tent at the edge of the plain. He saw Hakan and Highblade meeting up from opposite sides of the field, and they noticed him as well.

"Lord General!" called Highblade, unscathed as usual. "We are victorious this day!"

"They run," added Hakan, bloodied from many wounds, as usual, "like animals back to their masters."

The Lord General of the Rebellion stood beside his lieutenants and turned back to watch as the medics and priests and other soldiers started the long and dismal process of removing the wounded and sorting the dead.

Artorus would head out to pay his respects to the dead shortly. Though now, there was something to celebrate, this was but the first movement in a much larger overture.

"This day is won, gentlemen," Artorus said to his lieutenants, "but this battle is far from over. I estimate Kremaine's casualties at six or seven thousand – maybe more – and I'd like to find out what ours are. But, in the larger strategy, he's underestimated us once; he's not likely to do so again."

Artorus called for another runner and requested a meeting of the generals.

"I'd like to call for support from Orrogen and his Seventeenth Planar anyway," he went on to his lieutenants as people went about either rushing wounded back or collecting weapons and arrows. "I think we will need their help before the end of this. If we can end this decisively, we should."

Hakan snorted. "I think we can finish them without help."

"Of course you do," Highblade retorted. "You think you can kill anything."

"I can kill *you*, little elf-man," Hakan grumbled, eliciting a laugh from the other lieutenant.

"All right, Lieutenants," Artorus interjected. "I think your army has use of you still before you start the witty banter or the killing each other."

As his lieutenants complied and headed away, still debating, a commander approached the lord general with the slightest look of concern on his face. The officer saluted.

"Speak, Commander," Artorus said to the man as he returned the salute. "Is it the casualty count?"

"Um, no sir. It is High Commander Braïun, sir." Seeing the look on his lord general's face, the commander was quick to add, "He's not dead, sir, but he is wounded fairly badly. He requested your presence when you can see him."

Artorus breathed a sigh of relief and nodded. He would pay his respects to the fallen and he would see his friend, but at this moment, he had a meeting to attend.

The three generals of the rebel armies met shortly later in Artorus's command tent.

"I see what you mean, Vallon," Magron said in his gruff voice, "but the counts are in and Kremaine has almost twice the casualties we have. Now is not the time to play this conservative; now is the time to press the attack."

The tent was bustling with various command staff shifting maps and double-checking numbers.

"You don't know Kremaine like we do, Magron," Artorus stated. "I promise you that this attack will not represent his tactics for this entire battle. He has tested us, perhaps even underestimated us, but now he knows just what he's dealing with."

"Agreed," stated Warin.

"All right, gods bedamned," Magron submitted, "I'll hold off on the full offensive until Orrogen's troops get here. I guess I don't see the harm another couple regiments would cause us... aside from a smaller cut of the spoils."

Magron grinned from his stubbled chin. It seemed the general would stop shaving before each battle. Artorus had heard that his hair grew so fast that he would leave some battles with a full beard.

The three generals nodded to one another and left the tent to tend to their own armies. Though the Fifth Planar Army represented, by far, the smallest fielded that day, since most of their number were still in reserve within the woods, being center of the defensive line meant they still suffered some significant casualties. The latest report had placed the number of wounded close to three thousand men, and the dead, very near one thousand.

One thousand brave souls who stood resolute when Artorus called them to the rebellion. One thousand mortals who he promised a better future...

But his time to pay his respects to the dead would have to wait still a little longer. Braïun had need of him. The other wounded would need his attention as well.

Artorus made his way for the hospital tents. Mangled and dismembered soldiers met their lord general with hopeful eyes. This was not just another battle they had fought; this was the first day of victory against an empire that had enslaved them their whole lives.

Yes, there was pain; yes there was death; but so too was there hope and dignity.

Artorus found the place that High Commander Braïun was propped in his bed. The high commander smiled slightly as Artorus approached, but he was clearly in pain. The dwarf, despite injuries all about his upper body, began to straighten his hair with his hands. Artorus could only chuckle.

At a glance, Artorus guessed that Braïun's dwarven sturdiness might well have saved his life this day.

"The men are talking," Artorus said to the dwarf. "They tell of how High Commander Slick was stopping to fix his hair in the middle of battle again."

Sheepishly, Braïun stopped fussing with his hair.

"Just after," Artorus added, "he saved the entire defensive line with a heroic charge of his reserves." Artorus held the officer's eyes. "Thank you, friend."

In his wounded and bedridden state, Braïun made a motion that was likely some version of a bow.

"It is my duty, Lord General," he replied with a polite smile.

It was good to see that, despite his injuries, the dwarf once more had a smile upon his face. But, no sooner did Artorus notice it than it faded.

"General Vallon," Braïun began, but then he paused. "Artorus..." he corrected himself, "I feel I owe you an apology."

Artorus furled his brow. "For what reason could you possibly owe me an apology, friend?"

"Your wife and unborn child," the dwarf said, but then hesitated.

Even after all these years, Artorus felt the familiar sharp pain at the mention of Elsa and their child. But he listened intently.

Braïun closed his eyes. "You lost them so long ago…" He began thoughtlessly to fix his tangled beard with shaking hands. "My family…" The dwarf choked back tears. "I lost my family, and I thought I had reason to dwell in sadness."

"But you did, Orgron," Artorus quickly stated to his high commander, he himself feeling choked up. "You do…"

"Perhaps," the dwarf replied, no longer fidgeting with his beard, "but I cannot let it affect my ability to serve this rebellion. We have to stop the Planewars and we have to fight against these monsters that work to destroy us." He looked to his lord general with tears still wetting his eyes. "To do otherwise is to insult the memory of *your* family. This pain I've been feeling is the exact same pain that you felt all these years; I know it now. And I don't think a hundred years would lessen this pain…

"And there you stand… You who have felt that pain all this time." Braïun shook his head. "But you don't dwell in that place; you're stronger than that. You fight through the pain. You fight on *despite* the pain."

The dwarf strained to sit up just a little straighter. "And so, to do anything otherwise is a slight to your Elsa's memory and my sweet family too."

Artorus flushed with emotions.

"So," Braïun concluded as he quickly rubbed the tears from his eyes, "please accept my apology for how I have acted… For your wife, for you, and for my family – may they rest in peace – I pledge my life to this rebellion anew."

Artorus looked at the dwarf for a long moment. Though his attire and his hair were in such a disheveled state as he'd never before seen, and bloodied bandages covered many parts of his battered body, at that moment, this officer lying before him was more elegant and noble than any man in the Fifth Planar – than any being in all the Planewars.

Orgron Braïun was the truest soldier and truest friend Artorus had known in a very long time. He had to think on his words a moment.

"Your apology is accepted, my friend," Artorus said earnestly. "Please recover your strength now, and I will be calling on that pledge, to be sure."

"It looks much worse than it is, sir," Braïun said, half gesturing to his several wounds. "I should be back on my feet in another couple days or so."

Most members of his army, Artorus would have chided for such brazen heroics and remanded to bedrest for at least two weeks, but a dwarf was a creature of unequaled determination. Artorus could only shake his head. No one in these armies would be convincing High Commander Braïun to remain in this hospital bed any longer than a couple of days.

"Very well," Artorus stated, "then I want you to have command of our forces in the woods until it is time for us to depart." The general turned to look back on the wounded men behind him. "I'm going to need you to make sure that, no matter how the battle goes on the plains out there, these men stay hidden in the woods. I'll continue to cycle other fresh troops back into our reserves as well." He looked back to Braïun. "Our assault on the fortress is more important than this battle; even if the fight goes poorly – even if Kremaine captures me or I fall to his blade – we will need whatever components of the Fifth Planar that are still mobile to assault that fortress. That means these forces must remain hidden and protected. You understand?"

Braïun nodded thoughtfully. "Yes, sir; I understand."

Artorus was quite happy to have his high commander back, to have his friend back. And so Artorus left his friend to recover in the hospital tent with a pat on his good shoulder. The visit with the other wounded was unfortunately brief, as he would need to get to the morgue and then return to his command staff.

There was still a battle to fight. One day's success did not a victory make.

Chapter XX – The Battle of the Lakewoods (pt. II)

For six more days the battle between the rebellious armies and the Wizard-King's loyalists continued. Mighty forces clashed upon the open plain in the mornings and dead were gathered in the afternoons and into the evenings. The Lord General Kremaine had lived up to Artorus's descriptions and Warin's concerns; calculating maneuvers, vicious countercharges, and sheer ruthlessness had consistently countered the best tactics of the once-jubilant rebels.

The one success of the rebels, at a great cost in casualties, was ground. Having pushed the Imperial Legions relentlessly through sheer indomitable will, Lord General Vallon and his three armies were camped less than two miles from the steep terrain at the far end of the Lakewoods Plain, pinning their opponents against it.

Artorus wondered often over the past six nights, as he spoke to his injured and observed his dead, if the cost was not too great for the advances they had made. Many thousands lay dead, and the injured threatened to overcome their capacity to care for them. What could possibly prove to become even worse, dysentery had sprung up in more than one of the troop encampments and the officers of all three armies fought to prevent it from pervading their ranks.

Artorus couldn't stop himself from thinking he was playing right into Kremaine's hands. His initial impulse was to fight conservatively and let Kremaine's forces exhaust themselves with risky maneuvers. And yet, opportunity after opportunity seemed to present itself for the rebels to push forward, and it seemed each time, the opportunity ended up costing them more than they had guessed.

On the seventh day, a tenuous quiet held over the plain, as neither faction made an offensive. All armies took the opportunity to recover from days of fighting and injury and disease.

"We're going to have to do something about those ogres that have been tearing us apart," Artorus stated, looking over a map and several charts with the other two generals. "I haven't seen ogres so disciplined since the Battle of Annerak."

Magron had gained a fresh scar down the length of his left forearm, twisted and raw, as he still recovered from his arrow wounds from the first day of fighting.

Warin was looking particularly exhausted, perhaps showing wear from his decades of fighting in the Planewars as much as wear from the past week.

"And what is our latest troop count?" Warin asked, his voice raspy and quiet.

"The Thirty-Third is at a fighting capacity of eighty-six thousand," grunted the now fully bearded general as a pain shot through his arm; it had been doing that more and more over the past days. "Supplies are holding,"

"And I've still got twenty thousand good men from the Fifth Planar fielded," Artorus mentioned. "But a lot of good men are dead," he added as he lowered his head.

"Hm..." Warin contemplated a moment. "Well, I regret to inform you both that, after the ogres yesterday and the cavalry charges from the day before, the Second Planar has only about fifty-eight thousand fighting men still fielded. The dysentery, as you know, will soon be reducing that number further."

Each of the three were quiet a moment until Artorus spoke finally. "Well, let us hope those regiments from the Seventeenth Planar get here sooner than later... Until that time, we must simply continue the fight. It's true, we have the Legions pressed against the crags, but our scouts report that imperial reinforcements have been trickling in from beyond those cliffs, so our enemies still likely have almost one hundred ninety thousand fighting men. Those wolf riders that have been harrying us and the ogres on the northern flank are each proving troublesome. I'm just not used to prolonged fighting at this scale. Even the Battle of the Boils was spread out over a much larger area; none of clashes lasted longer than a few days." Artorus shook his head.

"Of the tacticians present," Warin stated, "only Kremaine is used to fighting like this. But that does not make him unbeatable. I propose we assemble a strike team of my best men for a deep incursion to rile up those ogres while they're still in the enemy's ranks. They can strike at first light. That should take care of that problem… and give them something to keep them occupied while they put down the beasts for us."

"Ah! Yes!" Magron added. "I watched Vayan himself do that to Kaladrius's Forward Ninth Army some years ago. One of the more exciting things I've seen." He scratched his bushy beard with his good arm as he continued. "And as for those wolves, if we can draw them into the Thirty-Third, I've got a unit of the biggest, ugliest greens that could shred them to bits with their pole axes. They train as an anti-cavalry unit. Those wolf riders have proved cunning, but it should work."

Artorus nodded. "All right then. I'll send a couple more riders to check on Orrogen."

He slowly got up before continuing, days of battle crying out from his aching bones.

"I suspect an attack just after daybreak. If I know Kremaine, he'll have spotted the signs of the disease catching on. I have half an inkling that we're just where he wants us to be. He's got to know that we're waiting for reinforcements as well, since the numbers game won't work in our favor." Artorus took a deep breath. "This is a bloody battle, but we knew that's what it would be… This is no skirmish for some bridge over a lazy river on a backworld, two gates from anything important; this is our moment. This is the fight to change it all, gentlemen."

Artorus looked over the maps one last time, looking for anything he might have forgotten. It was a habit he had made early in his generalship. Nothing else stood out to him.

"I'd say we're done then," he finished. "Thank you both. We are showing the Wizard-King just how serious we are every moment we fight this battle; his days of ruling this world are numbered."

The generals parted ways and returned to their battered armies.

Artorus had been cycling in new troops from the reserves in the woods in small numbers, keeping the men of the Fifth Planar Army relatively fresh; they would need it for their next task.

Artorus thought for a moment about the Wizard-King's fortress. He'd been to the location only a handful of times, but each time he was impressed with the massive and imposing architecture. The fortress of the Wizard-King could be spotted from miles away. Though the nearest thick woods were several miles from it, Artorus would not have them fashion siege equipment until the last possible moment. The speed of their travel would be paramount – and if all went according to plan, they would not even need to siege the fortress.

He had to continuously remind himself that the Wizard-King was the true fight for the Fifth Planar, because otherwise, the thought of keeping the majority of his forces in reserve while the Thirty-Third Homeworld and the Second Planar fought would sicken him bitterly.

It was not until well into the nighttime, as the lord general gathered what small amounts of sleep he could, that a rider returned with word of the other armies.

"What is it?" Artorus managed though his grogginess.

"My general," the soldier said in an uncertain tone, "*two* of our messengers have returned just now..."

"And?"

"A portion of Brakson's Twelfth Learden Army had separated from the main force, become surrounded, and then entrenched, and finally captured," the soldier said with his head lowered.

Damn, thought Artorus, *but I suppose we can't expect to harry the imperials endlessly...*

"How many?" the general asked.

"About fifteen thousand, sir, but the bad news..."

At this, Artorus shifted from his lying position to sit up.

"It's Orrogen, sir," the soldier said quietly. "The reason we hadn't heard back is because all of our previous riders were captured... probably killed... Just one of the riders got through. Seems the entire Seventeenth Planar is pitched in battle against the Fortieth Homeworld, under Lord General Vasz. The Wizard-King has blockaded most of the roads. The Seventeenth fight for their lives and couldn't spare the regiments even if they had some way to get them through the blocked roadways..."

The soldier kept his gaze on the ground, clearly ashamed to be bearing this news.

And Artorus was ashamed to hear it.

Speaking almost as much to himself as to the soldier, Artorus thought aloud. "This is bad... If we're to receive no help from Orrogen, then this battle could take much longer than planned. And, if it takes longer, Brakken will be able to better consolidate his forces..." Artorus arose from bed and put a heavy robe over his sleeping gown.

"Thank you, soldier," he said to his messenger, "please see to it that those riders are well fed and well rested; they will be needed again soon, I fear."

Lord General Vallon made for his command tent, about to call for runners to summon the other generals and the lieutenants, but he did not make it far.

A shrill horn sounded from the watches at the front: a night attack.

Before Artorus could even command it, runners were heading for the command staff, soldiers at watch prepared for battle, and others were quickly dashing from tents to equip for a fight.

Not good, thought Artorus as he rushed back to his tent to grab his sword. *No time for armor... Kremaine is a few hours earlier than I expected.*

He mounted his horse and sped into the night amid the maelstrom of half-awake soldiers.

Luckily, expecting an early morning assault from the loyalists, the armies were perhaps more prepared than they might have been, but few things in a battle are more powerful than surprise, and this attack could have terrible effect if Artorus did not rally the leadership quickly.

Apparently, though, that particular task would have to wait a moment.

Through the darkness and scattered torchlight, Artorus saw a spearhead of charging cavalry breaking through the poorly assembled defenses and charging directly for his command tent.

Kremaine still wants my hide, he thought.

"To me!" he called quickly. "They come this way!"

He whirled his mount around and drew Thordrin's Blade from its sheath, tossing the fine sheath to the ground behind, without a belt to which he could have clasped it.

Many soldiers did rally to the cry of the lord general. "Spears! Quickly!" he called.

The charging cavalry, though relatively few in number, had strength in both surprise and speed as they trampled dozens of soldiers who made their way to block them.

More soldiers came to the general, and he now had at least as many troops as now charged for him, but only he and a few others had horses, and they would not be much contest for the charging riders without more pole arms. A precious few spears and halberds were gathered.

The racing cavalry arrived, and with a thunderous crash they collided with the defenders. Artorus had managed to form a weak line of pole arms at the forefront and arrows had felled one or two more attackers, but they trampled many of the men as spears snapped before the mighty charge.

Shouting a battle cry, Artorus spurred his horse to meet the barreling cavalrymen. More spears and axes and swords flashed in the light of the half moon above as the riders, mostly bearing swords, hacked through the soldiers before Artorus.

A captain among the enemy riders locked eyes with Artorus.

"He is here!" shouted the lead rider.

"Come and take me!" shouted Artorus in return.

Artorus came to the lead rider and easily blocked a high swing.

Artorus found that most soldiers did not take much advantage of their mount beyond the obvious height and speed when fighting on horseback. With the weight of his steed and his left hand still holding the reins, Artorus lunged his horse into the other man's mount. Though fully armored and skilled at combat, the imperial was knocked slightly ajar from his saddle, and while attempting to reseat himself and bring his mount back under control, was run through by Artorus's blade.

Artorus ripped his sword free with enough time to block two more swings from another rider. Spears caught his enemy's back and Artorus finished him with a cut to the upper chest.

Ahead, two horsemen trampled a soldier below them, and Artorus charged forward. With a shout, he reared his horse onto its hind legs for it to kick at the rider to his left, allowing him two quick swings at the other rider.

The rider blocked one too few and he also fell to the ground. The horse under the other rider now fought with Artorus's steed, and they kicked and bit at each other with a ferocity only learned through the intense combat training of warhorses.

Artorus caught a glimpse of his surroundings as he maneuvered into a position to attack the rider in front of him. All around him there were still riders hacking the standing soldiers, but many of them had fallen.

A slash across his left arm brought Artorus's attention rightly back to the rider in front of him.

With a grunt, Artorus launched several attacks at the rider. The rider blocked, but only barely as their two mounts still battled beneath them.

This soldier was fast, but he was weaker than Artorus. Bringing his horse around another foot or so after blocking a quick horizontal strike, Artorus launched into another series of attacks – this time, powerful overhead swings from the shoulder. Two, then three, then four great clashes rang out in the fight as the full force of Artorus's swings were being blocked. A fifth and a sixth mighty swing were enough to break the man's guard, and he fell when Thordrin's Blade hacked through his helmet.

By now, the assault had failed as the remaining riders were set upon by many more soldiers who arrived from around the camp.

Now breathing heavily, Artorus checked his arm; the wound was not deep. He did not have time for a medic, however, and he rode off into the night to finish the task he'd started.

The leadership of the three rebellious armies rallied quickly enough, but the damage was done: in the night before dawn, the full forces of Lord General Kremaine managed to overpower and slaughter many thousands. Aside from the attempt on Artorus's life, each assault was quick and calculated. It was a precise attack by the loyalists.

Cursing the Wizard-King's name, Artorus and the other generals agreed that a rapid counterattack was needed. They rallied their armies for a countercharge, and they hoped to still accomplish the objectives they had agreed upon the prior day.

In another few hours of bloody fighting in the morning light, the armies crashed against each other like the sea against the cliffs. Men fought with desperation now and died or fell wounded by the several thousands. The ground was wet with the blood of mortals.

Artorus sat at his table in the afternoon, his fresh wounds now bandaged and the fighting done for the day. They had managed to push the loyalist forces back closer to the cliffs once more, but both sides suffered more heavy losses in the action.

"So, how are we to win this fight?" he asked himself aloud.

Artorus stared into the maps and charts before him, but they gave him no more answers than did his exhausted mind.

Mala would have a way. I should find her. He frowned, thinking about the report he'd gotten regarding his sister. Only a battle of hundreds of thousands of troops would allow Artorus to hear of Mala being injured and not go to her himself to check on her. *One too many tales of glorious battle I must have told... How could she have charged into a melee, despite my direct orders?*

In fact, after meeting around the fire that eve before the first day of fighting, Artorus had not seen his sister, Ty, Braïun, or the Sage since.

"You called for us, Lord General?" Warin said to Artorus from the side of the command table, standing politely.

Surprised that he did not even notice the general approach, Artorus looked up to see Warin nod respectfully to him as he approached the table.

General Magron arrived, looking rather exhausted as well; he'd likely been in the thick of the fighting. The prior wound on his arm was bandaged heavily, but bled through nonetheless – clearly having not had the time or attention to heal properly. Artorus wasn't quite sure how the general continued to fight, as he was fairly certain that Magron was left-handed.

Collecting himself, in the mild warmth of the spring evening, Artorus stood and saluted his generals. "I thank you for coming, Generals, I think it's time to reevaluate our situation."

They both nodded, and all three generals took a chair. This table had been set up on the field, closer to the front, since their armies had pushed far across the plain.

"Where are we at?" Artorus asked. "Give me all of it."

Warin nodded to Magron, and the larger man began.

"Hells, Vallon, we're not doing good. Those bastards can fight, and they sure don't pull any swings." Unconsciously, Magron rubbed his wounded arm with his other hand as he continued. "Even after we lost so many troops to push them back, those godsbedamned gobs and their wolves tore right through my greens; they didn't have time to get in position. The Thirty-Third Homeworld Army is at a fighting force of seventy-eight thousand if we're lucky. I've not seen fighting this damned bloody in a long time."

The disheveled man grunted in frustration as he shook his head.

"We're tired," he concluded, "but we'll beat those godsbedamned loyalists into the ground if we have to use our bare hands... I'd love to kick in Ethos's teeth myself."

Magron looked to Warin.

"The dysentery is spreading faster than we'd feared," began Warin, "so even if we hadn't lost so many troops to the fighting, the Seventeenth Planar would not be in great shape. My reports indicate something on the order of forty thousand men still in fighting condition. Nearly all of the one-thousand-man force that was sent to attack the ogres – some of the Second Planar's best – was captured hundreds of yards before their target... What's worse, we can barely erect new hospital tents to match the rate of men falling ill."

He paused to take a deep breath.

"Morale in the Second Planar is low, I'm afraid."

Artorus thought long on the topic and the other two men were silent with him. "Our fighting force on the field is not more than sixteen thousand at this point, but our spirit is strong. Of course, the Fifth Planar has the advantage of a huge reserve force..."

Artorus looked to the west, imagining the many thousands of Kremaine's men, eagerly awaiting their next engagement.

"This battle does not go well for us." Artorus could tell that defeat was laden in his voice. "I think it is in our interest to retreat, gentlemen. Warin, you'll be able to care for your men better off the field of battle. Magron, you'll have your chance at Ethos another day."

Artorus looked to each of the generals sitting with him.

Warin looked so very tired, but he maintained his posture well and he still likely outmatched the health of any man his age that Artorus had yet seen. Rustling his bushy white mustache in thought, he eventually nodded to Artorus in agreement.

Magron was looking pale, and he still cradled his wounded arm. His expression was slightly absent, but he eventually nodded as well. The defeat was obviously troubling to him, but his weariness would not likely allow for much more fighting and he knew it.

Magron raised his right arm and slammed a heavy fist into the table, then slumped back into his chair, and simply shook his head.

With a sigh, Artorus went on. "Then we shall prepare in the night and retreat at dawn. I shall draft a letter of notice to Kremaine." He looked to the older general, determined. "General Warin, this does not change our plan in the slightest. The Fifth Planar will make for the Wizard-King's fortress immediately. The secrecy of this maneuver is paramount."

Warin nodded again and then spoke. "I had been thinking on this, Lord General. I believe the afflicted men could make for a good excuse as to why the Fifth Planar did not have a significant representation on the field. We shall enact all of the precautions. I think you are right that defeat here does not affect the next stage of the plan."

Warin motioned to the simple map that sat on this table as he spoke. "It would have been much easier to remain unnoticed if the imperials were fleeing over the plateau and northward to Imren, but I believe, if your Fifth Planar is mobile before first light, General Magron and I can keep Kremaine's attention long enough to cover your movements."

Artorus took one more look westward, imagining Kremaine's forces. He had proved to be every bit the opponent Vallon had thought.

"Kremaine..." he murmured, shaking his head.

The Fifth Planar Army, the Thirty-Third Homeworld Army, and the Second Planar Army would retreat from the Lakewoods and leave the victorious Lord General Kremaine to his machinations... for a time.

"Then it is decided," Artorus stated.

He rose with some difficulty, his aching body protesting his every move. The other generals did the same.

Even in defeat, Artorus held his head high, his tone resilient. "It seems we have lost the Battle of the Lakewoods, gentlemen, but the Wizard-King and his slaves are sorely mistaken if they think this indicates this rebellion is finished." Artorus saluted the two generals before him once more. "It has been a great honor to fight alongside you in this engagement. I look forward to when we join forces again."

Artorus bade each general farewell, issued his orders to his command staff, and retired for the evening back to the woods, away from the battlefield, far from the encamped armies.

He had family that he had not seen in what seemed like a very long time.

The majority of the Fifth Planar Army had received word from the runners and was preparing to leave in the failing light of the evening.

Even among the chaos of an army preparing for march, Artorus found his half sister without too much trouble. Her horribly bruised neck, which she tried to hide behind a tall collar, had changed shades likely many times since he last saw her. But Artorus knew her other wound likely gave her more trouble.

"How is the leg?" he asked her, smiling through his exhaustion.

Injuries or no, it was good to see his proud little sister, that smile she wore so well.

"I thought you were going to scold me for that again," Mala said, a sheepish smile showing on her face. "I was waiting; I had several good rebuttals prepared. I couldn't very well send them through the runners."

"Actually," he said, "I was quite impressed with my sister's exploits on the battlefield."

Truly, it was his soldiers that were impressed – in the nights between fighting, they'd told tales of the Lady Andrius and her brave charge into the ranks of the enemy.

Artorus saw Typhondrius and Kellos both studying some tomes by what light they could use from a campfire.

"And where is Ormond?" Artorus asked.

"He is still drafting his charter of laws that he will propose once we've won the war," Mala replied with a smile.

"Good, good... Seriously, though, Mal," he said to Mala, unable to resist any longer, "you ought to be more careful. This rebellion needs you, and you're not immortal like our friend over there."

There was a brief pause in the conversation as they were walking slowly toward the campfire where their companions sat.

"You heard about the retreat?" Artorus inquired somberly.

Mala nodded, looking down, a hand coming up to rub her battered throat. "Somehow, I just thought there was no way we could lose, somehow we seemed... I don't know... unstoppable, I guess."

"Learned long ago," he retorted with a chuckle, "you're never unstoppable when the tides of battle are in motion."

They reached the campfire, and the two gentlemen stood and nodded to Artorus. All four took seats around the small fire as the soldiers moved about in the night, preparing for their secret departure.

"Though, I think many of the men felt much like yourself," Artorus continued, "but also like yourself, the men are mortals and the enemy which we challenge is not." Artorus looked to the Sage across the campfire. "Perhaps," he pondered, "if we were all more like Kellos here then we would not have to fear death. Our troops would walk about the battlefield like it was a garden in spring."

Artorus joked, hoping he might get one of those awkward smiled out of Kellos, but instead he looked thoughtful.

"Good general," the Sage began after a short moment, "I do fear death."

This was perplexing. Kellos, Sage of Delemere, was of the immortal number of Sages – the keepers of knowledge from time uncounted. So far as anyone knew, he was ageless and eternal. How could he fear death?

The Sage continued, "You see, death, like so many concepts, has more than one meaning. You probably assume that swords and arrows and spears will not destroy me, thus how could I fear death, yes?"

Artorus thought on that. *Hm. Is he immune to mortal weaponry? Would an arrow bounce off his skin, just like a Wizard's?*

Artorus nodded in response, just as the others did.

"Well, you are correct that I do not fear death from troops afield," he went on, "and yet I have little doubt that there is a way to end my existence on these many planes. In fact, I expect that my entire kind will one day be no more. It is the living things – mortals – that will likely never be destroyed entirely; not in a timeframe that a mortal mind could even conceive.

"The tree that falls in the forest is a shelter for many creatures until it finally dissolves back into the land and becomes more plants. The deer dies to feed the wolves and what is left dissolves just as the tree did. Even the single blade of grass, whether plucked up for food or whether it expires just where it first grew, becomes a part of something else.

"Having watched these many centuries, I've seen it countless times. Even the giants and elves and humans and orcs and dwarves and such races follow this theme, with one more element: consciousness. With the burden of thought, one could argue that death becomes something else for the so-called intelligent races. I have seen, though, that the things by which most mortals define themselves do not so much expire as they do metamorphose and are instead passed down to children and grandchildren. All the morals, the memories, and the ideals of a man or a woman are found in his sons and her daughters, his pupils and her friends – all the other beings with whom they share life, love, or blood.

"Though the tree that fell in the forest bears not the encumbrance of consciousness, if it did, it may fear death as you or I do. Yet, you and I can look to the fox denning in its hollows, the beetles feasting on its detritus, and the flowers growing atop it and see its existence continues beyond its life."

Artorus listened curiously to the Sage as the fire crackled softly at their feet.

"And a Sage's existence is knowledge. I will not die and feed the forest, nor will I ever have sons or daughters. Even what I do now, taking up a part in the Planewars and involving myself with mortals, is frowned upon by the Sages.

"So, you see, I do indeed fear death because with me will die, not only my physical form and consciousness, but so too will expire most of my knowledge. Write knowledge on paper, and it may one day burn or turn to dust; carve it into stone, and even the stone will eventually dissolve to sand."

The Sage stopped, and the murmuring of the fire was the only sound for a moment.

Typhondrius looked to the Sage. "But you share your knowledge with us now, master Sage. Will that not live on if any of us should for some reason outlive you? Or could we not pass this knowledge on to the generations that might outlive you?"

Mala added, "Is not all that you've shared with us since writing that letter simply knowledge of one form or another? Are you not fulfilling your destiny to teach the peoples of the twenty-seven worlds?"

"Yes," the Sage nodded to Typhondrius, "you may." Then he turned to Mala. "And it is, and I am. Yet this that I share now – indeed, all that I might share with you in our time together – represents but a grain of sand on the vast beach of the knowledge I have gathered in my time among the planes. It seems unlikely that I would be able to pass on even a moderate amount of this because, as you might come to see, the information I have is also not entirely practical or translatable; mortals tend only to remember that which, firstly, they understand, and secondly, is of use to them in some way."

The Sage looked distant a moment. His tone became serious.

"I have solved mathematical problems that mortals have not yet conceived numbers to propose, and I have contemplated paradoxes of logic that might just drive a sane mind mad. There are theories of the nature behind those things humanoids might describe as divine and those which might be called the mystical, which the language of mortals has not the capacity to even define fully. I hold knowledge of the physical multiverse which would confound even the most tenured lecturers at academy, and I keep hold of unanswered questions that the most curious philosophers won't dream for a thousand years yet."

That silenced the group.

Even when stated seriously as he had, the Sage claimed these things in his almost monotonous style, without so much as gesturing with a hand or raising an eyebrow. Truthfully, even stated emphatically by any other creature of the planes, these things would be clearly fabricated, and yet, from Kellos, Sage of Delemere, Artorus had no reason to doubt a single word. He had yet to hear the Sage exaggerate even once.

And, when he pondered the claims the Sage had made, it sent a chill down his spine as Artorus realized the sheer magnitude of some of them. The nature of the multiverse? Mind-bending problems of mathematics and philosophy? Paradoxes that could drive somebody mad?

The Sage simply spoke these things like they were unarguable facts, as a parent might tell a child that the color of the grass is called green. It was commanding and knowing, but not condescending or egotistical. The vibrancy of his powerful voice was likely the only thing that kept his manner of speaking from becoming exhausting. When Kellos spoke, the mortals listened.

Mala finally broke the silence.

"But Kellos," she began thoughtfully, "you will live forever; you could write entire libraries of books and leave them on each of the twenty-seven worlds to live on to whatever is beyond forever. And when these things all turn to dust, you could copy them anew."

The Sage nodded. "And in Delemere and the many monasteries of Sages across the worlds, such libraries exist now and are ever improving by the hands of diligent monks. Indeed, great effort is made at copying over the rotting scrolls and disintegrating tomes."

He paused, looking into the fire.

"While books can burn or age to dust, even the languages in which I write can be forgotten in time. But mortal life, resilient as it is, will construct new languages and carry on knowledge for time unknowable. I accept the likelihood that I will one day die, perhaps even more truly than you mortals. It is not something, however, for which I do not feel some anxiety."

The mortals thought on this until Typhondrius shuffled quietly.

"And what of the Wizard-King and his kind?" asked Ty. "Do they also fear death as you do?"

To think of a Wizard fearing their demise was a ponderous thought indeed. Artorus certainly hoped Brakken fretted as they rallied the people of The Vastness to their cause.

The Sage paused once more.

"Yes, I believe they do. Their actions seem to tell us they do, and I have no reason to believe their immortality is unlike that of the race of Sages. I am certain an end awaits Wizard-kind. And while I might fear that I cannot leave enough knowledge behind when I eventually cease, a Wizard collects power alone. And, in my time among the multiverse, I have seen that power is fleeting.

"So, yes, it stands to both reason and observation that Wizards do fear their end."

"So," Artorus mused, "Lord Brakken is as afraid of us as we are of him, is he?"

Mala laughed and added, "Perhaps we should simply let him know we understand his great burdens, and we will take his weighty rulership from him out of compassion."

"I do not see that being a viable option for you at this point," Kellos spoke quite honestly, to the amusement of the others.

Though Ty, Mala, and Artorus laughed, the Sage simply looked at them. He wasn't offended, but he didn't seem to see the humor either. That only got the group laughing more.

Despite all of the death and the gloom, somehow, seeing Mala and Typhondrius and this Sage gave Artorus a newfound confidence in the happenings of this rebellion. Truly, each of them had their own way of bringing a new wisdom and an entirely different perspective to this uprising, Kellos not least of all.

Artorus stood, stretching, as he spoke over the slowly dying campfire.

"Well, good Sage, this particular ever-living blade of grass must get some sleep. Yet another thing we know you have to miss out on, Kellos."

He smiled to the Sage and Kellos looked up to the general.

"This is indeed another trait of mortals for which I can find some envy. Dreams are often described as superior to the experiences of reality."

The Sage did not know what dreams were like. *He envies them?* thought Artorus. An interesting prospect, since dreams were so often filled with nonsense – hardly things a Sage should concern himself with.

Suddenly, Artorus thought of Elsa, if only for a flash.

The other three looked to him, as he contemplated his lost love. To see his late wife, even if only as a construct of his sleeping mind, was indeed a gift.

"It's different from reality; that much is true," Artorus said contemplatively.

He let the fading image of Elsa linger another second.

"Goodnight everyone; we have a very early day tomorrow, and it will not get any easier from there. I thank you each for your time this evening. It was just what a defeated, bruised, and tired general needed."

He bade them farewell and then retired to his tent.

Just as he knew he would, Artorus dreamt of Elsa again this night. Now that the Sage had pointed it out, Artorus did realize it was a thing of beauty – these rekindled memories of his – but with each dream it was the same: he would come quickly to realize that he was dreaming. After this point, he would force himself to remember the last time he truly did see Elsa: in the ashes of his home, little more than a charred skeleton. And just as his wife and unborn child did, the dream would burn away and be gone from him.

It was for them that Artorus fought – them and the millions like them.

The light of dawn was barely creeping past the horizon, torches still needed to see, when the armies were nearly ready to move. Artorus had already been awake for more than an hour, and many of his men had slept the prior afternoon so they could work straight through the night.

"Sir," Hakan said in what Artorus guessed was his best attempt at a hushed voice, "we only have to pack up the last tents and then we can move." The lieutenant met Artorus's eyes. "You're sure you still want to run from this?"

There was disdain in his voice.

"Dammit, Hakan," Artorus replied quietly, "you know this was our plan all along. Yes, I dearly wish we could beat Kremaine and his cronies into the earthen field, but us fighting here – even if we could change the tide of this battle – would only serve to squander our plans; you know that."

"We can beat them," Hakan said plainly.

"Are you going to disobey my orders, Hakan," Artorus said in a stern voice, "or are you going to get those tents packed up? You charge the field, and I swear to the fallen gods I will demote you."

With a disapproving grunt, Hakan nodded to his general. The fire-blood was looking somewhat worse for the wear of battle, but he still held his head high and grasped his sword hilt at his side as the long blade weighed down its sheath. He traipsed off into the darkness.

Out ahead of them, Artorus could see the other two armies assembling at the forested edge of the huge plain, their torches bobbing in the struggling light. Seeing it now, it was a sad reason to assemble so many thousands of proud soldiers, willing to fight against the evil rulership of the Wizard-King; but retreat was the reasonable act for the time being.

Could we still beat them? Artorus found himself thinking, picturing that look of determination of Hakan's face.

Lieutenant Highblade was right when he had quipped about his counterpart many days earlier; Hakan really did think he could defeat any enemy. Truthfully, as far as Artorus had yet seen, Hakan could. Though he lacked the finesse and talent of Highblade, Hakan was an impressive fighter for his unwavering determination and unfaltering strength.

Another half hour passed and the men were completely ready. By now, his admission of defeat should be reaching Lord General Kremaine, who surely watched the three armies drawing back toward the woods. Artorus guessed it would give Kremaine quite some pleasure this morning, which was why Vallon had been careful to end it with: *don't fool yourself, Kremaine; this is not the end.*

The Fifth Planar Army was mostly marching toward the woods that enshrouded the Brannus River, where it met Lower Woodslake on the southern edge of the Lakewoods Plain. Artorus and most of his command staff were some of the last to march.

The Thirty-Third Homeworld and the Second Planar both still remained on the Plain, beginning to trickle into the Lakewoods at the eastern edge. Those woods should cover the retreat of the two armies, attempting to still appear as three. Artorus could breathe a little easier knowing that he'd not be leaving these two armies to a slaughter.

It looked as though the sun would be breaking over the horizon any moment now. Artorus noticed a few torches still lit, but then another light seemed to appear out of the leading edges of the two retreating armies, as some of the troops were getting closer to the Lakewoods. It was different from a torch, far brighter.

What? thought Artorus, as he gazed into the dawn's light.

The light grew even brighter, a shimmering white unlike anything Artorus had seen, and then it seemed to burst into a larger blossom of oranges and blues and yellows, and a second later a loud pop raced across the grasslands in all directions, echoing off of far cliffs ahead and great trees behind. Artorus's heart stopped. He knew what this was.

The immortal Wizard-King, Lord Brakken, had come to this fight.

"This is not good," he stated dreadfully as the two lines of men now scattered, some of them aflame with Wizard's fire.

The lord general's hand went to the hilt of Thordrin's Blade. His muscles tensed and his breath became quickened.

Artorus and every other mortal on this field was faced with a choice: fight or run.

Artorus was not entirely prepared to make that choice with a rational mind. Days of fighting had weakened his will, and he was angry: angry with Kremaine for his endless deceptions and unrelenting tactics; angry with the Imperial Legions for being so blind as to follow murderous madmen; angry at this Wizard now just a few hundred yards ahead for all of the death and all of the pain – for *hundreds of years* of strife.

But this was not the time. To fight the War Maker now would be to fight him on *his* terms. They had to stick to the plan. The assault on the fortress was the most critical element of their plan.

"No!" Artorus shouted to the High Commander Braïun, hobbled as he was, assembling the nearest unit into lines for battle. "We cannot fight him here!"

"But, sir!" Braïun shouted back. "This is it! This is our chance to end this!"

Artorus hastily approached Braïun in the burgeoning light. Braïun had a cane to help support his weight, his body not nearly free of his wounds.

"It is *not*," Artorus insisted. "We *cannot* beat him here. He has come expecting battle and he will flee back to his fortress whenever it pleases him and maneuver his armies to protect him! It will unravel *all* we have worked for! It will make *all* the deaths on this field for naught! We must scatter and let him think we are afraid."

Artorus looked to the faces of the men quickly assembling. They *were* afraid. This was the immortal Wizard-King who had ruled over them and their fathers and their grandfathers, as far back as most histories tell.

Braïun looked at Artorus, now close enough to lock eyes, and frowned in thought.

"You're right, of course," he said more quietly now, "*fallen gods bedamned*. I just can't sit here and watch him slaughter those poor men."

What a brave officer Artorus had in Braïun. Even half crippled, the dwarf would marshal troops to charge an immortal Wizard.

"I know," the general said to his officer, his voice softer, "that is why we must not be seen at all. Order the men—"

Artorus was cut off by a booming voice that roared from the center of the scorched area where Brakken now stood. It was the voice of a Wizard. His magic somehow increased the power of his voice, and it carried well over the entirety of the mighty plain of the Lakewoods, echoing from the distant cliffs.

"Behold, mortals!" the mighty voice said, commanding, impressive, and powerful; dripping with disdain. "I am the immortal Wizard-King, Lord Brakken! You presume to stand against me, your king, and now you think you have the *luxury* of fleeing?"

From beside the Wizard-King, several of the men from the Thirty-Third Homeworld Army charged him, spears leveled at the huge being. Artorus could barely see Brakken turn his head toward them and they each froze, nearly a dozen of them.

No. Run. Scatter. Artorus could only watch desperately, as his mind cried for his body to do anything at all – anything but stand and watch.

The War Maker went on, completely unconcerned. "You have the opportunity to bow to my feet and beg for mercy, and you *may* earn a swift death. For the rest of you, *fire* shall cleanse you!"

His voice was menacing as it boomed, impossibly loud, to what surely must have been all the men on the vast plain.

Slowly, he'd been turning as he spoke to all the men around him. He raised his right arm, now pointed at the men who still stood frozen by unseen tethers.

Then, from among the ranks of the Second Planar Army, a battle cry rang out just as the sun began to break over the plain.

"For mortals!" A dozen more soldiers charged.

As he turned his hand now toward the men who had been charging him, the air in front of the Wizard-King's arm crackled and hummed and a bolt of lightning lit up the field and streaked directly through them. Even from where Artorus watched, the screams could be heard. At that same moment, arrows rained onto the Wizard and men charged.

Other soldiers, though, were running from the terrible scene. A few even fell to their knees at the awesome power of the Wizard. It was chaos. And Artorus knew all too well that chaos could be the deadliest element on the field of battle.

"Now!" Artorus yelled sharply to Braïun – and any other officer within earshot. "Get the hell out of here!"

Then a familiar voice roared from much closer to the ranks of the Fifth Planar.

"Die, you bastard!!"

Lieutenant Hakan charged the field, directly at Brakken.

"*Hakan!*" Artorus yelled.

But it was in vain as perhaps a hundred of the men nearest the lieutenant shouted, and charged toward the horrific spectacle now playing out on the field.

This can't happen! Artorus thought frantically, as more and more soldiers fell into line with the charging formation.

"Braïun!" he snapped. "Halt those men *immediately!*"

Artorus shouted similar commands to every officer he could find and went about marshaling all the troops he could back into their loosely assembled marching formation.

With a great and frantic effort, the lord general began to march the Fifth Planar Army hastily back into the woods that concealed them, but likely more than two hundred troops now charged toward Brakken the Cruel with their lieutenant.

Flames shot through the ranks of men, some soldiers were flung many yards back upon their brethren by unseen forces, lightning coursed over many, the earth trembled and broke, and unnatural winds reversed the flight of arrows. This was the sight of mortal efforts against an immortal foe; the mighty Wizard-King showed his powers. It was a nightmare.

Artorus, like all the men hurrying through the woods, could not take his gaze off of the sight. Hakan and his force charged forward still as most other mortals were by now running from the Wizard.

"Turn back, dammit!" yelled Artorus, but they were now well out of earshot.

Lieutenant Highblade had come up beside Artorus, and Braïun had also made his way to where the lord general had stopped to watch on a small outcropping over the river.

The mighty Hakan reached the Wizard-King from behind, just as he called flames down upon some of the fleeing men. He shoved his large sword straight through the creature's back.

The Wizard did not fall. He barely even seemed to notice the sword.

With a roar that could be heard even this far away, Lord Brakken spun about, tearing the large sword from Hakan's hands. Then, with unimaginable speed, the Wizard's left hand shot out and gripped Hakan's throat. Though the large lieutenant was over six feet in height, the Wizard-King stood nearly a full head taller.

Several of Hakan's men moved to attack the Wizard-King, but with a glance to either side, half a dozen of those men instead turned around and began to fight their own comrades. Still some men made it through the brutal melee, but their weapons only bounced off of the Wizard.

Brakken reached behind him and gripped the huge sword that jutted from his back, ripping it out of his own torso.

Despite all his might, Hakan only struggled uselessly against the unnatural strength of the War Maker.

Then, with a sickening hiss that could only just be heard from this distance, Hakan began to shake violently and, as though he were a water skin being drained, he shriveled before the eyes of the onlookers.

In a moment, Hakan stopped writhing and was lifeless.

The fireblood's armor slipped from his enfeebled form and fell to the scorched earth below. For the sheer horror of it, while the soldiers still fought one another or uselessly assailed the immortal, Brakken then raised the sword, paused brazenly, and stabbed the long blade fully through the withered remains of the lieutenant.

Artorus and his two officers gasped as they still watched in horror.

By this point, many of the men closest to Brakken were now simply running for their lives, abandoning weapons, shields, and hope as they fled the inhuman creature and the soldiers that were, moments ago, their most loyal friends.

In one last display of might, the Wizard shouted, burst into a huge ball of flame, igniting all of the soldiers unfortunate enough to still be close enough, and then was gone.

Silence gripped the plain a moment, but then the intermittent cries and steady moaning of burning and dismembered soldiers crept into the silence where the Wizard-King had been.

The two armies of the rebellion were in total disarray. It was at this time, in the increasing light of the morning, the Imperial Legion moved across the field to press the attack, even as the armies they meant to engage were not intending to fight them.

Some doomed few of the Thirty-Third Homeworld moved to face the attack, while most others scattered into the woods.

"What do we do?" asked Highblade in disbelief as he saw the Imperial Legions moving to sweep the battlefield.

"What *can* we do?" added Braïun as he stared at the dead and dying that littered the ground where the Wizard-King had stood.

"We do exactly what we were planning to do," Artorus said, finally breaking his gaze from the horrors on the plain.

His chest was aflame with emotion, but his voice was cold. "We march right for that bastard's home and we make him see that he can't kill all of us. We show him we are not afraid. We make him see that he does not rule us *anymore*."

Artorus walked off the small bluff and motioned for runners.

"Go and tell Warin – if he's still alive – that this changes nothing; we stick to the plan," he snapped to the runner, and then to the rest of the men around him, "*March!*"

The once-mighty army, having witnessed unbelievable horrors and watched the fall of their brave lieutenant, now marched solemnly through the woods. Though there were weeks between them, the Fifth Planar made for the very home of the creature that had just unleashed a furious hell upon their own and their allied armies.

If ever there was a time to doubt their task, it was now.

But on they marched. They had much ground to cover.

Chapter XXI – Braennor Hakan

A little more than three years ago, General Artorus Vallon had a high commander named Hakan. Nobody much liked him, but he was indispensable, nonetheless.

The fireblood was not necessarily of a great intellect, but on the field of battle, his skill was undeniable, both in the soldier's uniform and in the officer's. The large man from the plane of Ebbea had quickly climbed his way to high commander in Vallon's army through brilliant maneuvers and deeds of great prowess.

And Hakan had one quality that was more valuable than any skill: he was trustworthy. Even if he might not always be able to trust his actions in the moment, and while even a careful observer might miss it, where morals were concerned, Artorus could trust the fireblood completely.

Vallon had transferred numerous officers and even entire units out of his army if he didn't feel they could be trusted. More than ferocity or bravery or tenacity, trust was the quality Vallon valued most.

But even Vallon himself second-guessed Hakan's position as a leader from time to time. While every other officer in the Fifth Planar Army followed the same code as their general – the code of the previous general – and lamented in the job of dealing death, this man didn't seem to much care about that. While every other officer rued the wars they were forced to fight and mourned the deaths of their men, Hakan embraced warfare and lusted for battle.

"Fallen gods bedamned, Hakan!" Artorus shouted. "*What were you thinking?*"

As always, the fireblood's impressive frame was somewhat intimidating. Artorus could almost forget about the idiotic maneuver the high commander had just pulled, but not this time.

With the orders for a full retreat, Hakan had taken all the men he could and charged the enemy.

"I was thinking," the high commander stated plainly in his gruff voice, "that the Fifth Planar doesn't run away from a tough fight."

He looked directly into the eyes of his general. Though Artorus was a tall man, Hakan looked down at him.

The Fifth Planar had been engaged only hours prior with one of Brakken's other rivals in the Planewars, the Arch-Magus Vith. In fact, they fought with one of Vith's most elite forces, known as the Army of the Night. They were a fearsome assembly of goblins and orcs, with tactics unlike any force Artorus had faced. And they truly had a thirst for battle.

The Army of the Night was preparing to push the Fifth Planar out of the general vicinity of the worldgate on Ebbea. It was the gate that led from the plane of Ebbea to Vith's homeworld of Hael. Though Brakken the War Maker had long held a great stake on the plane of Ebbea, it was hotly contested among three other Wizards. This plane did not know peace.

Artorus glared into the cold eyes of his high commander. If it weren't for the fact that Hakan's move might very well have saved them their ground for the time being, he'd likely have had him demoted on the spot.

For now, though, a wave of the hand to dismiss him would have to do until he could better evaluate things.

Though the strange gravity of Ebbea played tricks on a soldier at all times, on the battlefield it could spell either victory or doom for them, depending on a few key elements. An army that trained on Ebbea and resided there for time enough to become accustomed to her gravity held a huge advantage over any other army. Historically, it made nearly every attempt to attack Ebbea from off-world impossible. Brakken had been very pleased to have Vith pushed out of the worldgate about three years prior.

The Army of the Night must have been training for this for months. Most armies would tie heavy stones to their men and have them practice for hours and hours to train for Ebbea. The typical sluggishness of an off-world army was nowhere to be found in these nighttime assailants. And they must have had agents on the plane, since they seemed to time their assault perfectly with the relief of Brakken's Eighth Ebbea Army by the Fifth Planar. But perhaps their greatest advantage: both the greens and the gobs came from this blasted plane. Whatever training a man or a dwarf or an elf might suffer to prepare themselves, an orc or a goblin has right down to his bones.

Even before the Army of the Night came through the gate, disease and bad food stores had weakened the Fifth Planar for the two weeks they held the worldgate; Artorus should have seen sabotage, where only coincidence was apparent.

But now they faced the whole of the mighty force of monstrous soldiers after they burst through in impossible numbers.

Battle was drawn again the following night. Living up to their name, Vith's generals took advantage of the excellent night vision of the orcs and the goblins to draw battle in the dark whenever they could.

Still reeling from the previous engagement, the Fifth Planar fared poorly. Things got much worse when Vith appeared and sundered one of the cavalry regiments with his terrible power, the very ground shuddering at his will.

Though the crazed Wizard left just as quickly as he'd arrived, after hours of fighting, Artorus saw no other way; his men were dying; he called the retreat of the Fifth Planar once more. This fight would have to be fought with more forces than his weakened, exhausted army, and for now it seemed Vith would gain a foothold on Ebbea. It could very well mean that Ebbea would be engulfed in war for decades to come. It might even mean a demotion for Artorus. But as a general, Artorus had a duty to his men; he could not simply let them be slaughtered any longer.

Then, as the majority of the forces were maneuvering to withdraw, Artorus could barely believe his eyes when a unit broke off and called for a charge. Thousands of General Vallon's troops charged against the order of their general.

"*Hakan*!!" Artorus screamed into the bloody night. "*I'll kill you!*"

Most of the officers looked with reservation to their general, who was obviously in a state they'd not before seen him.

"*The hells!*" the general roared at the officers around him. "Rally the men, we charge too! I'm not about to let those thousands of men die for nothing."

Cursing Hakan's name, the general organized a concerted counter-charge to push back the endless waves of orcs and goblins that fought so fiercely.

Fighting raged for hours more; so many thousands died by the time the sun rose once more that Artorus could no longer pay heed to casualties. The harsh gravity exhausted the men beyond any battle they had ever fought, but Artorus noticed something: no matter how much they trained for the task, the mighty Army of the Night had not been on Ebbea for months like the Fifth Planar had.

The orcs tired, their massive frames slowing them. The goblins never were courageous, and once the first few units of orcs broke, the goblins weren't far behind. By the time the first of the twin suns of Ebbea had risen over the battlefield, The Army of the Night was retreating back through the worldgate.

Artorus could hardly believe it. He bled from many wounds, and untold numbers of the Fifth Planar had died, but they were victorious. The worldgate to Hael was held, and a significant portion of Ebbea still belonged to The Vastness.

As the various troops tended to the wounded and collected the dead, a ragged Artorus wandered the field until he found Hakan. His lieutenant, Rreth, was reporting casualties to him along the way.

Spotting Hakan's huge frame from a distance, Artorus walked straight for him.

It seemed Artorus's face gave away something, because some troops parted and began to watch the spectacle as it played out.

Hakan turned just in time to see General Vallon's fist slam into his face.

Hakan reeled from the solid blow, but recovered almost immediately and returned the sentiment with an even more solid blow. Vallon was knocked hard to the ground in the heavy gravity.

Shouts were heard as men scrambled. Weapons were drawn and held to Hakan as Artorus brought himself slowly back to his feet.

"Should we throw him in the stockades, sir?" asked Rreth.

Artorus wiped the blood from his face and he couldn't help but laugh. "Should have expected that, I suppose," he lamented.

His nose bled steadily.

"No," General Vallon said after a moment of Hakan writhing in the grasp of the six men that held him. "Rreth, you know that you've been the only lieutenant since we lost Matheson. I think it's time we had another."

Artorus's gaze held that of Hakan, who was slowing his struggle as his general's words finally registered. This crazed fireblood might one day be the end of him. But his heart was undeniable.

"The bastard saved this battle for us," the general finally proclaimed, wiping the blood away from his mouth. "Let twenty lashes be his first recognition received as *Lieutenant* Hakan."

All of the men looked at one another. Hakan looked the most dumbfounded of everyone. But, finally, Rreth laughed heartily.

"Very well, sir," Rrcth said to his general. He extended a hand to the kneeling fireblood, as the other soldiers released their grip.

"Come on up, you lug," Rreth said to Hakan. "I've never whipped another lieutenant before. I can tell we're going to be fast friends."

Taking the hand, Hakan grinned widely and replied. "I think we will."

There was much to be done in the aftermath of the extremely bloody battle. The general did not get the chance to really speak with Hakan, outside of him shadowing while they issued orders, for several days after the incident. Once the Fifteenth Ebbea Army had arrived to relieve the Fifth Planar, Artorus finally sought out his newest lieutenant for a heart-to-heart.

"So, Lieutenant," he said, coming up beside the large fireblood as he oversaw the assembly of his units, "are you going to tell me what in the many hells gave you the idea you should disobey my orders for the second time in two days and charge an army of raging greens in the middle of a losing night battle?"

He looked at his new lieutenant and added, "I've been curious."

"Wasn't quite the way I saw it, General," Hakan replied in his deep voice.

Artorus looked at Hakan expectantly.

"You know," the fireblood began after thinking a moment, "my first assignment was with the Sixth Ebbea. Hell, I grew up on this rat trap. This place'll beat a man down. And, here, you sure fall hard. Once you're laying on that hard dirt, you got two choices, though. Either you get back up or lie down and let people walk on you like a bearskin rug."

The lieutenant paused to shout something obscene at a soldier who fell out of formation. He shook his head and spat on the ground beside him before continuing.

"Well, I met a lot of greens in my time on this damned place, and they fight like the hells. You can take a hit from a human blade, you can take a hit from a dwarven hammer, but you sure as hell don't want a hit from a green-ish axe. They'll kill a man and drink his blood. I seen it. They got about as much muscle as a bull, and they got an attitude to match. But they're used to things runnin' from 'em and armies retreating, that's what keeps 'em going. Nasty as they might look, you stand square with one an' you fight 'im... more times'n you'd think... he'll run."

The lieutenant finally turned to his general. He sniffed and shrugged as if there was no other conclusion to be made.

"So, that's what I did. Sometimes you just gotta keep trying even if it don't look so good."

He paused, adjusting his still-bleeding back. After a half moment of thought, he finished with "sir."

Shaking his head, Artorus chuckled. "Well, Hakan, the lashes are for disobeying my orders, and there will be more waiting for you the next time you disobey direct orders and endanger the men of my army. I only promoted you so that the next time you pull a crazy stunt like that, it might look to the rest of the men a little more like a lieutenant's initiative than a high commander's disobedience."

Artorus held the large man's gaze a moment longer.

"'Just gotta keep trying,' huh? Well, you keep doing that, Lieutenant."

Hakan laughed a slow, rumbling laugh. "Good enough for me, General."

Though, within two years' time, Vith's relentless assaults would finally gain him ground on Ebbea once more, long after the Fifth Planar was off to campaign on Learden, any tactician would have to agree it is all but assured Vith's holdings on the plane would have been at least threefold were it not for the heroic defenses of the Fifth Planar.

Hakan went on to win Artorus more battles and aggravate him unendingly in the process. But Artorus wouldn't have traded him for any other lieutenant.

And now Hakan was dead, slain by the horrific creature, Brakken the Cruel. He'd finally met an enemy he couldn't face down.

The bloodletting would stop soon; it had to.

Chapter XXII – The Long March to Certain Doom

Gnarrl, High Justicar of Lord Brakken, had waited patiently. His blades yearned for the blood of Andrius and Vallon and their friends.

At first he'd thought the vast battle would be a distraction to the rebel command staff and he'd have his chance to catch them all at once – a single fell blow to slice off the head of this fetid rebellion. It was a stupid assumption. At war is where generals are keenest; in battle their senses are heightened and they suspect an attack at all times from every direction. The generals stayed largely apart from one another, meeting only under heavy guard. His chance to strike did not come during the battle. He likely could have slain the Andrius woman and her elf, but then the generals would have been alerted to his presence, and he'd never have the chance to catch them unaware.

Gnarrl looked down into the desperate eyes of an unnamed soldier who lay upon the ground, still bleeding and looking fearfully up to the looming form standing over him. It was not the first such soldier Gnarrl had sought out, but this one bore the colors that Gnarrl wanted – the colors of the Fifth Planar Army. Looking down, Gnarrl could see where Lord Brakken opened the earth to take the soldier.

Lord Brakken...

The sight of Lord Brakken had been painful to Gnarrl. Something inside him ached, though he didn't know exactly what it was. Brakken was his king and his superior at arms; in more ways than one, he was the only father Gnarrl had ever known, and now Gnarrl had just two choices: return to him and tell him of his failure – and failure only brought shame and death – or bring him the heads of the leaders of this rebellion and change his defeat to victory.

This was exactly why he was now on the corpse-littered field.

"You," Gnarrl said to the soldier as he slowly drew his daggers.

Gnarrl's appearance was always one of predatory intimidation, but now – ravaged from weeks of eating rabbits and gophers in the rains of spring and sleeping in the mud and roots – he was a truly savage sight to the crushed man beneath him.

Shivering from the massive loss of blood where his crushed leg bled into the bottomless schism, the soldier had barely enough strength to plead, "N-no... P-p-please..."

"You will tell me where your army is going so that I can go and kill your leaders." Gnarrl grinned widely through the mud crusting his face, bearing his half-orcish fangs. "You will tell me; and I might end your pain... If you do not tell me, only torture stands between you and your inevitable death."

Moments later, the justicar approached Lord General Kremaine, cleaning his daggers and putting them away. Turning to see the walking spectacle that approached, the lord general made no effort to conceal his disdain once he recognized the High Justicar.

"Kremaine," Gnarrl growled, "I need men."

Gnarrl re-sheathed his daggers.

"Lord Justicar," Kremaine managed through his grimace as he forced himself to bow slightly to the half-orc. "I'm afraid I haven't any to spare. The scurrilous rebels have scattered in all directions, and I need every man I have to hunt them down and slaughter them..." His eyes flitted nervously to Gnarrl's daggers, and he carefully added, "as our Wizard-King has commanded."

The lord general eyed Gnarrl. He was obviously confused by the justicar's presence at the battle. Battle was normally no place for such a precision instrument.

"Fool," Gnarrl said plainly.

His cold eyes locked with the lord general's. Almost in the nature of conversing for Gnarrl, he reached back to the hilt of one of his daggers, so recently used. He barely noticed when he did it anymore – it was like a facial expression or a tone of voice. The lord general was visibly unnerved.

"You presume to refuse an order from the High Justicar?" Gnarrl's words crept from him. "I'm guessing Lord Brakken would be quite upset with me for disemboweling one of his lord generals – in front of his own troops, no less – but I just might make an exception for you, worm."

Gnarrl's voice was rough from weeks of travel, only just loud enough for all of the soldiers and officers who were pretending to ignore the conversation to hear.

Kremaine's face betrayed his fear. He knew that Gnarrl could kill him in seconds no matter how many troops were stupid enough to try to stop him. He knew Gnarrl would do so without a second thought. He had better choose his next words very carefully.

Bowing his head once more, Kremaine spoke through gritted teeth. "No, of course not, Lord Justicar. Take as many men as are needed; all soldiers of the Wizard-King's armies are at your disposal."

"Of course," Gnarrl repeated. "And do not try to follow me, Kremaine."

The justicar would not allow the blundering Kremaine to destroy all his careful work. If the lord general would find out the plans of the Fifth Planar Army from this battlefield at all, it would likely be a long time from now. His methods were nowhere near as precise as the justicar's.

Let Kremaine chase these other rebellious fools through the woods a while. Gnarrl had a reputation to regain.

The trapped soldier had told the justicar all about how most of the Fifth Planar had stayed in reserve for this battle, that they may sneak up the Brannus River to assault the fortress of Brakken himself. This was, of course, after Gnarrl had removed a few fingers.

Turning, the justicar pointed to one of the commanders that was standing nearby. "You. You will come with me and bring three dozen of your swiftest men."

The dwarven commander was rightly petrified at his selection. With a pale face, he turned to Kremaine for one last hope of escape.

Kremaine only nodded to him.

The dwarf, now looking quite sickly, turned back to Gnarrl, bowed low, and scurried away to find the troops he'd need.

Mala was already sore again from marching. It seemed to her that her legs would have remembered well the march to the battlefield only days prior. Admittedly, she did also have a deep wound in her left leg. The Sage had performed some healing techniques on it shortly after the skirmish, though, and it truly had healed much faster than Mala would have thought possible. But after walking on it for days, it was clearly not done healing – not entirely.

Her neck, too, still showed a sickly looking shade of discolored skin where that half-orc's hands had grasped her. It was a bruise that had lasted longer than any other she could remember, a slowly fading reminder of what battle truly was.

Wounds and defeat aside, it still felt good to be moving with the army now.

Only a year ago, she might have been filing missives for the allocation of timber resources, and now she marched with a rebellious army. This truth still caught her by surprise from time to time, when she gave it a space in her head.

She walked most days next to Typhondrius.

Her elven friend had been acting strangely ever since Lord Brakken had appeared; he was much more quiet than usual, none of his subtle levity to make their walk easier, and he rubbed his scarred ear almost incessantly.

Even before Typhondrius had surprised them by sharing some of his past, it was far from inconceivable to the noblewoman. Everyone had heard tales of the unequaled cruelty dispensed by the evil Wizard-King. And Typhondrius knew very little else for nearly a hundred years of his life. Surely, this was the first time Typhondrius had seen that inhuman creature since that night he nearly killed him.

Mala could hardly guess at the swirling emotions alight in her elven friend's chest.

The Fifth Planar Army made camp for the evening, among the thick woods. Mala found Typhondrius as the troops set up tents and unpacked foodstuffs.

"My good friend," she called to him as they settled in for the evening.

Typhondrius seemed almost startled by her as he looked up, but then he quickly lowered his hand from his ear and smiled weakly.

"My lady," he said bowing his head. "How is it that we have not seen each other in such a long time? Perhaps this is just the way of things when traveling with an army."

Mala smiled to the elf.

"Typhondrius," she said softly, "we've been walking very near each other for most of the day."

Typhondrius looked away, a slow realization coming to his expression.

Mala did not say anything for a time.

The two of them had relative solitude amongst the huge trees; it was an odd feeling. Despite tens of thousands of people packed into a small space near them, the mighty trees made their world feel somehow more mysterious; somehow larger.

Mala could only imagine the timber yield from massive old-growth trees like these. But most of the foresters made camps far closer to the edge of these woods, where the trees were much smaller and more manageable. Despite that, the yield from the Upper Brannus Woods was sought after for its quality. She likely sat among what could be turned to a significant fortune here in this more ancient part of the woodlands.

Even after all these years of serving the role she had, she was somewhat glad to have left it behind. Finally, she could admit freely that the majesty of these woods was a greater thing than all the carts and cabins and furniture and tinder in the world.

Thoughts such as these had perturbed her from the very earliest magisterial tasks she'd fulfilled. That was all a previous life now anyway...

But Mala could not avoid the topic by letting her mind wander these woods forever. Her friend had need of her.

"Please," she finally said to Typhondrius, "I know of what troubles you."

"My lady," Typhondrius began, "I do not mean to be such a burden to you. You have so many others to look after and I – I should be looking after you, my lady."

"Please," Mala repeated, this time more softly, "a friend is not one that looks after me, and a friend is certainly not a burden." Looking down, Typhondrius's voice was grateful. "You are kind, my lady, as always. I'm sorry. I've not known this sort of kindness for most of my years. It still sets me off kilter."

"I know that the Wizard-King troubles you more than my kindness, Typhondrius. I simply want you to know that I am here to talk if ever you should need me."

"I know..." he said, looking back up to her. "I simply must find the courage for myself to face it... All those horrible years. All those terrible memories... When the master came to the field, I was... I had... it was all just..."

Mala placed a hand on her friend's shoulder and another brief silence passed.

Sighing, Typhondrius looked around. "Where is master Kellos?"

"I believe he counsels with Artorus," she replied.

"Very well," Typhondrius declared. "Then with no others to look after but ourselves, I say we must do just that. Let us rest our wearied bodies."

Typhondrius's body was as tired as hers, surely, but his heart ached even more, guessed Mala.

"And... thank you, my lady."

Mala smiled comfortingly to him and they both retired to their tents for the evening.

It was only moments ago that the rider arrived, his journey doubtlessly slowed much by the thick woods. But the news he carried was important indeed.

The command tent had been assembled, which had been erected without several of the poles in order to fit it between the thick trees of what Artorus guessed were the Lower Brannus Woods. A small command staff surrounded him.

"... to inform you," Artorus continued reading to the small group, "that the numerous Imperial Legions that had beaten us nearly to exhaustion suddenly broke camp and headed for the worldgate. Rumors abound that..." Artorus trailed off.

The command staff, which now regularly included his sister, Typhondrius, and the Sage, all looked to him expectantly.

"It looks like our mighty Wizard-King bleeds," Artorus finally said, vindicated. "He bleeds and the other Wizard-Kings smell it in the water."

Artorus threw the letter to the table, where Highblade scooped it up and began to read.

"It seems," Artorus continued to the rest of the crowd, "Kaladrius has been maneuvering his armies for heavier engagement with The Vastness – or so it is rumored. And if this can be believed, then it is doubtful Phax or Krakus or Vith or Ziov are far behind that cue."

"Yes," Highblade agreed, nodding his head and staring at the letter. "After all our struggles against that blasted Wizard, we could use a few distractions. I hope it's true..."

"I must admit," Kellos stated to the group, "that if this information is credible, it does sound to be a likely assessment, good general. The

Wizards always look for a weakness amongst their enemies. My own observations would corroborate."

A murmur began among the group.

"I must apologize," Braïun said in a somber voice, though it fell within a brief pause in the noise from the crowd. "But all I can think of is three or four more of those terrible creatures descending upon us, confound it. We march to face Lord Brakken, and that task itself will be monumental..."

His voice was quiet, but it bore pain and anger, and it caught the attention of the group. The murmur faltered and an uneasy quiet seized the tent as they thought on the dwarf's words.

Artorus cleared his throat, regaining the attention of the gathering. "But I'm afraid this is not the reason for this meeting, gentlemen, lady. The letter and our off-world strategies can wait for our next military council."

Artorus smirked. "Would the High Commander Braïun please stand." Artorus held a hand out toward the dwarf.

A flash of guilt crossed Braïun's expression, as his last words still hung in the air. But he stood, wiping the guilt from his face as quickly as it had come, and he looked to his general with his head high.

Artorus lowered his arm. His tone became serious. "Officers of the Fifth Planar Army and leaders of the rebellion, I need not tell you what a loss we suffered with the death of one of the mightiest men this army has ever known. Lieutenant Hakan will be missed both in the camps and on the field for his leadership, his tenacity, and even for his bluntness, I think."

Highblade looked pained more than most, but many heads around the room lowered in sorrow.

Braïun, however, still looked at Artorus, confusion beginning to show in his expression. He tucked his beard nervously into its usual place in his belt.

"We will remember the time we had with Hakan. However, it is in the shadow of his defeat that we have reason to rejoice, as well. We must celebrate the soldier who will take his position at my side." Artorus's hand rose once more toward High Commander Braïun. "From this moment forth," Artorus went on, now louder and with more pride in his voice, "let us call this good man, Orgron Braïun, 'lieutenant.' Though he has only recently been promoted to high commander, he has long deserved his new title. As a dwarf of resolve, honor, skill, ferocity..." Artorus paused. "And, yes, impeccable fashion." A brief snicker ran through the tent. "I am proud to have 'Slick' as a lieutenant of the Fifth Planar Army."

The mood turned immediately, as a hearty round of applause broke out in the tent. Braïun, though, still stood looking gape-jawed at his general. Artorus could not help but laugh at the expression.

"Now spread the news, gentlemen!" Artorus called with the wave of his hand and the high command and others dispersed.

Lieutenant Highblade remained, as Artorus expected, and took Braïun's hand in a rigorous shake.

"I will miss Hakan more than I'll likely know at this time," Highblade said to Braïun, "but I'll be damned if I'm not ecstatic to have a little more tact amongst the lieutenants."

He smiled widely to Braïun, and the dwarf laughed back at him.

"I shall try not to disappoint," Braïun replied.

The dwarf fixed a lick of hair that had fallen out of place and all three shared a laugh.

The three stayed in the tent for likely another hour; they shared wine and stories of Hakan's greatest exploits. The stories could have gone on longer.

Eventually, though, the three leaders retired for the evening as well.

Artorus had noticed something that he had seen on neither Highblade's nor Braïun's face in some long days now – genuine happiness. They still had a very rough road ahead of them, but for this moment now, Artorus could feel safe in the knowledge that he had made the right choice.

The march through the thick woods continued for days. Mala's legs seemed to become accustomed to their torturous trudging through the never-ending woodlands.

The dysentery that had struck poor Warin's forces so strongly did afflict some of the Fifth Planar, but it was thankfully manageable. In his style, Kellos had provided invaluable advice for preventing further spread of the disease. He oversaw the sanitation of mess tents and the management of the stricken. He even had some sort of concern about the latrine pits, which Mala hadn't cared to become too involved with.

Through some great position in Koth's plan, it seemed as though their deception during the retreat had succeeded. The Fifth Planar Army did not seem to be followed closely. However, that did mean that, after their unfortunate loss at the Battle of the Lakewoods, their two companion armies had to suffer a heavy burden.

Mala sat in on the strategy sessions, and, by this point in their conflict, with or without military training, the various army staff seemed to view her as one of the leaders of the rebellion.

Reports had come in that Magron's Thirty-Third Homeworld Army was still fighting as they retreated through the Lakewoods and beyond. By those same reports, the majority of Warin's Second Planar, however, were largely either captured or retreating desperately into the surroundings of the great battle. It seemed Warin's deception of soldiers dressed to imitate the Fifth Planar was upheld, though. So, if things went according to plan, that would mean the Imperial Legions would be chasing what they thought were fragments of the Second Planar and Fifth Planar armies, as they continued to clash with the Thirty-Third Homeworld.

Still further reports came from wider-reaching parts of Myrus. Iron shipments intended for the war efforts of The Vastness had been mysteriously afflicted by bandits. Though, as Mala and Artorus knew, the shipments from the Enton Province, under the sympathetic King

Antioch, had actually been redirected to the rebels. Furthermore, some of the villages and towns where the Imperial Legions stored weapons or supplies were also found to be inaccessible or missing. Again, sympathetic mayors and nobles helped the efforts of the rebellion.

It had cost many lives – *too many* already – but it was quite difficult to say things weren't going well for them and their cause.

The situation was, with some unplanned variance, as it was supposed to be. Despite the Battle of the Lakewoods lost and despite armies being scattered and beaten, The Vastness was in a state of conflict. More reports had even surfaced from as far as Ebbea and Learden that unrest had arisen there as well. Perhaps most powerfully of all, the rumors of the other Wizard-Kings taking some action were verified from other sources, through Ayedd and Brakson. The word was spreading now across the multiverse. Artorus spoke of how it was only a matter of time until every one of the twenty-seven worlds knew: no longer must mortals obey Wizard-kind. Mala found it hard to argue with him.

And through it all, the Fifth Planar desperately hoped that Lord Brakken's attentions would remain focused more on the wayward armies and restless neighbors than themselves, that they might slip through the riverside woods to his very doorstep.

Mala had just exited one of the strategy sessions when she saw Lieutenant Braïun smiling as Artorus laughed – probably at some joke of his own. Her brother had a high opinion of his own sense of humor. And, truthfully, the whole scene was a heartwarming sight to see again.

Braïun had gone through a metamorphosis that no man should be forced to do, but lately he seemed his proper self.

"Good lieutenant," she began as she approached the two, "good brother." She smiled to each of them. "After serious injuries, horrid battles, and weeks of forced marching, I am so glad to see smiling faces."

The smiles both faded.

Though she meant it as a statement of encouragement, Mala immediately realized her folly. In noting Braïun's smile, she reminded him of why it had been scarce. The same thing had happened often after Artorus lost Elsa – Mala should have learned by now.

Braïun looked down, but Artorus nodded understandingly to his sister. He had probably tried his hand at cheering up their dwarven friend a dozen times already. Perhaps it was time for reinforcements.

"I've an army to run, an assault to plan, and a Wizard-King to defeat – and very little time to do it," Artorus said to the two of them with a smile. He nodded to Braïun. "Lieutenant." And then he placed a hand on Mala's shoulder. "Mal."

Braïun and Artorus shared a salute, and then the lord general left.

Braïun had been off his cane now for a day or two. He looked healthy, all things considered. Mala motioned for them to walk together.

Mala placed a hand on his shoulder. Mala knew this state; all too well she knew it. She said nothing for some time as they walked slowly through the thick woods. Braïun seemed happy to have the company at least.

Finally, the dwarf spoke, still not looking at Mala.

"I know why you walk with me, my lady. You wish to comfort me. I have already pledged my services anew to the rebellion."

His voice only wavered slightly. His convictions were true.

Mala nodded at his words and let a short moment pass before she responded. "Orgron, I know of no mortal in the multiverse who could fault your loyalty to our cause or your service to the Fifth Planar. But none of these things eliminate the pain. I know the pain you feel – at least I know something like it."

"I know I'm not alone in my pain, my lady," Braïun replied. "I know that you feel the same sort of pain; that *so many* do... I just keep thinking about how I will never get to see them again... I just wish—" He began to stumble over his words. "I just wish I could have seen them one last time and could have told them how much I love them..."

Mala nodded again and spoke in her calm voice. "I never had the honor of meeting your family, Orgron, but I can tell you one thing for certain: there was never any doubt in their minds or in their hearts that you loved them. None."

Braïun looked to Mala, thinking on her words for a moment. "You are likely right, Lady Andrius. I just – for some reason – I just can't stop thinking about it. I don't want it to interfere with my duties as an officer..."

Mala nodded in perfect understanding of what Braïun was saying. Even to this day, she thought frequently of Elsa.

It was no longer just a source of pain for her, but a source of inspiration.

"Orgron, may I ask you something about your family?"

"You may, my lady."

"In your most blessed moments with your family, what was it that you valued most about them?"

Braïun thought on that question for a long time as they walked.

He finally answered, "It was the joy of being with them, simply and truly; the peace and comfort of having my beautiful wife and our amazing children. I could hardly believe they were mine."

A wistful smile flashed across his face and Mala nodded in reply.

"You know of Artorus's late wife, Elsa, right?" she inquired after another moment.

Braïun nodded quickly and spoke as if to apologize. "And it is precisely this fact that I find most troubling. How can I claim any greater pain than Artorus? Than you or any other mortal who has lost loved ones to these Planewars? It is an insult to the memory of all the fallen mortals for me to falter."

"Please, this is not why I ask. In fact, I'm quite certain that Elsa would not have it – were she not with Koth now. She would say to you: 'please don't let me be a source of sorrow, I just couldn't stand it.' She never did want anyone fearing for her or pained by anything, really. She was peace incarnate, Orgron."

Braïun nodded, but was silent.

"Kindness," Mala said, looking out toward the huge trees that kept the two company. "It was her unending kindness that I loved most, though..."

She looked back to her dwarven friend. His hair and beard were kept as well as ever, but his eyes betrayed the wearied interior of the man. His physical wounds had healed nicely once again, his sturdiness still treating him well. Though dwarven healing may help the body, the soul heals differently.

"This," she informed him, "is the reason I mention my sister-by-law: because that kindness – that beautiful person she was – can never be lost from this multiverse. It lives on in me and it makes me strong.

"And the only reason Elsa is not still here to bring such light into my brother's life and to raise their beautiful child is because of the Wizards and their godsbedamned war."

Mala could feel her voice lose the calm and caring tone it normally carried. She let determination replace them. Braïun stopped and looked into Mala's eyes.

"For far too long," she continued, "the Wizard-Kings have caused this strife for us, killing countless mortals for their perpetual war. And Elsa, who once was a sister, a friend, and a role model, has now become an inspiration as well. She is still every bit as much those things she was in life, if only when I take the time to remember, but now she has become even more; she is a guiding light for me and for my brother and for anyone else who will remember her and fight to end these Planewars."

Looking to the dwarf, feeling a fire in her now, Mala concluded.

"And your family is the same, Orgron; they are now more than they ever were – if you can let them be. They can be those same beautiful, warm, loving memories, but they can be an inspiration too. An inspiration to stop these Planewars and stop countless more families from meeting the same fate."

Her eyes had glossed with tears, but she held them in.

A long silence followed, and the sounds of the army and the calls of the woodland animals filled the void. They had stopped in a small clearing not far from where the hustling men of the Fifth Planar finished striking camp for yet another long day of marching.

"Lady Andrius," Orgron said, "you are wise beyond your years. I once told your brother that you and he were the reason this rebellion would succeed, but he seemed to think it was more you than he." The dwarf smiled.

"I thank you for your counsel."

The call to resume the march rang through the woods and echoed on down the lines of troops.

Mala hugged her friend in the cool air of morning. She could only hope her words helped.

The two made their ways to their respective staff and the army began to slowly crawl through the woods again. There was still a long way to go.

Chapter XXIII – Magic

Typhondrius trudged through the dampened earth that fought for space with countless ferns and bushes and trees of all sizes. Though he'd always heard that elves had some spiritual connection to the sundry woodlands of the twenty-seven worlds, he did not feel quite comfortable amidst the trees. Typhondrius did respect the majesty of so many life forms living in harmony, it was true. But he rationalized his discomfort as a simple preference for warmth and cleanliness. Somewhere in the gentle elf, he knew the very essence of his elven heritage was being bred from his veins, generation by generation, by the Wizard-Kings' efforts to create a perfect servant race.

He had always heard that not every Dominance relegated elves to a servant class, though most that he was aware of did. It was an oppressive thought to imagine millions of elves across dozens of worlds who are raised from birth to be perfectly servile.

Though this really ought to have given Typhondrius resolve to fight against the Wizard-Kings, somehow it only challenged his courage further. Perhaps the Wizards truly were gods; perhaps their power did not stop at the awful might they wielded with their hands and with their minds, that terrifying sight he had seen with his own eyes once again on the Lakewoods Plain.

Perhaps Wizards truly did control the ultimate fates of mortals…

"My friend," Mala called to Typhondrius, thankfully breaking his concentration on such thoughts, "our scouts are reporting that the woods break ahead – not another day's walk. Already the trees are growing more sparse. Once we are out of the Upper Brannus Woods, we shall pick up pace greatly."

Mala's voice was always soothing to Typhondrius. All his life, he'd known only Lord Brakken and the refuse of the nobility that clawed their way closest to him. All Typhondrius's life he knew only the harshness of servitude.

Mala was peace, Mala was quiet resolve, Mala was kindness and compassion; Mala was everything that his life had not been.

"I only tell you," Mala went on, "because, if your legs have been as mine, you will have thought we were marching at a 'faster pace' all along. We must redouble our resolve for marching."

She smiled to him.

"Yes, my lady," Typhondrius replied, unable to keep a smile from his own face, "I believe we are of the same impression of these travels, and I do not believe either of us has ever marched with armies to decide the fate of worlds. Hard to even believe it still." He thought a second on that. "In fact, *can it be* believed? *By the master.* I've been spending too much time with the Sage…"

Mala's pleasant smile broke into pleasant laughter.

"Good Typhondrius," she said through a satisfied sigh, "I daresay you've changed quite a lot since we first met. I seem to recall a timid elf who could not begin a statement nor end one without bowing. Now, here on the precipice of victory, you make witty jokes. I must say: I like it."

Though Typhondrius wanted to tell Mala more, he sufficed with a simple truth.

"I believe you change all those who meet you for the better, Lady Andrius."

Mala's face reddened a bit at that.

"You," she managed, "my truest of friends, are far too kind. That is hardly the case."

"Your modesty, my lady, does not suit you. I think that there is no other among these many planes more deserving of praise."

"Well," Mala said, shaking her head, "we can talk at length sometime as to whether I'm deserving or not. In the meantime, we've got an army to care for."

She finally placed the scrolls she'd been carrying into Typhondrius's hands.

"I'd like you to look over these for me and tell me if our numbers match up. I still know no other who can see numbers like you do."

"It will be done, my lady."

He took the scrolls and bowed slightly to Mala.

"See!" she interjected. "There you go bowing again! I thought we were making progress here."

He smiled. "I believe there is some saying about an old dog and new tricks that applies."

Laughing, Mala turned and walked away. "Ninety-nine years is hardly old for an elf, my friend," she called back jovially. "You just need to take the *time* to learn."

He chuckled softly as the noblewoman trod back through the forest from the general direction she'd come.

The two had been walking as they spoke. In fact, Typhondrius could hardly remember a waking moment in the past several weeks that he was *not* walking. But, finally, the Fifth Planar Army seemed to be settling in to camp for the evening.

He made his way to find a tent in which to study these numbers. Perhaps the Sage would be available to help. Typhondrius was certain his command of the numbers was far superior to his own.

His uneasiness at the Sage's apparent similarity to Lord Brakken had dissolved almost completely by now. Even if the facial characteristics and the sound of their voices might be the same, the words they spoke and the actions they took could not be more dissimilar. This was a solace to the elf.

Artorus sat down hard. After many days of marching, this morning was the first real chance they'd gotten to practice their swordsmanship. Artorus was tired and he breathed heavily; he was feeling his age more and more lately. However, he also felt his swordsmanship improving some. He'd always figured Master Nightstar, back at the academy, was the finest swordsman in the twenty-seven worlds, and he could not learn any more from another teacher. He was wrong – likely on both counts.

Across from him, sitting with the lord general in the small clearing – the kind which was becoming quite a lot more common as the Upper Brannus Woods became thinner – was his lieutenant, Gregory Highblade.

"I must say, General," Highblade spoke through labored breath, "I think we're both losing our edge in our old age."

"I think you're just saying that to mask the fact that you nearly lost just now." Artorus grinned at his lieutenant.

Laughing some as he caught his breath, Highblade retorted, "It is always so sad to see old men becoming delusional with age."

A dwarven soldier approached the two in the small clearing, and both officers looked to him. He was young for a dwarf, not likely more than twenty-five, and Artorus didn't recognize his face immediately. A short beard adorned his chin and bushy eyebrows jutted from under the leather cap he wore on his head.

"Sirs?" he said in a timid tone as he saluted.

"Go ahead, soldier," Artorus said up to the soldier, not quite summoning the energy to stand for his return salute.

"Sir, I've been instructed to inform you that the meeting you requested has been assembled."

This dwarf looked to be desperate in his attempt to meet regulation. He stood rigid, his arms at his sides and his eyes straight forward, despite his lord general and his lieutenant lounging in the grass.

Artorus smiled to the young dwarf. "Maybe you haven't noticed, but things in the Fifth Planar aren't always so formal." He stood and wiped the sweat from his brow. "Especially not recently – what with open rebellion against the god-king and all."

Highblade arose beside his general and laughed lightly.

The dwarf looked very hesitant for a moment, glancing between the lieutenant and the general.

He finally replied, "I know, sir, I'm sorry. It's just... I've never actually spoken to you before."

"And this is cause for trepidation of some sort?"

His face becoming redder, the soldier replied quickly. "Um, yes, sir – I mean, no sir, I simply..."

Highblade and Artorus both glanced at each other and shared a laugh.

Highblade spoke, attempting to save the soldier from further embarrassment. "Young dwarf, I believe your message has been delivered and your lord general thanks y—"

"What I'm trying to say is," the dwarf interjected with sudden clarity, finally meeting Artorus's eyes, "thank you, Lord General Vallon... For giving us freedom, for once in our lives; *freedom* from the Wizard. He thinks he owns the multiverse. I can't wait to show him how wrong he is."

With another salute, he turned and walked hurriedly out of the clearing. The two officers stood in the small clearing in silence a moment until Highblade turned to Artorus.

"Well, that was candid," spoke Highblade.

Artorus nodded in thought.

"I think, my good general," he went on, "that these men of the Fifth Planar are changing."

"Well, they follow because they are soldiers of—"

"They don't follow you because you are their general, Artorus," Highblade spoke earnestly, cutting his general off. "They stopped doing that when you told them they could leave if they wanted; when you told them we were rebelling against the War Maker. That time is over. *Now* they follow you because you *inspire* them."

Artorus might normally have argued the point further, but he was somewhat humbled by the honesty in the lieutenant's voice. He nodded thankfully to the half-elf. "Well, I should get to my meeting then."

"The Sage?" Highblade asked.

"Yes, he has something he wants to discuss apparently."

"I hope he has some good news for us..." The half-elf chuckled. "Magic words that will make Brakken drop dead or some whatnot." Highblade smiled broadly. "Me? I'll stick to my blade."

He flipped his practice sword up from its resting place on the ground with a swift foot and gave Artorus a quick salute before each of them left the clearing in opposite directions.

Artorus went to where his command tent had been erected. This close to the edge of the Upper Brannus Woods, they could again erect the tent in its proper fashion. In it, he found three figures he had come to enjoy chatting with.

Mala, Kellos, and Typhondrius each greeted Artorus.

"Well," Artorus implored, "though I don't mean to be short, I do have another staff meeting shortly. What can I help with, Kellos?"

Kellos, after having his usual moment of thought, addressed the other three.

"I had Lord General Vallon call this meeting to complete a discussion we had started a short time ago."

Mala and Artorus shared a quick quizzical glance.

"Magic," Kellos stated plainly in his ever-commanding voice, filling the air around them. "I had stated a time would come that I would explain further the nature of this ability."

Artorus understood now what this meeting was about; he and his fellow mortals would now learn of the mighty power the Wizard-King wielded and – hopefully – how they could defeat it.

Mala looked as though she could barely contain her excitement, and if Artorus was being honest, he was feeling similarly. Not only were they lucky enough to have a Sage – one of the timeless keepers of knowledge – in their company long enough to teach them some sliver of his immortal wisdom, but he would also now reveal the very information that might just spell the success of this rebellion.

And justice for Elsa...

"Magic," the Sage expounded, "is the ability to bend reality to one's will. It is powerful, much of it is irreversible, and it is often nearly instantaneous. Also, it is not omnipotent; like most everything in this multiverse, it has been observed to follow laws and have limitations.

"I'll not reveal all I know on the topic, both in the interest of time and in the interest of retention. What I will reveal is the knowledge that I believe you three will need to succeed at your task. And I believe it bears explanation that I share this with you not out of a specific desire to see the race of Wizards defeated – as is your stated goal – I share it because it is information that I believe will introduce some balance into this equation. I see that Wizard-kind has grown to a level of imbalance that is dangerous to the multiverse, and I think mortals will be the ones to correct this. Exactly when and how, you may be the ones to determine, and so I will reveal some of what I know."

Artorus shifted in his seat. It was likely that no mortal outside of a Sage's monastery had ever heard what they were about to be told.

"Firstly," Kellos said in an almost-rehearsed sort of fashion, "magic has three branches from which all of its powers are derived. There is elemental magic which creates, destroys, and bends the primary elements to a Wizard's will. There is spatial magic which manipulates the space around us as well as things such as momentum and even what we perceive as 'time' to some degree. And there is psychic magic which manipulates the thoughts, emotions, and will of mortals.

"Secondly, know that magic is not what one might call a 'natural' force; it is of what I suspect to be a wholly supernatural origin. As such, it does not follow all the rules of this multiverse. For instance, in order to create fire on any plane of the multiverse, one needs fuel, oxygen, and a source of ignition. This is not so with Wizards, nor does the fire from a Wizard's origin do just as the fire of mortals does; similar properties of heat and the consumption of oxygen; quite different when it comes to fuel sources and ignition. And some Wizards have excellent control, such as igniting their entire body in flames, yet leaving their skin and clothing unscathed. Similar differences exist in the other branches of magical power, and the level to which a Wizard specializes in one branch or another can vary."

Across from Artorus, Typhondrius shifted uncomfortably. They each had now seen the fire from Brakken's own hands, but Ty had seen it much more closely than any of them.

Mala placed her hand on Ty's. The Sage went on to address the elf directly, motioning to him.

"Good Typhondrius, the mark on your head is from a Wizard's flame, is it not?"

Artorus cringed slightly at the Sage's directness. He'd never heard Typhondrius discuss his scar with anyone. From the day Artorus had found him, with the scorch still fresh upon his head and the wound very clearly going much deeper than that, he made it a point not to ask him.

Despite an initial flinch, Ty did not shrivel, as Artorus had expected. Instead, he glanced to Mala, took a deep breath, and responded to the Sage.

"You are correct, master Sage," he spoke directly, though his voice was still wavering slightly. "The immortal Wizard-King, Lord Brakken, himself did this to me."

Artorus was impressed. Something had been changing in Typhondrius these past years – and more so these past months. Artorus was proud to call him a friend and glad to have him as an ally in this rebellion. He had provided counsel and comfort to Artorus and his sister, he had invaluable insight into their enemy, and still, his greatest part in the rebellion was surely yet to be played.

"Yes," replied Kellos, "I knew simply from the patterns of the scars. And from those same patterns I can see that you did not recoil or pull away. It is highly unlikely that one would survive such an attack, and so I believe it indicates what most would consider to be great bravery that you stood and faced him."

'Great bravery?' Artorus found himself thinking. *It's true, isn't it? Ty is one of the bravest of any among this rebellion. He's the only one present to have faced the Wizard-King directly. Bravery indeed...*

Typhondrius had the look of a man who was forced suddenly to reevaluate all he had known, and had fallen into a deep, thoughtful stare.

"Now," Kellos continued, "Wizards have burned down entire forests, controlled the minds of thousands, bent space and time to their will, and shaken continents with their magic. It should be noted, also, that Lord Brakken is not the most powerful of their number by the assessment of the Sages. Yet even the greatest Wizards in the multiverse do have limitations to what their powers can do. You see, each time Wizards attempt to bend reality, it requires something of them. This brings me back to the three branches of magic."

Reaching one of his long, muscular arms out to the center of the table and, using only his finger, Kellos began to somehow carve into the hardwood. He had no implements and was not using his nail. Artorus simply watched in astonishment as the Sage carved a diagram into the table as though by fire. Indeed, a faint scent of smoke could be smelled in the tent.

"The first branch that I mentioned, elemental magic, is the ability to create, alter, manipulate, diminish, or negate the shape and mass of the primary elements of the multiverse. These elements are commonly considered air, earth, water, and fire, though there are those that argue more primaries exist or that combinations thereof form entirely new sub-branches. Using elemental magic is the most primal of magical forces and requires simple but precise movements of the body of the Wizard. While I know of no specific limitations within the laws of magic themselves preventing a Wizard from potentially creating or destroying entire mountains from half a world away or engulfing the entire sky in flames, the extent to which any known Wizard yet has manipulated the elements is limited to the approximate size of a small plain or intermediately sized lake or hill that is within roughly the eyesight of the Wizard."

Kellos continued to etch the hardwood as he spoke, creating a circle with a Wizard's hand at its center; a first line had already taken shape, and he began a second line extending from the center, each of them with various pictures and symbols.

"Spatial magic is not well understood, even by the Sages, and it is the most widely varied branch of magic. The space around us is a more complex thing than mortals could likely know. One commonly practiced and easily demonstrated example of this branch is the ability to shunt or transpose two spaces in the multiverse and the matter contained within them. I believe all present are aware of the technique commonly referred to as 'teleportation.' Simply put, this is the selection of two shapes in two locations and the exchange of all matter between the two. Other documented powers of spatial magic are somewhat lacking in consistency; it is said that an arrow's momentum or even the very time it takes to move out of its way could be at the whims of a powerful enough Wizard using spatial magic. Some have told of a sort of portal that can be torn into the fabric of space, and others have written about Wizards aging mortals to elderly beings before their eyes. This type of magic requires great presence of mind, even a meditative state depending on the desired effect, and seems also to be limited to the general vicinity of the Wizard, though the farthest reliably recorded distance teleported was across a small sea. This power does not seem to be able to pierce from one plane to another directly, though again, there is no specific limitation stating as such in the known laws of magic."

Finally completing a third arm to his concentric circle diagram, the Sage began to fill in the surprisingly detailed symbols attached to it in the elaborate pictograph.

"The final branch of magic is called psychic magic," the Sage continued in his lecture. "The Sages' understanding of this branch of magic is limited to the understanding of the metaphysical phenomenon known as the mortal mind, though it does indeed demonstrably hold sway over the thoughts, emotions, and actions of mortals to one degree or another. Memories, emotions, dreams, and perceptions can all be altered by a Wizard. Given the right circumstances, it is believed that every aspect of a mortal being's mind can be controlled by a Wizard. Simpler concepts such as 'protect me' or 'kill him' can be conveyed to entire groups of beings, as has been documented on numerous occasions as the 'stealing of souls.' To exert the most potent psychic powers over a mortal, a Wizard must have eye contact with them to at least initiate the bond, though the true extent of these abilities are yet unknown to the Sages. It has been theorized that Wizards must keep some small portion of their consciousness concentrating to keep this control over a mortal being, and, if confirmed, those Wizards that are well-practiced at this magic would seem to be able to split their concentration many dozens of ways and maintain it through wakefulness and meditation alike. The aforementioned mortal psyche being arguably more complex and nebulous then the physical universe, this branch of magic has much research yet to be made."

Kellos paused.

Staring into the carving now created in his table, Artorus was deep in thought. All the mortals had just heard more information than they could possibly digest here and now, he suspected. He'd have to think on this for some time.

But herein lay the secret to defeating Brakken, he was sure of it.

Kind of the Sage to take notes for me, Artorus thought as he peered at the diagram.

"So," inquired Mala finally, "the power of magic is not unlimited? Wizards are not all-powerful as so many believe?"

"No," the Sage replied, more quickly than he usually responded. "You wrote a letter to me decades ago, Lady Andrius, assuming as much, did you not?"

Mala flushed at this. "I can barely remember what that letter said, Kellos. I was only a child..."

"It contained some rather advanced hypotheses for one so young as yourself, at the time of writing," the Sage added.

Artorus couldn't help but smirk at Mala's embarrassment. He always did remember her as a highly curious youth. Many among the nobility apparently thought sagely pursuits were better left to the men. Obviously, they never tried to convince a teenage Mala Andrius of it, because they would have failed.

Kellos continued, "Wizards do have limitations. The Lord General Vallon has stated it before: a Wizard who visits a battlefield will cause much destruction. Always, though, they leave as quickly as they come."

Yes, thought Artorus. *Let's find Brakken's weakness, shall we?*

"I knew it," Artorus proclaimed, nodding. "I've watched it happen. So, just how much power does a Wizard control? Would we have, say, an hour before he was rendered helpless? How quickly do they regain their strength to hurl Wizard's fire?"

The Sage replied ponderously. "These questions, I believe, can be answered only very broadly. Lord Brakken, your most present target, is a singular being and is not represented by the specifics of any other Wizard, I have not seen such a display myself from Brakken or any other Wizard, nor have I heard firsthand accounts of such.

"I do know that reliable records of Delemere have described battles between Wizards lasting anywhere from a few short minutes to as long as six hours, unless exaggerations such as 'battled for weeks' or 'struggled through the dark days' can be extrapolated as somehow veritable. Histories, as written by mortals, tend to exaggerate figures such as this, it should be noted. That said, I should think that if there ever were a time for a Wizard to use every last power at his command, it would be in the fight during which his life ended. So I suggest you estimate liberally in your suppositions of Lord Brakken's longevity in combat, ranging likely in the number of several hours."

Artorus paled a bit. Hours – or days – fighting a Wizard did not sound like an exciting prospect. But there *were* limits.

"If there truly are limits at all..." Typhondrius added coldly.

Mala turned to the elf. "You have more information that could help us, friend? I think this would be the best time to reveal it."

Typhondrius looked to his audience, steeling himself. He swallowed hard.

"The master—" He shook his head with disgust. "I mean Lord Brakken... I can't say much for his abilities in battle..." The former servant closed his eyes as he continued. "But there were several who Lord Brakken did not deem worthy of gruesome death at his hands.

They were not consumed by flames nor crushed by stone nor suffocated where they stood nor shot through with lightning." He shuddered. "Most servants faced a fate such as this one day. Whether you might one day arrive late to a task or you had some simple misstep in the wrong moment... or... dropped a drink..."

Ty shook his head.

"No," he continued, "a simple death was not enough for the most *blasphemous* offenders. Those failed assassins and lord generals that committed the greatest follies, the greatest criminals of The Vastness – he stole their souls...

"It was an awful fate. Most of them became mindless drooling slaves, cursed to wander the halls of the fortress until they died of starvation, never eating any of the food that lay about the fortress any given day. But the *truly* unfortunate few he deemed worthy of such torture, he would have them eat and they continued to live as his playthings for untold years.

"There was a decrepit elf that we simply called 'Ghast,' who had wandered the halls as long as any of us elves could remember, paying some incalculable cost for some unknowable folly... He mostly held onto cloaks for visitors, but I could not bear to be in his presence. He moaned ever so softly, like a torturous pain was buried deep within him..."

Typhondrius shuddered once more as he paused.

"One night, when Lord Brakken had hosted some of the kings at the fortress, I had to stand by Ghast for a time. It was the worst night of my life, until the night I left the fortress... But I could swear upon the Wizards that he said a word to me... Just one word..."

Ty looked up to the others, tears welling from his eyes.

"He said 'help.' He was talking to me. He said 'help...'"

Typhondrius spoke now with hardness in his voice. "I *do not* believe Wizards have limits to their powers. I don't think this 'psychic magic' Kellos speaks of ever ends. I am certain that Ghast still wanders those halls as we speak, and he will remain tortured until his body has turned to dust... Though it sickens me to utter it, I consider myself lucky that he chose the flames for me that night."

Lucky to be touched by Wizard's fire... the thought lingered in Artorus's mind for an uncomfortable period of time as he looked upon the elf.

Four years now, and this was the first he'd heard Ty talk about the horrors he had witnesses in that fortress all those years.

Mala once again took Ty's hand in hers.

Artorus nodded gratefully to his elven friend. "Thank you, Ty. I know we've never spoken more of that night I found you outside of Brakken's fortress. I know how much it pains you to tell of it now. But I will *never* know the extent of your tortures serving that monster...

"I suspected this 'psychic magic' will be something we have to deal with. Still, I think our greatest resistance will come from the elemental and spatial powers of Lord Brakken. I've seen Wizards unleash them on armies before... We've seen what these can do to *my* army once already..."

Mala also nodded. "As horrible a fate as having my soul stolen might be, I fear more for the other things Brakken might do to our soldiers when we storm the fortress." She looked to Typhondrius. "And, my good friend," she reasoned, "Kellos tells us of how we can avoid this fate. We should all make the effort to avoid the eyes of Lord Brakken once we're in the fortress – and we should order the troops as such. Then we can effectively eliminate this particular threat."

"And as for the other magics," Artorus added thoughtfully, "I think Kellos has told us how to defeat those as well... A distraction of enough intensity might be able to break the concentration he needs to use this spatial magic, and if we can manage to restrict his movements well enough, we should be able to avoid his elemental powers as well."

"These are plausible theories," Kellos stated simply.

To Artorus, it may as well have been an enthusiastic endorsement.

He smiled to his sister. He knew that Elsa's justice was close now. A few dozen more miles, the element of surprise, and some luck, and the Wizard-King would be either captured or dead. His sister smiled back at him. He could barely believe that their victory seemed so real and present now.

Typhondrius cleared his throat, and the others looked at him. "I believe there is one aspect of the Wizard that we have not accounted for..." He appeared to be waiting for someone else to bring it up, but it seemed he would have to. "What of his ability to resist our weapons?"

The Sage nodded slightly. "Yes, the physical characteristics of Wizards are still something of a mystery to the Sages as well, but the prevailing theory regarding the resistance to bodily harm is that this is some extension of their spatial magic, though there are problems with this theory."

Kellos frowned slightly. Artorus guessed he was not used to wanting for knowledge on any topic.

"For instance," Kellos went on, "some weaponry has impaled the Wizards, or they have otherwise suffered what to a mortal would surely be injurious, without ever seeming to show any sort of wound for it. If spatial magic somehow stopped the weaponry from piercing them, as it may very well do in some instances, this would still fail to explain a woundless impalement."

He shook his head. "I surmise there could be more to it than mere spatial magic, but my information on the topic is inadequate to form much more than conjecture."

Hm, Artorus pondered. *Knowledge that not even a Sage knows...*

"Well, like the Sage has said," Artorus mentioned, "Brakken's magic is not limitless. Perhaps he will exhaust his ability to resist our blades. And, regardless of whether our weapons can actually hurt him, if we can manage to counter his three forms of offensive magic, then we can perhaps subdue him... Even if we must shackle him and chain him and blindfold him and gag him and throw him into a well and guard it day and night... eventually, he'll no longer be a threat to us; he'll no longer be in a position to lord his power over mortals and force them to war. Our goal will be accomplished."

Artorus had always felt it would be much safer to kill the beast, but he had known all along that their mortal efforts may just not be enough to slay a Wizard. It was a hard truth he forced himself to face. Capture would serve their purpose nearly as well, though.

Mala looked over to Kellos with a certain inquisitive flash in her eyes. "Noble Sage, I think that there is one more major aspect of magic that you have not yet revealed to us."

This was a shift in tone. Artorus was surprised at her accusatory air, but Kellos did not seem surprised in the slightest.

"You are correct, Lady Andrius," was the Sage's reply.

Mala waited to hear more from the Sage to no avail, so finally, she clarified her inquiry. "Do *you* possess these powers as well? Did I not see this when we fled my family's estate that awful night, when the imperial captain became suddenly... afflicted?"

Kellos thought a moment more.

"My lady, I have mentioned before that not all information is helpful or safe to know. This is another example of such knowledge, I believe."

"Well," Artorus's sister retorted, "tell me this... Are you not here to aid us in knowing all that we can know to even our odds against Lord Brakken and his kind?"

Artorus saw a steely determination in Mala's eyes. Artorus knew that determination all too well; he had lost many an argument to it. How would the immortal and wise Sage hold up to the indomitable Mala Andrius?

Kellos thought. "To some degree, yes. And perhaps you are forgetting that Brakken is a Wizard and I am a Sage."

"I know there is quite a difference, good Kellos," Mala added. "Is it not possible, however, that Sages also possess some kind of magic, and that Lord Brakken could have one or more Sages at his disposal? Indeed, did you not state yourself that most Sages would oppose your actions? Should we not know just how this might threaten our success and destroy the careful balance for which you seem to be aiming?"

Kellos frowned slightly, but still he spoke in his almost-rehearsed sort of tone. "It is very unlikely that Lord Brakken commands any Sages or that any Sage would take such direct action against us, Lady Andrius."

"Impossible?" she asked.

Another pause.

"No," the Sage finally replied.

Artorus looked at his sister's face and he saw that little girl back on the noble estate, so many years ago, who had just gotten her way from their mother. He saw the girl who had convinced her big brother to give her his sweet bread.

Had his sister really bent an immortal Sage to her will? He couldn't help but smile.

She waited for Kellos to continue with the slightest smirk on her face.

"Very well," Kellos began. "Sages, as the noble lady has surmised, do indeed possess the power of magic."

"Hm," Artorus let slip.

Despite his sister's and his theorizations, this was a rather shocking revelation.

So, just how are these Sages related to the Wizards? the general thought. *What might this mean?*

Artorus could see Ty's eyes narrow at the Sage. The elf's thoughts were likely even more suspicious than his own.

"It is," Kellos continued, "to every degree I am aware of, save one, the very same power that Wizards wield. To my knowledge, while Wizards' capabilities can vary to quite some extent, all Sages possess nearly the exact same prowess with their magic."

"So, you were wielding magic!" Mala exclaimed. "Was that psychic magic, then, that you used to convince that imperial captain to let us pass?"

"Yes," replied Kellos, "and with the brothers Hereditus and Orion before they departed. The former, I forced to speak as I wished, and the latter two, I imparted memories upon."

Wizards shared the power of magic with Sages. This could change much about how the multiverse viewed Sages. Artorus could understand why Kellos had been so hesitant to share this. He hadn't seen Kellos throw flames from his hands or teleport across any distances, but still, in a major way, he commanded the same powers that Wizards did.

"I wonder," Artorus asked Kellos, "what is it like to wield such power, to bend reality to your will?"

Kellos thought another moment. "Perhaps I may ask you: what is it like not to wield such powers?"

Artorus frowned.

"I suspect," the Sage went on, "our answers would be similar. Neither of us has known differently, so neither of us has a way to compare…"

But then Artorus came to another realization. "But, Kellos! Aren't you also immune to mortal weapons? Is that some trick of the spatial magic you mentioned?"

"While I've not had to test this ability nearly so often as Brakken surely has," Kellos admitted, "I have experimented some on my own flesh. It does seem to be impervious to harm from these standard forms of physical damage. And, while I am able to bend space to some small degree, it does not account for this trait on any conscious level. It is either an innate use of spatial magic, or it may yet be a fourth branch to magic, or perhaps merely a physical quality shared between Wizard- and Sage-kind. I do not yet have a complete theory on this."

Mala leaned toward Kellos, over the wooden table with the elaborate inscription now carved into it, with a glint in her eye.

"So what *exactly* is the relationship between the immortal Sages and the immortal Wizards? Tell us in detail, Kellos."

Kellos's tone did not change; his voice still even. "I'll not discuss this topic at this time. I have said already that I do have a theory. It lacks experimental or observational evidence; it is incomplete. This is not something I foresee to help you directly in defeating Lord Brakken or any other Wizard, so I see more danger in revealing it than in keeping it private for the time being."

Mala paused, at first looking like she would pursue the topic, but after a moment she leaned back, obviously feeling that one victory was enough for the evening.

She shook her head and sighed. "I don't mean to pry, Kellos. In truth, I am very thankful for all the information you've given us."

"It will be a great help," added Artorus.

"Yes, thank you," added Ty.

With a simple nod, the Sage concluded the conversation and retired to his own tent and his meditations, leaving the other three to sit and discuss what they had just learned and how best to train the troops.

They did not remain terribly long, however, as each was exhausted from marching.

The torches were lit as night descended upon the forest. Standing in the opening of the tent for a moment to stretch his legs, Artorus peered out at his army, nestled in the woods.

Not long now, he thought as he looked out into the dancing lights scattered through the trees and tents, and heard the hushed, hopeful conversations being shared in the night. *We have the last key to defeat Brakken. If we can show the multiverse that Brakken can be defeated, then they will know it is so with all Wizards.*

And if Wizard-kind can be defeated, then they will eventually end, and mortals will one day rule their own lives...

It was hours still before Artorus would retire to his bedroll. His thoughts were far too active this evening.

Chapter XXIV – The Final Obstacle

"Fallen gods be damned!" Artorus shouted, surprising some of those around him with his sudden display of emotion.

His mind raced as he processed the information he'd just heard. Not even a full day had passed since the nighttime conversation with the Sage, and the Fifth Planar had nearly reached the edge of the woods. Things should have been going as planned.

Artorus continued, forcing his words to come out more calmly, "Send messengers to the other generals of the rebellion immediately. Let them know the plan is compromised." A pause and a slow exhale helped him regain his senses. "Scatter, hide, fight as long as you are willing and able, but do not waste your lives."

"Sir?" asked the soldier who stood in front of his lord general, obviously hesitant to relay such an order.

"Do it."

Artorus then turned to Highblade and Mala, among various other army staff. All eyes looked to Artorus with concern; concern for their own safety, true, but likely more so concern that their indomitable general might be giving up.

"I still intend to get to Brakken and kill him," he assured them, "but if we should fail here, if we should die in a hail of arrows where we stand now, I want the others to know – to have *some* chance at surviving this. We have *enough* blood on our hands, dammit."

Artorus turned back to the messenger. "Inform Lieutenant Braïun as well, and be quick about it."

The man shook off his disbelief and nodded an affirmative.

After the soldier made haste to deliver the lord general's messages, Artorus quickly found a horse. Mala and Highblade did the same. The three of them rode for the butte that their scouts had located moments prior.

The short minutes passed at a gallop, dodging through trees, without conversation.

Cresting the massive rock that jutted from the now rather sparse forest, the three were forced to leave the horses in order to scramble up the steep slope. Atop the butte were already a small swarm of varied scouts and officers from the Fifth Planar Army, but they all made way as their lord general and his cohorts approached.

From the highest point for some distance, the Brannus River could be seen as it snaked across the land. It flowed from the looming mountains toward which they had been marching and down the hilly slope they had been climbing. Ahead, the woods grew sparser still and then stopped altogether.

Just beyond the edge of the forest was exactly the sight that Artorus expected. More than a hundred thousand men assembled to block their path.

Though he couldn't see it from this distance, Artorus could clearly picture the eagle and bear banners of the Ninth Planar Army: likely one hundred fifty thousand fighting men, fresh and prepared for combat. Artorus remembered how he had told the dissenting General Evvet that they would meet again on the field of battle, but he'd hoped to be wrong.

Artorus needed no counsel of his officers to know that the fighting power of the Fifth Planar was likely below sixty thousand by now – perhaps, with a very hopeful estimate, sixty-five thousand at best. They were tired from forced marching and from a long deployment, wearied by illness and by battle, and at their most hopeful numbers, outmatched by more than two to one. The distraught lord general scanned the landscape. The forest would protect them in a prolonged battle, but that is exactly what they could not afford. Even now, entire regiments of the Ninth Planar fanned out to cover nearly one hundred eighty degrees of their position near the edge of the woods, like some dark swarm, ready to consume Artorus's body, his army, and his most desperate hopes.

Is this the end of our rebellion? Artorus thought. *Will we be martyrs for a hopeless cause? At best, will we have only shifted the balance of power, that other Wizards might snatch up the worlds of Brakken's empire? Will we have done nothing for the mortals of this multiverse?*

Artorus dared not answer any of his questions.

"So, what will we do?" asked Highblade, his voice discouraged as he too scanned the terrible sight.

Artorus searched for the words, for the stratagems, for anything to tell his lieutenant, but nothing came – nothing he wanted to say aloud, anyway.

"We parlay," Mala said. "We know Evvet and he knows our task. You saved his life, Artorus. We can at least talk to him."

Both Artorus and Highblade looked at Mala in contemplation.

"We did already try talking…" replied Highblade, more contemplative than contradictory.

"Yes," added Artorus, "but what other options do we have? I think you're right here, Mala." He smiled weakly to his sister, despite the doom bearing down on them all. "You're always right, Mal."

Turning to one of the officers standing nearby, Artorus issued orders. "Find a clearing just inside the woods, send an emissary, and let Evvet know we meet there presently with only our lieutenants."

Some hours more passed as the Fifth Planar Army was in a strange place – not preparing for battle, but facing another army nonetheless; not scattering into the woods, though likely every soldier pondered it; so close to their goal, and yet so far now.

Mala advised most of the high command of the state of things as Artorus, Braïun, and Highblade made their way to a chance meeting to sue for a peaceful resolution. The messengers they'd sent to the other generals of the rebellion had been belayed until they could better assess their situation.

A formless hope still smoldered somewhere beyond what Artorus could dare to picture, more a feeling than a strategy.

Still more hours passed for Artorus and his lieutenants as they waited in the clearing, none but the horses, tied at the back of the clearing, to keep them company. These were painful, suspenseful hours. Conversation was sparse.

Artorus even got to counting the number of times Braïun fixed his beard.

He had reached twenty-three when the noise of riders approaching from the other side of the glade came through the tense silence.

Half expecting a full ambush, Artorus was almost surprised to see Evvet and his three lieutenants enter the clearing alone and with weapons sheathed.

Giving a glance behind Artorus and to either side of the clearing, the opposing general and his staff inched their steeds closer to the three men of the Fifth Planar Army.

Artorus and his lieutenants walked closer to the center of the clearing, and, finally reaching one another, Evvet and his lieutenants dismounted.

Evvet and his officers' armor each bore the golden emblems of their army. It was said that the eagle represented the swiftness of their riders and the bear represented the ferocity of their footmen. Somehow at this time, Artorus had a hard time imagining anything but those impressive stories he'd always heard of the great Ninth Planar.

"General Vallon," Evvet greeted Artorus. His hawkish face, with its sharp features and deep-set eyes, peered cautiously at Artorus.

"General Evvet," Artorus replied with a respectful nod. "How did you know we would be in these woods?"

"Come, Vallon," Evvet said in earnest surprise. "I've been keeping contact with Lord General Kremaine. You think he wouldn't notice the bulk of the Fifth Planar Army missing at the Battle of the Lakewoods? He was convinced he might still find you in the Lakewoods, but I knew you would strike right for the heart of your enemy. For all your skill at strategy, Vallon, you are a direct man. This is the most direct path, aside from marching your army straight up the highways."

Why didn't I see this? Artorus cursed himself under his breath.

"You read people well, Evvet," he said, maintaining his calm, though underneath he boiled. "That was why I invited you to that council in the first place; we needed people of such character and skill."

Artorus took a deep breath as Evvet merely held Artorus with that piercing gaze of his.

"So, this is the end, then?" Artorus chanced. "We are doomed to die here in prolonged battle – or worse: starved out, captured, and tortured, with our heads placed on pikes outside the War Maker's fortress?"

A small sigh escaped the other general. "Actually, I had hoped you would charge your haggard band from the woods to a glorious death," Evvet said with sincerity. "But here I am, at the request of your parley... It would have been easier not to have to face you, Vallon."

"And why is that?"

"Because..." Evvet hesitated. A short laugh escaped him as he looked down. Then he raised his gaze once more to Artorus.

"Because you were right."

"About?" asked Artorus curiously.

"About Lord Brakken."

A thousand thoughts filled Artorus's head as he watched for some sign of sarcasm or trickery on Evvet's face. None was found; it was not like him to deceive.

I was right about Brakken? Artorus contemplated frantically. *Has he not come here to stamp us out? Does he have it in him to disobey the Wizard-King? What is his game, dammit?*

Artorus's head cocked slightly to the side, he couldn't let silence be his answer. "You see now that he is evil?" Artorus guessed.

With a scoff, Evvet shook his head. "No, Vallon. I never questioned that Lord Brakken is evil – never. His twisted ways have enslaved men like you and me for centuries; his entire race is bent on the destruction of the multiverse as best I can tell... No, I know no more about

Brakken's evils than I did at our last discussion, but I did learn something important about him."

Artorus listened closely. The five present lieutenants did so as well.

"What I learned was that Brakken is afraid of you, Vallon."

Artorus nearly recoiled in disbelief.

"Yes," Evvet went on, "afraid. When I told him of your rebellion and told him how I suspected you would strike directly for him, he did not laugh; he did not scoff at your impudence or make some display of his immortal might; he instead called in every last one of the armies – those not already committed to search and destroy – to instead patrol around his fortress until your rebellion was defeated. He wanted protection. He was afraid."

Artorus could barely believe what he was hearing and a glance back to Braïun confirmed his lieutenants felt the same.

"When I last left your company," Evvet continued with determination, "I told you exactly why I would not oppose our Wizard-King: because I thought he could not be defeated; I thought he was immortal." His eyes were intense and his voice steady. "His actions have shown me quite clearly otherwise. He fears you will defeat him somehow."

"So—" Artorus began.

"So," Evvet interrupted, "I thought I could simply crush the Fifth Planar in glorious and tragic combat and continue on with my life, trying desperately to forget you and your rebellion for the remainder of my days."

As he spoke, he stared into Artorus's eyes with that intensity that left no room in Artorus's mind for suspicions.

"But I cannot... I cannot fight on the side of evil against the most just man I know... not when I now know it is *somehow* possible for him to win."

The general of the Ninth Planar Army breathed deeply and straightened his shoulders. He respectfully nodded once more to Artorus.

"General Vallon, with acknowledgement that I treated you and your companions wrongly, I will march with you to the fortress of Lord Brakken, so we *just may* end his evil rule."

Artorus heard a sigh of relief from Braïun behind him and he heard Highblade laugh in disbelief as the moment's tension bled away in an instant. He couldn't help but smile.

"Good general," Artorus said to Evvet, "I would welcome you as a brother at arms, and your apologies are not needed."

"And," Artorus added more introspectively, "I'll have to thank my sister for saving my life... again."

But Artorus paused, and his face darkened some. "Your army is vast and it is mighty... However... I'm not certain any more numbers will help us at the doorstep of the Wizard-King..."

Evvet and his lieutenants looked curiously at Artorus.

"This task – to kill the mighty Wizard – I think will require more subtlety and speed than it will might and valor." Artorus grinned to Evvet. "And the Ninth Planar Army has more might and valor than any. Tales of the great Ninth Planar were circulating well before I was in academy."

Evvet nodded in thanks.

"If it would suit the good general of the Ninth Planar," Artorus went on, "then I know of several other generals that could use a little of that might and valor right now..."

"Yes, we've been getting reports that Vasz's Fortieth Homeworld has Orrogen's Seventeenth Planar over the coals below the Feathertop Mountains," Evvet said. "And I believe Ayedd and Brakson have challenges of their own, despite the larger forces being redirected to the worldgates, if my reports are accurate."

"Hm," pondered Artorus, "it looks like your reports agree with ours..." He contemplated his options. "But, on further thought, I'm actually not sure if you could mobilize in time to help any of them very quickly."

"Agreed," stated Evvet. "We are weeks of marching from any of them. But you say you do not see a place for the Ninth in your assault on Brakken's fortress."

"Right..." Artorus was now deep in thought. "But didn't you say he deployed more forces to the vicinity?"

Evvet nodded. "He has nearly four full Imperial Legions, split into smaller task forces and roaming the mountains."

"How many do you think you can handle?" Artorus queried the other general.

"Mm, mountain fighting has never been a pleasure of mine." He shook his head slightly. "But we can split into task forces as well... I can hold a few choke points and make it very hard for them to come to the fortress."

Artorus nodded at this, stroking his beard.

"But," Evvet continued, "keep in mind that all of Central Province is wrought with roads, and we probably can't block them all. Some of them likely know these mountains much better than you or I. In fact, if they come by way of the Northwind Pass, then they will be yours to handle, surely."

"I would gladly welcome all the assistance you can provide," Artorus said earnestly, "and whatever legions do manage to line up outside the fortress, we will rain hell on them from the Wizard-King's own walls." He smiled mischievously. "Just imagine their faces as they try to siege the fortress of their own Wizard-King..."

Highblade laughed at the thought behind Artorus and grins were shared by the other men.

"Very well, then," Evvet proclaimed. "We will do what we can for you, Vallon." He gazed at Artorus once more. "Just don't let the lives of my men be forfeit to your damned ideals alone. I want to see you pull off this miracle and walk out of those mountains with Brakken's head... Damned if I know how, but I want to see you do it, or else we'll all be consumed in Wizard fire..."

The sun hung high in the sky over the small clearing in the Upper Brannus Woods, and within the hour the two generals had bade one another farewell. Within an hour more, the vast Ninth Planar Army was preparing to march for the Central Mountains, ahead of Artorus and his Fifth.

Braïun, Highblade, and the lord general had made haste back to the camp. They would need to move quickly in order to take advantage of their new ally's benevolence and still have a chance to defeat the Wizard-King. From what Evvet had told them, no less than four full Imperial Legions now patrolled the Central Province hunting for rebels, and his luck with the other armies was not something Artorus wanted to test.

As they got back, Mala stood outside a command tent with Ty and Kellos.

"Artorus!" she called.

"Mal!" Artorus returned with equal enthusiasm.

"I was afraid you might be ambushed."

As the three dismounted, Highblade laughed and Braïun was grinning. Mala glanced at the lieutenants.

"What? What do I not know?" she inquired.

"Well," Artorus said, before pausing to take a breath. He had to make sure he still believed what had happened himself. "It looks like you were even more right than we could have known."

Mala looked suspiciously at her brother.

"Evvet and the Ninth Planar Army have joined the rebellion," Artorus said, unable to withhold a smile.

"*What?*" Mala was obviously in disbelief. "How? *Why?*"

"I'd love to tell you the whole story now, but I'm afraid we'll have to make haste to get to Lord Brakken with any amount of surprise at all."

He nodded to each of his lieutenants and called other officers over to get the army ready to leave.

"Suffice it to say," he said back to his sister as the army began to take action, "that Evvet has always known just how evil the Wizard-King is, he simply now has some better motivation to do something about it. His conscience wouldn't let him crush us, like we all know he could."

Braïun added as he was addressing another officer before he left the group, "I believe it was something to the effect of 'I cannot fight on the side of evil against one of the most just men I have ever known.'"

The proper dwarf smiled widely, remounted his horse, and then tucked his beard back into his belt before riding away.

Mala blinked and shook her head, and spoke with an air of wonder. "Obviously there are others in this multiverse willing to stand against evil... I always wanted to believe it..."

Kellos shifted where he stood.

"What is evil, I might ask?" he posed to the group.

Artorus frowned as Mala and Ty turned to the Sage.

"I'm not certain we have time for another one of your philosophy sessions, good Sage," Artorus said.

He finished issuing orders to the last of the officers that were now each scrambling to get the camp struck and the troops moving.

"I do believe it may be of some import to you," Kellos replied, his always stoic face peering at the others.

Artorus fought the urge to huff at the Sage as many things raced through his mind. There were perhaps four Imperial Legions that would descend upon their location as soon as they found out Evvet's betrayal and even without their latest pause, the Fifth Planar was rushed for time.

But one does not dismiss the wisdom of an immortal Sage without either brazen ignorance or some form of insanity. The officers were already taking care of the preparations to depart. Artorus collected himself.

"Well, what do you mean?" responded Mala, with some signs of impatience beginning to show herself.

"This idea of good and of evil," the Sage began. "I've contemplated it at great length. I'm afraid it's not something I understand in the same way as you mortals do. More specifically, I do not believe they exist."

This caught the group off guard.

Evil is very real, Artorus thought. Evil was the cause for Elsa's death. Evil was the reason they now led this rebellion to make a change in the multiverse.

"So, Kellos," Artorus asked, slightly peeved, "are you saying that you don't think Lord Brakken is evil?"

"I do not," replied the Sage in his familiar plain tone.

"Kellos, how can you say that?" Artorus's voice began to rise.

His mind was worn from so many great obstacles he'd already fought and overcome just to get to this point, the Wizard-King himself still waiting to face them.

Artorus heard the frustration showing in his tone, but he could not withhold it.

"He destroys lives as easily as you or I pluck flowers and he feels less emotion about it. The creature has enslaved mortals for centuries and forced us to fight and to die in the Planewars for generations to no greater goal than his own power. Would you ever do such things, Sage?"

"I would not," the Sage replied, "and—"

"Because it is evil!" Artorus interjected. "Lord Brakken is an evil, vile creature and he has to be stopped."

Artorus suddenly felt like, here at the precipice of their victory, the Sage was challenging the morality of their task. He knew Mala agreed with him, even if she could conceal her frustration better.

"No, Lord General," Kellos replied calmly. "To answer your question, I would not do the things Lord Brakken does for many reasons; perhaps too many to even name here and now. Not because I call them evil."

The Sage paused, but he had more to say. He formulated his thoughts as he often did, so Artorus took a deep breath and waited to hear.

"You see," the Sage went on, "good and evil are concepts often touted as objective – perpetual, unchanging. This is, arguably, their entire purpose: constants of morality by which to measure all other things. They are the weight markings on the scale of the actions of mortals. I find this to be a fallacy – just as I do the concepts of right and wrong."

Artorus couldn't help but shake his head again.

"An example:" Kellos said as he motioned toward Ty, "Typhondrius, would you say that it is wrong to kill?"

"Well," he hesitated, "I would – I might…"

"Have you ever described killing as wrong?" the Sage prodded.

"Yes," Ty responded, collecting his thoughts. "Killing is wrong," the elf finally stated more definitively.

Kellos then motioned to Artorus. "And you, Lord General, have you ever killed?"

The Sage clearly knew the answer; all four of them did.

Typhondrius objected, "Now, that's different; killing in battle—"

Artorus stopped Ty's objection with a raised hand and a calm expression. "Yes, I have killed many, Kellos... So many..."

"And do you – or does anyone present – think yourself an 'evil' man or one who does 'wrong?'" Kellos asked plainly.

Typhondrius and Mala both shook their head as Artorus replied. "No. But, Kellos, to kill a man who is trying to kill you is different from killing somebody who is defenseless."

"Agreed," Kellos replied, "and so, the question becomes: is killing wrong or is it right? Or is it more accurately a subjective question? And, if it is subjective, then does that not make the definitions of 'right' and 'wrong' themselves likewise subjective?"

There was a pause as all three mortals thought on the Sage's words.

Ty finally spoke up, deliberate and careful in his choice of words. "I think I see what you mean, Master Kellos. Perhaps right and wrong, or good and evil are not so clearly defined as we might think. Is that it?"

Artorus interjected before the Sage responded. "Well, surely there are *some* things you think are good and *some* you think are evil."

He found he could not keep his thoughts from Elsa. Evil beings and evil actions had surrounded Artorus and shaped his destiny for his whole life, and some of the worst examples truly made him shudder.

"No," the Sage replied.

Artorus tried to think of a constructive way to argue the point, but was having trouble keeping his emotion out of the conversation. He was saved by his elven friend.

"A man killing another man just for the coins in his pocket?" Ty attempted.

"Misguided, perhaps," replied the Sage. "I would wish to know what this man would do with the coins; how the man who had them had gotten them; if a fight had broken out surrounding these coins, was it the killer or the killed that had escalated the violence beyond what one might consider reasonable in the situation? Were others present for this occurrence who would then need to be weighed in this moral evaluation? And, if so, could they have interrupted? The list of details goes on, and always does it make the concept of a moral 'right' or 'wrong' less clear with each inquiry."

"Hm," expressed Mala shortly thereafter. "So it is all merely a scale of gray; no black and no white to you, Kellos?"

"An apt analogy," the Sage stated plainly.

"And yet," Mala said carefully, "Koth draws a very clear line for us, Kellos. Truth and mystery divide the multiverse into shadow and light. Through Koth we can know truth."

Kellos looked almost uncomfortable at this statement, but Ty interjected again before Kellos could reply to Mala's statement.

"What then, Master Kellos, of the Planewars?" he asked seriously. "Are they not wrong? How many lives have been smashed to dust for the Wizard-Kings to sit in their palaces and torture their servants? How many cities have burned?"

Artorus could see Ty becoming impassioned as well. They all knew Brakken was evil. Ty probably knew better than most mortals.

The Sage turned his gaze to Typhondrius. "I shall take your other questions as rhetorical. Of the Planewars, though, having watched the multiverse these many centuries, good elf, I cannot say I believe there to be any other way for events to have unfolded. Though it may not be clear to see from within the confines of a mortal lifetime, the Wizards are as much a slave to causality as any of you. To say the Planewars are 'wrong' is to ascribe a moral evaluation to a metaphysical certitude. It would be as calling the wind malicious or the rain magnanimous; though both have effects we may benefit or suffer from, neither can be judged on a moral scale. This is the same for mortals and immortals alike. And, thus, if we cannot ascribe these moral valuations to the multiverse around us, they lose meaning and therefore cease to exist in any qualitative manner."

"But..." Ty sputtered a reply, but it faltered before it took hold.

Mala looked deterred as well. The Sage's pedantic style was difficult indeed to argue against.

"Well," Artorus stated after a moment, "there are certainly still some things that I know are wrong... Some beings I *know* are evil..." He breathed deeply. "But I can't say I don't see your point, Kellos."

"And that point is?" Kellos asked in return.

"That we should not be so quick to categorize an act as 'wrong' or a being 'evil' simply in order to avoid truly evaluating each situation..." Artorus swallowed hard. "But I still don't see how one so wise as yourself could not see Lord Brakken as an evil being. Even disregarding the acts he's taken in war, the actions Ty could tell us *alone* should be enough to judge."

His brow fell and his voice quieted.

"The Wizards are all evil... All of them... They took Elsa from me..."

He looked back up to Kellos, hoping the disdain he felt for Wizards and the dismay he felt about Elsa would be outshone by his determination to change the multiverse.

"They took Elsa and my child from me. I will destroy every Wizard in the twenty-seven worlds with my own blade if that's what it takes to end these wars."

The Sage looked into Artorus's eyes and Artorus was quiet. Though he'd never seen it on the Sage's face, Artorus thought he recognized empathy in Kellos's eyes, for one brief moment. Or could that possibly be sorrow?

In only a moment, that piercing gaze of the Sage became uncomfortable. It was likely nothing Kellos did willfully, but simply peering into those immortal eyes instilled an otherworldly sort of feeling. But Artorus blinked away the feeling, and Kellos directed his attention away finally.

After another short silence, Kellos looked to Mala. "So, what is the reason, Lady Andrius, that I bring up this topic, then?"

She looked up to him. Her thoughts were still elsewhere; she was not convinced by the Sage's rhetoric either, but she pondered his question, nonetheless.

"Because you think the men require more direction?" she guessed halfheartedly.

"No," replied Kellos. "The men and women of this mortal army – indeed of this rebellion – have in you and your brother all the direction they could need, I believe. It is not they who require the compass."

Mala thought more intently, letting the Sage's words hang in the air. "You bring it up," she began slowly, "because we must fully understand *why* we are rebelling against the Wizard-King if we are to be prepared to succeed."

"Yes," affirmed the Sage. "Though it may be easier to simply call Lord Brakken evil and his actions wrong, thereby making you and your cause 'good' and 'right,' what is your true reason for this rebellion if it is not that?"

Artorus still thought of Elsa. Words like *revenge*, *hatred*, and *pain* came to his thoughts, but Mala saved him from answering once more.

"We do it," Mala stated softly, looking down, "because people die every day, thousands of people across the multiverse, fighting a war in which they stand to gain nothing. So many people die every day, and if we can show this multiverse that there is another way, then we give them the choice to stop it."

Mala looked up to meet her brother's eyes and suddenly Artorus found his anger flowing out of him. Mala was right; she was always right.

This wasn't about good or evil, revenge or hatred or pain, it was about doing everything they could so that one day – perhaps even long after Artorus and Mala were gone, but *one* day – people could choose peace. One day, lives so beautiful and pure as Elsa's would not be collateral for senseless, perpetual wars.

"We do it for peace," Artorus repeated to Kellos.

"Peace," Ty echoed as well.

Kellos said nothing more, obviously satisfied with the conversation.

The Fifth Planar Army had broken down their tents and assembled to march on. After their discussion, Artorus and the others, still thinking on the words of the immortal Sage, helped the army finish their last preparations to leave.

Within the hour they were indeed marching again through those woods that had been their home for weeks now, at the very breach of the forest and climbing now through the foothills of the Central Mountains.

Not long now, Artorus found himself repeating in his head as they did so.

Walking with the sick and wounded, at the rear of the forces, Artorus and Mala were mostly silent. The weather was mild, and a soft breeze made the trees whisper as sunlight shone in broken patches across their pathways.

Somehow, it seemed suddenly like things might just work out for their rebellion. Despite his resistance as they were rushing to mobilize at the edge of the woods, the conversation with the Sage, like most he'd had with the immortal being, seemed to illuminate his shadowed path some.

Mala seemed to be pondering a similar subject as she turned to her brother with thoughtful eyes.

"Do you think that Kellos—"

She was cut off by a shout from the far side of the stretcher bearers.

"Attack!" someone yelled from through the woods.

It was hard to tell whether it was a battle cry or a call of warning, but the sickening feeling in Artorus's gut confirmed it didn't matter which it was – they both meant the same awful thing. Their carefully planned position could yet again be in jeopardy.

Thoughts raced through Artorus's mind in an instant.

Has Evvet betrayed us? Have we been followed? Is it the War Maker himself?

More shouts came from up ahead, nearly the opposite direction from the prior commotion.

"Damn!" Artorus exclaimed. "Mala, rally the soldiers here and protect the wounded! I'll go ahead to the other disturbance."

She nodded and the siblings parted.

Artorus rushed through the trees toward where he could hear the shouting. Sword clashes echoed through the woods.

After running for a moment, he suddenly felt a slight panic. Artorus had removed his armor and packed it on a mule before they began traveling; he had ordered most of his men to do so that they might travel as fast as possible. Cursing himself, he drew Thordrin's Blade and held it tight.

Ahead, seeing men through the trees, he called to them. "What is it?" he shouted as he burst into a clearing.

Roughly two dozen men were at the edge of the clearing, looking about for their enemy. Other soldiers began to approach the lord general as well, looking for direction as more shouts of battle sounded from around them and a few arrows flew overhead.

"We're not sure, General," replied a sergeant who was among the men. Then, at once, his face grew grim. "Sir! Behind you!"

Artorus spun to see a dark, harrowing figure roar as it leapt from the sparse bushes at the edge of the clearing. Shouts of surprise sounded from all the various people present as each of those who had not already done so drew their weapons.

Two unfortunate soldiers were between the general and the charging figure. They each fell to curved blades in their sides – stabbed, removed, and stabbed again. The ground of the small clearing, still wet from the morning's mist, was splattered now with blood. And Artorus finally got a look at the attacker, barely pausing while he ripped bloodied daggers from dying men.

The High Justicar of Lord Brakken, called *Gnarrl* by very few, had seen Artorus – and Artorus, him – just once before.

In meetings with lord generals and other high officers of The Vastness, Lord Brakken sometimes decreed orders or strategies in person. Always, a shadow followed him like a dark omen; a wraith of such origins Artorus never cared to imagine. But he had some twisted kind of sophistication about him at those meetings, like a ferocious dog, perfectly obedient when his master was present. His posture was straight and his demeanor reserved, despite an undeniable prowess and untold malice hiding just under the calmed exterior.

And now, here in the half-moment Artorus had to see this creature well, there was no sophistication and no obedience; the hound's master was not here. The heavy cloak that he guessed was at one point a shade of gray was now shredded and black with soil and blood. Tight, black leather, studded with dark bits of metal, had scrapes and tears as it clung persistently to the thick musculature of the justicar. He was hunched close to the ground and the daggers were gripped tightly in each massive hand, one held backhand, the other forward. Though he was easily over six feet in height, here, crouching in the muddy grass of the meadow, he was a low, sleek, predatory creature. Stubble grew thick on the face of the half-orc, which was slick with mud and marked by scrapes, drawing out his dark eyes that contained the speckled, sickly yellow of his orcish parentage. Those eyes locked with Artorus's.

And in the beast's eyes there was only wrath.

The assassin charged. Artorus gripped his blade tight. He was fast and he had bested many a foe, but he would need to be so much faster if he was going to survive this encounter. A cumbersome broadsword was no match for a very fast opponent with two quick daggers, but Artorus would have to make it work.

Some stories told that the High Justicar could not be defeated in combat; a mere shade that killed at his whim and left nothing behind but bloodied corpses. But indeed, it seemed that his sister managed to escape a fight with this half-orc, so Artorus would test the veracity of these stories... or die trying.

Dashing to the right, Artorus brought his sword down in a reserved strike, aiming toward the spot where he thought the justicar might be, but Artorus wanted to be able to retract quickly. The justicar was not under the blade and he dashed immediately for Artorus just as quickly as he dodged the attack.

The general knew his only hope to survive this fight was to keep the assassin at a distance and so he jolted back. Lucky not to be in his armor for this particular fight, as it turned out, Artorus stayed light on his feet as he swung once more; this time harder and in a horizontal motion.

Ducking again, well under Artorus's swing, the large half-orc tucked into a roll toward the human. Artorus kicked quickly at Gnarrl, landing a fairly solid blow and knocking him back away. As Artorus set his foot back down, he felt the searing pain of a long dagger cut along the inside of his right thigh.

Ignoring the pain, he lunged at the still-reeling assassin, aiming another sword strike for his head. Kneeling, the half-orc raised both his daggers overhead in backhand fashion and blocked the fine sword with them. Not wasting the opportunity, Artorus kicked hard once more, this time landing a blow in the assassin's face.

A roar erupted from the half-orc as he rolled back again, spitting blood into the air. Artorus moved to attack again, but the large gash in his leg slowed him. It was meant to.

Shouting, two more soldiers had rushed to the fight and now attacked the reeling assassin. With his daggers still held back-handed, he recovered almost instantly, blocked both swings, and deftly whirled behind one of the attacking soldiers, sliding his blade across the throat. He slumped to the ground.

By now, Artorus was upon the justicar once more, and, along with the remaining soldier, attacked the assassin with a series of sword blows. Metal struck metal as the half-orc blocked more swings and dodged others. The three combatants danced about in the small clearing as others were running to help their general.

The half-orc, despite any appearance of mere predatory rage, was still thinking through his fight. With most of the people approaching from the woods and noticing the general's attempt to keep his distance, Gnarrl rushed Artorus. Blocking all of his best attacks, the other fighter pressed toward Artorus, bringing those deadly daggers closer to Artorus's veins with every inch he moved. Artorus gave ground to the assassin, and the other soldier struggled to keep up with the two quick fighters, as they covered some distance across the grass and away from the trees.

Finally, after pressing Artorus back at least a dozen yards – probably farther – the justicar stopped suddenly and in a blur of cloak and flashing daggers, unleashed a surprise assault on the following soldier. The man fell to four deep stab wounds about his chest and neck.

Dammit, thought Artorus.

As he was focusing on keeping away from the assassin and he had just stepped onto his wounded leg, he was not in a position to strike him while his back was turned. The beast was all too smart; he had earned his reputation as an unparalleled killer.

Gnarrl turned back to his prey and growled through bloodied teeth. His fangs jutted from his swelling lips and his nostrils flared wide as the hate in his eyes seemed to grip Artorus like the very hand of death.

As the half-orc dashed forward once more, Artorus tried to keep him at bay with another strike of the sword, but he was slowing from fatigue and pain. The justicar, with incredible stamina, had not slowed at all and easily dodged the attack, closing on the general yet again.

For one brief moment, Artorus thought it was his end, but pure adrenaline took him, and just as the grizzled assassin slipped inside his sword's reach, Artorus shouted and dropped the fine blade for a flurry of blows from his fists, elbows, and knees – anything his worn muscles could muster.

Apparently, the assassin was as surprised by the maneuver as Artorus was, and no daggers found his flesh quite yet. Trying desperately to disarm his opponent, Artorus punched and kicked until he found an opportunity to grapple. The justicar was not the only one who could slip within the guard of his opponent's weapons.

Grasping tightly around the torso of the half-orc with both arms, Artorus pulled all his weight against him, straining to maintain his grip, and after he wrapped a leg around the back of one of his opponent's, the two warriors fell to the soft earth of the meadow.

Though the human managed to lock one of the half-orc's arms with his, in the fall, the assassin had positioned a dagger's edge between them. Artorus landed hard on the half-orc, but also, he felt the blade cut into his stomach.

This human was far more trouble than he should have been. Gnarrl's hatred had turned from a pure and flowing rage into unadulterated bloodlust. Gnarrl had not felt wrath like this in all his years of killing for the Wizard-King.

Gone was his plan to destroy all the leaders of the rebellion. Gnarrl had seen the Ninth Planar Army positioning to encircle the rebels, and he'd planned to simply take the captives from Evvet and deliver them to the Wizard-King. Instead Evvet joined this delusional rebellion. Was there no sanity left among the twenty-seven worlds?

Stripped away were the thoughts of regaining his glory at the feet of the War Maker. Even if he would die in doing so, he would complete this sole remaining task: he would slay Artorus Vallon in a display so gruesome, all the planes would tell stories of it for many years to come. And, if he could make off with the human's head, so much the better.

But now, only the wrath remained. This human would feel the unholy pain of the justicar's wrath.

The assassin's long daggers lost some of their usefulness in this hand-to-hand grapple, but Gnarrl raked the daggers' edges across skin and let the human feel his hatred, nonetheless. Just a slight shift and Gnarrl should be able to snap an arm or find a place to plant a dagger.

He had managed to put enough distance between the woods and the two of them, so soldiers were still running to catch up to the fight, but there were more soldiers up ahead. Gnarrl could hear the shouting as men approached from both sides. If he would have to slaughter this entire army to finally kill this Vallon, then he would do so. With a mighty surge from his exhausted leg muscles, he launched the general up and over him onto the grass behind and launched back to his feet.

The soldiers had arrived already. Gnarrl had only barely the time to orient himself to the new combatants before they attacked. Swords and axes and shields met with daggers, and Gnarrl kept an eye on Vallon as he slowly got back onto his feet and reached for his discarded sword.

The general was bleeding now from his leg and his stomach and a handful of other wounds Gnarrl had placed on him; with the blood flowed out his strength and his speed – the general would no longer be a match for Gnarrl's speed once he engaged him again.

Still there were more soldiers in the way – always something between him and his prey. One more soldier fell to a series of slashes, and then another to a stab to the throat; another to a dagger through her eye.

Gnarrl had fought probably hundreds of men in his life, but he was filled now with a wrath so pure that his daggers could not be stopped. He was rage; he was murder; he was death incarnate. He ducked attacks and planted his daggers in soldier after soldier. More blood covered the grass below as bodies fell one after another. At least a dozen men fell, but more came.

Finally, Gnarrl saw the general coming unwisely again to the fray. The time to end this hunt was soon; his time for redemption was upon him and he could no longer be stopped.

At that moment, he sensed a dwarf approaching from behind. Turning about, he sidestepped an apt swing and then reared and planted his daggers in both of the dwarf's shoulders, driving the long blades deep into his chest.

Seeing the face of this skewered dwarf, Gnarrl recognized him. He had seen this dwarf's wife and children at the tips of these same daggers... This was "Slick."

Gnarrl grinned at the thought of finally completing the job he'd started months ago. It seemed that the dwarf knew him as well because the look on his neatly kept face was one of utter shock and horrific disappointment.

Gnarrl would watch Vallon's face do the same...

But then it all went wrong.

"*No!!*"

A scream of pain came from behind Gnarrl, piercing the shouts and other sounds of the fighting.

Had time slowed somehow? The sound seemed to reverberate in and around Gnarrl.

It was Vallon's cry; his voice came from deep in his heart, crying out for this dwarf; it was the sound of loss. Not loss of a soldier, but loss of a friend.

Gnarrl's chest suddenly burst with pain. He felt hot and cold all at once, and the back of his neck twisted as muscles wrenched severely. The sweat that was hot on his brow a moment before became shiveringly cold. This was the feeling he'd felt that winter night in the bar some months ago.

At once, Gnarrl's entire life flashed before his eyes.

He remembered killing his mother for all she never did for him, but it wasn't right – he felt a wrenching sorrow as the image of it came to his eyes.

He remembered hunting and killing droves of greens that he thought might have been his father, never knowing for sure. But it wasn't the same as it had been – every green-ish bastard *was* his father; he could never kill them all, though. He could not even hate them all; there were too many orcs in the twenty-seven worlds.

He remembered entering the service of Lord Brakken's assassins and putting his impressive skills to use, but now the very thought of all he did sickened him.

He remembered rising through the ranks of killers as though the multiverse had not room for his ambition, but it was never ambition that drove him – he could see now it was desperation.

He'd hunted so desperately and for so long for *something*: could it be simple acceptance? Here on this bloodied field, he suddenly came to see that, if that was what he'd sought, he'd never found it; not from his parents, not from his assassins, and not from the Wizard-King. It was not something his blades could ever earn him.

This rebellion – the men of these armies – were not so united by some foolish ideal as they were by mere companionship. It was a nearly familial sort of affection.

Is this what he yearned for? How *could* it be? What use did this foolishness have for an assassin? The idea was ridiculous. Gnarrl wanted to laugh aloud. And yet, on this field of bodies – dozens splayed by his own hands – Gnarrl saw exactly what he was chasing all these years. The dwarf in front of him was twisting in agony, likely dying, and the men around him were truly affected by that.

No matter what use it had to him, no matter whether he wanted it or not, the assassin had been chasing it all his life. And no one would weep when Gnarrl died.

Gnarrl felt a strange sensation in his back. It tingled and it seemed to move through him. The hotness and coldness, the twinging muscles; they faded as this new feeling spread through his body.

Looking down, he saw a finely crafted blade protruding from his chest. It twisted slightly and then retracted back through his torso, jolting him some. Gnarrl slowly turned around to see a pained, bloodied, and exhausted General Vallon holding the large sword that now dripped with Gnarrl's own blood.

The tingling was sickly comforting, like a swig of strong alcohol to mask a fever. The blood flowing out of Gnarrl's torso seemed to wash over him like a soothing bath, even as his lungs struggled uselessly for air. His hands and feet could no longer be felt.

So, this was the final extent of Gnarrl's failure...

Artorus winced as Braïun fell to the ground, the twin daggers still planted in his shoulders, and the half-orc assassin stood half-dead, staring at Artorus with glazed eyes. More dead and dying were littered about the small meadow. This assassin had killed so many. Even Lord Brakken's killing seemed somehow reserved compared to the men and women who lay on the ground still gasping for air while their throats bled or their sides were pierced straight through to their lungs.

The massive half-orc fell to his knees with a loud thud. Still his eyes, which were only moments ago locked on Artorus's with hate and rage, now looked to him with a nearly child-like bewilderment. It was the look of a dullard, seeing something he did not fully comprehend. Somehow, Artorus pitied this half-orc now kneeling before him.

Pity? This creature was responsible for all the death that now surrounded them, for all the pain of these dying men, for the slaughter of the Braïun family, for trying to murder his sister, and for slaying the soldiers who swore to protect her. *Pity?*

With a shout, Artorus closed his eyes and swung Thordrin's Blade true, removing the head of the assassin.

Opening his eyes after just a moment, he saw all of the soldiers around him looking down to the disembodied head of the High Justicar, rolling to a stop in the muddied grass with the expression unaltered. Most of the other sounds of fighting had stopped and officers called orders to rally the disarrayed troops. And finally, the heavy body of the justicar slumped to the blood-soaked ground.

A pained noise came from Lieutenant Braïun and Artorus dropped his sword and rushed over to the fallen dwarf's side.

"Braïun!" Artorus shouted as he saw the look on the lieutenant's face.

His expression was not one of fear, nor even pain. There was a strange calmness on Braïun's face.

"You'll be all right, Braïun," Artorus tried to assure the dwarf.

Looking to Artorus with those strangely calm eyes, his beard still braided tightly and his hair combed neatly as blood soaked into them, Braïun spoke in a soft voice.

"Yes, sir, I believe we will be." His voice was strained, but his words were clear. "One way or the other, I believe we will be."

His eyes closed, and his breath became labored.

Cries of *make way* came from the crowd of soldiers around the fallen lieutenant, and they quickly parted as Mala and Kellos approached.

"Artorus!" called Mala, with the Sage in tow. "Are you all right?"

Then, stopping, she saw Braïun on the muddy ground. "No! Braïun!" She fell to her knees.

Her frantic eyes scanned over the bloodied lieutenant. Then she suddenly paused, and her eyes became alight with thought.

"You will live," she said to him determinedly. She rose and turned back to Kellos. "Please, Kellos, you can save him," she said calmly.

"Yes," the Sage said, looking down to the gasping dwarf, "I believe I can."

The Sage knelt down beside Braïun and began to inspect his wounds as Mala stayed kneeling at his opposite side.

Artorus, still breathing heavily and bleeding from his own various wounds, thought about the concept of Braïun dying here on this field. In truth, Artorus had seen the dwarf suffer many wounds, and like any dwarf, he always survived them admirably. None were quite like this. The assassin's blades were keen and they were precise.

Lord Brakken and his agents, whether they would end up defeated or not, may just have finished the job they'd started when they slaughtered Braïun's family. And dozens more were dead and dying around him.

It seemed no matter how hard he tried, he could not stop the death.

Not until the War Maker's head lay at his feet.

"Mala," he finally said softly, but with determination, "we must go."

"And leave our friend here to die!?" she replied, bitterness in her voice. The response came almost immediately, as though she knew he was going to say it. She did not look up from Braïun.

"Mala," Artorus continued, calmly as he could through his labored breathing, "Brakken is aware of our plans. It is only a matter of time before he realizes the failure of the Ninth Planar Army to stop us and calls any number of Imperial Legions to his fortress. We have no time. We may already be too late. If the noble Orgron Braïun is to die, then the most we can do for him now is to finish what he's started; what we've all started."

As though she knew this too before her brother said it, she was silent. Her eyes shut tight, and tears rolled down her cheeks. She nodded, placed a hand on Braïun's leg, said a quiet prayer to Koth, and then stood.

"We will go on ahead, Kellos," Mala said to the kneeling Sage.

"Yes," he replied while still inspecting Braïun's wounds, "I know. You will face Lord Brakken by your brother's side and—"

The Sage stopped himself and raised his head. His expression was odd – perhaps just contemplative, but maybe even slightly regretful – as he met with Artorus's eyes and then with Mala's. But then a nod said his goodbyes to the brother and sister, and he began to work with the wounded dwarf, muscled arms stretching out to place pressure on the bleeding wounds and wizened eyes looking over the mangled body.

Artorus called his orders to his men as other healers field-dressed his thigh and stomach. "We will leave a hundred men here to care for the wounded. Cancel the construction of the siege weaponry; by the time we will need it, it will be too late. Ormond will stay here, safe."

He looked once more down to the wounded lieutenant and tightened his grip on his sword.

Vallon, Lord General of the Rebellion, turned to the larger bulk of men now standing in the clearing. He swallowed the blood in his mouth and, with it, the pain from all his searing wounds. He summoned the will to walk and the strength to shout.

"All men who can still hold a sword, to me! We march for the fortress of the Wizard-King to show him, for Braïun – for *all* people – that he *does not* rule us!"

Those wounds that could be staunched were bandaged, and those who had fallen or would not last the night remained to find shallow graves soon. For the rest, the Fifth Planar Army marched one last time to face their enemy.

Chapter XXV – Agan Winnefore

Agan Winnefore had a reputation among the men of the Fifth Planar Army. In battle, he was like a running joke that had long since gotten old. Agan Winnefore, it was said, was the single worst swordsman in all the twenty-seven worlds. Stories were told of how soldiers of the Fifth Planar would have to fight harder with him added to their number than without him – perhaps even the worth of entire platoons compromised by the maladroit swordsman.

Ten years before the current day, Artorus Vallon was a still a captain in the Fifth Planar Army. He still had the invaluable leadership of General Hathey on the field, and he still had his beautiful wife at home. Artorus had a feeling that a promotion was in his near future, and he had a desire to know the men who fought for him. It seemed to be some part of what gave Hathey such charisma, and it felt right to the young captain.

And thus, every week or so, deployed or not, he practiced his swordsmanship in the very barracks and training fields that his men did. He fought against them in practice so he could better fight with them when lives were on the line.

"Good!" Artorus shouted as he dodged a very apt strike from one of his soldiers. "That is enough, soldier. I'm impressed with your skill."

"But, sir," the soldier said through gasps for air. "I tried... about as hard as I've ever tried... at anything in my life... I didn't lay a single blow on you."

Artorus smiled to his soldier, barely winded. "That doesn't mean you don't have skill. And, in fact, tenacity is at least as powerful a tool as skill in the middle of a pitched battle. Go ahead and switch with the next soldier and keep practicing. Next time I want you to be able to do that just as well for twice as long."

Still attempting to regain his breathing, he huffed, "Yes, sir! Thank you, sir."

The soldier saluted and hustled off to where the benches were. The captain turned to find a cloth. He wiped sweat from his face. The midday sun of Myrus was hot to him, even though the air was crisp with an approaching autumn.

"Um…" Artorus heard from behind him as he finished wiping his brow.

"'Um?'" Artorus repeated as he turned to see who he faced. "Is that your battle cry?"

Chuckling softly, a small man replied, "No, sir."

"Well then," Artorus said as he looked over the small human and tossed his cloth aside, "shall we begin?"

Looking hesitant, the man asked his captain, "Is this really necessary?" His voice was nasally and timid.

Seeing now that rows of soldiers were lining up to watch the coming fight, Artorus raised an eyebrow. "Have I fought you before?"

"No, sir," the soldier said with a smirk. "I think you would remember."

Now also seeing the large grins on the faces of all the men gathering – still growing in number – Artorus began to understand.

The soldier standing before him was not just small – he was quite possibly the frailest-looking being Artorus had ever seen. A malnourished elf might outweigh the man and would likely look more intimidating. His large green eyes bugged outward slightly, and his nose was crooked. His scrawny arms ended in comically oversized hands that seemed unable to properly grasp his training sword. The man wore some sort of pointy beard and mustache, but it grew so sparsely that it looked more like wisps of crooked hairs that might just fall from his face at any moment.

"You wouldn't by any chance be Agan Winnefore, would you?" Artorus questioned.

The small man bowed low with a flourish to the amusement of the gathering crowd. "None other," he said.

Artorus had yet to meet this soldier. He'd been transferred to his unit only that week.

With a sigh, Artorus said, "Then let us spar. As I hear it, you could use a pointer or two."

Shrugging at the seeming inevitability of the match, Agan moved into a combative stance. At least, Artorus guessed it was a combative stance. His feet were planted at about twice the width of his shoulders, legs stretched apart. His arms were both up above his head, and the practice sword wavered about in a strange quasi-pattern. Then, with an odd noise that wasn't quite a duck call, the soldier moved forward to attack.

Artorus did not move.

Agan missed.

Stumbling and nearly falling, Artorus caught Agan before he hit the hard ground of the training yard.

"Uh..." Artorus didn't quite know what to say.

"Sorry, sir." The man looked somewhat sheepish as laughter rippled through the crowd.

"Again," Artorus said, not believing this could be his truest effort. "I'd like you to try to hit me. Pretend I am your enemy."

After another beat, Winnefore attacked once more. With a wide swing, greatly overextending himself, Agan missed the captain by at least a foot. Painfully slow, Agan brought his sword back two seconds later for another attack, Artorus blocked the strike easily, and Agan reeled back. Two more incredibly slow and amazingly inept strikes followed, both also easily blocked, until Artorus reached out with his practice sword and tapped the soldier on his chest, eliciting a yelp of pain.

More laughter came from the spectators. Artorus still refused to believe this was the best the man could do. He shook his head. "Again."

Three more rounds followed, and all were worse.

Finally, Artorus called a stop to the sparring, and Winnefore stood gasping for air. He thought on his words a moment. "I apologize to you if this is offensive," Artorus said, "but is this truly the best you can do?"

More laughter erupted from the watching soldiers.

Swallowing as he still breathed heavily through his large nostrils, the frail man looked up. "Yes, sir. I'm sorry if it doesn't meet with your approval."

"Well..." Artorus searched for the words. Perhaps swords were simply not his strong suit. "Is there anything that you're better at?"

Another chuckle rippled through the other soldiers, and Artorus realized the context of his question.

"Than fighting? I could have made a respectable jester, I suspect," Agan said as his breathing finally slowed some. "Perhaps a writer – or, wait – a *philosopher*."

Agan had a wide grin on his face. Artorus supposed that the others couldn't so much laugh *at* Agan if Agan, too, was laughing. It was a joke they all shared in. Agan almost seemed to enjoy the attention.

"And yet," the captain said to the soldier, "you stand here and practice your, um, swordsmanship?"

"Sir, I did not choose a life of military service," Agan said earnestly to his captain. His eyes suddenly held a seriousness that Artorus did not quite expect from the small man. Those green eyes shone bright in the light of the open yard. "*By the fallen gods*, did any of us? When I was ten years old, I knew – everyone in my family knew – that I would be relegated to field work, or a road maintenance crew, or courier service; anything but soldiery. Of course, most men are doomed to soldiery, but even at ten, my stature and skill were obvious. I would make a terrible soldier. And my father had been a courier for the nobility.

"But our magistrate had other ideas for my family... You see, my father, the courier *and poet*, Tyrus Winnefore, had written some works that some considered to have sentiments against the Planewars. And such blasphemy is not tolerated in The Vastness. I and my four younger brothers were doomed from birth for actions my father had taken before any of us was born…

"We don't have the choice," Agan said more quietly, looking down. "No, I can only do the best with what I have; play the hand I am dealt…"

The crowd was quiet. The words were spoken to each soul present, in truth. Every mother had dreams that her boys would get assigned to any task other than warfare. The chances weren't always great, but hundreds of thousands of men kept the roads and tended the fields and worked the dockyards of The Vastness. Millions, however, fought the wars of their Wizard-King.

Artorus looked at Winnefore another moment, trying to figure him out. "But you fight with passion,"

He meant it. Very few soldiers in Artorus's unit would still have that sword in their hand, round after round, for all their peers to see, if they fought as poorly as this man did. There was an undeniable passion to Agan, that he continued despite it all. It certainly seemed that he honestly did seek improvement, though Artorus could not see much of a chance for it.

"Yes, I do," Winnefore said. "And if it were up to me, I'd find a beautiful wife, have several children, and never pick up another sword." He looked to his practice sword and added, "Wooden or otherwise. But since this is my lot in life, I must do my best. I may die an inglorious death; I might die a failure – I probably will – but I won't die a man who felt sorry for himself, who didn't strive to better himself."

Those green eyes held the captain's confidently. The crowd was still quiet.

As Artorus looked at the man, for a moment he somehow saw so much more than the frail, helpless man before him: he almost saw a lion… a giant-slayer… a champion of the planes. Agan Winnefore was much, much larger than he appeared.

"Very well," the captain said smiling, "then keep practicing."

Turning to the crowd and raising his wooden sword high into the air, Artorus shouted. "Let's hear it for Agan the *Mighty*!"

The crowd erupted in laughter and applause, and Winnefore began once more to bow in a flourish to each side of the training yard.

In all reality, the army had a near infinite need for support staff. Artorus would have Agan transferred to the runner teams, perhaps. He seemed lean... not exactly agile, though. But, wherever Winnefore ended up, when battles became heated, even runners and medics and scribes and waterers were not safe. The sword practice was important.

It was only weeks later that the General Hathey promoted his Captain Vallon to Commander Vallon, as Artorus had hoped. The life of a commander was a busy one indeed. As he now led *thousands* of troops, Artorus had all too little time to practice with the men after that, and it was another two years before he heard anything more about Agan Winnefore.

Eight years ago, the Fifth Planar Army had been embroiled in a pitted battle amid the harsh heat of Learden. With many other forces from The Vastness, they fought a host of Kaladrius's greatest armies for the strategic advantage of one of the larger continents on this plane. It was a massive engagement that spanned the greater portion of a large badlands that was known as the Boils. Blood spilled and swords clashed as the many great armies fought for Dominance. The result of the battle would likely determine the balance on Learden for many years to come.

The armies of The Vastness fought hard. At every skirmish, their losses were not as harsh as the enemies', and at every turn they gained a little more ground. But Kaladrius had devoted many of his forces to this place, and the armies of The Vastness were still dreadfully outnumbered. They would have to continue fighting for many months to come if they were to stave off the hordes of enemies.

And the greatest impediment to victory was a device that Kaladrius had introduced only recently. The goblins had their magic mud, and a great deal of damage it could inflict, but the alchemists of the enemy Wizard had discovered something altogether more horrific. It was a weapon that could hurl flames for many yards; flames that stuck to whatever they touched, like they were made of tar; flames that burned as hot as Wizard's fire. Many good soldiers died under its horrible wrath.

And so the Great Battle of the Boils raged on, with neither force yet a clear victor and the numbers of dead mounting.

It was in the fifth week of the huge battle that the lord generals of The Vastness met. Four were here on Learden at this time. Though Hathey was no lord general, he waited inside the meeting tent, and though Artorus was certainly no lord general, Hathey had brought him along. Artorus had been told that Lord General Kremaine, Hathey's superior, wanted Hathey at the meeting, though why Artorus was here was still mysterious to him.

"This is foolhardy," one lord general called. "We do not have much fight left in us, and we only squander our resources here. Our forces should be withdrawn and redeployed more strategically. Let Kaladrius have these Wizard-forsaken badlands."

"Yes," replied Lord General Kremaine condescendingly, "in battle there will always be losses – and in heavy battle, heavy losses. But do not confuse loss of troops with foolhardiness. If we can win here, we may just push Kaladrius from Learden for good."

"Not with those fire machines, we won't," a general added from the other side of the tent. "You realize my Twelfth Planar has lost the better parts of six regiments in the past three days of fighting. *Six...* That's *thousands* of men doused in flames and burned to bones *in minutes*. We've not seen a wrath like this before! Not short of a Wizard's touch."

"Yes," agreed the first lord general, "how do we continue to fight *that*? The intelligent thing to do is strategically withdraw. We can better manage this threat in smaller engagements."

"Well, our meeting here is to discuss the options before us and their implications, lord generals," stated Kremaine in his even tone. "If history is any indication—"

A messenger burst in, interrupting the lord general. "Sirs! The Northwest Plateau!" he spat frantically, searching for the words, but everyone in the room already knew what he was referencing.

The place that the armies were calling the Northwest Plateau was where the Fifth Planar was currently deployed, along with portions of other armies as well. It had proven to be a superior vantage point from which to scout much of the Boils. There had been constant skirmishing on and around the plateau, but the majority of the heavy fighting was on fields far from that point. Nonetheless, the Fifth and others had been rotated onto guard duty for this vantage point, so as not to let it slip into the control of Kaladrius and his armies.

"Kaladrius," the soldier huffed, trying to recover his breath. "He has somehow mobilized *six* different armies... and he marches to the plateau right now! ... Battle will be drawn within the hour!"

Six armies? Artorus thought incredulously.

Much noise erupted from the various generals in the tent, issuing orders to mobilize armies and calling for their command staffs. But each lord general knew the truth: the Northwest Plateau was far enough from the bulk of their forces that they would not arrive in time to support the Fifth Planar. Kaladrius's forces must have been planning this for some time to execute such a sudden and surprising move with so many of their units, unnoticed and unheard until the very eve of the attack.

Artorus felt it, and he saw it on his general's face: the Fifth Planar Army was in grave peril.

The meeting was finished without resolution as each leader hastened to issue orders to their men, and Artorus made haste back to the Northwest Plateau with his general.

It was nearly a dozen hours later at a full gallop that Hathey's retinue approached the Northwest Plateau, and what they hoped would remain of their army.

Several other armies of The Vastness were coming a few hours behind them to meet the forces of Kaladrius in what might prove to be one of the largest battles of the engagement thus far.

But it was all too likely that the armies of The Vastness would have to face the armies of Kaladrius – six of them, if reports were to be believed – in newly won entrenched positions on the higher ground of the plateau. This could spell disaster for The Vastness in the larger strategies, but it surely had already visited disaster on the Fifth Planar.

Hathey knew as well as Artorus did that, by this point, their proud and mighty army should be little more than charred remnants of what it was, so they were both quite shocked to see the ranks intact as they reached the back side of the plateau. The forces of Kaladrius hadn't even managed to completely encircle the Northwest Plateau yet.

What has happened here? thought Artorus. *Has Kaladrius only just arrived?*

The general and his small retinue hastened to take their opportunity and climb up the slope, into the huge maw formed by the enemy armies closing around them.

The men of the Fifth Planar were formed into their flawless battle lines, and the bulk of the army was alive. They were in the midst of battle with the greater masses of *six* other armies, but they were *alive*.

It took very little time for the general to meet with his lieutenants and gather what had happened so far, while the enemy completed their encirclement, possibly dooming the general right along with the rest of his men. Artorus doubted his general would have had it any other way.

Since he was still waiting for the runners to tell him the location of his regiment, until he knew where he should be, Artorus waited and listened to the reports.

"... outer defenses at the edge of the plateau fell almost immediately... and as they approached, we formed our lines, sir," one lieutenant was saying.

"Yes, but we didn't have much time!" another interrupted, his tone excited. "We rushed the men to their formations, but before we'd even finished, several units broke formation... they charged. They charged directly for the fire machines!"

"How could this happen?" Hathey was saying in slight disbelief. "Where were you?"

"Well, sir," the other lieutenant replied, "it all happened in an instant. By the time we'd figured out what was happening, all we could do was watch them burn. They burned by the hundreds, by the thousands even..."

"But then it happened!" the other lieutenant interrupted again. "They just kept pressing on, until the fire machines were overtaken! I don't think the forces of Kaladrius expected it any more than we did. Everybody was stunned. There were hundreds of the fire machines, but once our regiment had broken through, they raced down the lines and destroyed them."

"So that's when we called the full charge, sir," stated the first lieutenant. "Our window would have been slim, but Kaladrius's armies were in disarray from their long forced march to get here and then the sudden loss of their fire machines... We charged and we pressed them back, right off of the plateau. The Fifth has the high ground and the defenses. We're outnumbered and we've suffered heavy losses, but the estimates are that Kaladrius has lost at least twice as many as we have so far."

"We believe that was most of their fire machines, sir!" the second lieutenant exclaimed.

Hathey was deep in thought. "So we should easily be able to hold out until our reinforcements arrive, and Kaladrius has overextended himself. They will be caught in a bloodbath, and they don't have their fire machines..."

The runner had finally returned to Artorus, but he had a strange look on his face. Was it regret? "I'm sorry commander, but your regiment is..."

"Is what?" replied Artorus, but the conversation behind him caught his attention once more.

"Which regiment led the charge?"

"It was the seventy-seventh regulars – Vallon's regiment!"

"*What?*" Vallon spun about in shock. "But I wasn't even present! Who rallied the unit?"

"A man," one of the lieutenants said. "They are calling him by some title... They were chanting it... Was it Hagan? Hagan the Mighty?"

"*Agan Winnefore?*" Artorus questioned in disbelief. "*Agan* the Mighty?"

"Yes!" replied the lieutenant. "He might just have won this day. He *might* just have won us this entire engagement. Agan the Mighty!"

Even here, farthest from the battlefront, the men surrounding the officers heard the name and returned the victory cry.

"Agan the Mighty!! Agan the Mighty!!"

Hundreds shared in the call.

In the ensuing hours, the armies of The Vastness came to surround and engage the six armies of their enemy.

In the following days, as the many other armies of The Vastness held strategic points to prevent their enemy reinforcing the desperate armies, they battled fiercely until Kaladrius's forces had no choice but surrender.

Brakken's forces had captured tens of thousands. It was the most significant capitulation ever to occur on Learden – one of the greatest in the Planewars, or so the men of The Vastness were saying.

In the continuing weeks, it became clear that Kaladrius would be unable to regain any strategic position among the Boils, and their remaining forces called for the retreat.

The Vastness had won the Great Battle of the Boils, and it was estimated Brakken would have nearly unchallenged control of this continent on Learden for some time to come.

While most of the armies celebrated with strong drink and warm women on the eve of their victory, Hathey met with his officers. The general often met with various officers after the end of an engagement, and he'd called for Artorus. As Artorus approached, Hathey awaited his commander on a bluff overlooking the retreating armies – a truly epic sight to see from a vantage as hundreds of thousands of soldiers moved toward the horizon.

The third sun dipped toward sunset, lighting the entire sky aflame as the clouds burst into brilliant shades of pinkish-red on a backdrop of blazing orange.

"Come, see what prize our fallen have purchased," said General Hathey as his commander came up beside him. "It is a momentous sight, don't you think?"

"Yes..." Artorus said, deep in thought.

"What is it?"

"We lost so many… My regiment is a ghost of what it was just weeks ago. The victory was sound, to be sure, but I feel as though I failed my men…"

"Curious," Hathey said.

"Curious?" questioned Artorus plainly. "Have you not taught your officers that each death is to be mourned?"

"Indeed, Commander," replied Hathey. "Indeed each death should be. I have spent every evening for the last month observing our fallen… But it is curious that the leader of the men so inspired to fight for him that they charge to certain death and all but win the greatest engagement of recent memory… should think himself a failure."

Hathey spared a glance to Artorus, gauging him. Artorus hadn't seen it that way.

They drank in the sight for another moment. The smell of dust lingered in this place always, but never more so than now, as the marching armies left the entirety of the badlands in a thick haze, which only served to further accentuate the effects of the brilliantly setting suns.

"You had heard of the soldier named Agan Winnefore before a few weeks ago?" Artorus finally asked.

The doumir let out a short sigh. "I'd heard about that one… Nothing particularly good, I'm afraid," he added with a tinge of curiosity to his voice.

"Yes," Artorus continued soberly. "Most thought him a failure… I suppose he proved them wrong, didn't he?" Artorus found that a fond smile had wiped the somber expression from his face.

"Agan the Mighty…" Artorus repeated to himself.

"You know, I'd been putting some thought into your soldier in these past weeks." Hathey had turned from the awesome visage to look at Artorus. "He was brave and honorable, beyond even most in the Fifth Planar. In fact, I do believe this Agan Winnefore exemplifies two of my primary philosophies on tactics."

Hathey smiled as he looked at the commander. Artorus looked back expectantly.

"Yes," the doumir went on. "Well, the first is that a man's capacity for greatness has nothing to do with how he fights or what rank adorns his uniform. Truly nothing."

Artorus smirked. Thinking back to that sparring match, it almost sounded like something Winnefore might have come up with himself. And, more than anything, it was true. Artorus nodded his agreement.

"And perhaps more importantly," the general added with a reverent tone, "one is not always defeated when one dies. True, a great warrior might live through a thousand battles, but some pay the ultimate price to attain their victory. Even as he died in flames, he likely didn't know how far-reaching his actions would be. But, Agan the Mighty truly was victorious this day. Histories will tell of him."

He peered back at Artorus. "And of the commander of his regiment, no doubt."

Artorus rather doubted his name would grace any pages of the Sages' histories. But his general's words were powerful, nonetheless.

"Commander Vallon," Hathey said.

Artorus turned to regard his superior.

"Surely you had wondered why I brought you to that command meeting, just before the battle at the Northwest Plateau."

"I did, sir."

"Well, I had half a mind to do it before, but now there is no question. I'm promoting you to high commander."

"Sir?" Artorus couldn't help but question what he'd just heard. Artorus had only recently made commander. When he entered the armies as a foot soldier, the thought of a title like *high commander* was inconceivable to him.

"I won't have any resistance on the idea, Vallon." Hathey waved a hand dismissively. "Besides, we both know there will have to be some rearrangement among the regiments after this battle." The general finally turned back to the view of the vast withdrawal that stretched nearly as far as the eye could see. "I think you've got the talent for leadership, Vallon. It is not a resource to squander in these Planewars."

Both were silent again, as the words sank in for Artorus.

The visage, too, sank in for Artorus. The blazing suns that fell upon the same horizon to which the huge mass of men retreated. The sight was glory for the Dominance; the sight was relief from what seemed like endless fighting; the sight was victory.

And Artorus's thoughts returned again to his scrawny soldier from the training yard those two years ago.

"I do believe you're right, sir," Artorus said. "Agan Winnefore is victorious even in death; he has won this for us. His name will be remembered in the pages of history and tactics when they describe the Battle of the Boils... Agan the Mighty...

"They could kill him, but they could not defeat him."

Chapter XXVI – The Immortal Wizard-King

I've done this once before, thought Typhondrius as he scurried across the sloping landscape in the dark of night. *Only, this time, I return to the place from which I once ran.*

His ear ached, but he did not rub it. His lungs cried for air even as he filled them with it. His legs seemed like they were screaming for him to stop, after the soreness of weeks of marching, but still he forced them to run up the hill.

The sun was beginning to light the sky from its hiding place below the horizon, a beauteous eruption of reds, pinks, and oranges creeping up from sight unseen.

To elves, sunrise is a sacred time, no matter what world they are on, no matter how many suns.

This is the last sunrise for Lord Brakken. Typhondrius's thoughts rang through his mind. *The creature I always thought would kill me one day, shall die by* our *hands.*

"There!" a whispered cry rang from someone just ahead. "The fortress!"

Typhondrius's elven eyes had long been fixated on the ominous form resting amongst the mountainous slopes ahead, but now the majority of the army could see it. The pace doubled as the many thousands of men struggled to gain as much ground as possible while the veil of night still clung. Typhondrius's heart raced.

"Let's go!" Mala hollered to the soldiers around her. "This is it! This is the day we become truly free!"

The excitement was nearly palpable in the air about the men as they made their final charge toward the huge fortress ahead.

Mala had never seen the mighty fortress of the Wizard-King. She felt at once both relieved by the sight and frightened. Seeing now, in front of her very eyes, the great palace of which she'd only heard stories made it so much less mystic; so much more reachable. And also, seeing the massive stone pillars with spiked battlements and great parapets, hewn from the very rock of the immovable mountain, Mala was intimidated too.

Braïun had worked with several of the high commanders and commanders on specialized combat tactics in storming fortresses. Now more than ever, Mala was thankful that she had attended most of those sessions. His work would be put to the test.

Well, she thought, feeling her heart flutter at the rush of emotions, *we came all this way for this chance. We have more than fifty thousand men and we have the indomitable will of mortals.*

She looked around for her brother, but could not see him.

No matter, she thought, a smile spreading across her lips as she ran through the rising dawn, *we will see each other at the door of the fortress, when we both walk through.*

"To the fortress!" she shouted to the men once more. "For Braïun! For our families! For freedom!"

Scanning the horizon for silhouettes of any Imperial Legions that might be waiting for them, Artorus was relieved to find none.

"If the Imperial Legions are here," he huffed as he ran beside Highblade, "they'll likely come from the flanks of the mountains."

Lieutenant Highblade nodded. "All of the officers have been briefed, Lord General. They shall hold them long enough for the task to be done."

It was a strange feeling – running toward the greatest enemy known to mortals, to face that all-powerful being; to be this close to the fruition of so many years' work; to face the destiny of the multiverse.

Artorus thought once more of his beautiful wife and of what their child might have been like, and the burning muscles in his legs quieted as his lungs filled with cool morning air.

The light of dawn was now fully upon them, and they were close enough to hear the cries of the guards as they saw the mass of the Fifth Planar Army rapidly approaching their gates.

"We make for the gates!" Artorus shouted to the men around him, breaking the hush of the many footfalls, and he heard his officers repeating the cry. "We take all the battlements, and we hold the fortress! *We hold*!"

Already he could see the guards rushing to close the huge doors to the fortress, but Artorus knew something most did not; Ty had supplied many great secrets to the general in their years of planning. So ancient was the metalwork of the massive building and so rarely were the doors moved that most of the guard thought they couldn't even be shut, and, if it was possible it would take fifty men an hour per door to do so. From this distance, the rumors seemed to be true, as the Fifth Planar Army raced up the steep roadways toward those barely creeping doors and panicked guardsmen.

Arrows began to rain upon the attacking army, and Artorus heard the cries of the stricken. Still, they charged. Stones began to fall upon them too, and Artorus heard bones snapping under the sickening thud of the rocks. Still they charged. Shields raised from the lines of guards formed around the great entryway and Artorus spilled yet more blood. And still they charged.

The few guards present at the gate had fallen quickly to the massive surprise attack, more mortals giving their lives ignominiously in service of the Wizard-King. Within minutes, Artorus and many of his soldiers were inside the fortress.

"In here! More of them!" echoed the call of an unknown soldier from one of the many hallways.

Sounds of fighting could be heard.

Lord General Vallon breathed deeply, and his wounded leg was screaming to him with the pain of a forced run, but he was now reserving his strength as he stood in the main entry hall of the fortress, a turtle shell of shields protecting them from the various deadly things that rained from the slats in the high ceiling. So many men of the Fifth Planar Army raced through the entryway into the various antechambers and stairways that led to the battlements – sergeants, captains, and commanders each took platoons of men and made for their own objective within the thick walls.

Screams of battle echoed through the many chambers.

Soon the hail of attacks stopped as one of the first strike forces obtained its objective. Again, Artorus gave a thought of thanks to Typhondrius for his knowledge of the fortress, and another to Braïun for his superior planning.

"Artorus!" called Mala from the entryway.

"Mala!" he returned with a smile. "Have you seen Ty?"

"Yes, he was just behind me, he will be in shortly," she said, also breathing heavily.

Mala came to stand with Artorus and Highblade as they conferred with various other officers over a map Ty had drawn months prior. They continued sending groups to their own tasks.

"Good," Artorus said as he looked back to the map. "Our main strike team should be arriving momentarily." Looking to one of the commanders that stood with them, he continued, "Now you start trying to get those doors shut as soon as all our men are in – you don't worry about anything else, you hear? This is your task now, Commander Laran."

Commander Laran was a doumir, like the late General Hathey. But much unlike the late general, Laran was a typical doumir, with none of the grace of elfdom and none of the might of dwarves; outwardly, he was merely a frail dwarf with light eyes, pointed ears, and a patchy beard. But Artorus knew him well, and Laran was one of the most determined men ever to serve under the flag of the Fifth Planar.

With that determination lighting those eyes and his sturdy hand axe grasped firmly in his fist, the officer nodded to his general.

"Yes, sir."

He would hold this fortress no matter what came for them.

At that moment, Typhondrius burst into the main entryway, sword clutched in his hand and several dozen soldiers in tow. Artorus cocked his head at the sight.

Typhondrius looked... heroic. Now, here in the very halls he'd fled a few short years prior, he seemed determined to fight against the Wizard-King. This was a hero their rebellion could use.

"I never thought I'd see that," he mused to Mala.

And, on his sister's face, Artorus could see it now. Why hadn't he seen it before? She harbored some feelings for Ty. It was so clear, here and now. Artorus wanted to laugh out loud that he hadn't seen it before in all the years of visiting the estate and talking with the both of them. Perhaps Mala did not even know it yet.

But there were far more pressing matters at the moment. That conversation would have to wait.

Within moments, other officers took the task of the map, and several hundred of the most elite of Artorus's men rushed inward toward the very heart of the fortress with Artorus, Mala, Highblade, and Ty at their fore.

The elf directed each turn through the twisting corridors. Elaborate marble statues of Brakken lined many of the hallways, between expensive tapestries and huge paintings. Shouting and other sounds of battle could be heard from outside the main structure, as the Fifth Planar Army was overtaking the fortress.

Occasionally a group of guards would come into their path and the mighty soldiers would make short work of them. This selection from the Fifth Planar was a force to be reckoned with – shock troops and extremely skilled officers, with perhaps the most skilled man Artorus had ever seen hold a blade: Gregory Highblade. These guards were of little concern to the general.

"This is not good," said Ty through labored breathing.

Mala, Highblade, and Artorus looked to him as they rested a moment in a large hall that had many stained glass windows shining with the light of the early morn.

"We're close," he continued, "but I believe the guard has been doubled, or even tripled, since I was here last. Evvet certainly raised some concern with Lord Brakken when he told him your plan..."

"Guards we can deal with, Ty," Artorus said determinedly. "You just point us in the right direction."

"No, you don't understand," Typhondrius added, "the number of High Guards could likely be—"

"No, I don't think you understand, Ty. We have to get to him as quick as we can; what is the way to the throne room?" The general pointed his bloodied sword to the large double doors at the end of the long room, "This way?"

Ty nodded.

"Then this is the way we go." Then, to the mass of soldiers crowding the room, "All right, this is the final moment, men. Many of us will not survive this. Make peace with your family, your friends, and your gods, for now we face our destiny."

Artorus breathed deeply and raised his sword toward the doors once more.

"Go!"

The surge of men that were still pouring into the room crashed against the doors. But behind the huge doors, now splintered into a thousand pieces, Artorus saw what Typhondrius was worried about.

Ahead, clogging the narrow hall that led to ornate carpeted stairs and the very place Brakken would be, if all went as planned, were dozens and dozens of guards. Each was heavily armed and more heavily armored, and the corridor was narrow. This was the War Maker's High Guard, prime among all of his soldiers and loyal to the death.

Our numbers won't help us here, Artorus thought as he tightened the grip on his sword.

"Looks like it's my turn," Artorus heard from his side.

Turning he saw his lieutenant staring straight down the corridor and smiling.

"I'm afraid these look like they might be a bit too much for you, Lord General. You save your strength."

Before Artorus could even reply, the half-elf gave him a wink and then bounded down the hallway, long blade flashing in the light of the stained glass that lined this corridor.

What followed could only be described as a work of art or a massacre – nothing less. Gregory Highblade was peerless with a sword and each guard learned this in turn. The long sword was not even as effective in the relatively tight corridor, but it swung about, deflecting strikes, passing shields and finding the places between plates of armor that made screams of dying fill the long walkway.

Most soldiers of The Vastness had likely heard of Gregory Highblade, winner of nearly every sword tournament he'd ever entered, decorated from a hundred duels, and favored sword champion at the Planar Games for many years now.

Surging into the hall behind Highblade, Artorus, Mala, Ty, and every soldier that could fit followed the skillful lieutenant. Any of the guards that survived the deadly blade of the lieutenant – few as they were – only faced the charging force that followed.

Expecting the cramped space to aid the elite guard of Lord Brakken, the assailed men quickly realized it only reduced their chances of surviving the advancing blade master, and most of the remaining guards scrambled up the staircase to reach the larger room beyond, where they hoped to even their odds.

As the guard regrouped above the stairs, Highblade finished off the last remaining guards from the hallway and charged up the staircase.

"Wait!" called Artorus. "We will fight them together!"

But the lieutenant did not stop.

The skilled half-elf reached the top of the staircase where a dozen of the heavily armored guards still waited to engage him. First one and then three and then six elite soldiers came for Highblade.

Artorus reached the bottom of the staircase and began to climb, but one of the fallen guards rose to his feet in front of him, bleeding, but not dead. The general engaged the soldier while several dozen others waited behind him, trapped in the corridor. With higher ground and heavy armor, the soldier rebuffed all of Artorus's attacks, but past the guard, Artorus could still see his lieutenant.

Spinning, Highblade dodged the swords that swung skillfully toward him, and his long blade moved to the backs of knees and to the sides of breast plates, finding the spots with no armor and drawing the blood of the guards. One by one, they fell to the ground shouting in pain. Highblade didn't have the time nor need to bother finishing off the wounded as he continued clashing swords with the guards. The troops of the Fifth Planar awaited the charge at the bottom of the staircase.

But then something strange happened.

As Artorus fought with the guard, trying desperately to fell the persistent fighter, he saw the scene at the top of the staircase play out from below. The image of his lieutenant suddenly wavered violently. They were waves of heat. The guards all stopped attacking the lieutenant as some looked back behind them, and others tried to run in horror. The noble half-elf only stopped his fighting, turned back, and looked to his general with reverence. A respectful nod was cut short as flames erupted and engulfed Gregory Highblade and all those that surrounded him. Some screams were heard, but mostly the hallway filled with the terrible roar of the volcanic maelstrom above and the air of the hallway rushed up toward the flame.

"No!" screamed Artorus.

The guard, distracted by the terrible sound and sudden flash of light fell to Artorus's sword jabbing straight through his neck guard. Behind him, he heard the gasps of disbelief at the fiery display above from both Mala and Ty.

Lord Brakken was here.

Both of the mightiest men ever to serve in my army, Artorus thought in horror, *both fallen to this despicable creature; both lives destroyed by this monster.*

He stared up to the furnace still burning at the top of the staircase, engulfing the entire opening. He climbed the stairs and Mala attempted to stop him.

"No, Artorus!" his sister called to him over the roar of the flames. "You will be killed!"

"No, Mala," he called back to his sister, still staring at the wall of fire, "this is the moment for which we've planned. We wait until the fire is just low enough and then we charge Brakken."

Artorus finally turned back to his sister, Ty, and the many other soldiers who were waiting behind them. Their faces each betrayed fear, so Artorus was sure to show none.

"This is the moment we've waited for," Artorus pointed his sword up the staircase to the roaring flames. "We will go to that room and we will take our freedom from the Immortals."

Some of the faces remembered the impossible task for which they strived from the very beginning, remembered their every reason for fighting the immortal Wizards, and they steeled their nerves.

Then a voice from further back called out, "But how can we beat that, sir? His magic is too strong!"

"No," replied Lord General Vallon firmly, "he can be beaten. Remember what we discussed: avoid his eyes at all costs, move directly for him, keep him distracted with our motions, and do everything we can to detain him. Even if our swords cannot hurt him – which I intend to test fully – we will still defeat him; we will make him know that he does not rule the lives of mortals *anymore!*"

Artorus breathed deeply as he saw the faces of his family and his friends and his army, and he heard the sounds of the flames dying down.

Now with more courage in his eyes, his voice louder, he continued. "*This* is the day all the twenty-seven worlds will remember as the fall of the immortals! *This* day, eternity ends!" And with that he turned and raised Thordrin's Blade in front of him, shining in all the colors of the flames and the stained glass all around. "For Highblade! *To glory!*"

The battle cry was echoed by all in the hallway as they charged up the staircase to their destiny.

Laran looked out of the massive doors, still open barely wide enough for a man or two to pass. With the last of the vanguard, the Fifth Planar Army was now entirely within the walls of the mighty fortress.

"All right!" he shouted. "Let's close it!" Then something caught his eye. "Wait."

He stepped out of the doors and onto the packed earth of the road that was smeared with blood, all of the bodies either swept off the road or brought into the fortress. The light of day now fully illuminated the landscape, and just over one of the various ridges that sprawled the mountain landscape he saw a dark form creeping.

It was an army. It was an Imperial Legion.

As soon as the commander noticed it he heard the calls of alarm from atop the walls as well. "Imperial Legions approach!"

"Hm," was all that escaped the commander's throat as his determined eyes stared down at the sight.

Soldiers rushed to his side. "What do we do, sir?"

"All right," he replied, "let's close it up. If these bastards are going to try to take the fortress from us, we'll make it hell for them."

He didn't move from where he stood as the soldiers started to head back into the fortress.

"Sir?" one of the soldiers said back to his officer.

"Go ahead, soldier," Commander Laran said, still looking out at the quickly approaching sight.

"But, sir," the soldier contended, "we can't shut it with you still out here."

"Of course you can," he replied. "Can and will. It will take at least twenty more minutes to get it closed the rest of the way, and we can't know if it will even open again after that. I won't have it once that Legion gets here." The commander turned back to his soldiers in the bright light of morning. "And *somebody's* got to try to reason with them."

"Sir," the soldier began to argue.

"Soldier," the commander interrupted, "I'd hate to have our last interaction be a disciplinary beating. You close that door, and Lord General Vallon will be out with the head of Lord Brakken by the time this Legion gets here. We won't have a thing to worry about. Until then, the high commanders will issue orders."

Silenced, the soldier nodded to the others that waited to close the door. The tremendous grinding sound of metal joins moving against their will began again as the massive doors slid slowly across the packed earth, inch by inch.

Before the doors closed the rest of the way, Laran looked back up to the top of the massive fortress. He could still see some smoke coming from two broken windows near a suspended walkway.

We'll give you the time you need, Lord General, he thought, *but I sure hope you've got some miracles planned for us out here...*

Typhondrius watched Artorus run up the stairs and disappear into the flames and smoke. His heart stopped in his chest. His eyes had not left these flames since they first sprang to life at the top of the staircase. He'd not been so close to a Wizard's flames since the fateful night so many years ago, when it touched his very face and scarred him for life: the night he'd first met Artorus Vallon.

The flames were low, not the roaring inferno that they'd been a moment ago. But still they were the flames of his former master: a

Wizard's flame. The heat was familiar to him, as a recurring nightmare rekindles deeply buried fears.

This is the moment, he thought, his chest bursting with anxious energy. *Either now or never will I stand against the flame of Lord Brakken.*

He swallowed hard, gripped his sword firmly, and glanced to Mala beside him. Her face showed nothing but immutable determination. With her at his side, he did not hesitate before the fires as they both lunged in.

Artorus opened his eyes. It was the first time he'd been immersed in a Wizard's fire and he planned not to do it again. In the split second he had to notice himself, it seemed the flames did not catch him alight since they had burned down enough, but his truer test stood before him now.

Standing in front of Artorus, perhaps thirty feet away, was the immortal Wizard-King, Lord Brakken of Myrus. The extremely tall form was well-muscled, rippling fibers under every portion of exposed skin. His robes were of a deep, rich gray and they were lined in shimmering gold, with a blood-red sash hanging over one shoulder. The creature moved smoothly and with purpose.

This must have been some kind of meditation chamber, as it was very large and circular, with many bright decorative windows. A ring of the same lush carpet that covered the stairs at the outer edge, and little else, adorned the room. There was some design on the floor. Was it the same design Kellos had carved in their table?

Artorus averted his eyes before they met the Wizard-King's. Sensing an attack, he immediately darted to his right, sword still gripped well in his right hand. He felt the electricity in the air as a bolt of lightning shot barely past him, singeing his left arm and striking the stonework behind him.

The wounds from the High Justicar were far from healed and all of them cried out as he jolted his body in a quick charge toward the Wizard. He picked a spot on the Wizard-King's chest – one of his ornate medallions that hung lazily from his neck – to look at instead of his eyes.

The Wizard-King made little effort to evade. Artorus didn't expect him to, particularly. With both hands, he swung Thordrin's Blade hard from the right, in an arcing attack for the neck.

Brakken raised his left arm, and the sword barely sunk a quarter of an inch into the thickly muscled forearm. Artorus wished he had some disbelief about the situation, but it was truthfully quite close to what he expected. Thus, he was prepared when Brakken's right arm reached out for him. Ducking quickly, he rolled to his right, now mostly opposite Lord Brakken from the rest of the attacking men that poured through the scorched opening to the room.

His goal was to keep Brakken distracted while they figured out how to destroy this beast. So far, so good.

His sister and Typhondrius were first among the incoming attackers and they each took their own swing at the Wizard. Both deflected off of Lord Brakken's back similarly to how Artorus's blade impacted the Wizard's arm, but it was enough to distract him from Artorus's attacks.

Each of the Wizard-King's moves were relatively slow, not because he lacked speed, but because his every motion exuded the power of an immortal, and each of his moves were deliberate, patient, and deadly. As he turned toward Artorus's sister and her friend, he moved both of his arms in slicing motions and the air in the room began to swirl about.

As quickly as he could, Artorus hacked his sword at the Wizard-King's right leg, connecting solidly, but again only sinking a fraction of an inch into the creature's flesh. None of these wounds Lord Brakken was collecting seemed to be bleeding, much less having an effect on the Wizard – more than a slight distraction and some tears in his clothing, anyway.

But a distraction was just what Artorus wanted. The motions that Brakken was making with his arms were thrown off ever so slightly by

Artorus's strike and the whirling currents that were quickly collecting speed in the surrounding space of the Wizard-King dissipated into a mere breeze.

Excellent, thought Artorus as his brow began to bead sweat. *So we can affect him with our swords...*

A roar of some kind came from the War Maker as his spell was defeated. He whirled about to face the crouching general, this time with much more speed. Before Artorus could react to the Wizard, his right foot came up and connected with Artorus's chest.

Like an entire mountain had uprooted itself and hurled all its weight at him, Artorus felt the force of the Wizard connect with his torso. He was flung back at an alarming speed and he skidded across the floor for many more feet. His lungs had no more breath as he gasped to reclaim oxygen once more. He could feel the ribs that had broken in his chest.

Through his pain, though, and the entire room spinning about him, he did notice as dozens of soldiers were now swarming about Lord Brakken and each took their best swing at the Wizard-King. Some attacks he fended off with his arms and others he simply let bounce off of his chest and back.

With his massive arm, the Wizard reached out and grasped the head of one of the soldiers. Despite his every effort to writhe free, the Wizard-King merely squeezed his large hand and crushed the soldier's helmet. With his other arm, he swung around and impacted the head of another soldier. The sickening sound of skulls breaking echoed through the large chamber. Still the soldiers fought the Wizard.

As more and more forms entered the combat, the Wizard-King became completely surrounded. Then, with even greater speed than before, Lord Brakken suddenly moved in a swirling pattern of arm movements, extending upward, until his arms stopped above his head and the wind that had come and gone before returned in force.

The wind came with such ferocity that it shook the stained glass windows and whirled about in the center of the chamber, where Brakken stood. The air currents came closer and closer until they formed a whirlwind around the mighty Wizard. Each of the soldiers that Artorus could still see through the increasing wind was now forced to cover his face from the gale. Then the wind came closer still, even tighter to the frame of the Wizard whose hands were still extended above him, and then it burst outward in all directions. Through the ringing in Artorus's head and over the frantic gasping of his lungs, the sound of the storm roared in Artorus's ears.

The prismatic glass gave way to the blast of air as everyone around the Wizard-King was thrown back. Several soldiers flew through the emptied frames where the windows had been, falling to their deaths amid a waterfall of sparkling colors. But still more soldiers came from the stairway and flooded the room as quickly as it had been emptied.

Artorus had managed to avoid the blast of air from his position already on the floor and he'd managed to regain a bit of his breath. He pushed a disoriented soldier off of him and attempted to stand, despite the many complaints of his aching body.

But one of the soldiers near the front of the group made a mistake. He froze in front of the charging group, causing others to stop and to run into each other. His eyes were locked on the gaze of the Wizard-King.

Fallen gods be damned, thought Artorus.

Some of the soldiers paused to see what was wrong with the frozen man.

"He is dead now!" the general shouted through a fit of coughing, as his lungs burned and his ribs shot pain through his chest. "He is the Wizard's man, now!"

Artorus couldn't imagine many of the soldiers heard his sputtering commands, but it turned out not to matter much, as the soldier began to attack the men around him. Some of the men were still charging at the Wizard, nearly reaching him now, but many were stopped as the soldier whirled about attacking his own friends.

As that spectacle played out, Artorus found his feet and regained the grip on his sword. At that moment, two of the soldiers came to Lord Brakken, swords high. The Wizard-King ducked and placed his hands on the stone of the floor. The two men that had just reached the Wizard suddenly flung like stones from a sling directly past the Wizard-King. They each screamed as they flew like dolls across the room. One scream was cut short as the soldier slammed into the stonework of the room and the other faded quickly as the soldier went out the window and disappeared.

As many of Artorus's soldiers that were still standing were distracted with the fighting amongst their own number and the others regaining their feet, Lord Brakken stood again and extended his arms out in front of him, bent at the elbow, hands in fists.

"No!" Artorus tried to call. "Stop him! Magic!"

It caused tremendous pain for Artorus to try to shout, so he scrambled to get closer even as he finished his enfeebled commands.

A few soldiers were attacking the Wizard, but their blows did nothing. Waves of heat again began to emanate around the Wizard-King. Lord Brakken shot his hands outward, palms opened, and he shouted.

The few soldiers that attacked the Wizard-King and the others who were still rushing to get to him were all engulfed in a massive torrent of flame that exploded from around Brakken and shot forward to the hallway opening which had still been smoldering from his last touch. Screams were again muffled by the horrible roaring of flame as Artorus and all the others that were not engulfed by the jet of flames were forced to back away from the heat. The sickening smells of burning clothing, melting metals, and searing flesh filled the room.

Artorus could still see Mala to his right and Ty to his left, along with a number of his troops flanking the great fireball that hid Lord Brakken. He was now dripping with sweat as he forced his chest to breathe again, and the lord general began to issue orders to all those who could hear him. It was still painful to try to call out, but Artorus could again form full sentences.

"All right!" the general shouted through the waves of heat and labored breaths. "As soon as we can stand the heat, we all swarm Brakken at once! We're going to tackle him and try our best to hold him! Your swords aren't of much use, so worry more about getting a hold of him – and avoid those eyes!"

Soldiers all nodded as they passed along the word, and each faced the massive fire before them. Artorus blocked the heat from his face as he waited once more for the inferno to die down. His broken ribs were nearly immobilizing and, as he still gasped for air, he began to wonder if he had a collapsed lung. He had never hoped to suffer a kick from the Wizard-King. Artorus knew he was strong, but he couldn't have previously comprehended the sheer power this evil creature commanded in his very limbs, magic aside.

But Artorus didn't have the luxury of succumbing to his pain just yet.

We can do this, he attempted to convince himself. *We* have *to*.

With some significant luck, the power of many mortals might just be enough to overcome that Wizard's strength.

Typhondrius wiped the blood from his face. He'd not suffered such wounds since the last night that he was in this fortress, and his skin scraped easily against the stone floor as he was flung by the Wizard's powers of air. He bled and he was bruised, but not badly. He still had his wits about him.

He'd lost his sword in that blast, but there was a growing collection of them about the floor as more soldiers fell, and Typhondrius had procured another.

The fire was waning, though the horrifying heat was still intense. From where he was, Typhondrius could see Artorus readying to charge, along with more than a dozen of the elite men of the Fifth Planar Army that still surrounded them. Typhondrius knew from Artorus's face that Mala was still alive, likely readying for a charge of her own from the other side of Lord Brakken.

Once more, Typhondrius swallowed his fear as he readied himself to walk into Wizard's fire.

The flames reduced and the figure of Lord Brakken became visible once more. He almost looked… tired…

Thick, black smoke poured upward and swirled about in the domed ceiling of this room, and the fires of the Wizard-King died to mere spits of flame about the floor. All of the mortals charged.

At once, likely near twenty weapons struck at the Wizard-King and still they had little effect. Soldiers also lunged for the looming figure. Typhondrius found himself too slow to get into the direct fighting since so many people crowded Lord Brakken by the time he was close. He circled about the outside of the fighting forms, looking for an opening.

Lord Brakken was now making several noises of frustration as his long arms moved about, snapping bones and flinging mortals from the fray. Just as one soldier would gain a firm enough grasp on the Wizard-King, he would simply shrug them off as though they were children in a wrestling match with a giant.

Then Typhondrius saw Mala. She was stabbing into Lord Brakken's side with her sword, as a soldier clung to the monster's back.

His heart froze as the Wizard-King, still snapping bones under his fingers, turned toward Mala.

No! Mala! thought Typhondrius desperately.

But now, here in the very face of the terrible, sinister thing that had ruled his life for a hundred years – his former master – Typhondrius found it difficult to move. These strong soldiers, trained for war their whole life, were being flung from the Wizard-King like rag dolls, so what use would Typhondrius's scrawny form have?

It doesn't matter, he told himself, *this is for Mala!*

Just as the Wizard-King had nearly faced Mala, with a shout Typhondrius lunged in between the two.

All these years, he thought as his heart raced and Lord Brakken now faced him, *all these years, I feared you more than anything. I called you "master," and I groveled before you.*

The Wizard was about two feet taller than the elf. Staring at the huge creature's chest, where Typhondrius's eyes were level, he looked directly up to Lord Brakken's eyes.

Not anymore, Brakken. I won't let you take her from me. Typhondrius was never as sure of anything as he was of the words that rang out in his mind at this moment.

The Wizard-King's eyes were dark – perhaps darker than anything Typhondrius had seen in his life. They seemed to swirl with power, with anger, with... *hatred*. But Typhondrius saw something he did not expect as well: vulnerability, fear, desperation. These were not the eyes of a god; they held in them anxiety and insecurity; they held in them a whole range of emotions; it was almost... mortal.

Typhondrius heard a desperate shout from Mala to flee, but Typhondrius didn't care so long as she was safe.

"I'm not afraid of you anymore," the elf said to the lurking visage that loomed over him.

Then, the dark eyes of Lord Brakken flashed with something – some distant power – and Typhondrius felt a sinking feeling in his gut.

All of the fighting around Typhondrius – the shouting, the swinging of the swords – everything seemed to slow to the crawl of a snail. And Lord Brakken's eyes burned the elf's soul with some unholy flame he'd never known. He wanted to scream or to cry or simply to die, but he could do none of these things; he could do nothing at all besides stand and stare into those demonic eyes, frozen in time.

"I know you, don't I?" the Wizard-King's voice boomed in Typhondrius's mind, louder than anything the elf had ever heard. He felt as if the sound alone might break his bones, but somehow he knew there was no sound at all.

The Wizard's mouth did not move, but his voice was unmistakable as his eyes bored into the elf's skull. The words echoed a thousand times through the embattled chamber and the frozen forms of his friends.

Typhondrius spoke without moving his own mouth; his voice sounded distant to himself as it echoed, the world around him still frozen in place.

"Y-yes," he managed.

Lord Brakken laughed – a deep, menacing laugh. "That ratty little servant that spilled the drink! That explains the mangled face."

Typhondrius's fear gave way to anger.

"I once called you 'master!' I once obeyed your every command! But now you are my foe! Now we will defeat you! I'm not afraid of you, Lord Brakken!" he found himself shouting defiantly, the echoes amplified.

Another dark laugh came from the Wizard-King. "You should be."

Then, like a poison had entered every vein in Typhondrius's body at once, he jolted in sharp pain. He tried not to cry out, but it all seemed fruitless. His reverberating screams filled the large room and then melted into an entirely different noise, like perhaps the roar of a waterfall, then finally settled into something of a muffled droning sort of tone.

And all things became suddenly gray to his eyes and Typhondrius found he no longer had control of his body.

He stood, unmoving; unthinking.

Without willing it so, he heard his own thoughts betray him: *I am ready to serve you again, master.*

The Imperial Legion seemed to stretch forever. As far as anyone in that fortress might care, it could. Commander Laran breathed deeply of the mountain air as he stopped on a relatively flat spot in the road to the fortress and waited for the huge force to arrive.

Who could say which secret pass or winding backroad this Legion might have taken to slip past the Ninth Planar? Or perhaps they were already closer to the fortress than the Ninth Planar when they ascended into the mountains.

But the lord general had expected the Legions to come one way or another.

Despite the doom, the morning on the high slopes was beautiful. The air was crisp and cool. Birds of prey could be seen soaring the drafts along the mountainside from afar, seeing all that played out this day.

I wonder if they'll be the only ones left to tell of the events of this day, thought Laran.

First two, then ten, then several dozen soldiers of the Imperial Legion crested the hill to the flat space. Each soldier leveled a spear or a drew a sword at the commander, who stood steadfast against the swarming army, his own weapons sheathed, no motion to attack.

A call rang through the ranks of the Imperials, and the army ground to a halt, still mostly on the steep slope. Soldiers parted and a general appeared – a lord general, if Laran remembered the legionnaire markings correctly.

After a short silence, the lord general staring into the eyes of the doumir, he spoke. "Who are you?"

"I am Commander Laran," he replied, "of the Fifth Planar Army, of the rebellion against the Immortals."

Laran's voice was as determined as ever, but the Imperial legionnaires laughed at this comment. Laran hadn't expected any different.

Scoffing as he glanced to his advisors and officers that surrounded him, the lord general replied to the steadfast figure.

"'*Rebellion.*' Yes, this is why we're here." He shifted his stance, outwardly showing his displeasure with even speaking to such a man. "If you willingly flee the fortress and release any hostages, I will at least attempt to garner you and your men a quick execution. Do this not and—"

"Lord General," Laran interrupted calmly, "I am here to deliver terms of surrender to you."

Another round of laughter echoed through the ranks of the Imperial Legion, and the lord general, clearly displeased with being interrupted, raised an eyebrow.

"This rebellion is claiming this world," Laran continued. "Not for ourselves, you see, but for *all* of us – for *mortals*. We want you to join the side of justice instead of fighting the unending war for the undying warlords."

The doumir stood alone among the thousands that marched for the fortress. All weapons were still leveled at the small man, as silence seized the mountain slope. He breathed in the fresh mountain air as he waited for the inevitable answer.

With a sigh, the lord general merely waved a hand, and all of the soldiers around him moved to attack.

I had to try, Laran thought. *Now, then, let's see if I can prove my resolve.*

Laran unslung his hand axe from his back with his right hand and caught the first soldiers spear with his left. Swinging around, he planted his axe squarely under the soldier's chin and yanked it out just as fast. Swinging the spear he now held in his left around, he shattered it in the neck of the next soldier, then planted his axe in the chest of a third.

There were far too many, though, to make any difference here besides a bit of time. And the mass of troops closed quickly to overwhelm the commander.

Dropping the splintered shaft of the spear and letting the axe stay buried in the poor soldier's chest, he reached to the sturdy dagger sheathed at his side, under his right arm. Pulling it out and flipping it to a throwing grip, he found his target.

Even as the dagger left his hand, he felt several spears and swords slide into the flesh of his back and sides. The small blade flew true, but the lord general was not terribly close and there were several soldiers in the way.

As Commander Laran fell to the onslaught, he saw the dagger stick into the right arm of the lord general, eliciting a roar of pain. That small bit of pain was nearly worth the overwhelming pain of a dozen weapons that bit into his own flesh.

It rests upon your shoulders, Lord General Vallon, the doumir thought. *It was an honor to stand at your side.*

Commander Laran, the noble doumir that stared down the Imperial Legions on the sloped road before the mighty fortress, died with a grin on his face.

Having mangled or killed many of the soldiers that were trying to engage him, the Wizard-King suddenly stopped, facing away from Artorus.

"This is our chance!" he shouted as best he could to his men. "*Now! All together!*"

The remaining eight men and Artorus all pounced onto the huge Wizard. His strength was immense, but perhaps the force of so many at once would be enough to subdue him... The mighty Wizard struggled, Artorus heard a scream from somewhere in the pile of bodies as all of them writhed against the immense strength of the creature. Artorus imagined the Wizard's hands crushing some poor soldier.

But the mass of mortals stayed mostly on top of Brakken.

It's working! Artorus thought with excitement, *we can do this!*

Another scream sounded, this time the sound was from right next to Artorus.

Daring to glance away, he looked up to see Ty with an extremely bizarre look on his face.

He was pulling his bloodied sword from the back of one of the soldiers.

No, not Ty! Artorus thought. *No!!*

Two of the soldiers released their grip on Lord Brakken in order to defend themselves from the possessed elf.

"No!!" cried Artorus as he strained with all his remaining might.

He felt Lord Brakken moving under the pressure of the last few remaining mortals. And then, with a tremendous cry, the huge Wizard threw the last mortals off of him.

Artorus looked around from where he now lay on the ground, his head spinning and his ribs searing with pain once more. No more soldiers yet came from the still smoldering hallway, as only smoke trickled out the top.

He forced himself to stand once more, shaking the pain from his head and blinking to realign his vision. It didn't work very well. His head must have struck the floor hard this time. But he could make out some of the action in front of him.

Lord Brakken extended a hand toward the two soldiers that still worked to fend off Typhondrius. They each screamed a blood curdling cry as they began to shrivel to husks. The screams quickly fell to whimpers and then exhausted. Another hand shot out toward where three more soldiers regained their feet and the air crackled as lightning jumped from the War Maker's large hand and coursed through each of them; more screams filled the chamber. The last two soldiers gathered their courage and charged the Wizard, but he grabbed both of their heads as swords bounced off his torso. With a sickening crack, he rammed the heads against one another, and both soldiers fell to the ground.

Artorus couldn't tell where Mala was.

Artorus tried so hard to move, but his body ached such that every inch took immense effort. His movements were as through molasses, and his muscles strained to fight it. It was all going wrong. They couldn't subdue the mighty Wizard, his magic did not yet cease, and he didn't even try to run – he didn't have to.

As the lord general tried to steady his vision, he could now at least make out the figures still standing in the room littered with bodies: Artorus, Mala, the possessed Typhondrius, and the Wizard-King. They had brought many more soldiers of the Fifth Planar on this strike force, but Brakken must have launched that last jet of flames all the way through the hallway where the elite guard had been and into the larger room beyond, as no more had yet made their way into this chamber.

Mala screamed and charged. "You *shall* fall to us!"

No... Artorus saw the scene play out in slow motion. *Not Mala, too...*

Mala charged, swung her sword true, and the Wizard-King caught the blade in his right hand, twisting the steel in his inhuman grasp. With his left, he reached across and then slammed into Mala with a back-handed blow. She flew back and landed hard on the stone floor. Her mangled sword was still clutched in the War Maker's hand.

"*No!!*" Artorus cried.

Artorus's body snapped out of its shock in an instant and adrenaline rushed through his veins. Feeling returned instantaneously to his muscles and his legs found their strength to stand once more. He planted his feet firmly enough to launch into a charge as his grip on his sword tightened.

He rushed at the Wizard-King's back, ducked beneath another backhanded swing as the Wizard turned to face him, and sliced twice deeply into the Wizard's gut. Artorus jumped back to avoid the bent sword that clashed to the floor from the Wizard's other hand and twisted further into a spike of mangled steel. Lunging forward once more, Artorus plunged Thordrin's Blade deep into Lord Brakken's chest.

This time, the sword went through his flesh, but Artorus could see it clearly now from so close; Lord Brakken *allowed* the blade to pass through him. Though his robes were now hardly more than singed tatters across his torso from all the sword strikes and flames, he was no more wounded than had the sword bounced off him like all the rest.

The Wizard-King looked down at the hilt of the blade that stuck out from his chest. Slowly, he began to laugh. His laugh, maniacal and sinister, built until the sound filled the bloodied chamber entirely. Artorus still held the handle of his sword as he struggled to remove it for another strike. Finally, as Artorus wrested the blade free, he stood an arm's reach from the seven-foot-tall monster, and he no longer tried to avoid his eyes.

Artorus looked up to the dark, menacing orbs that sat deeply in the sockets of the Wizard-King's face. The immense figure stopped laughing.

Holding Artorus's eyes, Lord Brakken spoke with his powerful voice. "Foolish mortal. What did you hope to accomplish here? Did you think that your mortal weaponry could harm a *god*? Did you think that you had any hope of taking my worlds for your own? As though your own kind would bow to *you*?"

"No," Artorus spat back to the Wizard, "we came to show you that you do not rule mortals so easily!"

Another laugh filled the large room. "Oh, no? The mighty Artorus Vallon... It is a shame such a brilliant general fell to these delusions of grandeur. You could have had a future in my Dominance." The Wizard-King cocked his head to the side. "Now your future is only *death*."

Too late, Artorus heard the soft footfall behind him. Then, searing pain shot through his lower back, up his spine, and down through each of his legs.

Typhondrius, a friend for so many years, the elf he'd saved on that fateful night so long ago – or what was left of that elf – stabbed Artorus just under his backplate which had been jostled loose from all the action. The sword slipped next to the spine; a deep, piercing wound that stopped all feeling from Artorus's legs in a jarring spasm. Reflexively, as the strike still tore into Artorus's back, his elbow came back and connected squarely with Typhondrius's face, knocking him to the floor.

Artorus dropped Thordrin's Blade to the side and his legs no longer held him up, but before he could crumple to the ground, a large hand shot out and grasped his neck. Artorus's vision blurred, and he felt the enormous pressure from his neck swelling his head, fading nearly everything he could see to a single, dark red blur.

Artorus heard the scraping as Lord Brakken lifted the twisted sword from the ground at his feet. Artorus still clung to the slightest vision and he saw the look of pure satisfaction on Brakken's face.

A thousand sounds all wavered in darkness, and then light came back to Mala's perception. Her skull screamed with pain, but it didn't matter. She shook her head in an attempt to align the sounds with her swirling vision.

A terrible feeling gripped her chest.

Get up! she told herself. *Get up* now!

With all the strength she could muster, she lifted her head, pulling her aching shoulders with it, and sat up. It was dizzying, and yet the pain of it helped to realign her senses.

She saw Lord Brakken gripping her brother's neck, holding him just above the blood-splattered stone of the floor, where it looked like Typhondrius was lying as well. The Wizard held a twisted sword by the base of its mangled blade, not even bothering with the hilt of it. It was poised to stab her brother through the heart.

No! she thought as she scrambled to find a weapon.

No! Her senses did almost nothing for her as her hands felt around for something – anything – that could save Artorus.

No!! She could feel tears flowing from her eyes.

Lord Brakken thrust the twisted blade through Artorus's chest.

"*No!!*" she screamed, piercing the air of the chamber.

The Wizard-King released her brother's neck, and he crumpled to the floor, twisted sword still protruding from his chest. He quivered as breaths came shallow to him.

"No!" she screamed again.

Then Mala felt the hilt of a weapon; she didn't care what it was. She swung a long axe around in front of her as she tried to stand. Her legs were unstable, and she fell as soon as she got to one knee.

Lord Brakken, hatred on his very breath, laughed lowly at the sounds of suffering. He slowly turned to face Mala. She did not avert her eyes; too powerful was her hate.

"You killed him!" she screamed at the ominous figure who took one step toward her.

"Yes," replied the booming voice of the mad Wizard. "And I think you'll be too much trouble to keep around as well. So you shall join him in the many hells."

The Wizard-King held Mala's eyes as he slowly raised his right arm. Heat enveloped his tattooed arm, swirling about and coalescing above his hand. Where the heat converged, a bright flame erupted, hovering above the Wizard's hand.

Artorus found he was not quite dead yet.

The redness faded, but darkness now crept into Artorus's vision from the edges. He heard weeping, as if from very far away. He felt his blood flowing from his chest and chills began to shake him.

Finally, the sounds of more soldiers entered the room – the heavy footfalls of armored men. But they were too far away; as far as Artorus's senses told him, they might be a thousand miles away. They couldn't reach the Wizard-King in time.

Through his blurring vision he managed to catch sight of his sister on the ground, desperately clinging to an axe, with Lord Brakken standing over her, his heavily muscled, tattooed arm raised high, and flames spilling from his hand like liquid.

It can't end like this, Artorus thought. *Not Mala...*

More shudders shook him where he lay. He was so very cold.

The flame in the Wizard-King's hand flared into a bright jet of angry fire, and he began to slowly lower his hand toward Mala.

Artorus tried to scream; tried to get up and cut off the War Maker's head; tried to do anything at all, but his body could not. His blood pooled around him on the cold stone floor, and Artorus knew death was near.

The soldiers were too slow, in their heavy armor. Artorus could hear their clamoring echo through the chamber into his failing ears.

Lord Brakken's tattooed arm leveled at Mala and then a great flare burst from him.

But something else happened at just that moment – something Artorus could not quite comprehend. A strange popping sound came to Artorus's ears, and then a burst of wind erupted into the room, dispersing flames.

Artorus's vision could barely keep up, but he saw now; he saw what happened. Another form had entered the room. Was it another Wizard? The blackness crept ever closer to the center of Artorus's vision. The figure was tall, nearly as tall as Lord Brakken, but with a shaved head. He wore robes of brown.

It was Kellos. When had he entered?

Artorus could not react to the new sight as a fit of coughing gripped his throat, blood welling up from his chest, but still he held to his last vestige of sight. Kellos was here. He was here to save Mala.

Kellos must have moved quickly because Lord Brakken seemed stunned. Then, with the same speed, Kellos swung his strong arms in a delicate pattern. First his left hand swung down and then up to hold perfectly still in front of him. Another burst of air filled the chamber, hissing violently, and Lord Brakken's right arm seemed to flail to his side. Then, Kellos performed a similar motion with his right hand, and another burst of air sliced through the room. Lord Brakken's right arm detached and fell to the floor with a thud. Bright red blood flowed from him.

Brakken, standing at first in amazement, suddenly noticed himself and saw his arm on the floor. A scream came from the Wizard-King, like nothing Artorus had ever heard. Lord Brakken screamed so loudly that he doubled over. The wailing of a hundred men and the roaring of fifty lions would not have made even half the sound that came from Brakken – even to Artorus's muffled hearing, the scream was pain; it was fear. Artorus was sure that, if the windows had not been shattered already, they would have broken to this cacophony.

Then, as Brakken crouched even lower, the thick stone floor shuddered with the sound of thunder and great cracks formed in circles around the Wizard-King and raced outward, spreading over the floor, climbing onto the walls and creeping onto the ceiling.

Soldiers stumbled at the intense spectacle, some falling from the crumbling floor out to the deadly heights without.

Then, with a popping sound, Lord Brakken was gone, his scream silenced.

Artorus had been using his remaining worldly might to stay somewhat sideways, and that failing, he fell back onto the floor and his head slapped the stone.

Where at first there was a strange silence with the end of Brakken's otherworldly scream, a rumbling now replaced it as the cracks across the ceiling grew, and the entire chamber began to shake.

Though he thought the blackness had taken Artorus's vision entirely, he suddenly saw a wonderful sight.

Mala leaned over him. She was bloodied, her nose was likely broken, and one eye was hemorrhaging. Tears streaked down her battered cheeks, but she was alive; very much alive.

Artorus wanted to laugh with joy, but only coughing escaped him.

Soldiers rushed about, mostly trying to escape the collapsing room. Artorus heard pieces of stone begin to fall as the rumbling and the shaking intensified.

"Artorus," he thought he heard his sister say. "Artorus!"

He wasn't sure if he still had some fragments of vision or if his memory simply held Mala's image before him. Her voice was heavenly, soft and pure, like light pouring over him.

"You told me once, a long time ago, that this would end one of two ways..."

She was speaking to him, he was sure of it now.

Or it was a dream?

"You said it was between victory and death. But Kellos is here! He *hurt* the Wizard-King with his magic. Did you see it? The Wizard-King *bleeds*, Artorus! If he bleeds, he can die. *Wizards* can die!! The multiverse will know, Artorus. The twenty-seven worlds will hear of Brakken and our rebellion."

Artorus felt his heart failing, and his short, labored breaths had long since ceased. Was Mala stroking his hair? That would feel nice.

"You will die now, my sweet brother; Koth show you to your final resting place."

Artorus felt Mala's hot tears splashing onto his face. Somehow through all the immeasurable pain, the devastating cold, and the enveloping numbness, he felt it.

"You will die, but so too will you be victorious. You will have death *and* you will have victory."

More stones fell, and the room was surely on the verge of collapse as soldiers likely scrambled every which way in their attempt to escape, but Artorus noticed almost none of it.

As the formless chaos played out in the large room around him, Artorus Vallon, hero of the rebellion, died on the bloody stone floor. And as he passed from the multiverse, his sister's whispered words, loudest he had ever heard, went with him.

"Victory and death..."

Chapter XXVII – A Change in Weather

The skies darkened as rain clouds defied the late summer and crawled across the bright evening. The weather foretold the sentiment of the myriad peoples of Myrus.

A woman ran to market before it was to close.

"Please," she tried desperately to convince the merchants as they packed up their goods. "My baby is sick – my wee boy! We need food! I's got some coins. Almost enough…"

The vendors seemed more concerned about the weather than the paltry coins in the woman's hands. They each shook their head or looked away as they finished packing their things.

The woman could only hang her head and stare at the measly fortune in her trembling hands. She looked exhausted in the steadily darkening street. She tucked the coins back into her coin purse and walked to the overhang of the tavern before she was soaked by the coming downpour.

There, two old men sat on their stools, observing the street and talking to one another, though neither seemed to be a great listener. Apart, they'd likely be mistaken for one another, but together, an observer might note that one had fewer teeth. Neither had them in abundance.

"I tell you," the toothless old man said to the other, tapping his gnarled wooden cane against his stool, "no way that damned Kaladrius would be so brazen if it weren't for that fool's rebellion. Bah! *A truce?*" The man forced a chuckle. His voice was rough.

"Could be true," the other man mused without looking up from a small project he cradled in his hands, his voice a little more melodic than his companion's, "could be true. But who's t'say he's not offering a truce fer real? Maybe join forces with The Vastness? Fight together?"

He shrugged to himself, still focusing on whatever lay in his hands.

"You're a fool for even questioning it!" The toothless man glared over at his companion for a moment. "Don't even think for a second it's honest. Not a moment of peace crosses that evil creature's mind."

He tapped his cane three more times.

"I suppose," the other man said.

The item he held was a small wooden idol. He was whittling a figurine with a dull old knife.

The toothier man whittled a moment longer in silence as the other man kept shaking his head and mumbling to himself.

Without looking up, the whittling man went on, "Supposin' the rebellion's caused some trouble. But I don't think the Wizard-King had to execute quite all them folks..."

"The hell he didn't!" The man rapped his cane hard against the stool. His voice grew more gruff and a little frantic. "Fools thought they could take over The Vastness! Thought they could kill our god! The fools deserved their punishment; not a one general deserved to keep his head, most of those rebels done burned alive, they did. By the Wizards. A hundred thousand executions's not enough I say!"

"Maybe so, maybe so..." The man stopped whittling and frowned deeply, accentuating the wrinkles that creased his face.

He closed one eye, cocked his head, and moved his thumb over the right arm of the figurine. It was a figurine of Lord Brakken.

"And they even hurt our Wizard-King... They fought his own legions from the walls of his own fortress..." the whittling man shook his head in disbelief. "Yer right, you know. Yer right they deserved what they got. A hun'red thousand ain't enough."

"Every one of them," repeated the man with another three taps of his cane. "But they say a few folks scurried off." The man set his jaw. "I'd turn them in if I saw 'em; I would. Sure as Wizard's fire."

"Mm-hm," agreed the other man as he began again to whittle.

The woman, who at first had stood in silence, found herself drawn into the conversation. Her trembling from the cold was replaced with an angry sort of trembling.

"How can you say that?" she demanded.

"Eh?" questioned the toothless man. "What's that, girl?"

"How can you say that?" she repeated. "Even as you sit n' talk, the bodies o' them people're still warm in the Wizard-King's fortress... them what's left is trapped in their mountains or else they's hunted across the worlds like dogs..."

"Damn right, girl," the man replied with another rap of his cane, "the dogs they are!"

The woman's eyes began to tear up as she spoke. "All they's wantin' was peace fer us! Fer you and fer me and fer yer families!"

Thunder rolled through the village as the first drops of rain began to spit up tiny plumes of dust on the road.

"My little Garon is sick," the woman continued, looking down at her work-worn hands. "Even iffin' he makes it, he'll just get shipped off t'the armies in another nine years."

She shook her head.

"Can protect him from hunger an' cold, and maybe can protect him from sickness... but can't protect him from the Wizards and their wars..." Tears now fell from her face, joining the drops from the sky.

The toothless man gave a huff. "Girl, I'll assume that your youth blinds you to the way of things. Nobody challenges our god for his throne. The Planewars is just life, t'ain't nothin' to be done 'bout that." He rapped his cane again on his stool once more.

This earned a tearful glare from the girl.

"There were someone tryin' to do sumin' 'bout it," she spat, "and you two was just laughin' 'bout them gettin' burned up!"

"All right, girl," replied the toothier man. He had once more stopped whittling his figurine. He was using his hand that held the dull knife to gesture widely. "All right," he repeated. "So, supposin' that those folks only did want peace. How were they goin' ter get that? Hm? Wit' more fightin'? By grabbin' power fer themselves?"

A few more tears rolled down the woman's cheek and she looked away. "All's I know's I'm fightin' every day…" She spoke softly as the sound of rain began to overpower the conversation. "Fight the price at the fruit stand; fight that look the 'pothecary gives me when I can't afford the powders for Garon; fight the thought that my boys'll be fightin' some Wizard's war 'fore long…"

She wiped the tears from her eyes.

"Maybe 'twas stupid," she murmured, "but all they wanted was peace fer us – and they's willin' to fight Wizards fer it."

A clattering bell sounded over the rain that now came down in a steady deluge. Shouting was heard along with the bell, and a rider clambered down the now-muddy street in the rain.

"He attacks!" the rider shouted as he stopped his ringing and came up to the three people under the overhang. "The Wizard-King Quirian has broken the Hundred Years Truce of the Oldgate! He attacks Myrus!"

"What?" the toothless man stood sharply, using his cane for support.

"His armies march right over our defenses," the man said, shaking his head under his large hood as rain dripped from the sides.

"Fallen gods be damned!" the old man shouted, rapping his cane hard against the wood of the deck. "I'll bet Kaladrius won't be far behind."

"Not at all," agreed the other old man, shaking his head in wide strokes. "Not at all. Talk of truce! Ha!"

The rider cocked his head to the side as his horse trotted restlessly in place. "You haven't heard? Kaladrius's Dominance is in turmoil. There is an open rebellion on Voryn now. And they say Phax is dealing with his own troubles on Munos. Ziov may also have his own troubles. Some wonder if all the Wizards aren't facing their own uprisings…"

The rider shook his head again. "These rebels in The Vastness may have doomed us all… But it sounds like other Wizards suffer from it as well…"

The old man with the figurine looked down at it, rubbing the still-rough parts in contemplation. "Our king," he said softly, "our Wizard-King will save us..."

"Bah!" spat the other old man, flipping his stool to the side. "The one-armed Wizard! His day is done now. Myrus will belong to one of the others."

He turned to the woman, who stood silently.

"Peace, huh?" he snapped at her, rapping his cane once more against the deck, violently. The crack of the wood rang out through the din of the rain. "Well, this is the *peace* yer precious rebellion has brought us!" He spoke again, more to himself. "Young people and their damned fool ideals..."

"Your Wizard-King requires the service of all able-bodied men in this village," the rider interjected loudly, his horse flinching from the thunder that echoed in the skies. "That does include any sons of age, m'lady. If any of you can use a sword, I suggest you ready it."

The rider set his teeth a moment, then spurred his horse with a loud *ha!* His bell began in clamor again as the messenger sped into the rainy dusk.

He left the three stunned people under the meager protection of the rotting overhang, as rain beat the ground in waves now and thunder rolled through the darkened village.

Part Three End

Epilogue – The Council of Kings (pt. II)

A heavy fog rolled into the darkened valley, the mountain retreat but a pinpoint of light in the gloomy world. It always snowed here. Little warmth clung to the valley as kings of men huddled once more in the small building. The same candelabras lit the space poorly. It was as though the oppressive gravity of this world afflicted even the light.

Duke Garreth Jacob peered across the table at their meager gathering. There were only four other noblemen here. The doubting King L'Ardent was not present, but neither was King Horrin.

Garreth's thoughts wandered as he kept his left hand in the pocket of his robe. There he held an item which spurred him to call this meeting.

"Almost two years has it been since last we met..." Garreth spoke in a contemplative tone, his thoughts racing about.

"Not nearly the number we had before," King Nimmion added, his voice nearly a whisper.

King Morris Nimmion II was a frail-looking man, with wiry limbs and deep-set eyes. He still had the same dark circles under his eyes as he had two years before – perhaps worse than they were. His weakened appearance did not make him look quite kingly, despite the royal attire. This place was, in fact, his mountainous retreat.

"Twelve were there two years ago and now we have only five, duke. Did you invite everyone from last time?" Nimmion asked pointedly.

Garreth nodded, and a murmur spread through the other four rulers.

"Then they could be revealing our intentions as we speak!" Nimmion cried.

"Well, regardless," added King Tristran, shaking his head, "this Artorus Vallon of the infamous rebellion in The Vastness is dead and gone."

King Blaine Tristran was a fairly large man. His voice was deep and his arms thick. He had a certain brashness to him that was almost charming. Duke Jacob was glad he had accepted his invite, if he was perhaps a little too blunt.

"And," he concluded, "those that joined him are now headless; their Wizard-King saw to that."

"Not all of them," High Count Jolliard interjected.

Mastus Jolliard ruled over a loose collection of lands on an island chain among thousands of others, upon the world known as Aiya. He always wore fine garments, with luxurious cloaks. His demeanor was extravagant, but Garreth had always guessed his intentions to be honest. He was rather well regarded by his people, as Garreth had heard it. And the mere fact that he had traveled two gates to be here, for each of their secret meetings, spoke highly of his commitment to the concept they discussed.

"But I think we're missing the point here," Jolliard went on. "The Wizard-King of that Dominance, Lord Brakken… He was *wounded*; lost an arm as I heard it. His Dominance is in disarray. These mortals have not accomplished nothing at all."

"Hearsay," replied Nimmion. "I doubt if a Wizard was wounded by this Vallon."

"Well, if it is true," Duke Jacob interjected undeterred, "this would mean that Wizards can be hurt – which would mean that they can be killed."

Still, Garreth could not keep his left hand from returning to his pocket.

"Well," added King Fadran, the last of the kings who had come, "I hate to sound like I'm agreeing with Nimmion…" This earned a scowl from the other king. "But we all know that a Wizard can't be harmed.

Didn't Horrin go on about that when last we were here? Hasn't Vith survived countless assaults of mortal weaponry? I heard he was once speared through the heart and he laughed at the man – before blasting him to the many hells, of course."

King Fadran was a boisterous and heavyset man who wore thick kingly robes. His province saw some of the fiercest fighting in the Dominance within living memory. A casual observer might think him unfazed by the trials he'd faced, but Duke Jacob guessed it was a defense of his to project strength, where woundedness might otherwise show.

"Yes," Duke Jacob replied, "but it was no mortal that claimed Lord Brakken's arm…"

He paused, contemplating if he himself believed the words.

"It was a Sage."

The nobles reacted sharply to the revelation.

"How can you know a Sage did this?" King Tristran questioned with an obvious air of disbelief. "Sages are not warriors, and they are certainly not freedom fighters. It sounds like a children's tale, if you ask me."

"Oh no," replied Jolliard from under his thick cloak, "it is quite true. My sources confirmed it. In fact, it is in the very monastery of Delemere on Myrus that the last rebels still hold out. A couple of the generals, some of the soldiers, and the Sage himself. They say the Sage of Delemere controls magic, just like the Wizards do. Some even say *all* Sages can."

"Preposterous!" exclaimed Nimmion.

"Well, we shall find out soon enough," spoke Duke Jacob before argument could again overtake the five nobles.

He withdrew from his robe and threw to the table a new letter, where the letter from Vallon had sat two years ago. It thumped heavily to the hardwood.

"I have a letter from the new leader of the rebellion on Myrus: Mala Andrius." Duke Jacob spoke with determination. "Not only does she confirm all of these facts, but she has offered counsel with herself and this Sage, should we be able to make it happen."

He raised an eyebrow and grinned at his audience.

High Count Jolliard smiled thoughtfully. "A conference with an immortal Sage... So, perhaps it can be done... What if all we need to secure a victory against the Arch-Magus is a willing Sage to guide us and hurl his own immortal magic at our enemy, when the time comes to face him?"

"That," added Fadran, "and more armies than you've seen in your lifetime, High Count. Even the whole of my province has maybe four hundred thousand in force at any time. I'd suspect we would need fivefold that, at least. And that's assuming any of those damned lord generals would even follow me to war against their own Arch-Magus."

"Perhaps," replied Nimmion sharply, "and if the Sage can really wield magic, but we might not have to worry about any of it, you fools! Not if Vith's agents are descending upon us now. Do none of you realize? Jacob told all the twelve kings of this meeting! Any of them that are not here could be in the Wizard-King's throne room now, spilling our story and begging for his life!"

His scowl deepened. "I suspect that damned old fool, Horrin, the most; he—" King Nimmion was interrupted by pounding on the front door.

All five of the noblemen froze in fear as silence gripped the room tightly.

Another knock echoed through the chambers of the small building. Of the five men around the table, expressions ranged from cautious curiosity to sheer terror.

Duke Jacob swallowed hard and nodded to two of the servants, who were also serving as guards for their secret meeting. They slowly made their way to the door.

Upon opening it, a gust of wind and snow roared into the chamber. It accentuated the cold feeling of dread that Duke Jacob had in his gut already.

Five men entered the building. Four were royal guards and one had all the trappings of a king. The man was tall, and he carried himself well, but all of their faces were concealed by heavily furred hoods, caked in snow.

The king reached up and pulled back his hood to reveal a short beard and kempt hair of speckled white. It was King Horrin, and his expression was calm and determined.

The five men in the room sat in disbelief; none had expected him – Nimmion least of all as his mouth still hung open from his last words.

Finally, Duke Jacob spoke cautiously to the newcomer.

"Good King Horrin." He bowed his head slightly. "We did not expect you to return. From your words in our last meeting, we thought you would not commit to a rebellion. I dared to hope, but..."

Jacob's thoughts trailed off. He could only wait in suspenseful silence as all the kings of men did.

King Horrin carefully met the eyes of each of the men in the room. The moment seemed to stretch on as torchlight sparkled in the steadfast eyes of the monarch.

"Yes," he began in his regal tone, "well, things have changed, have they not?"

The End

Appendix I: Ranking of the Armies of The Vastness

Wizard-King

High Ministers of Military

Lord Generals

Generals

Lieutenants

High Commanders

Commanders

Captains

Sergeants

Enlisted Men

Appendix II: Glossary of Characters

(By last name, as applicable. Race, Dominance, titles/ranks, and pseudonyms mentioned for each, as applicable. Information accurate to date SCS 343, when the novel begins.)

- **Andrius, Balia** – (Human. Dominance: The Vastness. Title: Lady.) Mother of Artorus Vallon and Mala Andrius. Previously married to Horus Vallon, then remarried to Lord Thorton Andrius. Deceased prior to the events of Victory and Death.
- **Andrius, Mala** – (Human. Dominance: The Vastness. Title: Lady.) Sister to Artorus Vallon and friend to Typhondrius. She is helping to lead a rebellion against The Vastness.
- **Andrius, Thorton** – (Human. Dominance: The Vastness. Title: Lord.) Former Magistrate of Timber Management in Forus Province on the Great Continent of Myrus, residing outside the city of Keldt. Deceased prior to the events of Victory and Death.
- **Ayedd, Hakim** – (Human. Dominance: The Vastness. Rank: General.) General of the Nineteenth Homeworld Army. Known to Artorus Vallon only by his reputation on Myrus.
- **Braïun, Orgron** – (Dwarf. Dominance: The Vastness. Rank: Commander.) Soldier of the Fifth Planar Army. He becomes involved in the rebellion against The Vastness early and comes to the Andrius estate by the request of Artorus Vallon.
- **Brakken** – (**Wizard**. Dominance: The Vastness. Title: Wizard-King. Pseudonyms: Lord Brakken, the War Maker, Brakken the Cruel, Brakken the Eternal.) Immortal Wizard-King of The Vastness and primary opponent of the rebellion by Artorus Vallon, Mala Andrius, and cohorts.
- **Brakson, Antonius** – (Human with some elvish ancestry. Dominance: The Vastness. Rank: General.) General of the Twelfth Learden Army. Known to Artorus Vallon through their interactions on Learden and Myrus.

VICTORY AND DEATH — 499

- **Evvet, Symon** – (Human. Dominance: The Vastness. Rank: General.) General of the massive Ninth Planar Army. Known to Artorus Vallon through their interactions on Ebbea, Learden, and Myrus.
- **Fadran, Thaddeus** – (Human with some dwarvish ancestry. Dominance: Terris Omnius. Title: King.) A robust and hearty king of a large, regularly war-torn, militaristic province on the world of Hael. He received and supports the letter from Artorus Vallon.
- **Fadrus** (**Wizard**. Dominance: Various. Title: Wizard-King. Pseudonyms: Master Fadrus, Lord of the Darkness, Bringer of Worlds.) A Wizard known only from the histories of the Planewars. Shortly after Wizards came to power, he slew his master and the first Wizard-King, Gorrithas, and took the empire for his own. His knowledge and power allowed for Wizard-kind to cooperate in opening all of the worldgates beyond the original twin worlds. Records of his exploits stop abruptly at the onset of the Planewars, approximately SCS 0.
- **Foloss Quirian** – (**Wizard**. Dominance: Eternity. Title: Wizard-King. Pseudonyms: Eternus, Quirian the Eternal, The Deal Maker.) One of the more powerful Wizard-Kings, ruling the entirety of one of the original twin worlds. He and Lord Brakken have forged the "Hundred Years Truce," which keeps a peaceful hold on the Oldgate between the original twin worlds.
- **Gnarrl** – (Half human/half orc. Dominance: The Vastness. Rank: High Justicar. Pseudonym: the Blade of the Wizard-King.) The orphan assassin who has climbed the ranks of Lord Brakken's empire with a bloodthirsty ruthlessness. He is one of the most skilled fighters in the multiverse. The position of High Justicar is the chief assassin and spymaster of The Vastness. He is tasked by Lord Brakken to track down the rumors of rebellion on Myrus.
- **Hakan, Braennor** – (Human with mixed ancestry of other races. Dominance: The Vastness. Rank: Lieutenant.) A large human, hailing from Ebbea and possessing ancestry of other races, at least including orcish and elvish, though possibly including more. He is brash and boisterous. He serves as a lieutenant of the Fifth Planar Army and he has earned the trust of Artorus Vallon, despite his violent nature.
- **Hathey, Magnid** – (Half elf/half dwarf. Dominance: The Vastness. Rank: General.) General of the Fifth Planar Army immediately prior to Artorus Vallon. His mixture of races is known as a *doumir*. Among innumerable other lessons he imparted to Artorus Vallon, he is also the reason Artorus was eventually promoted to general. Deceased prior to the events of Victory and Death.
- **Hazzin, Jerrald** – (Human with some orcish ancestry. Dominance: The Vastness. Rank: Sergeant.) A promising fighter and loyal soldier of the Fifth Planar Army. One of the men selected by Artorus Vallon personally to join the rebellion and come to the Andrius estate.
- **Highblade, Gregory** – (Half human/half elf. Dominance: The Vastness. Rank: Lieutenant.) One of the most skilled swordsmen of the multiverse and twice

decorated as the Grand Champion of Swords in the Interplanar Games run by the Interplanar Society, which is one of very few neutral parties in the Planewars. The games are held every three standardized years in Jayce, a city on Mortis which is also stately neutral from the Planewars. Gregory Highblade has served Artorus Vallon for years and is promoted to the position of Lieutenant of the Fifth Planar Army after a previous lieutenant dies in battle.

- **Horace, Keldon** – (Human with some dwarvish ancestry. Dominance: The Vastness. Rank: Captain.) A leader of some regard within the Fifth Planar Army, whom Artorus Vallon has withheld from further promotion, as he intends to utilize him in his rebellion. One of the first men selected to join the rebellion and come to the Andrius estate.
- **Horrin, Meriwether** – (Human with some elvish ancestry. Dominance: Terris Omnius. Title: King.) King of a small but wealthy province on the world of Hael, with a long-standing reputation for the stability of his domain. He attends the Council of Kings, at the summoning of Duke Garreth Jacob, though he opposes the ideas set forth by Vallon on the premise of the Wizard-Kings' invulnerability.
- **Jacob, Garreth** – (Human. Dominance: Terris Omnius. Title: Duke.) Rules about one third of a small but strategically important province in Terris Omnius, on the primary world of Hael. He is young (compared to the other leaders of his Dominance) and idealistic. He received and enthusiastically supports the letter from Artorus Vallon.
- **Jolliard, Mastus** – (Human. Dominance: Terris Omnius. Title: High Count.) He is the ruler of a loose collection of islands on the plane of Aiya. He traveled far to attend the Council of Kings, betraying an earnest interest in the words of Artorus Vallon.
- **Kaladrius** – (**Wizard**. Dominance: Empire of Steel. Title: Wizard-King and Emperor. Pseudonyms: Kaladrius the Mighty, Emperor of Steel.) Emperor of a Dominance known as the Empire of Steel, and one of the constant rivals of Lord Brakken. He controls portions of the worlds known as Voryn, Learden, and Munos, with his seat of power on Voryn, though he clashes with Brakken mostly on the plane of Learden.
- **Kellos** – (**Sage**. Dominance: The Vastness.) One of the immortal race of Sages. Sages are the keepers of knowledge for the twenty-seven worlds. He contemplates the multiverse from his monastery in Delemere, in the mountains of the Winterlands, on the Great Continent of Myrus. He has taken an interest in the actions of Artorus Vallon and Mala Andrius.
- **Krakus** – (**Wizard**. Dominance: The Collective. Title: Wizard-King. Pseudonyms: Krakus of the Slaughter.) A Wizard-King who some consider mad even by the standards of Wizards. His seat of power is on a protected world known as Herth, though he battles constantly with the numerous other Wizards who attempt to control the neighboring world of Ebbea.

- **L'Ardent, Phillip, III** – (Human. Dominance: Terris Omnius. Title: King.) A middle-aged king of a large, unruly province on the plane of Hael. Subject of much punishment from the Arch-Magus. Missing a hand. He entertains the prospects put forth in the letter from Artorus Vallon, though he is skeptical by nature.
- **Magron, Loren** – (Human, with some dwarven ancestry. Dominance: The Vastness. Rank: General.) General of the Thirty-Third Homeworld Army. Known to Artorus Vallon through their interactions on Myrus.
- **Nimmion, Morris, II** – (Human, with some elvish ancestry. Dominance: Terris Omnius. Title: King.) King of a small province that produces ore for the empire on the plane of Kyrin. He hides his elven lineage. It is his retreat on Kyrin at which the Council of Kings occurs.
- **Ormond, Landais** – (Human. Dominance: The Vastness. Title: Lord.) He is city administrator of Manara, in Forus Province on the Great Continent of Myrus. He plots with Artorus Vallon and company to rebel against The Vastness.
- **Orrogen, Däruth** – (Dwarf. Dominance: The Vastness. Rank: General.) General of the Seventeenth Planar Army. Known to Artorus Vallon through their interactions on Ebbea and Myrus.
- **Phax** – (**Wizard**. Dominance: Infinity. Title: Wizard-King. Pseudonyms: Phax the Omnipotent.) Known primarily as the Phax the Omnipotent, this Wizard makes his primary home on the world of Munos in addition to controlling nearly half the world of Ki'Maren. He clashes with Lord Brakken mostly on the plane of Munos.
- **Rreth, Averett** – (Human with some dwarvish ancestry. Dominance: The Vastness. Rank: Lieutenant.) He is lieutenant to the Fifth Planar Army, under General Artorus Vallon. He has served under Vallon for years.
- **Tristran, Blaine, IV** – (Human. Dominance: Terris Omnius. Title: King.) A large and somewhat brash human who rules a conflicted province on the world of Hael. He constantly fights back invasions from the plane of Mortis. Received and wants to act on the letter from Artorus Vallon.
- **Typhondrius** – (Elf. Dominance: The Vastness.) Friend to Artorus Vallon and Mala Andrius. Being born to servitude directly under the Wizard-King, Lord Brakken, he was denied a surname. He previously was a servant, but is now helping to lead a rebellion against The Vastness. He carries a large scar on the side of his head, a testament to his time with Brakken the Cruel.
- **Vallon, Artorus** – (Human. Dominance: The Vastness. Rank: General.) Half brother to Mala Andrius and friend to Typhondrius. He is attempting to lead a rebellion against The Vastness from his position as general of the Fifth Planar Army.

- **Vallon, Elsa** – (Human. Dominance: The Vastness.) Was wife to Artorus Vallon and carried his unborn child. Both deceased prior to the events of Victory and Death.
- **Vallon, Horus** – (Human. Dominance: The Vastness. Rank: Sergeant.) Was a sergeant in the Nineteenth Planar Army, died serving on Munos. Deceased prior to the events of Victory and Death.
- **Vith** – (**Wizard**. Dominance: Terris Omnius. Title: Wizard-King and Arch-Magus. Pseudonyms: The Magus, The Giantlord, The Ogrelord.) The Wizard-King whose seat of power is the world known as Hael, with a complete rulership of Kyrin and at least some stake on the planes of Aiya and Ebbea. He is the only Wizard known to field the race of giants in combat, and he profits greatly by allowing the export of ogres to other worlds, though he retains by far the larger number for his own ranks.
- **Warin, Leon** – (Human. Dominance: The Vastness. Rank: General.) General of the Second Planar Army. Known to Artorus Vallon through their interactions on Learden and Voryn.
- **Ziov** – (**Wizard**. Dominance: The Imperium. Title: Wizard-King and Emperor. Pseudonyms: The Eternal Emperor, The Dwarflord, Lord of Lizards.) Known primarily as the Eternal Emperor, this Wizard-King makes his primary home on the embattled world of Ebbea. With their sturdiness lending well to service on the gravity-stricken world, the Eternal Emperor commands more dwarves than any other Wizard-King. He is also the only Wizard to employ the race known as lizardfolk en masse.

About the Author

Russel Frans was born and raised in the San Francisco Bay Area and moved to Spokane, WA in 2016 with his wife and son. He has been a creative writer for most of his life, but he has not chosen to step into the world of novel publication until *Victory and Death*, in 2024. When he is not using what shreds of free time he has to write, he enjoys board games, reading, and the beautiful distinction between the four seasons offered by the Inland Northwest.